Together

LIKE THIS

Friends Like This Book Five

BETHANY MONACO SMITH

Together Like This

Bethany Monaco Smith

Author's Note

Normally, this is where I let you all know you can find triggers for this book listed on my website, however, this book features discussions of suicide/attempt and self harm.
If these are triggering for you, please put this down until you feel you're in a space to read about these topics. And if you are dealing with thoughts of suicide or self-harm, please don't suffer alone. Reach out. Help is always available.
In the United States call 988 or text 741741
For all other triggers, please visit my website,
www.bethanymonacosmith.com

To anyone who has ever been afraid of the fall... but jumped anyway

Chapter One

Snuggle Me

Sarah

I HAVE TO PEE.

My eyes flash open and I squint, looking around my dark bedroom until my eyes land on the clock.

6:10

Damn it. I'm never getting back to sleep now.

"Mm." An arm wraps around my waist, pulling me closer.

"I've gotta pee," I whisper.

"No. You're cozy," Joel says, burying his face in my neck and simultaneously lighting me on fire.

This might be a slippery slope. Actually, I think it's more like when Clark Griswold waxes up the bottom of his sled in *Christmas Vacation*, then goes soaring down the hill and across town. There's fire and mayhem involved.

That's *definitely* what this is. But I can't stop myself. It's not like anything is really *happening*.

But it's not *not* happening, either.

Does that make sense?

Does anything at 6:12?

Whatever.

1

"I'll be back soon," I whisper and ease out of his grasp, then climb out of bed as he complains.

When I first asked him to sleep over, I thought it was all for me. Now I realize it's for him, too. I could say we're getting different things out of it, but I know we're not, even if I don't like admitting that fact.

After using the bathroom, I make my way back down the hall, already dreaming of coffee because no matter how cozy Joel makes me, I won't be able to fall back asleep. Especially since I have to be up in a half hour, anyway.

I'm almost to my bedroom door when I hear a soft tapping. I tilt my head and look into Rae's room. Rae's *old* room.

There's tapping again. I walk through the empty room and pull the curtains open. I'm greeted with my sister's smiling face. She waves, then motions for me to lift the window. Confused, I unlock it and slide it up, then climb out, shutting it behind me.

"Hi," I say softly. "What are you doing here?"

She smiles a bubbly smile at me.

My sister can be the most dramatic, emotional girl in the world, but when she's happy, she's effervescent. Her happiness is contagious. After what she's been through the last few years, it always makes me happy to see her like this.

"Come sit, and I'll tell you."

She pulls me over to the lounge bed and sits down.

I sit down next to her, narrowing my eyes slightly. "What's going on?"

"I have something to show you."

"Before 6:30 in the morning? You're being weird." I shove her shoulder.

In response, she whips her hand out of the pocket of the hoodie she's wearing—Aaron's, of course—and holds it up.

Oh. My. God.

I grab her hand, my eyes widening more each second.

"Grandma's ring?" I ask.

Her smile grows as she nods.

"On a very specific finger?" I continue.

She nods again.

"Oh my god!" I screech, pulling her into my arms. "When did this happen? How? Tell me, tell me!"

She laughs, bouncing a little. "It happened last night."

"Last night? Of course. The anniversary. Oh my gosh. How did he do it?" I smack her thigh. "Why aren't you over there still having crazy hot sex?"

She laughs again. "We already did plenty of that. He's sleepy." Her face is adorable. I'm sure she's imagining him asleep in their bed. "I snuck out because I... wanted you to be the first one to know."

Her eyes fill with emotion and I pull her into my arms again. "I love you, Rae baby."

"I love you too. And since we're going out with everyone tonight and you're working today, I wanted to make sure I got to tell you in person."

I pull back and take her hands. "Tell me everything."

After twenty minutes of gushing over the extremely romantic and sexy date and Aaron's perfect proposal—seriously, he nailed it—we end up snuggled under a blanket, chatting.

"You know, now that I'm living with Aaron, you could move into my old room. It's bigger. And the window's right there. That way Joel has less distance to walk when he climbs in."

She gives me a troublemaking smile, letting me know *she* knows exactly who is in my bed right now.

"No. I could never live in there. Even if you aren't here, it still feels like your room."

She looks out at the backyard. "Part of me misses it. I love our apartment, but I never had a moment of sleeping here for the last time and saying goodbye."

"Well, at least you know you'll still like it here if you and Aaron fuck it all up again." I smirk at her.

She elbows my side. *"Not* funny."

I shrug and smile.

"And what exactly is going on with you and Joel?" she asks, lifting an eyebrow.

"Nothing."

I answered that way too fast.

"Okay, then. I believe you," she says, nodding vigorously.

I toss my head back and look up at the sky. "When I figure it out, I'll let you know."

"Fair enough."

The alarm on my phone goes off and I pull it out of my bathrobe pocket and silence it.

"Ugh, that means I need to get up and get ready."

"That's okay. I should probably sneak back to the apartment before Aaron wakes up." She reaches over and wraps her arms around me. "I'll see you tonight, baby. And remember, tell no one about this."

I smile as I lean back. "My lips are sealed."

She climbs off the lounge bed and offers me a hand. I take it and stand.

"Have a good day at work."

"Have a good day getting laid." I wink at her and head back inside as she walks down the deck stairs, laughing.

Sighing, I close the window and lock it, then look around Rae's room.

Nope. I could never sleep in here.

The emptiness of the room still feels jarring, though. I'm crazy happy for Rae and Aaron, but I miss my sister. I knew it would happen eventually—especially given how hot and heavy she and A have always been—but I was never going to be ready for it.

Rae has always been my safety net. She catches me when I'm falling, cleans me up when I'm a complete mess, and has my back whenever I mess up. When I first moved in here, Mom and Dad let me sleep in her bed with her until I felt more comfortable. Even then, I ended up in the small bedroom I'm in because it was closest to hers. I didn't want to be without her.

I hate being alone. A product of my shitty early childhood before my parents adopted me. Which may be why I called Joel my first night without Rae here. The room felt hauntingly empty, and despite how happy I was—and am—for my sister, it made me sad.

I'm not sure if it was a moment of weakness when I called Joel, but I did it, and he showed up two minutes later—like always.

"You okay?" Joel asks softly, sitting on the edge of my bed.

I bite my lip and look away. Not much can make me cry, but feeling lonely always does the trick.

"It's stupid," I whisper.

He toes his shoes off and lays down next to me, staring into my eyes. "I doubt that."

"I miss Rae. I'm crazy happy for her and Aaron. They deserve to have their own place... but I—"

"Miss her. That's normal, Sarah. You two have lived together most of your lives and spent the last two years sharing a bedroom. This is sudden. Of course you're going to miss her. You know she'll always be there for you. You'll be welcome there any time. Except when they're busy. But you should be used to that part by now."

I bite back a smile and shake my head.

"It's more than that, though. It's the shift in our relationship, too. I knew it would happen, eventually. I'm just not ready yet."

Joel pushes a stray hair off my face and looks into my eyes with his captivating wildcat ones. They start a grayish green at the edges and transform into a beautiful golden bronze by the iris.

"I know. I've felt the shift, too. My relationships are changing with both of them as well. It's okay to feel sad about that. It's part of growing up. We'll all always have each other, but it'll keep changing as we get older." He kisses my forehead. "All the more reason we need to hold on to each other now. If you can't crawl into Rae's bed anymore, you're always welcome to crawl in mine." Though his voice is soft, his eyes dance.

"I might take you up on that."

Our faces inch closer together. His breath tickles my nose. Our eyes lock. My stomach twists, yearning for him. But I can't. Can't take this further just because I feel vulnerable.

It's not that I don't want him. It's not that I don't have big feelings for him. Both of those are true, and they have been for a while. But I can't play fast and loose with Joel. He's everything to me. If I can't do it right, I'm not doing it at all. Some lines can be crossed, but others could destroy everything.

With Trevor, I jumped in with both feet. It was easy. Maybe that's because I was young, or maybe it's because he never meant to me what Joel does. Either way, if I kiss Joel tonight, there's every chance I'd let it go too far.

Instead, I flutter my eyelids shut and take a deep breath, breaking the intensity of our gaze. Then I roll over, pull the blankets up, and say, "Snuggle me."

He laughs and shimmies further under the sheets before wrapping an arm around me. With his body nestled against mine, I feel safer. Relaxed. And finally, I fall asleep.

"Hey," Joel says, walking into the room in nothing but low-slung exercise shorts, and rubbing his eyes.

I smile softly at him. He's the best snuggler. Probably why we've spent every night sleeping in the same bed since then. Hence the slippery, icy, probably-going-to-crash-and-burn slope that we're sliding down right now.

"You're a liar," he says.

"Hm?"

"You said you'd be right back." He wraps his arms around me and kisses my nose. "You lied."

"Sorry. Rae showed up and—"

"Rae? That early? Why would she..." He steps back, a wide smile on his face.

Rae mentioned Joel might suspect last night involved the big question since he helped Aaron set up for some of it.

But I'm not giving him the satisfaction of an answer.

"Did something happen with her and Aaron last night? Something *good?*"

I look at the ceiling and shrug, then say, "I don't know what you're talking about. We just drank coffee and had some sister time."

He steps forward, sweeps his hands under my tank top across my ribs, then kisses me, pushing his tongue into my mouth.

Okay. Sometimes we kiss. But unlike my sister, I have no delusions about them being *friendly*. I know they aren't. Which scares the hell out of me. I don't want to be alone, but I'm not ready to be with him, either. I'd like to say I try not to give in, but I don't. I match him stroke for stroke, bringing one hand up to the back of his neck and playing with his hair.

He inhales sharply and presses his body into mine, deepening the kiss.

South of my waistband things are heating up, but I'm trying to ignore it. Some lines can't be crossed.

And this is when I focus on work. Focus on the day ahead. Don't stress over this. Even though, inevitably, when we're done hanging out with our friends tonight, we'll end up in the same bed again, still no clue what the hell we're doing, but doing it anyway.

Slowly, Joel untangles our tongues and lifts his lips off mine.

"Liar," he breathes against them, then steps back. "Your mouth doesn't taste like coffee."

That jackass.

He gives me his signature troublesome smirk, the one that melts me to my core, even if I like to pretend otherwise.

But two can play at this game.

I shrug again. "Don't know what you're talking about. Anyway, I've gotta get ready for work, so I'll see you tonight. Have a good day," I add in a sultry voice. Then I kiss his cheek and sashay past him and into my room, knowing he's gaping at me the whole time.

Joel

"Thanks," I say, lifting the cup of coffee to my lips as I exit the bakery. It takes everything inside me not to go upstairs, bang on Aaron and Rae's door, and find out what happened last night. The only thing stopping me is that I don't want to find them *banging.*

Sarah thought she was being funny this morning, changing the subject and walking away with that sexy sway in her hips. Joke was on her, though, because my clothes were still in her bedroom. So I gave her a minute, followed her inside, then pressed her up against her door and kissed her until she was sputtering for words and had to rush to get ready. The twinkle in her eye as she left said it was all worth it.

I got dressed and came down to the bakery for some coffee. It's not the fanciest coffee in the world, but it's a decent cup, and Mackie's mom always keeps interesting flavors on rotation. This is some kind of roasty-caramel flavor, which with some vanilla creamer does the trick of waking me and my taste buds up.

Rather than cross the street and cut through Sarah's backyard, I take the longer route, walking down the side street Sarah once lived on with her biological mother, then turning down Front Street and heading toward my house.

When I swing the front door open, I'm met with the sound of clattering in the kitchen. Toeing my shoes off, I walk down the hall and find my brother in the kitchen.

Jesse turns to stir something on the stove and says, "Hey little bro. What's up? Want some hash browns?"

I plop down at the kitchen counter. "Yes, please. I'm starving."

"Didn't have breakfast with Sarah?" Jesse asks with a smirk.

I grimace, and he laughs.

"What, do you think I don't know?"

I don't even know. At least not what we're doing.

But honestly, this is karma. I gave Rae and Aaron shit for years. Now it's coming back around to me.

"Shut up and feed me."

"Someone's hangry," he says with a laugh, placing some hash browns on my plate. "Want some eggs?"

"Please." I shove a forkful in my mouth. *Fuck, those are good.* "When did you learn to cook like this?"

He glances at me, then looks down. "Something I learned living with Carrie. I guess one good thing came out of our relationship."

Jesse and Carrie were planning on moving to Albany together, where they'd both gotten jobs. Actually, they made it as far as moving in together when Jesse found out Carrie had been talking with some other guy. She hadn't cheated, but things were headed in that direction. What Jesse thought were growing pains in their relationship was actually things slowly falling apart. When he called her out for talking to this other guy, again Carrie didn't seem to know what she wanted, at which point Jesse told her it obviously wasn't him and ended things. Now he's living back here for the summer while he figures out his next career move.

The first few days home were spent with him moping and crying. Then he switched to staying piss-drunk for a full forty-eight hours. He's still mad and hurting and occasionally getting drunk off his ass, but for the most part, he's leveled out.

Of course, there was the one night he gave me a nice long drunken speech about how stupid it is to hand your heart to someone and fall in love, especially if they won't love you back.

I tried not to let it get to me, but it was hard not to think of Sarah. She's nothing like Carrie, and I think she's being honest with me, but that doesn't make it easier to be in love with someone who isn't ready to open up and actually love me back. *I'm not going to push her.* Doesn't mean it isn't a challenge some days. Trying to give enough of myself without setting myself up to be completely crushed.

He lets out a sigh as he sets his plate of hash browns in front of him and leans over the counter.

"Well, look at the bright side. Your whole life is in front of you now. Even if it means you spend a summer crashing with your parents."

Jesse grimaces, then grabs a paper off the counter and hands it to me.

"Not so much on the parents."

I look down at the paper.

Joel and Jesse,
The other night we were invited by some friends to spend the

summer exploring Europe with them. After thinking it over, we decided we couldn't pass it up. They had a private jet leaving this morning. By the time you read this, we'll probably be in the air! What a whirlwind! We'll be back sometime in mid-August. We transferred extra money to the account that auto pays the credit card balance, so order food as much as you need to. Have a wonderful summer and we'll check in soon. If there are any emergencies, call the Hansens or the McKinleys, and they'll help out until we can get home (if need be). Love you both,
Mom and Dad

I let out a wry laugh and shake my head as I toss the paper onto the counter.

On-brand for my parents.

"Well, they left a note, at least," my brother says.

"Yeah. Great."

"Hey, I'll be here all summer." Jesse grins at me. "And I can cook now."

"Yeah, that's something, at least." I eat the last few bites of my hash browns and say, "I'm gonna pass on the eggs. I need a little more sleep. You'll be at The Rooftop tonight, right?"

"Definitely. Wouldn't miss it," Jesse says.

"All right. See you later."

I grab my coffee and head upstairs. When I get to my bedroom, I flop down on my bed.

I can't believe my parents up and left in the wee hours of the morning. Except I can believe it because they do shit like this way too often.

My parents can be wonderful. They're kind, generous, and never the type to flaunt their wealth. Most people in my life have no idea how much my father is actually worth. It's well into the millions. Not only was he CFO of a company that deals with government contracts manufacturing vehicles, aircraft, and drones; my great-grandfather invested big in real estate in New York City with the small inheritance his father left him when he passed. He sold it all off in the late eighties and made 500 percent back on his investments. Our family has been set ever since.

While it's nice not having to worry about money and getting to do plenty of fun shit—like having a lake house to live in with my best friends or a beach house to go to whenever we want—it doesn't replace having my parents actively involved in my life.

I get it. I was an oops baby. Jesse was too, but they hadn't officially decided they weren't having any more kids until after him. Then I showed up. They were burned out, I'm sure. Four boys is a lot. Especially with my oldest brother Jared, who was and still is—even at age twenty-eight—an utter pain in the ass. Jonathan, who is five years older than me, was always easier being quiet and introverted, but again, four boys is a lot to handle—especially if you weren't planning on having that many.

Don't get me wrong, my parents never said anything to make me feel like they didn't want me. I know they love me and support me. But they aren't *here* for me. They had checked out by the time I was in middle school. They were looking at early retirement and traveling the world, something they always wanted to do. Even when I was little, their focus was rarely on me, unless I specifically asked for their attention. They weren't mean about it, they just weren't there. By the time I was in high school, they were off having adventures, and I was living here with Jesse or alone most of the time.

Staring up at my ceiling, I let out a long breath.

I have a good life, but I also have some mild attention issues. It's why I like being the wittiest guy in the room and having all eyes on me. Like Sarah, I hate being alone. But while it sends her spiraling, I adapted by becoming the kid always with his friends, who could show up at their house any time and be welcome. I rarely have to be alone unless I *choose* to be. Of course, as Sarah has noted, things are changing with Rae and Aaron moving in together and all that.

Sarah might not realize it, but I cherish every night with her because it's another night I'm not alone.

This is where Aaron and Miles would call me a sap.

I try not to come off as clingy, even though I feel that way sometimes, like I'm always poking at the people in my life and silently asking, "Do you love me?"

It's probably why I was so cranky when Rae brought Aaron around for the first time. She was *my* best friend. Then I met him, and he gave me a huge smile, said he liked baseball, and I realized he would be *our* best friend. I'm lucky I ended up with the five of them in my life, but I'm especially grateful that Rae and I stayed so close. She's the sister I never had.

I grab my phone and text her.

Me: How was the anniversary last night?

I'm surprised when I get an immediate text back.

Rae Rae: Good.

Me: Just good?

Rae Rae: It's always good with Aaron. ;)

Me: Gross. I wasn't asking about the sex.

Rae Rae: What were you asking?

Me: I think you know.

Rae Rae: Do I?

Me: You're impossible!

Rae Rae: Maybe.

Rae Rae: Meet us at the apartment at 5 and walk down to The Rooftop with us?

Me: Sounds good. See you then. Love ya!

Rae Rae: Love you too, Joelskies! And thanks for helping out with everything last night. ;)

I'm not sure if I'm more or less confused than I was before I texted her, but hopefully I'll find out tonight.

I set my phone down, roll over, and grab my body pillow. It's infinitely less cozy than Sarah, but I'm tired enough I pass out, anyway.

I wait near the corner across from the bakery for a couple of cars to go by, then cross the road.

As I'm stepping onto the sidewalk, the door next to the bakery that leads to the apartments swings open and Rae and Aaron step out, holding hands and chatting.

I stop in place and stare at them. I'm out of patience.

"Hey, Joelskies," Rae says when she sees me, acting like there's nothing going on.

"Hey, man," Aaron says.

"Are you two engaged?"

Aaron laughs, then looks down at Rae, who beams up at him. Then she turns to me and sticks up one finger. I assume she's flipping me off until I realize it's her ring finger and there's a gorgeous ring on it.

My chest swells, bursting with happiness and excitement for them. After everything they've been through, they deserve this.

I feel tears trying to make their way to my eyes, but I push them down. It's always been a joke that Rae and I are the dramatic ones. We are freakishly alike sometimes. And of the guys, I've always been the most emotional.

Putting on a know-it-all smile, I say, "It's about damn time. We've only been waiting for fifteen years."

"Hey," Aaron says, taking mock offense, "I didn't even tell her I was going to marry her until eleven years ago, *thank you.*"

I pull Rae into my arms for a bear hug. She squeezes me back and says, "Thanks for helping to make it perfect."

She steps back and I take her in. I love it when she's happy. Maybe because she's so expressive, her pain is more palpable. In the same way, her happiness is effusive.

"You look happy."

"I'm stupidly, ridiculously, perfectly happy." She turns and looks up at Aaron with starry eyes. He looks at her with so much heat in his gaze I want to vomit, then he grabs her and kisses her possessively.

I roll my eyes, then make a dramatic retching noise.

"I know you're excited, but could you maybe... not?"

Aaron laughs as he pulls his lips from hers, then smacks my shoulder.

"Oh, I absolutely can and *will* make out with my *fiancée.*"

He says it, and Rae visibly swoons. I love them being happy and all, but they are nauseating. That's how it's always been with them. They're disgustingly in love or everything is a dumpster fire—thankfully, I think we're past the worst of the flames now.

"So, you told Sarah this morning? What about everyone else?" I ask as they find some sense of decorum and start walking down the sidewalk.

"Oh, you know, we've got a plan," Rae says with a smirk.

Their favorite thing to do is tell people in over-the-top ways. Like when they first started dating and Aaron and Jesse staged a fight.

"Actually, we could use your help with the friends tonight," Aaron says. "We're telling the parents at brunch tomorrow."

"Cool, I'll send mine a carrier pigeon to wherever the fuck they are tomorrow."

Aaron winces. "They're gone again?"

I shrug. "For the summer."

Rae loops her arm through mine and says, "More time for you to spend with us. Now, about tonight..."

She tells me her plan, and I'm excited to be the one helping them pull off the surprise announcement this time.

Sarah

"What? I thought she quit?"

My eyes drift sideways as a nurse says to one of the secretaries, "No. She failed the drug test. Cocaine, I heard."

I roll my eyes and turn around, heading over to the room where my fetal monitoring patient is.

"You okay in here?"

"I'm okay, but she flipped over," the woman grimaces, then continues. "I tried to fix it, but it's still not picking her up."

"Okay, let's see what we can do."

I glance at the readout to see how long ago the movement dropped off, then reposition the belt.

"Hopefully, she'll stay around there for another ten minutes. If not, just give me a yell. My name's Sarah."

"Okay, thanks."

I walk back out and see an empty room that needs clearing and a wipe down.

I get to work doing that. It's not the most glamorous work, but it's closer to what I want to do than most other jobs, and they pay me well. I feel lucky that the OBGYN office I work at was willing to hire me for summers and school breaks only. It probably helps that I have a great relationship with the CNM and nurse practitioner here. She's my provider, and we got talking at one of my appointments about how I wanted to work in this field eventually, and she gave me her number. When they had an opening, she let me know, and I think she talked me up pretty heavily, too.

It's a good place to work, not as toxic as a lot of other places I've experienced, but healthcare breeds it. Long hours, chronically understaffed, not always great pay, heavy burn out.

I'm not exactly selling this, am I?

It's what I've always wanted to do, though. Originally, I just wanted to be a nurse, but as I worked as a nursing assistant, I homed in on what I enjoyed, and that's obstetrics and gynecology. I graduate from my three-year nursing program in one year, and then I'll be moving right into a graduate program that will certify me as nurse midwife and a women's health nurse practitioner.

This is a step on that journey, though I'm hoping to work part-time here as a nurse when I've graduated. There's a large hospital where we do all of our practicum for our nursing program up by SUNY FL, so hopefully during the school year, I'll be able to work part-time on their OB unit.

I finish stripping and cleaning the room, then carefully remove my gloves, wash my hands, and check on the woman having the fetal monitoring done.

"Hey there. Did she stay put this time?"

"Yep."

"Good." I step all the way into the room and pull the belt off and give her tissues to wipe the gel off her stomach. "Just one minute."

I step out of the room.

"Hey, Alissa, I have your OB patient. She just finished fetal monitoring."

"Oh, perfect. I'll grab her. Thanks, Sarah."

"No problem."

Usually the nursing assistants don't take care of the fetal monitoring patients, but because I'm in the nursing program, they give me some extra responsibilities.

Glancing up at the clock, I see it's about time to head out. I'm excited for tonight, and I can't wait to see how Rae and Aaron tell everyone.

I do a quick walk through to make sure no other rooms need cleaning and no one else needs anything.

I'm heading to the employee area where my stuff is when I hear, "Sarah? Sarah, honey! Are you busy right now?"

Shit.

Rather than answer, I spin around and look at one of the nurses. "What's up, Alma?"

"Well, Dr. Wilson has a patient he needed to squeeze in. His nursing assistant has to leave, but I was wondering if you could stay. It shouldn't take too long. She'll be here in ten minutes."

Say no. It's okay to set boundaries. I have plans. It's not my doctor. Say no. Just say no.

Alma looks at me with puppy dog eyes.

Crap.

I should've said no.

That quick appointment took almost an hour. Now I'm rushing through a shower, feeling more stressed than I was at work. I don't want to be late. I know my friends won't care, but I don't want to miss out on anything. Plus, I've been looking forward to this.

We're going to a new restaurant called The Rooftop. It has four levels. A brewpub type of restaurant on the ground floor with live music. A club style area for those twenty-one and up—won't be going there for another year—then there's an entertaining area on the third floor, able to be rented out for gatherings or parties. Finally, there's the rooftop. It looks out over downtown Ida and has a lounge feel. There are even gas fire pits scattered throughout. You can order appetizers and light fare from the restaurant and have it brought upstairs. The focus is on relaxing with friends and enjoying food and drinks throughout the night. They even have plenty of alcohol-free cocktails. It opened a few weeks ago, and we've been stalking their social media and looking at the menu constantly because it seemed so cool.

There will be a big crowd there tonight, and I'm excited. In addition to the six of us, Trevor, Hyla, Amanda, Jamie, Jesse, Maia, Vince, Nick, Leigh, and Braden will all be there.

After toweling off and quickly styling my hair, I get dressed and head downstairs.

My parents are sitting in the front room, chatting and drinking wine. I'm glad I'm going out tonight. They look like they want to get a little *dirty*.

"Should I avert my eyes?" I ask, walking into the room, shielding my eyes.

Dad laughs. Mom's cheeks are a little pink. Not sure if it's because she's embarrassed or from the wine. It's a little weird, but I love seeing my parents like this. It's strange to think that they're only forty. They had Rae so young, they're still a young couple themselves, and it's clear they're still having plenty of *fun*.

Mom doesn't answer my question, instead asking, "Heading out?"

"Yep. We're going to check out The Rooftop." I look down at my watch. "In fact, I better walk fast."

I walk over and give them each a kiss on the cheek. "Love you guys. Have fun tonight. I'll be home late, or I might stay with Rae and Aaron." I know I won't, but I want them to have *fun*. I'll come in through the window and I won't be able to hear anything from my room, anyway.

"Okay, if you stay somewhere else, let us know," Dad says. "Have fun and tell us how it is. Love you, honey."

"Love you guys, too."

I wave and head out the door.

On the list of things I'm grateful for in life, my parents adopting me is number one every single time. I was more broken than they possibly could have realized when they got custody of me. In some ways, I'm still learning how much my early childhood damaged me. Being in a safe place let me process it, even if I still did plenty of stupid shit. They loved me through it, though. They always do.

I wish I could say I've healed from most of it—I guess I have. I haven't healed from all of it, though. And my biological mother, though I wish she weren't, is still a big trigger point for me. That's why I decided to cut off contact a few years ago. I'm healthier and happier because of it.

I make my way downtown and head for The Rooftop.

When I get there, I give them the party name and am escorted to the elevator that leads to the roof. When the doors open, revealing the beautiful rooftop, I find everyone immediately. They're the biggest party, settled in lounge chairs around a fire pit with a table along the outside filled with food. They're also chatting and laughing loudly. I love my friends.

"There she is!" Amanda yells as I walk over.

"Hey, guys."

I'm surprised for a moment to see my cousin Dani sitting with everyone, but then I remember she's in town visiting Grandma and Grandpa. I'm excited because I don't get to see her nearly enough. She's one of the cousins Rae and I are closest to, and she's a ton of fun to be around. Saucy, spunky, and does not take anyone's crap. She's like a snarkier version of Rae.

People shout greetings back as I lean down and kiss Rae's cheek. Her ring is conveniently obscured by a sweater, and she's nestled happily against Aaron. It makes my heart so happy seeing her like this.

I make my way around the large circle, exchanging a wink with Miles before sitting down between Joel and Mackie.

"How was your day?" Joel asks, making me a plate and pouring me some sparkling juice.

"Long," I sigh. "But not bad. Way better now." I smile at him, trying not to be too obvious that part of that is because of him. It's probably pointless, though.

I grab the sparkling juice and am about to take a drink when Joel stops my hand. He nods toward the other full glasses around the fire, and says, "Now that everyone is here, I'd like to make a toast."

Everyone quiets down and looks at Joel. I'm confused for a second until I see the twinkle in his eyes and know exactly what's happening.

"Here's to our first night at a place that will inevitably become a frequent hangout. To all of us being home for the summer and having a great time together. To Chuck at the bar for sneaking me some actual champagne." He looks in Chuck's direction and gives a tiny nod. Chuck is a year older and used to play baseball with the boys. "And to Rae and Aaron for *finally* doing what we've all been waiting for. Congratulations on your engagement. Cheers!" He quickly drinks and everyone else is in the midst of saying cheers or drinking when they process his words.

I smirk as I look around.

Then Amanda shrieks, "What?!"

Miles leans forward at the same time as Mackie and asks, "Seriously?"

Rae and Aaron smile at each other, then she dramatically stretches her arm up, before bringing her hand down, no longer obscured by the sleeve of her sweater, and says, "Yep."

"Oh my god!" Amanda, Mackie, and Hyla yell at once, reaching over the firepit and grabbing her hand.

Congratulations and details about the engagement are given, and the rest of the evening is spent enjoying good food, plenty of champagne, and eventually roasting marshmallows.

It's after eleven at night before we finally disband and head home. Joel walked home with Jesse because he was bordering on sloppy drunk. His drinking picked up after Rae and Aaron made their announcement. Though Rae took him aside and talked with him, I'm sure he was still trying to drown his sorrows.

I'm walking back to our block with Mackie, Miles, Rae, and Aaron. Rae's arms are looped through mine and Mackie's as we giggle, walking together and whispering about all the dirty things Rae did with Aaron last night and this morning.

"You know, we can hear you," Aaron says about halfway home.

"Like you don't already know what happened," I tease.

Miles laughs as Aaron shakes his head.

When we get to our house—my house? I don't know what to call it now that Rae has moved out—we exchange hugs and goodbyes.

"You want to come over for a bit?" Rae asks, squeezing me tightly.

I look over her shoulder at Aaron, who is talking to Miles, but keeps glancing at Rae.

"Nah. I'll be fine. Have fun with your fiancé."

Rae beams at me. "That I can do."

When she lets me go, I give Aaron a big hug. "Congratulations. I'm so happy for you two."

"Thanks, Sarbear. And thank you for always believing in us." He lowers his voice and whispers, "For the record, I believe in you and Joel."

Then he steps back and winks at me before wrapping his arms around Rae.

We all wave to each other, then I watch as Miles crosses the street and Rae and Aaron walk toward the bakery with Mackie. I turn toward the house and glance up at my parents' bedroom window. Seeing the light on but the curtains drawn, I make my way to the back of the house, unlock the gate, and head up the deck stairs before climbing through the window. I do my best to ignore the emptiness of Rae's old room, and hurry into mine.

After stripping out of my cute clothes, I throw on an oversized tee and tiny sleep shorts, then climb into bed.

I lie flat on my back, close my eyes, and inhale deeply, in and out, and try to relax. I will myself to go to sleep, but sleep doesn't come. Toss. Turn. Change position. Change position again. Maybe if I lay on my stomach. Nothing works.

I open my eyes and silently scream at my ceiling.

Fuck it.

I violently toss the sheet off, grab my phone, throw on my sweatshirt, and give in to what my body and heart want.

Joel

Soft footsteps pad across my bedroom floor. Sarah's warm hand sweeps across my back as she slides into bed with me. Her movements are slow, deliberate, filled with grace. There's never any uncertainty when she does this. She wants me, no matter how much it terrifies her. Not that it's surprising tonight.

Sarah and change mix about as well as oil and water. And that's all this last month has been. Now Rae and Aaron are engaged, and while I know she's thrilled for Rae, it's another change. Another hole in the armor of consistency Sarah is used to wearing.

Her sky-blue eyes roll over my face, then she bites her lip and smiles. I'm a goner. I always have been for her. Ever since we were little kids and she'd work the puppy dog eyes on me—or anyone—to get what she wanted, I couldn't resist her.

Sliding a hand up her rib cage, I roll on top of her, intertwining our fingers before stretching her arms up and pinning them above her head.

My heart ticks up, falling into rhythm with hers as our lips meet. Those soft, supple pink lips swell under mine, and she wastes no time taking what she wants. Her tongue in my mouth, her body molding against mine.

I squeeze her hands tighter as I draw my lips away, moving them down her neck as she moans.

With the flex of her arms, she rips her hands down, wrapping them around my back and pushing me onto my side. She throws a leg over the top of mine and our lips meet again.

She pours herself into me.

And I wish she'd say it.

I wish she'd say what's vibrant in her eyes. What's radiating from her heart.

But she won't do it.

She's too afraid. Afraid to lose her safety. Her peace. Me.

What she doesn't understand is she never could.

Never.

Not because we're like Rae and Aaron. No, we've never been that volatile. Our relationship is softer and understated.

She'd never lose me because loving her is like breathing to me.

And I know how pathetic that sounds, but it's true.

She could eviscerate my heart, put it in a blender, feed it to me, and I'd eat every bite and beg for more.

I'd walk in front of a bus before I'd walk away from her.

And that's how she deserves to be fucking loved. That's how I'll keep loving her. She might not know how to fully accept it, but I'll keep giving it, praying one day she'll finally be ready to let it all in, let it wrap around her and sweep her into the safety of us.

But it won't be tonight.

So, I turn my attention back to her lips, her tongue, and her soft yet sculpted body pressed into mine. I run my fingers through her hair and revel in this high, always painfully aware that tonight might be the last time I feel it.

Chapter Two

Mess It Up

Sarah

"MORNING," JOEL MUMBLES, FLOPPING back into my bed after using the bathroom.

"Hi," I murmur, rolling over and pulling him to me. "It's cold this morning. It's supposed to be June."

He chuckles. "It *is* June. It's June in Ida. Don't you remember the year it snowed on the Fourth of July?"

"Ugh. Don't remind me. I want warm. I want summer. You think we can go to Charleston?"

He chuckles. "We did talk about going this year, but never did." He pulls his phone out and taps around.

I shield my eyes from the light of his phone screen. "What are you doing?"

"Seeing when spring break is next year so I can book the beach house."

I prop myself up on my elbow. "Really?"

"We can't drop everything and go now, but we can still go. Plus, spring break falls over my and Rae's birthdays this year. It will be the perfect birthday trip. And you in a bikini will be the perfect present."

I give his shoulder a shove, then bite my lip and look down. When he says things like that, it feels like we're doing more than we are. It scares me and it makes me feel guilty.

"Hey," he says softly. "I'm just kidding."

I stare at him for a beat, then smile and say, "No, you're not. But if I wear a bikini, you have to wear a Speedo."

He laughs at that. "No fucking way."

"Mm. Your loss, then. I'll have to get one of those one-piece suits with a skirt at the bottom and cap sleeves. Ooh. Or a wetsuit."

I'm laughing so hard I don't feel the bed shift, and that's when he pounces on me, tickling me as I screech and try—not very hard—to get free, but then he drops on top of me, going limp so all of his weight is on me.

"Joel. Get. Off."

I give him a shove and he falls onto his back, laughing.

We lie in silence for a few minutes before he takes my hand and says, "Sarah?"

Crap.

That's his serious, I-need-to-talk-to-you voice. Maybe I took the flirting too far.

Though my instinct is to change the topic or say I need to use the bathroom, I know Joel well enough to know it would only delay the conversation. He's like an elephant. He never forgets anything.

Isn't that the saying? *Elephants never forget?*

He gives my hand a squeeze, reminding me I haven't answered.

"Hmm?" I try to keep the tone of my voice even. I don't want him to think I'm nervous about where this is going. Even though I am.

"Can we keep doing this?"

"Keep doing what?" I ask, trying to hide my breathiness. My heart is slamming in my chest. I don't want to have to turn him down again. I don't want to tell him I'm not ready yet. Not again. I'm scared he'll give up on me if he asks again and I say no or not yet.

"Sleeping in the same bed. I..." he trails off and takes a deep breath. "You told me you weren't ready for more yet, and I agreed. Do you remember what I told you? When we talked after Valentine's Day?"

I swallow hard.

"Tell me again."

I remember every word, but I want to hear him say it again.

"I understand this is hard for you, and I won't push, as long as you're honest with me. And even if you want to take it one tiny step at a time, that's okay, too. I'll be here. Spending time with you is my favorite thing, and I'm happy however we do that. Just promise me if you ever decide you don't want this, you'll tell me. Don't lead me on, that's all I ask."

"Joel, I—"

"I'm not asking for anything more. I'm not asking for a promise that this is the next step toward us being something. There's nothing like late nights in a big bed to make me feel horribly alone. I like sleeping next to you. Will you stay in the master with me at the lake house? There are two closets and that private bath, plus a foldout couch, so if you don't want me in the bed, that's okay. I just—"

I grab him and wrap my arms around him, pulling him to my lips for a hard kiss.

It's stupid. Every single time I do it, I recognize the lines we're blurring, but when I kiss him, I stop caring. And right now, I want him to know how loved he is. I'm not holding back *because* of him. I'm holding back *for* him.

Joel might've had his parents around, but they were often in the periphery. Joel hates loneliness like I do, and I never want him to feel lonely. Sharing a bed is win-win. Whatever we're ready for or not, we can keep doing this.

"I do love a big closet," I tease as I pull away. "I can't promise—"

"I know," he whispers.

"But I'd like to keep snuggling with you. You're the best snuggler."

He kisses my forehead.

"And don't worry, I'll make it clear to everyone there are two beds, so in their eyes we'll be roomies, okay?"

"Thanks, Joel." The words are simple, but the way our eyes lock and the intensity of our gaze tells the weight behind them. How thankful I am for him respecting my boundaries, for not pushing me, even when the rules I set twist around and seem crazy.

"Of course."

He wraps an arm around me and I rest my head on his shoulder.

After a little while, both of our phones go off. He grabs his and shows me a group text from Rae.

Rae: On our way to Syracuse for the appointment. We'll keep you all updated!

Today is Aaron's appointment with the specialist about his hand. He's been nervous, and I know this topic brings complicated feelings up in their relationship. That night shaped so much of them and their future and their relationship.

I roll over and grab my phone.

Me: Love you guys! Sending all the positive vibes.

Joel: Hoping for the best. Call if you need anything.

Miles: Well, fuck me, y'all are actually up early for a change. Tell A it'll be okay, and you try not to stress too much. Love ya.

Mackie: Too early, but I love you guys, and ^ all of the above.

Rae: Thanks guys! Love you.

Joel sets his phone down as I drop mine onto the bed.

"I hope it all goes okay," I say.

"Me too," Joel says, and I can feel his anxiousness. His relationship with Aaron was rough for a bit after Aaron's injury and subsequent spiral, and I know he feels guilty about it.

Joel bounces his leg while chewing on his cheek.

Distraction mode engaged.

"Hey, how about we go down to Marion's for breakfast? I bet she'll have those amazing homemade bagels if we get there this early. Then we can have some fun with last minute shopping and setting up for tonight."

I get a beaming smile for that. "Sounds perfect."

He leaps out of bed, rips my curtains open—which makes me groan and cover my eyes—then starts getting dressed.

I shake my head but smile and climb out of bed as well.

Rae

Aaron bounces his knees, then runs a hand through his hair and cracks his knuckles.

I place my hand gently over the top of his interlaced fingers, my ring shimmering under the bright hospital lights as I do.

"Ace," I whisper.

His eyes snap to me, then he takes a deep breath. "Sorry. I'm nervous. Ridiculously nervous."

"That's okay. This is a big trigger for you."

He pulls one of his hands from under mine, then wraps it around my back and pulls me close, kissing my head. "I love you, Beautiful. Thank you for being here with me."

"I love you too, Ace, but don't thank me for that. You know there is nowhere else I would ever be."

"I know. My mind is just fucked up right now. The doctor is running late and all I can think is he won't give me the time of day like the last time and—"

"Last time, I wasn't with you. And that's my fault because I was treating you like crap. I'm sorry for that. We have no idea if this doctor will be the same. Hopefully not, but he's not going to blow you off, because I will body block the door and not let him leave until he gives you the time you deserve." I smile at him, and he finally laughs.

He leans over and kisses me. "I love you," he mutters against my lips.

And my heart soars. You'd think we'd just started dating, not that we're engaged.

Yep. Still love saying that.

I'm about to kiss him again when there's a quick knock on the door and it swings open.

Aaron sits up straight as the doctor—who is younger than I thought he'd be—walks in.

"Hi there, Aaron?"

We both stand and Aaron shakes the doctor's extended hand. "That's me. And this is my fiancée, Rae."

"Nice to meet you both," he says, quickly shaking my hand. "I'm Doctor McCarthy. You can call me Max, though. Sorry I was late, I squeezed someone in last minute this morning and

I've been behind since, but it's important to me that I take time with each patient."

I squeeze Aaron's hand and look at him like, *see?*

He sits at the computer and pulls up Aaron's files. "So, you injured your hand several years ago?"

"Correct," Aaron says. He's using his coach voice.

"And you're a pitcher?"

"Was," Aaron says, clearing his throat.

"He's on hiatus. He's a pitching coach now," I say sweetly.

"You'd like to pitch again?"

Aaron takes a deep breath, a pained expression crossing his face. I grab his hand and hold it tightly.

Doctor Max looks over at him and smiles softly.

"I would love to be able to pitch again," Aaron says, voice thick with emotion. "I just don't want to get my hopes up."

Doctor Max nods in understanding, then spins the stool he's on toward us.

"And you've had some treatment?"

"Some PT and OT, but it only helps me manage it. If I miss a session or doing my exercises, it gets stiff and painful."

"Have you ever had a consult before?"

Aaron bristles slightly. "Yeah. The guy spent five minutes with me and said I wasn't a candidate for surgery."

Doctor Max looks at Aaron like he's crazy. Then he shakes his head.

"That's the kind of doctor I aspire to never be. A healthy teenager who was in pain and wanted to continue their baseball career? Ridiculous. You're absolutely a candidate for surgery. A good one, too."

Aaron's demeanor changes and he lets out a sigh of relief.

Doctor Max smiles, and looks back at the computer, pulling up the X-rays. "Okay, so the fractures occurred when?"

"Around this time, three years ago."

"And when did you first seek treatment?"

"Uh, around six months later," he says, looking down.

I squeeze Aaron's hand tighter and try to push my emotion down. I don't love looking back at that time in our relationship or how this all happened in the first place.

Doctor Max looks between us. "Can I ask how the injury happened?"

Now *I'm* the one looking down. Aaron rubs his thumb over my hand, then looks Doctor Max square in the eye. "I beat the shit out of the guy who sexually assaulted her."

Doctor Max nods. "Hope the fucker got what he deserved. I'm going to make sure we do everything we can to get you pitching again. There are no guarantees, but you're young and healthy, and with surgery, I'm confident we can move in that direction. Hop up on the table for me."

As Doctor Max examines Aaron, he tells us about the plan. They go in, rebreak the fingers or even cut away some bone, then realign the fingers. After that, he'll wear a cast for four to six weeks. Once he's cleared by the doctor, he'll start PT and OT again, and this time, hopefully, he'll be working toward an end goal of getting back or close to the pre-fracture state.

"Your season starts when?" Doctor Max asks, going back to the computer as Aaron comes back to me.

"We start regular practice again in January, then the first game is in late March."

Doctor Max pulls up a schedule. "That should be good. I'm booking into October at this point. How does the week of the twentieth work for you?"

Aaron chuckles. "Never thought I'd say this, but I can't do that week. We're getting married that weekend."

Doctor Max smiles at that. "That's absolutely fine. Let's look at November instead. How does the eighth sound?"

Aaron looks at me and I smile back.

"Sounds good," he says softly.

"Perfect. The checkout desk will get it all scheduled and give you all the details for any pre-op testing, when you'll need to be here, everything like that." He pulls a card out. "If you have any concerns or questions before then, this has all my contact information on it."

"Thank you," Aaron says, voice thick with emotion.

Doctor Max nods, and grabs his files, then says, "Thanks for trusting me with this. Take care."

"Take care. Thanks," I say as he leaves.

Aaron and I stand up. He looks at me in disbelief, then pulls me into his arms. I hold him tight as I say, "See, Ace? It's going to be okay."

He blows out a breath and chuckles. "I hope so. Whew. Trying not to get my hopes up, but the idea of pitching again? Hell, not having my hand ache constantly? That would be amazing."

"I think it can happen," I whisper.

He gives me one last squeeze and lets me go, his face still covered in emotion.

"What do you say we check out, then grab some lunch before we head home?"

"Sounds perfect, Beautiful. Let's go."

He takes my hand, and we walk out of the room, both cautiously optimistic of what this could mean for his future.

Joel

"Congrats, man. That's awesome," Trevor says, smacking Aaron on the shoulder.

"I wish I was fully excited about it instead of anxious," Aaron says, buttoning up the charcoal gray dress shirt he's wearing.

"Reframe it," Miles says. "You've got it all wrapped up in how it happened and what it means for baseball. Focus on the fact that it causes you pain in your daily activities and, at the very least, the procedure *will* help with that."

"What's the date again?" I ask, flicking through my phone calendar.

"It's all subject to change, but November eighth."

I nod and add it to my calendar. "I'll be there."

Aaron stops mid-button and turns to me. "You don't have to."

Before I can say anything else, Jamie says, "I'll be there too."

Aaron turns to him with a smirk. "You mean, if your coach *lets* you. You'll either be playing in the league or at a D1 school. That's more important than my two-hour procedure."

He looks between all of us. "Rae and my parents will be with me. Rae will keep everyone updated, so no one needs to miss school or anything. Now, it's not happening for another four months, so I'd much rather focus on the exciting things that are happening before that, specifically my engagement party tonight."

"To that end," Jesse says, descending the basement stairs, "let's have a toast."

"You're going to give it?" Aaron asks, lips pulling flat.

"Damn straight." He gestures for each of us to take a shot glass, then fills each one with bourbon. He holds his glass up and says, "Here's to a night of celebrating Aaron and Rae being the nauseating couple we love—and lovingly mock—and all the fun wedding shenanigans to come. Cheers!"

We all clink and drink, then Jesse, Miles, Trevor, and Jamie head for the stairs, but I grab Aaron's arm. "Can I talk to you for a second?"

"What's up?"

"I want to be there. For your surgery."

"Joel, I appreciate it, but you don't need to be there."

"I *want* to be there. For you. And for Rae. But especially for you." I try to keep the emotion from my voice. The guilt. I didn't show up for him the way I should have when everything happened with his hand. I didn't encourage him to get treatment, I gave him a truckload of shit when he couldn't play, and I was an ass to him when he was in a downward spiral. He'd always been the steadfast one, and when he wasn't anymore, I treated him like shit rather than see the pain he was in. Some best friend I am.

He appraises me, then puts a hand on my shoulder. "You know we're good, right? We talked through all this shit a long time ago. I don't hold on to any of it. You shouldn't, either. We're good."

He gives me the same stupid smile he gave me the day we met. The day I knew I'd found a lifelong friend.

"I know, but you're my best friend, I want to support you. When everything else happened... I fucked it up."

Aaron is the kind of person who would walk over hot coals for a fucking stranger. He'd never give up on any of us. He never has. When he needed me the most, I let him down. He may have let it go, but that doesn't mean I have. See: needing to make sure my friends know I love them and they love me back.

Aaron lets out a little chuckle. "You're my best friend, too." He looks up at the stairs. "Which is why I would like you to be my best man."

My chest swells with emotion.

"Really?"

"Of course. I mean, I'll have other people up there, but you're the one I want standing next to me."

Oh, fuck. That's gonna do it.

Tears crest in my eyes.

"I'd be honored, A."

"Come here," he says, extending an arm and pulling me into a hug. I sniff as I pull away and he laughs. "I knew that would get you."

"You're an ass."

That just makes him smile wider and his eyes dance.

"You love me," he says.

I roll my eyes in response.

"I suppose," he says, taking a last look in the mirror, "it might be good to have you there for surgery. Especially for Rae's sake. She won't show it to me, but I know she'll be a mess."

"Well, of course. It's Rae. I'll definitely be there."

"Hey, are you two done making out down there?" Trevor calls, coming part way down the stairs.

"Yeah, you might want to hurry up. I have it on good authority that your fiancée looks incredible. You *might* want to get your ass moving so you can see her," Miles says.

If there's a way to light a fire under Aaron's ass, it's getting him riled up for Rae.

"Coming," he yells back.

"That's what she said!" Jesse calls from upstairs.

I shake my head as we walk toward the stairs. Aaron looks back at the couch and smiles.

"What's that look? Oh god, please tell me you haven't had sex with her on that couch."

He laughs. "Surprisingly, no. I did have a dirty dream about her there, which she discovered and almost fulfilled."

"Gross."

"I was actually thinking about the morning after I lost my virginity."

"Why? Did something happen between you two?"

He glances at the couch again and smiles as he steps on the stairs. "Mm. Not technically, but something *could* have. And for me, it was the moment that started it all."

"You guys were fucking ridiculous," I say with a headshake.

He stops and gives me a smug grin. "Pot meet kettle."

Then he walks up the stairs, laughing the whole way.

Jackass.

Sarah

"You look gorgeous!" I run my hands through Rae's styled waves one last time to make sure they look perfect, then she twirls around as Mackie, Hyla, and Amanda whistle and clap.

"And that dress..." Amanda says. "Damn, girl."

"Well, I did buy it with him in mind," she says with a cheeky smile. "I'm glad it still fits. I'm not the same size I was during senior year." She runs her hands over the sparkly green dress she wore to homecoming senior year.

"I think you look even better in it now," I tell her.

"Definitely," Mackie agrees. "He's going to get an instant boner."

"Mm. I hope so. Especially after this morning. The appointment might've gone well, but he's still anxious about it. I want to take his mind off it."

"That dress will have his mind on only one thing: you and how hot you look in it," Hyla says, wiggling her eyebrows.

"Agreed!" I shout, then grab the champagne and pour us each a glass. "Here's to Rae getting married to the man of her dreams, making us all believe in love, and giving Aaron an instant boner in that dress!"

Everyone laughs and clinks their glasses together.

"Oh, by the way, I talked to Leigh, and she has the date all set for us," Amanda says.

"I can't wait to see you in wedding dresses, Rae baby."

Rae puts her hands on her cheeks and shakes her head in disbelief. "I can't believe I'm getting married. In just over four months! It's crazy. I'm so excited. And praying we can pull it off."

Amanda waves her hand in dismissal. "I told you, it'll be fine."

Amanda jumped in to be Rae and Aaron's wedding planner. Rae offered to pay her, but Amanda said she needed the experience. Although, honestly, Amanda doesn't even need to finish her degree to be a planner. She is talented and has everything figured out. As soon as Rae and Aaron announced they were getting married at the barn on our grandparents' property, Amanda narrowed down what they wanted for food, flowers, and decor, and got it all booked. Now she's working on their honeymoon. If the phrase head bitch in charge were a person, it would be Amanda. She could easily be a mafia boss.

My phone chimes, letting me know it's time for us to go, and we all slide on our heels, grab our clutches, and walk out the door.

"Are you ready for him to see you?" I ask Rae.

"You're acting like I'm in my wedding dress," she says.

"No, if you were in your wedding dress, I'd probably be crying."

She wraps her arm around my back and rests her head on my shoulder. "I love you. Thank you for putting this night together. Everything is gorgeous."

We're at The Rooftop, and the entire roof is decked out in white and light pink streamers and flowers with plenty of white twinkle lights and tea lights everywhere.

"Excuse me, I helped too," Joel says, walking over from the stairwell. "Aaron's about to come up the elevator, so get ready to be gross."

She smacks his stomach, then says, "Thank you too, Joelskies."

The elevator dings and Rae steps away, standing a few feet away from the doors. I open my camera app, ready to take photos of the look on Aaron's face.

Joel wraps an arm around my back, sending a bolt of electricity through my spine that nearly disorients me until Rae says, "Hey, Ace."

I start snapping photos as his mouth drops. He takes her in as she smiles adorably at him, then slowly spins around. He takes two big steps to her, stopping just short of grabbing her, and looks her over one more time.

"You wore the dress."

"You always told me you wanted to be the one to take it off."

Aaron leans in and says something to her in a growly voice as Joel mutters, "Gross."

I snap one more picture as Aaron grabs Rae by the back of the neck and crushes his mouth against hers.

"Okay, I'm ready to be anywhere else," Joel says.

"Yep, me too. Let's go."

Joel extends his elbow to me, and I take it, letting him lead me to the rest of the party.

As far as engagement parties go, I think this one has been a massive success. We embarrassed Aaron and Rae a little bit, did a dramatic retelling of their relationship, had some incredible food, and the music has been on point. Joel and I spent a lot of time curating the right mix of music for each part of the night.

About twenty minutes ago, we started the slow dance mix, full of sweet and sexy love songs that make you want to be in the arms of the person you love—even if admitting that isn't your strong suit.

It's me. Hi.

After spending the night reliving the tumultuous start of Rae and Aaron's relationship and now swaying in Joel's arms, I wonder if we're more like them than I thought we were. I've always said we're different. Rae and Aaron were destined to be together, and we could all see it from a young age. The chemistry sizzled between them, even if they were too stupid to notice. I never thought it was that way for Joel and me. Sure, we always had a connection, we understood each other, but I thought it was different. When I look into his eyes now, I'm not so sure about that.

My mind goes back to our very first kiss at the beach house in Charleston during that game of truth or dare. I wanted to slug Aaron when he dared me to do it. I assumed he was leaning into our sibling-like relationship and trying to get under my skin, but now I wonder if he saw the spark between us and was trying to poke at it, like we all often did to him and Rae.

I was with Trevor, and I was fully into him. He was the most perfect first boyfriend I ever could've asked for. I remember my hands shook as I texted him to ask if Joel and I could kiss for the dare. Why did I even do that? Why didn't I tell them all to fuck off? Was I trying to prove a point? That I didn't have feelings for Joel? And if so, was there a part of me that thought I did? Looking back, I'm not sure if I was nervous asking Trevor because I was afraid he'd get mad or if I was afraid he'd say yes.

Then he *did* say yes. All bravado, never back down from a dare, had to prove a point, I told Joel it was fine. He came closer, smiled like he always does—and it made my stomach flutter, though I didn't show it—then leaned in and kissed me.

Closed mouths, lips touching, but I remember the crack of electricity I felt. A surge that didn't make sense to me. I loved Trevor. I *wanted* him to be the one. The next day, I told Rae I had felt a spark—something Joel and I had both lied about in the moment—but it made me miss Trevor more. And that was true, but it was because I was desperate to get back and kiss him, to feel *us*. Trevor was peace and comfort and safety. He was fun and flirty. Good in bed. He understood me, stuck by me through my bullshit, but before I ever kissed Joel, I started getting a gnawing feeling in my gut that it wasn't quite right. After I kissed Joel, it became harder to ignore, but I willed it away. I blamed myself. I figured I was holding back from Trevor somehow. I tried to open up more, but ultimately, I had to accept the truth—I didn't feel the connection to Trevor I wanted to feel. I'm sure we could've worked it out and had a nice life together, but I think by the time we were in our thirties, we both would've been aching for more.

Breaking up with him gutted me, but who was there with me that night? Besides Rae... Joel. Always Joel. He always shows up when I need him, and when he does, I feel safer.

When Vanessa called me senior year, right before I cut her out of my life, I got drunk, and Joel carried me out of the party even as I screamed that I hated him. He rubbed my back as I puked. He held me as I cried. I tried so hard to deny it, but there was *always* something there. Something between us. Maybe not like Aaron and Rae were—crazy, undeniable chemistry even as kids—but there was safety there, understanding. Trevor understood me. I understood him, but we learned to do that. With Joel, it has always come naturally. Like our souls knew what the other was feeling. How is that possible?

It was a year and a half before I kissed him again. After his eighteenth birthday party. It had been a bitch of a day with Rae and Aaron's massive fight, then Aaron and Jesse's fight and Jesse needing stitches. We were both exhausted as we sat on the back deck, beers in hand, lamenting it all. I asked what he wanted for his birthday. He said he wanted to kiss me. My stomach flipped, my body went haywire, but I couldn't deny him his birthday wish, so I leaned over, grabbed his shirt, and pulled his lips to mine. He settled for a slow, soft kiss, but I didn't. I took him to his bedroom and kissed him for hours, our tongues dancing, our hearts beating together, and both of us falling into something we didn't want to admit.

We were playful until prom, when we kicked it up a notch. Grinding in his bed. His hot lips on my naked chest, my hand on a certain hardened muscle until he was groaning my name.

The next day, I was horrified. Lines were crossed. Lines I wasn't ready to deal with. I told him it was just for that day, and he told me he'd take whatever I'd give.

But that was just it. I wouldn't give him anything. I thought I could put a stop to it all. Though I saw the hurt in his eyes, he let me do it. Then we went to school and started hooking up with other people. We both pretended it was fine. But it wasn't. I missed that connection. Then, after another year, he was there for me again, right when I needed him, and I gave in. We've been inching forward since then.

I glance up at his gorgeous face, stubbled with light brown hair.

Emotion hits me square in the gut as I stare at him. I'm so thankful for him. For how patient he's always been. If it were up to him—well, we'd probably be at a joint engagement party with Rae and Aaron right now.

Tears well in my eyes, as I feel both grateful and guilty—he's given me so much and I keep holding back.

I sniff back tears, praying he won't notice, but it's Joel. He always notices.

"What's wrong?" he asks, tilting his head to the side and looking down at me as one hand cups my cheek.

"Just thinking of us. How we got here."

"And that makes you sad?"

"It makes me... emotional." My voice drops as I look into those intoxicating eyes of his. "You've always been there for me."

"And I always will be," he breathes, like it's second nature. Like nothing else could possibly be truer than that.

I nod against his shoulder, but can't bring myself to say what I'm thinking.

But what if I can't do that for you? What if I'm not enough? What if I mess it up? No. What happens when I do mess it up? Because that's inevitable. I'm not sure I'll ever be able to give him what he gives me.

I hold him tighter and try to will the conflicting emotions in my chest away. How much I love him. How badly I want to take things further. How scared I am to ruin it all.

And this is why I keep him here. He's safe here, and I can't lose him. Losing him would destroy me. I'll keep opening little pieces of myself to him, and slowly, we'll get there.

Hopefully, I won't fuck it up when we do.

Chapter Three

Never Be Alone

Sarah

"I'M OFFICIALLY BASEBALL-ED OUT," Rae says plopping down across the table from me.

"Probably because it's not really baseball. It's a bunch of dudes talking about numbers and scoring and what every pick means for this season of baseball." I roll my eyes.

"Yeah, I've never been more grateful that Aaron has no intention of going pro. I mean, if he wanted to rehab hard and try, I would support him fully and learn all about this shit, but thank God I don't have to." She jerks her thumb toward the other room. "The guys are all eating this up. Even Miles. I'm glad I can just be the supportive fiancée and then come hide in here for a while."

"Well, you're more than welcome." I pick up the tray of brownies we brought off the chair next to me. I wasn't hiding them, *I swear.* She smiles brightly as I slide them across the table to her.

It's day two of the MLB draft, and we're at Jamie's house for the second day in a row. His parents opened their large home to anyone who wanted to come watch with them. Of course, that includes Amanda, Aaron, Joel, Miles, Trevor, Rae, me, Mackie, the boys' baseball coach, many of Jamie's teammates, some of our other friends who have dropped by here and there, and even random members of the town, not limited to Maia's dad, Leo, a massive baseball fan. Even Grandpa stopped by for a little while.

The back door swings open and Mackie walks in carrying a tray of iced coffee.

"I come bearing coffee," she says, sliding the drink tray onto the table and sitting down next to Rae.

"Hallelujah," Amanda says, grabbing the one with her name on it and dropping into the chair at the head of the table. "I'm exhausted."

"Draft fatigue?" Rae asks, reaching for her iced coffee.

Amanda doesn't really answer, just half-heartedly nods while taking a sip.

Mackie, Rae, and I look between each other.

"Mands?" I ask.

"Hm?" she looks around the table.

"We don't lie to each other. Unless it involves attempting to hide our true feelings for the boys in our lives." Rae looks at me with a wicked smile.

I match her evil grin and lean forward. "What can I say? I learned from the best."

She kicks me under the table and we both laugh before turning back to Amanda.

"Seriously, what's up?" Mackie asks.

Amanda sighs and sets down her coffee. "I'm nervous. Nervous if he'll be drafted, where he'll be drafted, but most of all, what it means for us. We agreed when we started dating that if we were still together at this point, we'd decide on all of this together, but really, it's not my decision. I'm here to support him. And I'm happy to do that, but this is going to change everything. No matter where he ends up, his trajectory is going to be the majors, which means people are going to be watching him. He's going to have money, attention, ball bunnies—"

"Ball bunnies?" Mackie asks.

"Yeah, you know, the girls who chase after the baseball players. Show up at their hotels when they travel, try to get them to party with them. Cheat."

The word rolls off her tongue, and she looks down.

I reach for her hand and squeeze it tightly.

"Are you worried about that with Jamie?"

"He is the sweetest guy I've ever known. He loves me. But fame and money can change things..." She swallows hard. "Even if it doesn't, you saw what that girl pulled last year with Rae. Imagine that on the scale of professional baseball. I'm not sure I'm ready to deal with that. And I'm trying not to say any of this to him because I don't want him to worry about it. I want him to focus on his future and what comes next. This is exciting. I'm excited too. But it's scary knowing everything will change and knowing the distance between us is likely going to grow. It's not easy. I'm worried that, one way or another, this will tear us apart." She snorts at herself. "And now I sound depressing. I swear I'm not a basket case. This just brings those insecurities to the surface."

"I understand," Mackie says.

"I think we all do," Rae says. "Relationships are hard. Falling in love is hard. It's scary and the only reassurance you have is your trust in the person you're with."

My stomach churns at those words, but I push them away.

"How would you feel?" Amanda asks Rae. "If it were Aaron? Would you be... worried?"

Rae blows out a breath, then smiles softly. "No. It would suck. But I'd also just tell the rest of the world to eff off and go with him anywhere. That's how we are. I would never believe anyone who tried to spin stories that he cheated. I know he never would.

But Aaron and I have also been through it. We've learned a lot. It sucked, but it made our foundation stronger."

Amanda nods slowly. "I trust Jamie. He could have gotten rid of me as soon as he met my brothers."

We all laugh at that. Well, I try to, but Rae's words about trusting the person you're with are still rolling through my brain.

"Whoa," Amanda says, looking at me. "Why do you suddenly look like you got hit by a bus?"

"I'm... fine," I sputter.

Amanda's brow furrows. "I thought we didn't lie to each other."

"See the prior caveat to that," Rae says, reading my mind. Or maybe I'm way too obvious.

"Come on," Mackie says. "You've heard the gamut of my relationship drama and Rae's. Hit us with yours. That's what we're here for."

I pull my cheek between my teeth, then glance toward the living room. "You said it comes down to how much you trust the other person. What if you don't trust yourself? What if he can't trust me?"

"Is that really how you feel?" Amanda asks.

Rae's foot brushes over mine as she gives me an empathetic look. She knows why I don't trust myself. Mackie has an idea. Amanda... she's never seen the worst of me.

"I've fucked up a lot of things. And I... I'm scared I'll mess it up. At some point, I'll struggle or I'll spiral and I'll ruin it."

Mackie shakes her head. "I call bullshit on that. I think you're scared and using that as an excuse."

"You've seen me bounce off the bottom, Macks."

Rae stares at me for a moment, then gently says, "I'm not calling bullshit. I'm sure that's what the voice in your head is telling you, but the thing is, when you love someone, you fight through the hard moments. Yeah, Aaron and I aren't a great example, because we didn't nail that initially, but we've learned a lot since then. And Joel is different. He's steadfast in a way I've failed at being in the past. More importantly, he loves you. And the way he loves... nothing stops that. When you love someone, when you make the choice to give them your heart, it's scary as hell, but it comes back to that trust. Trust that you'll be there for each other, that in those hard moments, the other person will pick you up. Real love doesn't run because there's a storm, it stands stronger. It outlasts. It survives."

Thanks, I want to cry now.

"Only you can decide what you're ready for and when," Amanda says softly, squeezing my hand. "But don't sideline yourself out of fear."

Silence falls over the table for a moment.

Am I ready?

My gut still says no. It's easier now. I'm taking one online course and working part-time over the summer. When school starts again, I'll be in classes and practicum for at least sixty hours a week. It'll be a beast. I want to be able to commit to him. Do it right.

That's why I'm taking it slow. Rae and Aaron didn't build their foundation well enough. This gives us a chance to do that. *Slowly.*

There's a gasp and then a shout from the living room. We all leap out of our chairs and dash out of the room. We skid to a stop in the living room just in time to hear the announcer say, "And in their tenth pick, the New York Metros choose eighteen-year-old Jamie Henderson from Ida New York." The room erupts in cheers, drowning out the announcer reading Jamie's stats.

Any fear Amanda was feeling before melts away as she leaps into Jamie's arms and kisses him. When he sets her down, they're both teary-eyed.

"You did it, baby," she whispers. "I'm so proud of you."

I can't help but smile watching them. After another kiss, Jamie turns to Aaron, who also has tears in his eyes, and they share a long hug.

Everyone congratulates him and all the craziness begins again as Jamie's phone rings and he, Aaron, and their coach figure out all the logistics.

Across the room, Joel catches my eye and shoots me a wink.

My stomach whirls and I remember why all my fears and uncertainties are worth it. A simple look across the room makes me feel like no one else ever has.

We'll have fun. Enjoy each other. Talk. Build it all up. *Slowly.*

Joel

Jamie made the fucking pros. I know we all saw his potential. We hoped it could happen. But damn, he actually did it.

I grab a water bottle from the kitchen counter and take a long drink as I walk over to the window that looks out on the expansive backyard. That's when I notice Trevor sitting alone on the back deck. I give him a lot of credit for being here with all of us. He didn't have to come here and support Jamie, but he did, knowing it would hurt.

I turn and grab another bottle of water, then head downstairs and out the basement door to the back deck.

"Hey, man." I walk over and sit down next to him, extending the water bottle.

He takes it and nods, then opens it and drinks some.

"Got anything stronger?" he jokes.

"Sorry, there are parents supervising this one and small kids around. Most I could get you is a cup of coffee."

"I'll stick with the water."

He looks out at the backyard again.

"Do you want to talk about it?" I ask.

He lets out a wry laugh and runs a hand through his hair, then looks up at the clouds.

It's surprisingly cool for mid-July, but I'd rather that than sweat my balls off.

"I knew it would be hard, but I thought my excitement for Jamie would override everything else. Spoiler alert. It didn't. Honestly, after the immediate moment, it socked me in the gut. All I keep thinking is... could that have been my future? I know I was never as good at ball as Jamie or even Aaron, but I was a great third baseman and a solid hitter. I was rising in the ranks on my team at college. Now my knee hurts when I walk up the stairs. Not how I saw myself going out. I wanted to at least have a chance."

"You played like hell as long as you could. Not to mention you've handled losing baseball like a champ. You might wonder what if right now, but you're going to end up on the right path and those questions will fade. Any idea what you want to do?"

"Not sure. I've thought about a few different things. Right now, I'm leaning toward sports management. You can do all kinds of stuff with that, from athletic director jobs to becoming a sports agent. I'm going to have Aaron set me up with your coach when we get to school and see if he can offer me some guidance."

I smile at that. "It'd be good to have you involved with the team. Most of the assholes have graduated, and with Aaron and I being upperclassmen this year, we get a little more of the run of the place—well, I guess A has no matter what, being a coach."

"I would love to see him in action."

"He is both calming and terrifying when he gets in the zone."

"What about you?"

"What about me?" I ask.

"You ever thought about playing pro?"

"Fuck no. Jamie is a badass for going after that lifestyle. I don't have any desire for that. I play because I love the game, I like the competition, and I have way too much fun out on the field. This year I start my core courses to be an athletic trainer. It'll set me up so I can work for a school district, a college, even privately. I always knew I wanted to do something with sports, but I learned more about a lot of this stuff after Aaron was injured. Athletic trainers help develop plans to prevent injuries, not just monitor injuries. It's a nice combination of planning and sports. I think it'll be a good fit for me."

Trevor chuckles. "Looks like, other than Miles, none of us are giving up the game any time soon."

"It's been a formative part of our lives. Why should we?"

"That's true." He's quiet for a moment, then says, "You didn't have to come out here and sit with my pathetic ass, but thank you. You're a good friend."

A knot forms in my stomach at those words. *I don't feel like a good friend.*

"I don't know about that."

He turns to me, brows dipping in. "What? Why?"

I blow out a breath and meet his gaze. "I need to talk to you about something."

"Oh boy, what drama could there be now?"

Though I want to roll my eyes, I don't, instead forcing myself to say the words I need to say—ones I should've said months ago. "I have feelings for Sarah."

His eyes narrow, but then a slow smile spreads across his face until he breaks into a deep laugh. A guffawing laugh. A head-thrown-back, holding-his-stomach laugh.

"What?"

"It's hilarious if you think we all don't fucking know that. It's obvious."

Great.

"So, you're not pissed at me?"

"Why would I be pissed at you? Sarah and I haven't been together for a long time. It wasn't like you were some underhanded asshole who tried to steal her away from me."

"Yeah, but you guys were together for a long time. And there's bro-code."

"Fuck 'bro-code.'" He puts finger quotes around it. "It's been obvious for a while how you two feel about each other."

"I'm sorry. I should've talked to you sooner."

"It's fine. All I care about is that you respect my friendship with her. The romantic feelings are long gone, but the depth of friendship we built will never fade, and as long as you don't act like some jealous prick about it, we're good. It took a while for me to be okay with it, but she was right. We weren't meant to be. When I see her around you, that's obvious. Hopefully, that means my perfect woman is still out there. With sinful curves and long hair for wrapping my hands around." He rubs his hands together, practically drooling. "And if she's a redhead..." he whistles. "My point is, you two are right for each other... even if it takes her some time to get there."

"Yeah, she moves at a glacier's pace, but I feel her heart opening more. She agreed to share a bedroom with me at the lake house."

"Congratulations, man," he says, slapping me on the shoulder. "You might make an honest woman out of her yet."

I roll my eyes in response.

"Remind me never to talk to you about this again."

He chuckles, then takes a deep breath. "Well, thanks for a fun distraction, but my head is still not in the right space for all this. I'm gonna head out. I'll come back later if you guys are still here."

"Might go out for dinner to celebrate."

"All right, just let me know." He rises from the chair. "And Joel?"

"Yeah?"

"Thanks for checking in. You *are* a good friend. And you're good for Sarah. Those walls will come down, eventually."

"Thanks, Trev. Later."

"Later."

He walks up the small hill along the side of the house toward the driveway. I sit for a few more minutes until it starts to sprinkle, then head inside.

When I get back to the living room, Arizona is calling their last pick of the day.

"Arizona picks Tanner Hauser from Westchester, New York."

Aaron smiles softly as Rae kisses his cheek and whispers something in his ear.

I walk over and clap him on the shoulder. "Nice job, *Coach.*"

A second later, his phone vibrates. He looks down at it as Rae and I read over his shoulder.

Tanner: Thank you. Seriously. Thank you. Glad I gave you a chance ;)

Aaron rolls his eyes as we all laugh at that.

Sarah strolls over and hands me her half-finished iced coffee. "Pretty great day."

I take a long sip and stare at her. "Yeah. It definitely is."

Sarah

I'm lying on my bed, staring at the ceiling, my mind on the events of the day. Hearing Amanda's fears but seeing them wash away when Jamie was drafted made me wonder if my fears would wash away if I gave in to Joel.

I run my hand over his ribs and gently poke him.

He rolls over and tosses an arm around me. "Why are you awake?"

"Just thinking."

He pries one eye open and looks at me. "About what?"

Lots of things. All the things.

For a moment, I don't answer.

His other eye opens and he props himself up on his elbow. With his other hand, he sweeps some hair off my face before sweetly asking, "What's on your mind?"

"What do you want out of your future, Joel? We saw Jamie get a big part of his future handed to him today. Rae and Aaron are a few months away from getting married, and they both know what they want to do for careers. What about you? What do you want?"

He drops down onto his back and takes my hand.

"Happiness," he says softly. "I mean, I know it won't always be like that, but at a base level, I want happiness. Doing a job I enjoy—even if it's not perfect. Coming home to the person I love—even when it's hard. I want to love someone and be loved. Build a life and a family. Raise kind kids who know they're loved and wanted, and who never question if their parents love them."

Tears stream down my cheeks because I know he's talking about us. In different ways and at different times, we didn't have the love we deserved. We felt alone. Isolated. Not something I ever want my future children to feel.

Tears come faster when I realize that when I imagine that future, when I imagine having a child, Joel is the one there with me.

I roll over, my wet face slamming into his chest as I wrap my arms around him. I'm afraid to tell him I want the same things.

Afraid to make a promise I'm not sure I can keep, but like usual, he doesn't force me to.

He kisses my head and whispers, "Most of all, I want to hold my wife like this every night, look into her deep blue eyes, and tell her she's not alone, and she never will be."

I snuffle back tears as he holds me tighter and kisses my forehead.

Why can't I just live a little? Jump off the edge?

Because jumping without a plan is how you crash into the rocks and die.

I throw my leg up over his and melt into him.

My muscles relax, and my heartbeat slows down.

Eventually Joel's grip loosens, and he snores softly.

I lift my head off his chest, reach up, and kiss his cheek, then breathe, "You'll never be alone, either. I promise."

I tuck my head back against his chest and drift off to sleep.

Chapter Four

Have Fun

Sarah

MOVING DAY.

I can't believe this year we get to move into the lake house. Part of me will miss the convenience of campus, but most of me will not miss any of it, especially not sharing a bedroom—except, you know, with Joel. But that's different. I think.

Grabbing one of the boxes from the few left in my pile, I make my way across the driveway to the moving truck.

When I get to it, I pause and reposition the box so I can slide it in easier. It's not heavy, but it's bulky. It has all my favorite blankets and some sheets in it.

"I see your boxes are labeled master bedroom. Interesting."

I jump at the sound of Trevor's voice and drop the box I'm holding. Quickly spinning around, I slug him hard in the shoulder.

"You scared me!"

"Ow," he rubs his shoulder. "Easy. That's one of the few places that still works correctly. I need a good arm to jack off with."

"Don't sneak up on people, then," I huff, crossing my arms over my chest.

He laughs as he leans down and picks up the box, then sets it in the back of the moving van before sitting down on the edge.

"So, sharing a room with Joel, huh?"

Shit. I should've told him.

Trevor grins at me. "Relax. Joel told me about it. And whatever it is you two are doing. Or *not* doing."

I groan and run a hand over my face.

"Come here," he says, grabbing my elbow and pulling me down so I'm sitting next to him. "What's going on with all this? And don't say nothing. I know you better than pretty much everyone. I know you have feelings for him. Why are you holding back? And don't say because of what happened with us. No bullshit."

He knows me too well.

"I'm gonna screw it up, Trev."

"Probably," he teases.

"Seriously. At some point, I'll do something stupid or mean or I'll spiral out of control and he'll be the collateral damage. I'll lose him. I'm not... ready yet. I need to be sure I'm strong enough."

He nods slowly for a moment, then says, "Nope. Still bullshit. You're going to make mistakes. That's how relationships go. This idea that you're not enough as you are or that you can't handle this... it's a lie. A lie you're telling yourself because you're scared. The only way you're going to screw this up is by worrying so much about it that you hold yourself back for too long and it becomes a self-fulfilling prophecy."

I glare at him.

"Ah, I hit a nerve," he says with a smile.

"I want to take it slow and be my best self. Is that so bad?"

His smile grows. "No. If that's really why you're doing it. Either way, whatever pace you're going, you love him, right?"

I'll take any other question for five hundred.

He elbows me. "You can tell me. We made it through, Sarah. It's okay."

"It's not. Because I haven't technically even told him yet."

"Doesn't surprise me." He sighs. "Look, if you have feelings for him, you want to be with him eventually, and you're good with where things are now, why are you being so dramatic about this? Have fun. Enjoy this. Because one day, you're going to look back on this as the time you were falling in love with him and building your relationship. Wouldn't you rather look at it happily?"

"I hate you," I grumble.

"No, you don't and you never could."

"Ugh. When did you get so wise?"

He chuckles at that. "I think Braden was right. Maybe trees knock some wisdom into you when you run into them."

"You two would joke about that."

"Hey, we both won our battles with the trees."

I roll my eyes, but can't help the laugh that creeps out.

He gives my thigh a squeeze and stands as Rae, Aaron, and Joel walk down the driveway toward us.

I stand up, too, and Trevor leans in toward me and whispers, "Don't forget, *have fun.*"

"All packed?" Rae asks, smiling.

I glance at Trev as he goes, and he shoots me a look that's pure mischief. *Asshole.*

"Uh, I've got a couple of boxes left inside."

"We'll grab 'em," Joel says, grinning at me and melting me more than the hot weather today ever could.

Stupid, hot jerk.

Rae follows my gaze—which is locked on Joel—as they go and elbows me.

"You're hot for him," she sing-songs.

"Shut up."

"Like you didn't give me all the shit when I was doing this with Aaron."

"Maybe," I say with a smile.

"There they are, Ma," Grandpa says to Gram as they round the corner of the house.

We hurry over to give them hugs.

"What are you doing here?" Rae asks.

"We couldn't let our girlies leave without saying goodbye," Grandpa says.

"We'll miss you," I say softly.

As Rae hugs Grandpa, Gram wraps me in her arms.

"Looking forward to living at the lake house?" she asks.

"Definitely."

"Especially with a certain roommate?"

She lets me go and we watch Joel and Aaron carry the boxes over to the truck.

"We'll see," I say coyly.

Gram smiles knowingly. "Don't be scared of the fall, sweetheart. It's the best part." She steps back as Aaron walks over and kisses Rae, and Joel strides over to me.

"All packed. What do you think? Ready to go?" he asks.

Another pinch of nervousness hits my stomach, but I push it down.

Trevor and Gram are right.

Joel is letting me call the shots on what happens when. I should be enjoying this.

Flirting with him makes my heart race. His smile brightens my mood. Snuggling in bed with him makes me feel safe and cared for.

"Yeah," I say brightly. "I'm ready."

Sunrise, Sunburn, Sunset by Luke Bryan blares through a speaker in the kitchen of the lake house.

I grab a bottle of water off the kitchen counter and wipe some sweat off my brow. We've been unloading the moving van for the last hour, but it seems like we've barely made a dent. It doesn't help that it's only ten-thirty in the morning and already eighty-five degrees.

Rae leans against the counter next to me, grabs a water bottle, takes a glug, then mutters, "Why is it hotter than Satan's ass crack?"

I choke on some water, manage to swallow it, and laugh.

"What? It's an accurate description," she says.

"At least that means we can go for a swim later," I say.

She opens her mouth to respond, but before she can, Aaron calls, "Hey, where does this one go? It's not labeled."

Rae turns to him and her eyes widen. I turn as well and see Aaron standing there, shirtless, chest glistening with sweat. I stifle a laugh as Rae sputters for words. Aaron smirks, drops the box, and walks over to her.

I shake my head as he grabs her waist and kisses her. "It goes upstairs, right?" he mutters against her lips.

"Definitely. In our bedroom."

Aaron grabs her hand and leads her toward the stairs, occasionally kissing her as they go. I choose not to tell them they didn't take the box. No wonder the first thing Rae did when she got here was make their bed. She must have some psychic horny vision.

"Ow! What the—?" Joel stops and looks down at the box he bashed into. "Why is that right here?"

"Because Aaron had to go..." I clear my throat. "With Rae."

He rolls his eyes and pushes the box out of the way with his foot. "That didn't take long."

He sets the box he's holding by the kitchen island, then comes over to me and takes the water I'm holding out to him.

"Eh, can't really blame her. All these shirtless guys walking around." I poke his pec, enjoying as he flexes it against my finger.

He cocks an eyebrow, smiles, and moves closer, pushing that firm chest against mine.

"You like my chest?" He takes my hand, lifts it, and drags it down his chest, then to his abs. "What about these?"

I'm panting.

"You okay?" he asks, leaning down and brushing his lips over my ear.

"Yeah. Yep. Okay. Just... hot." *No, Sarah. That was the wrong word.*

"Me too." His lips barely press into the skin of my cheek with the word. Then he steps back biting his bottom lip as he laughs.

He turns and walks away like he didn't just set my entire body on fire for him.

Well, two can play at that game.

Joel

The cool lake feels incredible after loading, unloading, and unpacking boxes all day. It's ridiculously humid, and even the lake breeze wasn't doing anything to cool us down.

Aaron and I climb back up the ladder to the dock, ready to race and jump in again, but once we're standing on the dock, we see Rae and Sarah strutting across the backyard toward us.

Holy fuck.

Aaron grins and whistles at Rae in her black and pink color-block bikini, but my eyes are trained on Sarah in a sinfully gorgeous baby blue bikini that is so perfectly fitted it's molded to her skin.

"Come on," Aaron says, smacking my shoulder.

Huh? Oh, right. Dock. Jumping in.

Pulling my gaze from Sarah, I spin around and line up on the dock with Aaron. Trevor, leaning against the side of the small attached boathouse says, "Three, two, one... go!"

We take off running, but halfway down the dock, I realize someone else is on the other side of me. As we get to the end, Sarah flies past me, jumping into the water before Aaron or me.

We follow her in, and when I get above the water, her smiling face is the first thing I see.

"Beat ya."

As Aaron climbs back up to the dock, I swim closer to her. "You think you're funny?"

She shrugs. "Maybe."

Then she takes a big breath and dives under the water again. I follow her as she swims under the dock. When she pops up again, she turns to look at me, smiling mischievously.

Biting my lip, I swim over to her and run my finger over the strap of her bikini.

"I thought you said you were going to wear a wetsuit."

"Mm. That was for Charleston when you said I'd be your present. Today and this suit are all about me."

"Oh, really?"

She moves a little closer, her feet brushing mine as she treads water.

"Mhm. I'm enjoying myself. Having fun. Like this."

She wraps her arms around my neck and her legs around my waist, then smashes her lips against mine, kissing me hard, but just as I'm settling into it, she pulls away, winks at me, then swims out from under the dock.

Damn it. I'm going to get her back for that.

After eating some pizza for lunch, everyone has been lounging in the backyard, on the dock, or been playing in the water.

Sarah is laying out on a towel next to Rae. Aaron is next to her, a baseball cap pulled over his eyes as he sleeps. I swear he can sleep anywhere, anytime.

Seeing the sunscreen sitting next to Sarah, I grab it and rub down my arms and shoulders, then I poke my toes into Sarah's side. "Can you help me?"

Her head pops up, and she squints at me, so I shake the bottle at her.

"Oh. Sure. Your back?" she asks, getting to her feet.

"Yeah. Well, I haven't done my chest yet either."

She runs her hands across my back, spreading the lotion out and rubbing it in.

"I can handle that."

She's methodical about spreading the sunscreen over me, taking her time, feeling every muscle.

I thought this would be a fun way to tease her back, but I think we're both enjoying it.

When she's finished with my back, she spins me around and starts on my front. She inhales sharply as she rubs her hands across my pecs, then down my abs, but it's me who can't breathe when she squats down in front of me and rubs her hands along the waistband of my swim trunks.

"Sarah..."

She stands up and tilts her head to the side. "That good?"

"Mhm. That's good. Thanks."

"No problem," she breathes, but I notice her breathing is heavy.

"Okay, I'm gonna go, um—swim some more."

"Have fun," she says, lying back down on her towel.

I walk over to the dock, then take a running start and jump off the end, letting the cool water wash over me and settle me down.

If it keeps going like this, sharing a room with her might kill me.

The girls split off from us for some girl time after dinner. I'm getting ready to climb into the shower when Sarah walks into the room.

She grins at me when she sees me standing here in nothing but exercise shorts—shorts I'm now realizing are white and am wondering how much they reveal.

Don't look down at your junk. Don't do it.

She strolls over to me and runs her hand down my chest. "Is this your way of getting me back?"

"Getting you back for what?" I ask innocently.

Her eyes narrow, then she puts on a fake pout. "Are you saying you weren't *having fun* with me today?"

I poke her cheek, right where one of her dimples usually forms, begging it to pop out.

"Oh, I had plenty of fun. I enjoyed teasing you as much as I loved you teasing me. In fact, you might've gotten me a little excited." I grin at her, but my eyes widen as she drags one finger down my stomach, tracing the line of my abs.

"Me too. Maybe we should finish teasing each other," she says smoothly.

I am not smooth at all. My voice cracks as I say, "What do you mean?"

She glances toward the bathroom. "You were going to take a shower. Maybe you should take a bath. With me."

Holy shit.

"Naked?"

Jesus, I'm dumb.

"Yes. Naked."

"And what do you want to do?" I ask, some smoothness returning to my voice.

She inhales sharply. "I thought we could... relieve some tension. There's a lot we can do without doing *that.*"

"You want us to touch each other?"

"I was thinking more like touching ourselves. At the same time. But maybe each other, too. If you want to."

"I want to," I breathe.

"Okay. I need to get some clean clothes. Can you go run the water in the tub?"

"Absolutely," I whisper, then kiss her cheek.

My heart is pounding as I step into the bathroom and run the water in the large whirlpool tub. With two faucets, it doesn't take too long to fill up.

I pull my shorts down and toss them in the laundry basket before climbing into the tub and letting the water fill the space around me.

I'm relaxing in the hot water when Sarah walks into the room. My eyes trail down her body as she slips her robe off, taking in her perky breasts, the soft but lightly defined curves of her stomach, and her toned legs.

She slides into the water with a hiss, then settles in, giving me a dazzling smile as she glides her toes up my shin.

I lift one eyebrow in question.

"What? I thought touching was a part of this," she says with a smirk.

"Just tell me when you're ready." I grin back at her.

She shakes her head softly. "I need to relax first."

"Come here," I say softly.

She looks at me skeptically.

"Trust me."

She moves toward me, then spins around when I ask her to, her fingers brushing my legs.

"Lean back," I whisper as I bring my hands to her shoulders.

"What are you doing?"

"I thought touching was a part of this."

I rub my hands over her tight shoulders, gently massaging the muscles.

"Are you worried about school starting?" I ask.

"Not really worried. Stressed, I guess. I'm always stressed until I settle into the new routine."

Not surprising.

"You know I'm here if you need anything. If there's something I can do to make it easier on you."

Her breath hitches, then she mumbles, "I'm ready."

"What?"

"You told me to tell you when I was ready to..."

"Oh," I say, trying to mask my sharp inhale. I got lost in massaging her and talking. Forgot about *the other thing.*

She slowly glides away from me and turns back around, leaning against the opposite side of the tub again. She brings her knees up and runs her toes up my shins, resting her feet against me.

"You still want to?" she asks.

I nod, my throat dry and my dick hard as granite.

She tilts her head back as she runs a hand over her boobs, pinching her nipples before trailing that hand down into the water. I know where her hand is by the little gasp she lets out and the way her body tenses.

I move my hand lower too, massaging my balls before fisting my length and rubbing up and down.

Sarah's other hand works one of her breasts as her body flows in rhythm with her hand. God, she's sexy. I'm trying to capture every moment, commit it all to memory. She's perfect.

When she moans, I yank my hand away, that tingling feeling already hitting the base of my spine. I'm so fucking horny for her I can't think straight. I go to sleep with blue balls almost every night, but she's worth it.

"Oh," she breathes, eyes drifting closed as her arm tightens and she picks up her pace.

I thrust into my fist, clinging to the edge of control. I want to watch her before I let go.

Her hips roll faster as I steady my pace.

I let out a groan as my fingers brush my tip.

My eyes are locked on her. The tiniest movement of her throat as she swallows and gasps for air. The way her chest rises and falls. Her fingers rolling back and forth over one nipple. Her body tightening more with each second.

Her breathing quickens, then her head drops to the side as she whimpers and cries out, her toes digging into my legs as she does.

"Oh, fuck," I groan, my abs tightening as I explode.

She's still riding the last of her high as I collapse against the tub and let my heavy eyes close as my heartbeat pounds in my ears.

After a moment, her hands skim up my legs until she's between them. I flash my eyes open to see her shimmering blue eyes, flushed cheeks, and a gorgeous smile. The smile grows, and in a sudden, fluid motion, she lunges forward and slams her lips into mine, gliding her tongue into my mouth.

Then she climbs onto my fucking lap, and thank God we did all that, or she'd be able to feel how desperate I am for her right now.

She wraps one arm around my back, the other snaking up into my hair and twisting the strands.

I hold her tightly, dipping her back slightly as I melt into the intensity of this kiss. It's been a while since we've shared this kind of kiss. Probably since Valentine's Day.

She wraps her other arm around my back, pulling me closer as she unfurls our tongues and lifts her lips off mine.

"That was amazing. We should do that more often."

She kisses my nose, then climbs out of the tub, wrapping herself in a towel before heading into the bedroom. I'm still staring, mouth agape, wondering where that came from... and if there's any chance it means we're moving forward.

Chapter Five

Something

Sarah

NURSING PROGRAMS ARE NO joke. Especially accelerated ones. This isn't even the fastest track available—those go year-round—but it's the fastest track for traditional college students, taking three years instead of the typical four to graduate with a bachelor's degree. Monday, Wednesday, and Friday we have full class days with long lectures, typically going from eight in the morning to six at night. One of those days, I'll also have a clinical in the evening. Tuesdays and Thursdays are spent fully doing clinicals. And twice a month, we have clinicals on Saturday morning as well.

Today is the first day back at school, and there is zero time for adjustment. You're expected to study and maintain your skill set over the summer because we pick up right where we left off the year before. It's exhausting, but I love it. Mom always says I thrive in chaos because of my early childhood. I don't know if she's right, but I do work well under pressure. It's like it helps my brain work at full capacity. When things have to be done well and handled quickly, that's where I shine. Give me too much time to do something, and I'll forget about it or get bored and move on to something else.

I yawn and stretch as I walk out of class for our twenty-minute break before the lecturing begins again. Quickly checking my phone, I see a text from Gram and pause to respond to it.

Gram: How is your first day going?

Me: Busy. Already.

Gram: Good. It'll keep you out of trouble. Love you, sweetheart.

Me: Love you too!

I put my phone away, thinking about whether I want to settle for crappy vending machine coffee or walk over to the next building for a cup from one of the cafés when my gaze connects with a set of hazel eyes so piercing, I can feel them in my soul. Or maybe that's just because it's *him.*

Smiling, I make my way over to where Joel is waiting, leaning against a wooden column, backpack slung over one shoulder, and wearing his signature charming smirk.

"What are you doing here?" I ask. I thought most of his classes were up at the far end of campus in the athletic building. "Were you waiting for me?"

"Just got done with class. I knew you had that long lecture today. Thought we could grab some coffee during your break."

"Wait, class? I thought you were at the opposite end of campus. Even you can't run that fast. And how did you know when my break is?"

He chuckles as he stands up straight, then leans in and kisses my cheek.

"I snuck a peek at your schedule. You wrote your break times in purple glittery pen. And I told you my classes were at the opposite end of campus because the surprise and happiness on your face when you saw me is a high I wish I could bottle and feel all the time."

Oh, my sweet Lord.

I've known Joel most of my life, I've seen the many sides of him, but this? This combination of sweet, sexy, thoughtful, smoldering... swooniness—if that's even a word—is a new level. And I'd be lying if I said it didn't leave me feeling a little hot and bothered.

His smile grows, and he bites his lip, adding a hint of devil to his otherwise sweet look.

Forget it. I'm melting.

"So? Coffee?" He extends his arm, and I nod as I take it.

"Oh shoot, I left my purse in the classroom," I say, looking back at the door.

Yep, I definitely would've ended up with vending machine coffee.

"Babe, please. I'm paying. And you're getting an extra shot of espresso and plenty of whipped cream on your latte, just how you like it."

My eyes light up as my heart pounds.

Why is it the simplest things that affect me like this?

"Thank you," I say, voice breathy, but I can't help it. I'm starry-eyed over him. Head over heels.

He's just so wonderful. Caring. That's it. There are many sexy things about Joel, especially physically, but the way he cares—the way he loves—that is by far the sexiest thing about him.

What's that thing Rae always says?

Oh, yeah.

I'm so screwed.

Hopefully literally.

You know, whenever I'm finally ready for that.

Joel

"Hey, what's up?" I ask Aaron as I stroll into the baseball locker room. Regular practice doesn't begin until second semester, but we have one weekend practice a month. Though Aaron often works with other players on the team, he texted me and said Coach wanted to talk to us.

Aaron shrugs from where he's leaning against the lockers. "Don't know. Just know Coach texted me. He's running a few minutes late. What's up with you? How's your first day been?"

"Pretty good. Got to take Sarah for a coffee during her break."

"Are you going to tell me what the hell is going on there? Or are you going to keep pretending it's nothing?"

I lean in, smirking like an asshole. "Payback."

He rolls his eyes and shakes his head. "You know, Rae and I are getting married in a month and a half. You *could* let it go."

"And stop picking on the two of you about what idiots you used to be? Where's the fun in that?"

"Says a current idiot."

I hold up one finger. "No. No. I know *exactly* what I'm doing with Sarah. Unlike with you and Rae Rae, I know what Sarah is thinking. I know what she wants. I know what she needs. And I'm giving it to her."

"I'll skip the *dirty* and ask... what does she need?"

"Support, patience, and to know she's loved unconditionally."

Aaron stares at me for a beat, then nods. "Okay, I'll rescind the idiot comment. But to be fair, you're older. You didn't have to deal with this stuff in elementary school."

"You're the one who said you were going to marry her one day under a damn slide. Don't act like you haven't always wanted her."

He gets a giant dumbass smile on his face and looks lost in thought for a second before saying, "Yeah. Okay. I was an idiot for not locking it down then and there."

I chuckle as Coach walks up.

"Wilkinson. Cooper. Thanks for coming. I have a couple of things I need to discuss. Come on into my office."

We follow him inside, taking seats in the chairs in front of his desk.

"What's up, Coach?" Aaron asks, his intense voice on. Not sure if he's worried or just ready to spring into action.

"Well," Coach says, dropping into his chair, "first, thank you boys for connecting me with your friend Matteny. He's a good kid and I'm working on some ways to get him involved with the team. Second, Cooper, I'm officially putting you on the roster as a closer for this season."

Aaron's eyes get massive. "But I haven't even had the surgery yet. What if—"

"If something goes wrong or doesn't work out—which I doubt—we'll cross that bridge when we come to it. And don't worry, you'll remain the assistant pitching coach as well, but I want you out on that field. You have too much talent to let it go to waste."

"I'll second that," I say. "It'd be good to be on the field with you again."

"Which brings me to the third thing and the main reason for this meeting. I've unfortunately lost several players over the last few months. One was a pitcher. One was an outfielder. But two were catchers. It would've put us in a pinch with only one catcher. Then said catcher—supposed to be a transfer student this year—messaged to tell me he wouldn't be attending after all. Now, I remember coming down to see you boys play, and if I recall, Aaron, you had quite a rapport with your catcher."

Aaron and I glance at each other.

"Uh, yeah. He's one of our best friends. We've played together since we were six. Miles," Aaron says.

Coach nods. "I pulled the small file I had on him when I realized he attends school here as well. I remember offering him a spot on the team, but he said he was ready to turn his focus elsewhere. What I'm wondering is if that has changed, and he might be interested in playing again. Or if you could convince him to," Coach says with a smile.

Aaron looks at me and raises his eyebrows. Then we both smile.

"I think we might be able to twist his arm," I say, loving the idea of getting to play with both of my best friends again. With Aaron being injured senior year, the last great game we all had together was the state championship. Of course, we had no idea it would be the last amazing game we had together. To get a do-over? Another chance to have a blast doing something I love with my best friends? Count me the fuck in.

"Good. If you manage to pique his interest, tell him my door's open any time."

"Will do," Aaron says. "Anything else, Coach?"

He smiles. "One last thing. Good work with Tanner."

Aaron nods. "Thanks, Coach."

"All right, get out of here. I'll see you in two weeks for our first practice."

"Yes, sir," we both say, then head back to the locker room.

The bright sunlight stings my eyes as we step outside the athletic building.

Aaron looks down at his phone, smiles, then quickly types a text before looking at me. "I'm going to meet Rae before she heads over to Promise. I'll see you back at the house and we can gang up on Miles?"

"Sounds perfect." I bump his waiting fist, then walk the opposite direction.

One more class, then it's back to the lake house.

Rae

I suck in a deep breath before opening my car door and walking across the pavement to the entrance of Promise. I don't get chills down my spine when I walk past the spot where a gun was pointed at me anymore—at least, not usually. It still weighs on my mind some days, though. An extra important reminder not to take a second for granted.

I flick my badge over the keypad and the lock buzzes. When I walk in, I'm greeted with the familiar sound of chatting and the orange-vanilla scent Kristen always uses in the diffuser.

"Hello," I call, walking around the corner so I'm facing the main desk. Kristen is there with one of the younger interns, Elsa, and a redhead I don't recognize.

"Oh Rae, I'm glad you're here," Kristen says, standing up and coming around the desk, the redhead following. "I'd like you to meet our newest intern. She's a transfer student who took Jackie's spot," she says, referencing one of our students who left the internship program after changing her major. "This is Chelsea." She turns to Chelsea, who is about my height with stunning curves. Her long auburn hair flows down her back, and damn—I think I have a tiny girl crush on her. "Chelsea, this is Rae McKinley. She's a junior as well, though I have her on a bit of an accelerated track here. If you need any help, she's your go-to girl. I'll have you spend some time shadowing her to get the feel of things here."

"Great." Her voice is soft when she speaks. Though she holds herself confidently, she seems a little shy.

I extend my hand. "It's really nice to meet you."

"You too. Rae, right? I totally space on names until I hear them a few times."

"Yep. Rae McKinley." I get a big dumb smile on my face. "Actually, you don't have to commit to remembering the last name right now."

Kristen laughs at that. "Rae's getting married in a few weeks."

"Oh! That's so exciting!" Chelsea fawns, eyes dropping to my ring. "That's gorgeous."

Heat rises to my cheeks, but I'm still smiling. "Thanks."

"Well, I need to get a little more work done before I head out for the day. Rae, would you mind giving Chelsea the full tour?"

"Sure!" I lean in toward Chelsea. "I'll try to make it fun."

"I heard that," Kristen calls with a laugh.

"Get some work done!" I yell after her.

Chelsea's eyebrows shoot up. "Wow. You two are comfortable with each other."

"This is my third year here and we've been through a lot. I'm going to put my stuff in the back. If you want to bring your purse with you, I'll show you where we keep our belongings. Although, when I'm working out front, I usually keep it up here."

I start off down the hallway with Chelsea at my side.

"So, getting married?"

"Yep. In case you can't tell by my perma-giddiness, I'm excited."

She laughs at that. "How long have you two been together?"

Hm. I never know exactly how to answer that.

"Well, technically a couple of years. But it's complicated. We've been best friends pretty much our whole lives. It was always building to this."

"That's awesome."

"So, where are you from?"

"I'm from Birch Lake, if you know where that is."

"Oh, cool. Yeah, I'm from Ida, so you're like forty-five minutes from us."

"Us?"

I laugh at myself as I open the door to the back room where there are cubbies for our bags and coats.

"Sorry. I grew up with several best friends and we all go to school here together. Our other friends joke that we're a hive mind. I guess they're right about that sometimes."

She smiles brightly. "That's really cool. I have a couple of friends back home, but haven't really met anyone here yet. I mean, it's only the first day..."

"Hey, if you're up for making some new friends, we're having a barbeque tonight. My best friend's dad owns a lake house, and a bunch of us live there."

"How many of you guys are there?"

I chuckle at that. "There's the original six—me, my fiancé Aaron, my sister Sarah, and our friends Miles, Mackenzie, and Joel—his dad owns the lake house. Our other friend Trevor who just transferred in this year lives with us, and so does Amanda, who is from Woods Junction. We met her here freshman year. We're kinda wild, but in a low-key way, if that makes sense."

"I'm not sure, but if the invite's open, I'd love to come."

"Sounds great. Now, let me give you a little tour."

Joel

When I walk through the front door of the lake house, I see Miles and Aaron in the kitchen. Miles is busy cutting vegetables while Aaron is mixing something in a large bowl. Some kind of dessert, probably. Ever since he learned to cook, he's been obsessed, especially with desserts.

I drop my bag on the coffee table and walk over to the kitchen, catching Aaron's eyes as I do. He gives me a little nod.

"Hey, anything I can do to help?"

Miles quickly sets his knife down and spins to face me, one eyebrow cocked. "Since when do you help in the kitchen?"

"Wow. Rude. I know I'm useless at cooking, but I can open hot dog packages, form beef into a patty, and skewer spiedies with the best of them—without stabbing myself."

Miles smirks at me and grabs the skewers. "Congratulations. You've got yourself a job."

I quickly wash my hands and get to work skewering spiedies, trying to prove I can do it without stabbing myself, because I come close every single time I do it.

"So, Joel and I had a meeting with Coach today. He says he's going to put me in as a closer in the spring."

Miles glances at Aaron and smiles. "Good. You fucking deserve it."

"Hell yes. Can't wait to be out on the field together again," I say.

"You ever miss it?" Aaron asks.

Miles tips his head back and forth. "I don't know. Sometimes. At first, it was nice to feel a little free from that after doing it for so many years. I'm definitely missing playing now. Maybe we should start doing pickup games in the summer when we're home."

"We could do that," Aaron says, then turns so he's fully facing Miles. "Or you could be a catcher for the Sea Dogs."

I choke back a laugh. "Really? Just going right for it?"

Aaron shrugs as Miles sets his knife down and steps back, looking between us.

"What the fuck are you two going on about?"

I look at Aaron. He's the coach, he should do it.

"Coach called us in today because he lost all of his catchers this season. He specifically requested we talk to you about it."

Miles's eyes go wide. "Oh. Really? I'm surprised he even remembers me."

"Oh, he remembers you. Remembers how well you and A played together. And seemed the slightest bit... *miffed* that you turned him down. He wants you on the team. And selfishly, we were thinking how awesome it would be to play together again. Plus, Trev will be involved with the team behind the scenes in some capacity."

Miles looks between us. "I want to talk to him first."

"I'll set it up," Aaron says, whipping out his phone.

"All right then."

Miles steps forward again, picks up his knife, and continues chopping vegetables.

Behind his back, Aaron and I exchange a smile, then a fist bump.

"Yeah, yeah. Get back to work," Miles says, but when I turn back toward the counter, I see him smiling ear to ear.

Sarah

First day of nonstop lectures is *done.*

Hallelujah. It always takes a little time to get my brain back into school mode.

When I pull into the driveway of the lake house and park my car, I see Rae walking up the front porch steps with a girl with deep auburn hair and curves for days. Don't think I know her.

I hop out of my car and grab my bags.

"Rae baby! Wait up!"

She and the girl turn before they get to the door.

"Hey, how was the first day?" Rae asks as I climb the deck stairs.

"Long," I huff out as I get to the top and walk over to them.

"Chelsea, this is my sister, Sarah. Sarah, this is Chelsea. She's a new intern at Promise. Transfer student."

Chelsea extends her hand. "Nice to meet you."

"You too."

Chelsea subtly looks between Rae and me.

"Looking for the resemblance?" I ask with a smile.

"Kinda," she laughs.

"I'm adopted," I say.

Rae wraps an arm around my back. "Yep. We were best friends first, then the universe decided I get to keep her forever." She rests her head on my shoulder.

I love when she says it like that. It reminds me of the little girl who quickly became my best friend. The one who has always tried to cheer me up through the worst moments, and who was crazy excited for me to officially be her sister.

I pop a kiss on Rae's forehead and Chelsea smiles.

"What do you think?" Rae asks, lifting her head off my shoulder and moving to the door. "Ready to meet everyone?"

"Bring it on," Chelsea says.

Rae swings the front door open and Chelsea and I follow her in.

"Damn," Chelsea breathes, looking around.

"It's pretty awesome," I say, happily dropping my bag by the door. My stomach growls as the scent of food grilling drifts in from the back deck along with the sound of laughter.

"Looks like the party has already started," Rae says, leading the way past the kitchen and the large dining room table to the sliding door. "Hey." She steps onto the deck and everyone turns to look in our direction. "I brought some fresh blood."

Chelsea and I step onto the deck.

"This is Chelsea. I work with her at Promise. She just transferred here, so I thought I'd bring her over to meet everyone and hopefully gain some new friends."

Miles immediately turns from the grill and flashes her his signature charming smile. It's not at full wattage, which means he isn't trying to hit on her. *Yet.* "Hey, nice to meet you. I'm Miles." He gestures to the grill. "I'm the resident cook around here."

"Rude! I help!" Mackie yells from the far end of the outdoor table. "I'm Mackenzie. Nice to meet you!"

Amanda waves from her seat next to Mackie. "Hey, I'm Amanda. I'm the most recent addition to crazy town. Hope you'll stick around and join us. Although, once they have you in their clutches, there's really no getting out." Amanda winks at her and Chelsea laughs. The mere fact that she's not overwhelmed gives her points.

"And that's—"

"Well, well, who do we have here?" Trev cuts Rae off as he walks onto the porch.

Rae spins to face him. "A new friend, so be on your best behavior."

"No promises." He smirks at her. Then Chelsea slowly turns to face him and his expression changes. His eyes light up like a kid on Christmas morning seeing the room stuffed with presents.

Their eyes lock and her cheeks tint pink.

"Hi," Chelsea says breathily, unable to take her eyes off him.

Trevor, though enamored, maintains some smoothness as he steps over and shakes her hand.

"Nice to meet you. I'm Trevor."

His eyes roll over her face, landing on her lips.

I elbow Rae, who nods in agreement. We are *definitely* watching a love at first sight meet cute. Or at the very least, connection at first sight.

"It's nice to meet you. I'm Chelsea. Rae said you just transferred up here this semester. So did I."

Trevor breaks into a full charming grin now. But it's more than the kind he uses to hit on girls. There's something deeper in his eyes. "Maybe we can get to know campus together."

"I'd like that," Chelsea says, swallowing hard.

Damn. They've both got it bad.

Before Trevor can do anything crazy like grab her and kiss the hell out of her, Aaron steps onto the porch.

"Hey, Beautiful."

Rae turns to him with her swooning eyes, watching him as he strolls over. "Hi, Ace."

He wraps his arms around her and gives her a deep kiss as Joel and Mackie boo in the background.

Chelsea chuckles. "Are they always—"

"This nauseating?" I ask. "Yep."

"But it's better than them being whiny, emotional messes," Joel says.

Rae sticks her middle finger up at him as she untangles her tongue from Aaron's.

"Oh, yeah. Chelsea, this is Joel," I say. "He's—" Why did I almost say he's my boyfriend? He's *not* my boyfriend. I mean, he kinda acts like it sometimes, but he isn't. We've established that. I stumble over my words, trying to find the right thing to say. "He's. He... um..." Joel is amused by this and makes no attempt to save me. Thankfully, Rae does.

"His family owns the house," she says.

Joel holds his hand up to his chest. "That's all I am to you?"

Rae rolls her eyes. "He's also like my very annoying brother and was my first best friend. We're where this little group began. The OGs." She holds out her fist across the table.

"The OGs," Joel says, bumping her fist.

"And they never let us forget it," Aaron says, taking Rae's hand and leading her around the table. He sits down next to Joel, then pulls Rae onto his lap.

"Absolutely nauseating," Chelsea whispers to me with a smirk.

I like her already.

Her eyes quickly drift away from me when Trevor says in a smooth, deep voice, "Chelsea."

He pulls out a chair for her. I chuckle at that. Trev has always been good with that stuff. Outwardly, it might look like charm, but it's not just that. He genuinely cares. He likes to take care of people. Maybe that's why he was drawn to me. It's one of the things he and Joel have in common. Though they're very different people, they're both incredibly caring and they have good hearts.

I guess if I have a type, that's not a bad one to have.

Chelsea sits down, and I sit down next to her. Trev is about to sit down on the other side of her when he asks, "Chelsea, can I get you something to drink? We have beer, wine—"

"Something non-alcoholic?" she asks.

"You like fruit punch?" he asks.

She laughs. "Sure."

"I'll be right back."

"Hey, what about the rest of us?" Joel teases.

"Fuck off. You live here," Trev says, heading back inside.

I smile at Joel, who runs his toes up my leg in return. My eyes flare, and I wish there were an easy way to tease him back right now. With no better ideas, I lift my other foot and brush it over his, twisting it around and tickling the bottom of it. He bites at his lip, then hooks his foot around my other leg, slowly tugging it toward him and causing me to slide forward in my chair.

"What are you two doing?" Amanda asks.

"Nothing," we say at the same time.

He drops his foot off my leg, and we both scoot back in our chairs, but he leaves his toes gently resting over mine.

"Here you go," Trev says, returning to the table and sliding a glass of fizzy fruit punch in front of Chelsea, and opening a bottle of tangerine seltzer for himself. *Interesting.* Trev isn't obsessed with alcohol or anything, but usually when we're all sitting around relaxing and grilling, he drinks beer. I can't help but wonder if he's choosing not to because Chelsea isn't drinking any.

Chelsea grabs her drink and takes a sip. "Ooh. That's really good. What is it?"

"Fruit punch and," he lifts his can of seltzer, "tangerine seltzer."

"It's delicious. Thank you."

"Hey, the meat is about ready. Someone want to grab all the rolls, condiments, and sides?" Miles says, more as a command than a question.

Rae looks at me, then says. "I'll get them."

"I'll help, Rae baby."

"Me too," Mackie says, standing up.

Amanda stands as well and says, "Chelsea, want to give us a hand?"

She steals a quick glance at each of us, then says, "Sure. Happy to help."

"Smooth," Miles mutters as we walk inside.

Rae busies herself pulling things out of the fridge, while Amanda asks the important question.

"What is happening between you and Trevor?"

Chelsea's cheeks go pink. "I don't know. I swear when I saw him, it felt like my heart stopped. Obviously, he's drop-dead sexy, but when he touched my hand, I felt this—"

"Tingly feeling? Like you've always known him, and like you'll know him forever?" Rae asks.

Chelsea's mouth forms a little 'O'. "Yes. How did you know that?"

Rae's eyes dance as she looks out the window at Aaron. "Been there. *Still* there."

"I feel like I'm getting way ahead of myself. I just met him. But damn it, I want to *know* him." She looks at Rae. "I'm so glad you invited me here tonight."

Rae laughs. "I had a feeling about you. Guess I was right."

"Is he a good guy? I mean, you all seem pretty nice, but he's not a jackass player who's going to break my heart, is he?" She looks down for a moment. "I've been through enough."

"Trevor is *amazing*. Truly. He can pick up girls, but he doesn't play them. He has never been that type," I say.

"Yeah, we don't hang out with those types of guys," Rae reassures her.

"Sometimes you just date them to avoid your feelings for the love of your life," Mackie deadpans.

Rae rolls her eyes hard. "It's been four years! I was sixteen." She shakes her head as she looks at Chelsea. "Some things will *never* die."

"Nope," Amanda teases. "And I didn't even know you then."

"Anyway," I continue, "Trevor is caring and the absolute best boyfriend."

Chelsea's eyes widen. "There's nothing going on with you guys, is there? It seemed like there was something between you and Joel."

Amanda cackles at that, so I shoot her a death glare. She blows me a kiss in return.

89

"Something," I mutter.

"What was that?" Amanda asks. "It was a little garbled."

"Shut up. We're not talking about Joel. We're talking about Trevor." I look back at Chelsea. "There's nothing going on with Trevor anymore, but we were each other's first... everything. I'm not saying that to freak you out. He's incredible, but it wasn't the right fit for us. We're good friends now, but that's all." I sigh and look between the girls. "And if you need reassurance about that..." I sigh as all the other girls look on, amused. "I might possibly have feelings for Joel."

"Surprised you didn't choke on those words," Mackie says.

Ignoring her, I look at Chelsea. "Trev's been hurt, too. But I promise, he's one of the good ones."

She smiles sheepishly. "Okay. Thanks."

"You guys done with your girl talk?" Miles asks, sticking his head in the door. "I'm fuckin' starving."

"Coming," Rae calls. She shoves a dish, rolls, or condiments in everyone's hands and we make our way back outside.

After setting everything in the center of the table, we all sit down. This time, Rae takes the chair next to Aaron instead of his lap. Miles sits at the head of the table and proclaims it's time to eat.

We all get our food, and Trevor adorably fills Chelsea's plate with everything she asks for. Once we're all sitting, I notice Trevor rest his arm along the back of Chelsea's chair and gently play with her long auburn hair. I watch Chelsea's reaction, and see her put her hand on Trev's thigh and squeeze. Trev moves a little closer in return.

I rip my gaze away from them when Joel's toes brush mine again. He gives me a smile so sexy I feel like molten lava is coursing through my veins.

I try to focus on my food and not breathe too heavily. When I glance at Chelsea out of the corner of my eye, I realize she's doing the same.

As I munch on the array of food in front of me, I can't help but wonder if one of us is about to catch fire.

Joel

"Tonight was fun," I say as I lie in bed, waiting for Sarah to finish in the bathroom.

She walks out looking fresh faced but tired. "Yeah, it was. I was waiting for Chelsea to mount Trevor, though. That was some insane chemistry."

"Pretty sure they're making out on the couch right now," I say.

"They seem like a good match. I hope it will be for him."

"Is it weird for you?" I ask.

"Trev and Chelsea?"

"Seeing him with someone else. I don't have an ex like that, so I have no frame of reference."

She lies down next to me, staring at the ceiling.

"Now? No. The only thing I feel is excitement for them. If it had happened within a few months or even a year after breaking up, it would've been hard. But we made our way back to friendship, and that's what I feel for him."

I nod, then stare up at the ceiling as well before taking her hand.

"What would you have done if Chelsea had been interested in me?"

She swallows hard and fidgets for a moment.

"Well, I would've had to sit next to you." She pulls her hand from mine and slides it up to my neck, twisting her fingers through the hair at the base of it. "Do something like this." She rolls onto her side. "Then, if that didn't work, I'd do something like..." She trails off, then drops her lips to the crook of my neck, kissing the spot just above my collarbone. My dick hardens instantly.

"Sarah," I groan.

"Good to know that would've made it clear how I feel about you."

I refrain from asking how she feels about me, instead letting her kiss across my chest and show me with her lips.

I thread her hair, twirling my fingers around the shining blonde strands.

Another moan escapes before I can help it.

She pulls away suddenly, and I assume it's because she's freaked out. Whatever, another night, another case of blue balls.

Maybe I'll jump in a cold shower after she falls asleep.

But then I hear her bedside drawer open and close. She shakes something up, opens it, then closes it again after a moment. She turns to me, rubbing her palms together, then drops her lips to my neck again, intermittently licking and sucking this time.

"Fuck," I mutter, hips rolling toward her before I think better of it.

Then, before I realize what's happening, she pulls my boxer briefs down and wraps a hand—covered in her favorite warming lubricant—around my shaft, then massages my balls with the other.

Through my haze of pleasure, I manage to mumble, "What are you doing?"

"Consider it payback for the coffee this morning," she whispers, lips brushing my skin. "If that's okay."

"Mhm," I murmur in confirmation.

She smiles against my neck, then moves her hand up and down. The sensation makes me groan, and I have to focus hard to keep from losing it too quickly. I want to enjoy this. The feel of her skin on mine. The sexy noises she makes as she strokes me. She brings her other hand down, gently squeezing my balls as she teases me, going slow and changing the pressure as she glides her hand down my length.

"Sarah," I rasp, thrusting into her hand.

She follows my cues and tightens her grasp as she strokes me faster, taking me right to the edge. God damn, she knows how to touch me. This hand job is more intense than any sex I've had in my life.

And she's not slowing down. She sucks on my neck again, and I'm done, my dick pulsing as I moan her name. I can barely breathe when she's finished with me. The only time I've ever come harder was when she went down on me.

She runs to the bathroom, grabs a towel, wipes her hand, and then my stomach. Carefully, she pulls my boxer briefs back up, then tucks me in before going into the bathroom again.

I'm nearly asleep when she returns and snuggles next to me, resting her head on my shoulder and draping her arm over my chest.

When she takes care of me, allows herself to be vulnerable like this, I think she's more ready for us than she realizes, but if she's still too scared, if this is all she can give me, I'll take it without complaint.

Chapter Six

Nothing is Logical in Love

Sarah

"HERE'S TO RAE. WE all wish you a lifetime of messy, complicated happiness and all the thrills and joys that come with it."

"Thank you, Momma," Rae says. Then she looks around the private room of the tea house we're at. "And thank you all for being here today. Yesterday I was spoiled rotten and had so much fun at my bachelorette party, but I'm grateful to spend today with all the incredible, supportive women in my life."

Yesterday was *quite* the day. We spent the day and night in New York City, having a spa day, lunch at an upscale sushi restaurant, then shopping, followed by dinner with the boys at a premier steakhouse. While we had our adventures, the boys were busy playing a game against the New York Metros. Between Jamie being drafted to the team and Aaron having connected with their pitching coach, Marc Demoda, over the summer, some big strings were pulled. Safe to say the boys had a hell of a day. Especially since they won. Last night we spent the evening having a combined bachelor-bachelorette party in a massive hotel suite—which Joel is to thank for. He refused to tell me how much he spent, but I know it was *a lot.* Of course, halfway through the drinking and games, Rae and Aaron disappeared so they could *celebrate* on their own. We left early this morning to come back to Ida—by limo.

Now we're having lunch at a local tea house which has a private room for events. They provide a ridiculous number of tea options, plus finger sandwiches and an array of homemade desserts.

Rae's right, this table is filled with amazing women. All of our female cousins are here, along with our aunts, Mom and Gram, Aaron's mom Cathy, Miles's mom Katie, Mackie's mom Linda, and our closest friends—Mackie, Amanda, Hyla, Chelsea, Maia, and Leigh.

"Before we eat, we have a special gift for you. Rather than everyone getting you a gift for this party, we asked them to contribute to this—an idea Gram, Sarah, Amanda, and I came up with," Mom says, getting up and taking a beautifully wrapped large box from a nearby table.

Rae looks at it in awe as it's set in front of her, wrapped in shimmery gold paper with a rose gold bow.

"Open it," Mom says softly, sitting back down beside her.

Carefully, Rae unties the bow and pulls off the wrapping paper before lifting the cover off the box. Inside is a stunning photo album. On each page is a letter written from a woman at the table with their advice on love and anything else they wanted to include for Rae. There is also a picture on each page of Rae with that person.

Rae opens the cover and slowly flips through.

"Oh my gosh," she breathes. "Thank you all." Her eyes fill with tears. "This means so much to me."

"A few of us thought we'd read our letters aloud, if you'd like to hear them," Mom says.

Rae nods. "I'd love that."

Mom takes the book from Rae and begins. Tears and laughter flow freely as a handful of us read our letters. Mom, then me, followed by Mackie, Katie, and Cathy. Then the book goes to Gram.

"I suppose there's a reason we decided I should go last," Gram says with a sniff. "Before I start, I want you to know writing letters is a tradition I started many years ago. Each year on a grandchild's birthday I write an updated letter to them with my thoughts and advice. Before one gets married, I write a final version to give them on their wedding day. This, my girl, is yours." She clears her throat and begins.

"My dear, sweet Rae, I want to start this letter by telling you how proud I am of the woman you have become. Watching you fight for the things you want. Watching you discover your purpose in life. Watching you fall in love.

"From the first moment you brought that sweet golden-haired boy around, I knew he would be the one for you, even if you two kept us on our toes waiting for the moment when you'd realize that."

She pauses and we all laugh.

"The love that has grown between the two of you has been beautiful to watch. I know your kind of love because I have experienced it myself. It is the kind of unshakable and unmovable love that lasts a lifetime.

"With that, I'd like to pass on some words of wisdom that I have learned over the years.

"First, know that life is not a straight line. It doesn't matter how you think it should go or will go, it won't go that way. Things will happen when you least expect them. Things will happen out of order. Things will challenge you and confuse you and even the things that seem the hardest may land you precisely where you need to be. Don't try to force things that aren't working. Don't try and move down that straight line because someone said you should. Find your place and your path.

"Next, concerning love, do it. Whatever it is. Do the crazy things. Do the wild things. Do the frustrating and annoying things. Laugh at the ridiculous fights. Revel in the hard moments because they will strengthen your love. Trust in Aaron and yourself. It is so clear he is the man you were made to love and that he loves you incredibly deeply.

"Finally, my dear, a reminder of something that I know you have struggled with in the past—I need you to love. Not partially. Not with uncertainty. Not with your brain. I need you to let go. I need you to love so deeply you can't see the surface of the water anymore. I need you to love with your heart and believe that it will lead you precisely where you need to go. I'll try to remind you of this as often as possible. You're like your father, always looking for the practical, logical answer. Stop. Nothing is logical in love. It's warm and endearing and confusing and uncertain and powerful and requires a leap of faith like nothing else in life. Do it. Love unapologetically. Love in ways you didn't know you could love. Trust your gorgeous, wonderful heart and it will always lead you right where you should be.

"In closing, I want you to know the depth of my love for you knows no bounds. Go live your life in the fullest ways and open that heart to the immense amount of love it deserves.

"All my love. Gram."

Yep. Good thing she saved it for last because the entire room—including a server who paused to listen—is ugly crying.

"Thank you," Rae blubbers, hugging Gram tightly for a few moments.

"Well, who's ready for some food?" Mom asks, wiping her eyes.

Rae clears her throat. "I, um...just need a minute." She grabs her phone and walks onto the nearby balcony—to call Aaron, I'm sure.

Everyone else gets up and wipes their eyes before milling about the room, looking at all the food.

I take a moment and excuse myself, going downstairs and out the back door to the small parking lot. Leaning against the building, I try to steady my breathing, but I can't stop crying.

Gram's letter to Rae hit somewhere deep inside me, especially her words about love. I may not hold back in the same way as Rae, but there's no denying that I have been.

"Honey?"

I look over and see Mom standing a few feet away, but I still can't stop my tears.

"Oh, baby. Come here." Mom pulls me into her arms, letting me cry against her shoulder. "What's wrong?"

What is wrong? How do I explain this?

"Love," I whisper, for lack of anything better.

She steps back and smooths her hand over my cheek before tucking some stray hairs behind my ear.

"You love Joel?" she asks, getting right to the point.

I nod slowly. "Yes."

"Why does that make you cry?"

"Because I want to tell him that, but I can't," I choke out.

"Why not?"

Wiping some tears and trying to get a deep breath, I say, "Because I can't give him that love—or me—yet. Not all of it. Not everything he deserves. I'm working so hard, and I'm proud of myself, but I don't feel like I have enough of myself to give to a relationship. I don't want to set myself up for failure. If I try to split my focus or get too stressed—I'm scared I'll mess it all up. If I want to do it right, I need to wait. Go slow."

"Does Joel know that?"

"Yes. He's been so patient and understanding. All he's asked me for is honesty."

"Then what's the problem?"

"I want to go slow, but my feelings aren't slow. They're fast and reckless. I'm scared if I tell him how deeply I feel for him, but can't give him all that yet... eventually, he'll get tired of it and leave me."

"Oh, honey..." She takes my hands in hers. "I've seen how Joel looks at you, how he cares for you. I don't think you ever have to worry about him leaving you. Deep down, I think you know that. I know it's hard for you, but you have to trust in that—in him. If he says he wants honesty, telling him the truth about your feelings is important."

She steps back and wipes a few tears off my cheeks.

"I agree with that," Gram says, coming to stand next to Mom. "I guess I did a number on everyone with that letter. Rae just came in from the balcony after crying on the phone to Aaron. I didn't mean to bring down the mood."

"You didn't," I tell her. "But you know how to make the most of your words."

"I'm going to sneak back upstairs and check on Rae," Mom says. "I love you, honey. Think about what I said."

"I will. Love you too." Mom walks inside and Gram takes my hand. "What's your wisdom for me?" I ask.

She laughs at that. "Oh, the same as always, I suppose."

"Something about opening my heart, right?"

She nods. "Yes, but you don't have to push yourself. Take your time, think about what you want and what you can give, but don't be afraid to tell him what he means to you. I don't think it will hurt either of you to tell him that. In fact, it might bring you closer and strengthen your bond. You have a beautiful heart. Don't hide it from him."

I nod, knowing she's right. She's always right. Her and Mom. It's scary sometimes. But I suppose they've learned some things over the years. I hope I can be as wise as them one day.

"You're good at that."

"After seventy years, I may have picked up a thing or two. You will too, as you grow. It also helps that I was listening to the end of that conversation with your mother."

"Oh, so you cheated."

She shrugs, giving me a wily smile that shows the spunkier side of her that Grandpa loves so much. "Used it to my advantage."

"Well, either way, I appreciate it."

"Come on, honey, let's go back inside and enjoy the rest of this day."

She wraps her arms around me and leads me inside, my mind turning her words and mom's over and over. I don't know if I'm ready to tell Joel I love him, or deal with the emotions that might come with that yet, but I'm not sure how much longer I can deny it, either.

Joel

As far as bachelor parties—or in our case bachelor weekends—go, Aaron's has been epic. This weekend has been a fucking blast. From playing with all of our friends on a major league field to making a fuckton of awesome memories that we'll laugh about for years to come, I couldn't have asked for it to go better.

Now, Miles and I are leading everyone onto my back deck for the final part of the bachelor weekend shenanigans.

Most of our closest friends are here. A few guys from the team, along with all of our Ida friends, Jamie, Trevor, Nick, Vince, Braden, and my brother.

"Shit, man," our first baseman, Ricky, says. "This is awesome."

The back deck is lit up with large bulb white string lights. There's a cooler with beer and other drinks, wings of every kind on the table, and several pizzas.

"Food and drink are over there," I say, gesturing to the table and coolers beneath. "Pool is heated to ninety degrees or there are comfortable chairs and heaters on the deck. There's wood set up out back for a bonfire. Eat, drink, and be merry!"

Though I didn't outright say it, I've saved the hot tub as a sort of VIP section for our closest friends.

"Hell yes," Miles says, lowering into the hot tub, followed by me, Jamie, and Trevor.

"This is seriously the perfect way to end the night," Aaron says, looking fully relaxed as he leans back in the hot tub.

A car door slams, then my phone goes off.

"Who's that?" Aaron asks.

"Don't worry about it," I say, climbing back out of the hot tub and grabbing a towel.

I head inside and find Rae and the girls.

"Ready for my grand entrance?" she asks.

"Are you?" I ask, lifting one eyebrow.

"She's about to be," Amanda says devilishly, lifting a bag of clothes.

In a flash, she and Sarah have Rae stripped down to her swimsuit, then covered back up again in a trench coat, big sunglasses, and a baseball cap pushed down low.

I have no idea how I'm going to get through this without dying of laughter.

"Okay, I'm going to head back out there and set the scene. Come out when you hear the music."

When I get back outside, my brother is sitting along the edge of the hot tub, dipping his feet in. I climb back in, trying to hide my smirk. I can't do it, but that's okay, because it works well with the lie I'm about to tell.

"What's going on?" Aaron asks.

I glance at Miles like we might be in trouble.

"Look, it's not a big deal," I say. "We might've hired—"

"A stripper?" Aaron growls, crossing his arms over his chest and standing up.

Forgot how intimidating he is when he's pissed.

"Dude, chill," Miles says. "It's a bachelor party necessity. Plus, she's technically a *personal* stripper. She'll even—"

"Fuck that. I told you two I didn't want a stripper. You know the only girl I'm interested in seeing even close to naked is Rae. Why would I ever want to do more than that? What the hell is the matter with you?"

He is hilarious when he's angry. He loses all common sense. Like we'd ever do something that could hurt Rae like that. And he knows well enough that we'd kick his ass if he tried.

Miles and I exchange a glance, then Miles says, "Well, she's already here, so at least let the boys have some fun."

Before Aaron can argue, Miles turns on the music. Music Rae specifically requested. First, she chose *Do You Wanna Touch* by Joan Jett and the Blackhearts. Kinda perfect, honestly.

Rae struts out onto the deck right on cue.

Aaron is watching with his arms crossed and a grimace on his face.

She strolls over to the hot tub and, in a deep Long Island accent, says, "This the groom? He's *cute.*"

Aaron shakes his head. "Listen, I'm sorry, but—"

Rae, God love her, commits to this. "Now, now, there'll be time for all that. You just sit right there and enjoy this, honey."

She moves—not too terribly—to the beat of the music, making her way around the deck and dancing in front of each guy. She teases that she's going to open the trench coat several times, but doesn't do it.

When she gets back to the hot tub, she looks at Aaron, who is still glaring.

"What's wrong? You don't like this song?"

Her Long Island accent game is strong. I am trying so hard not to laugh. I look over at Miles, who is stoic, but I can see the laughter he's forcing back.

Rae looks at Miles and says, "You, you tall drink of water there. Can you put on the other song we discussed?"

Miles smirks and grabs his phone, putting on *Dress* by Taylor Swift.

At this point, she leans down and runs her hands over Trevor's shoulders. "You busy tonight, honey?" And something about that makes Trevor realize it's Rae, and he nearly starts laughing.

Aaron is red-faced as Rae makes her way back to him, hands on her hips.

"Now, what's the matta, honey?" She leans forward and looks at him, her face just inches from his. "I thought you liked this song." She drags a finger down his chest and pulls her bottom lip between her teeth. I clock the second Aaron realizes it's Rae. His arms drop, his posture softens, and a grin crosses his face.

"Mm. I do like this song," he says, climbing out of the hot tub. He undoes the ties of the coat, letting it fall open, then steps back and looks her up and down while whistling. "Damn."

She smirks at him and moves closer. "Does that mean you're ready for the full show?" She asks, never dropping the accent.

Aaron cocks an eyebrow and hungrily drinks her in.

He lowers his voice and leans in toward her. "If it's a private show, does that include touching?"

"That could be arranged. Lead the way, handsome."

Aaron takes her hand and leads her in the back door. Half of the guys are slack-jawed that they just witnessed that. The other half are doing everything in their power to keep from laughing hysterically.

"What the fuck..." Jamie mutters.

Jesse looks between Miles and me. "You're just going to let him go with her? What the fuck is wrong with you two?"

Miles's neck is tight as he fights back laughter. My stomach hurts from holding it in. Trev looks like he's about to bust a nut, and across the deck, Nick—who also figured it out—is cackling.

"What the hell is the matter with you guys? You think this is funny?" Jamie yells, standing up. "I'm going to—"

"You're going fucking nowhere," Trevor says, as we all burst into a fit of laughter.

"What are you laughing about?" my brother asks.

"I can't—I can't believe you didn't know it was—" I wheeze, trying to catch my breath.

Miles is laughing so hard he can't talk.

Nick strolls over. "Did you guys not notice she was a pretty bad dancer for a stripper?"

"And do you really think Aaron would go off with some random girl?" Trev asks.

"You're asking what the fuck is wrong with us? What's wrong with you?" Miles says, wiping tears of laughter from his eyes.

I lock eyes with my brother and say, "I thought you, of all people, would figure out *exactly* who that stripper was."

I'm stifling laughter again when realization finally hits him. His shoulders slump and he shakes his head. "It was Rae. Of fucking course, it was."

Jamie pinches the bridge of his nose, then splashes some water at us. "Jesus, you had me pissed and ready to kill A. That's why he had a sudden change of heart when she got closer."

"Yeah, why do you think he leaned into her when he got out of the hot tub?" Nick laughs.

Gross. Don't need to think about my best friend with a boner. Or wonder what they're doing in the spare bedroom upstairs. Actually, there's no wondering about it.

"So, the groom left. What else do you have in store for us? Some actual strippers?" Ricky calls.

Miles and I exchange a smile, then he whistles. The rest of the girls appear on the back deck to cheers and applause.

Sarah climbs into the hot tub and sits down next to me, holding up her fist. "I think we nailed it."

I bump it, agreeing. "We definitely did."

"What a day," Sarah says, the picture of exhaustion as she climbs into the bed. "Can you believe we were still in New York City this morning?"

I laugh at that. "No. We crammed a lot into this weekend."

"That we did. I'm assuming you boys had fun golfing and then having lunch at that swanky club your dad is a member of."

"We did. I had so much good food this weekend I'm not sure anything else will live up to this for a while. How was the bridal shower today? What was the deal with Rae crying? I freaked out for a second when she called."

Sarah inhales deeply, then looks up at the ceiling. "We had everyone write letters to Rae and we put them in a photo album. They're full of love and advice. But Gram got us with hers."

Rolling onto my side, I wrap an arm around her waist and rest my head next to hers. She turns slightly and looks at me.

"What did it say?"

"Basically how she always knew Aaron was the one for Rae and reminding her—and all of us—the importance of opening up to love and fighting for it. To do crazy things and hard things in the name of love and to love fully and deeply. Rae was crying. I was crying. Most of the room was crying."

"You were crying?" I whisper.

She turns more, fully on her side now, and stares deep into my eyes. "Yes."

"Why?"

She takes a few breaths as she searches for the right words. "Because I could feel my own uncertainties and fears about love in her words. I understood the complexities of it all, but the importance of opening up despite that."

I tuck a strand of hair behind her ear and then get lost in her eyes for a moment. "That sounds like a lot."

"Definitely. Beautiful, though."

For a few moments, we lay like this, arms wrapped around each other, faces almost touching.

She looks down and chews on her bottom lip for a moment before looking up at me again.

"Joel?"

"Hm?"

"I..." She closes her eyes and takes a deep breath. When she opens them again, they roll over my face. She sweeps her hand across my cheek. "I missed you today."

Moving closer, she tucks her head against my chest.

"I missed you too," I whisper, but my heart is beating fast because I know what she almost said.

I've known how she's felt for a while now, but this is the closest she's come to admitting it. She might not be ready to say it yet, and I won't push her, but it's another moment of intimacy that inches us closer to the line and lowers another piece of her armor. More importantly, it tells me what I need to know. She wants me. Wants us. Wants a future together. That's all that really matters.

After pulling the blanket up over us, I wrap my arms tightly around her and kiss her head, thinking the words *I love you* as loud as I can, hoping she'll feel them and know how much she means to me and that I'll always want a future with her, too.

Chapter Seven

Sloppy, Reckless

Sarah

I JOLT AWAKE AT the sound of a train whistle and almost go tumbling onto the floor, but Joel grips me tighter, pulling me on top of him. It takes me a minute to remember where I am, then it all makes sense. Normally a train whistle doesn't bother me. But I'm not usually right next to the tracks. Aaron and Rae must've gotten used to it.

"I know. It's fucking loud," Joel mumbles, not opening his eyes.

Rae and Aaron had no intention of spending the night before their wedding apart, and since Joel and I were up late with them going over all kinds of last-minute things, we decided we'd just crash here on the couch. Plus, Joel and I wanted to make sure we keep Aaron and Rae on schedule.

I try to rest against Joel's chest and enjoy the last few minutes in bed—or on the couch, I guess—but I'm in the wrong position. I slide down his body a little, so my head can rest comfortably against him, when I feel something... hard.

"Sorry," Joel mutters, reaching to adjust himself.

I catch his hand and thread my fingers through his. "You don't have to apologize for being turned on. Especially if it's by me," I mutter, brushing my lips over the skin of his neck.

"It's always by you," he whispers. "You were pressed so tight against me last night I couldn't help it. And you smell amazing."

He kisses my neck, and I almost moan.

Two can play this game.

I suck the skin of his neck into my mouth.

He grips my ass with one hand and moans my name.

"Wow, I thought we were supposed to be the perpetually horny ones," Aaron says with a laugh. Joel and I freeze in place. Aaron looks at Rae. "Quick, get on the kitchen counter."

"Don't tease me. I'm going to miss you." She kisses his neck, and he groans.

"Gross," Joel says in a cough.

"Says the guy with his hand on my sister's ass. Check yourself before you sass me."

Joel yanks his hand off my butt like it's burning him, then I quickly sit up. Aaron fights back a smirk as Rae shakes her head.

"Are you ready to go? Or do you need a minute?" Aaron asks Joel, eyes dancing.

"Fuck off. I'm ready. Let's get Miles and—"

There's a knock on the door. "I come bearing coffee!" Miles yells through the door.

"Or he'll find us," I say.

Aaron opens the door and Miles strolls in followed by Mackie and Amanda.

"I think that's our cue," Aaron says, wrapping a hand around the side of Rae's neck.

"Just think, next time you see me, I'll be in my wedding dress."

Aaron inhales sharply. "Can't fucking wait. I love you, Beautiful."

"Love you too, Ace."

He gives her a long, slow kiss. The kind that makes me giddy for them rather than nauseous.

When they pull away, Aaron winks at her, then steps back.

Joel rises from the couch, giving me an adorable smile offset by a smoldering gaze. He walks over and kisses Rae on the cheek. "Happy wedding, Rae Rae. Have fun getting ready."

She ruffles his hair. "You too, Joelskies. Don't get my almost-husband drunk, please."

"Scout's honor," Joel says.

"Like you were ever a scout." Rae rolls her eyes.

"Have a good morning, ladies," Miles says. "Don't worry, I'll keep the boys out of trouble."

With one last lingering look between Rae and Aaron, the boys head out the door.

Mackie and Amanda set all the coffees on the table, and we all sit down on the couch.

"So..." Rae says, "what were you and Joel doing?"

Amanda and Mackie's eyebrows go up.

"Sorry, I can't hear you over the sound of it being your wedding day!" I exclaim, willing to do anything to change the subject.

"And as the bride, you have to do what I say." She grins at me. "I thought you two were about to start humping. Spill."

I groan, but give in. There's no way of getting around it when she's like this. "Nothing happened. But he may have been a bit... hard. For me. And he does things to me... anyway, nothing was going to happen on your couch. Even if we were alone, we probably would've just kissed and teased each other. *Maybe* there might have been some touching. But we haven't crossed any other lines since Valentine's Day, okay?"

Rae takes me in, then smiles, grabs her coffee, and takes a drink. "Okay. *Now* we can focus on me."

We all laugh, and Amanda whips out her checklist, making sure we have everything we need as we drink our coffee. Once we're done, we pack everything we need and head to Gram and Grandpa's farmhouse to get ready.

"You look so beautiful," I say, circling around Rae as she stands in the living room of Gram and Grandpa's house.

Rae is bursting, bouncing in place. "I hope he thinks so, too."

"You know he will. Now, you go wait by the tree, I will go get Aaron, then Dad will meet you when you're finished with your first looks."

"Okay," she says with a nod, then she grabs me and pulls me into her arms. "I love you. Thank you for helping make today so special. The wedding hasn't even started, and it's already been amazing. I couldn't ask for anyone better to stand up with me. I'm so lucky you're my sister."

I squeeze her back, trying hard not to cry. "I love you too, Rae baby. I will forever be grateful I got you as my sister. But now we have to stop this because I don't want us to have to redo our makeup."

She laughs as I let her go. "If you think I'm not wearing ultra-waterproof mascara, you're crazy."

"Come on." I take her hand and lead her to the front door. I hold the train of her dress to make sure it doesn't drag on the ground too much, and follow her to the large tree in front of the house.

I let the back of the dress down when we get there, then step in front of her, taking in her gorgeous A-line gown with an intricate lace top and a tulle bottom. The tulle is lightweight and airy. The whole dress is a deep cream color with a thick rose gold sash that sits at the waist, adding color to the dress without being overpowering. She looks absolutely stunning.

"Okay. I'm going to get Aaron now. Just be careful with him. You look so incredible..."

"Instant boner?" she giggles.

"And he needs to be able to walk down the aisle." I quickly kiss her cheek, then squeeze her hands. "Love you."

"Love you too, baby," she says.

I turn and head for the side of the house where Joel said Aaron was waiting. As I round the corner, I see him standing there, cracking his knuckles as usual when he's nervous.

"Hey."

His eyes snap to me, lighting up immediately with anticipation. I don't know why this moment catches me, but it does.

"Sarah McKinley, are you crying?" he teases.

"Trying not to," I snuffle. "You two have been a lifetime in the making. Seeing you dressed in your suit..." I shake my head. His deep bronze suit is perfectly tailored, and he's wearing a rose gold tie that matches Rae's dress and accessories. "Anyway." I blink back my tears. "Your girl is waiting."

He breaks into a grin, then steps forward and pulls me into his arms.

"I'm so happy for you."

"Thanks, Sarbear," he says as he steps back.

I nod toward the front of the house. "Go see your girl."

"Happily." He squeezes my hand, then walks toward the front of the house.

I watch him go, feeling drunk on love—and I'm not even the one getting married.

I turn and walk toward the back of the house. As soon as I round the corner, my eyes land on Joel, who is talking to Miles and Jamie. He stops mid-sentence when he sees me and walks toward me, taking in my V-neck dusty pink maxi dress. It's stretchy, with a banded waist and hugs every curve of my body to perfection. My hair is tucked back in a low bun with a few loose tendrils framing my face.

"You are... breathtaking," he says as he stops in front of me, eyes still rolling over my body.

"You look pretty handsome yourself." I tug at the lapels of his suit. The groomsmen are all wearing light brown suits with pale pink ties.

"Rae all ready?" he asks.

"Yep. Looking stunning."

He inhales sharply, eyes filling with adoration. He sweeps one hand up the side of my face and rests his forehead against mine.

"Someday, we're going to be standing like this, with you in a heart-stoppingly gorgeous wedding dress. I don't care when it happens, but I know it will, and I'll be as much of a puddle for you then as I am today."

"Joel!" Miles yells. "We've gotta go. Come on!"

My heart pitter-pats as I imagine it. Being wrapped in his arms in a wedding dress, about to become his wife? That thought makes my body flush and fills me with desire.

It scares the shit out of me, what it will take to get to that point, but I know it will be worth it. And I want it.

Joel brushes his lips over my cheek, then pauses and whispers in my ear, "I love you. I hope you know that. And we're going to have a beautiful future."

One last peck on the cheek, then he stands up straight, grins at me, and turns toward the boys.

They walk down the small hill toward the field, and I watch Joel until he's out of sight.

We're going to have a beautiful future.

I hope he's right about that.

Joel

I'm standing at an altar next to my best friend, who is craning his neck, trying to get a look at Rae like he didn't just see her a few minutes ago.

"Breathe, man. It'll be any second now."

He takes a breath and tries to relax his shoulders, but he can't.

"I'm just... ready. After all these years, I finally get to marry her."

An instrumental version of *You're Still the One* starts playing, and Aaron's gaze on the end of the aisle intensifies. A second later, Rae is standing there with her dad.

Aaron inhales sharply, then takes a steadying breath.

"God, she's beautiful," he murmurs.

And she is. Even I feel emotional watching her walk down the aisle. Seeing my two best friends finally get their happily ever after is the best feeling in the world.

Once she gets to him, they're both teary messes, and I'm trying not to add to that. I gaze across the aisle at Sarah, and my heartbeat ticks up. I meant every word I said to her before the ceremony. It's going to be us someday. Hopefully not too long from now, but I'll wait if I have to. No matter how badly I'd like to sweep her into my arms and make her mine forever.

Her gaze lands on me and she smiles softly and gives me the slightest wink. I said I would never push her, but seeing her in that dress, dreaming of marrying her? It's hard not to push, not to want to cross every line and deal with the consequences of that later.

What's that thing Rae says?

I'm so screwed.

Hopefully literally.

Yeah, right.

After a beautiful ceremony, complete with personalized vows and the kind of kiss that made me want to vomit, we took eight thousand pictures. It was pretty fun, though, especially when all six of us were together. I love having Amanda, Jamie, Hyla, Trevor, and now Chelsea as parts of our little group, but there's something special about the moments when it's just the six of us. It's like everything else washes away and we're those same six kids who became best friends in kindergarten. I couldn't have asked for better friends to grow up with, and I'm thankful I got to watch Rae and Aaron finally make official what we all knew was coming since those years in elementary school.

After pictures, we made our grand entrance into the barn, and Rae and Aaron immediately shared their first dance. Aaron danced with his mom and Rae danced with her dad. Now, we're finishing our meals—we all got to order off small menus from Yo Taco! and Burgers and Sh!t, which are set up in the driveway outside the barn. It's classic Aaron and Rae to do something like that.

It's about time for Sarah and I to make our best man and maid of honor toasts, but we decided to combine them into something special.

Rather than do a large head table, Rae and Aaron opted to do small tables of four to eight people. Rae, Aaron, Sarah, Miles, Mackie, and I are all sitting together while Trevor, Chelsea, Hyla, Amanda, and Jamie sit at a table next to us.

I glance over at Sarah, who gives me a little nod.

We both stand and head over to the DJ, who gives us a mic.

"If I could have your attention, please," I say, drawing everyone's gaze to Sarah and me.

Sarah takes the mic. "We're so excited to be here to celebrate Rae and Aaron *finally* getting married." Everyone laughs at that. "Joel and I each have a few words to say, and then we have a special surprise for Aaron and Rae." She looks over at them. "I see your skepticism, but trust me, you're going to love it." She takes a deep breath. "I was lucky enough to grow up with Rae for a sister. She has a beautiful heart. She's kind and forgiving and she put up with all my drama. Though, to be fair, I put up with my fair share of hers." Sarah winks at Rae, who laughs. "But one of the most beautiful parts was getting to watch an innocent childhood friendship blossom into a very real, complex love story. One that was not always easy, but showed the true meaning and depth of love and all it can survive and triumph over. A love like theirs is hard to come by, and getting to watch it unfold has been truly incredible. I can't wait to see all the wonderful things life has in store for the two of you. I love you both. Happy wedding."

Sarah raises her glass of champagne as Rae wipes away a couple of tears and mouths, *I love you.* Everyone clinks their glasses together, then dings their silverware against them for Rae and Aaron to kiss—which they happily do.

I take the mic from Sarah and try to control the emotions I'm feeling. I'd rather not be the one to cry through this.

"I could stand here for hours telling secrets and stories, both funny and embarrassing, but tonight is about the two of them. What a roller coaster it has been to watch them finally admit their feelings and fall in love—even if it was imperfect at times. Their resilience and ability to hold on to each other in the hardest, most complicated moments is proof that they have what it takes to make it through anything. A love like Aaron and Rae's is rare. It is all-encompassing and constantly overflowing.

Their love touches everyone they know and seems to grow stronger every day. I'm lucky I got to see it from the beginning, the very moment it all changed. When Rae took Aaron's hand and led him across the backyard and simultaneously changed both of our lives. I got a new best friend, and I got to watch my first best friend—more like my sister—slowly fall in love with the person who was made for her. And that has been an honor. Which is why Sarah and I decided to go back to the beginning and show everyone how far they've come and just how long they've truly been in love."

I nod to Amanda, who sets up the screen and projector.

"Aaron and Rae danced to a beautiful song called *I Will Always Be Yours* by Ben Rector. But it's not *their* song. Their song, by the same artist, is called *Love Like This.* And Sarah and I may have underhandedly convinced them that it was too slow for a first dance song. That may be true, but really, we wanted to use it for our own purposes. So, now, set to their song, is the story of their love."

Amanda turns the lights down and starts the video we put together, perfectly timed to *Love Like This.*

A hush falls over the room as their song plays and pictures of them from early childhood through to their relationship now play, lining up with certain lyrics to the song. Many of the photos are not only of them, but of all of us. I've seen them plenty of times over the last few weeks as Sarah and I worked on the video, arranging the pictures to be just right. Tonight, my eyes are drawn to the two of us. In many of the photos, we're standing together. My arm is tossed over her shoulders or she's smiling up at me. Then there are the photos from prom, where we're looking at each other with excitement and nervousness.

With Aaron and Rae, it was obvious from a young age what was between them. But as I see the flashes of Sarah and me in these photos, I wonder if it could have been there for us, too.

If I'd realized before she got with Trevor, if we'd have ended up together instead. What could have been mixes with what I want us to be, and my gaze lands on her. She's looking back at me, eyes filled with emotion, like she's thinking the same things.

She reaches down and gives my hand a gentle squeeze as we get to the last part of the song. This was the hardest part of the video to figure out, because we couldn't put it together until today. Their videographer was amazing and gave us the footage of the ceremony as soon as it was over, and while Rae and Aaron took their couple pictures, Sarah, the videographer, Amanda, and I snuck off to add the last piece to the video. Through the last chorus, a video of the two of them at the altar, exchanging rings and kissing, plays. Seeing it again set to their song catches me. Tears stream down my cheeks as the video ends, and Sarah and I turn back to Aaron and Rae, who are out of their seats and coming over to us.

Rae throws her arms around me. "Thanks, Joelskies. That was beautiful."

I squeeze her tightly, then kiss her cheek. "Happy wedding, Rae Rae. Love you."

"Love you too," she breathes, then turns to Sarah. "You stole a bunch of those from the box in my bedside table, didn't you?"

Sarah laughs and wiggles her eyebrows before pulling Rae into her arms. "Maybe. Had to find the best ones."

Even Aaron is wiping his eyes as he thanks me.

With the whole room still focused on us, I raise my glass. "Here's to Aaron and Rae and a life full of love."

The whole room cheers and whistles, then clinks their glasses. Rae and Aaron kiss, and I high five Sarah.

We nailed it.

Sarah

What a night—and day—it has been. Rae was incandescently happy, and that made my heart feel so full. Right now, though, my heart is full for a different reason. I'm in Joel's arms.

Rae and Aaron left about a half hour ago, ready to get their honeymoon started. Aaron is surprising Rae with a suite at the local hotel tonight before they head out to their honeymoon in Spain tomorrow morning. They'll be there all week and get back home next weekend.

The party has been winding down since they left—lots of slow dancing. Amanda has a team of people coming to clean up the space tomorrow, so tonight is all about relaxing. And here, in Joel's arms, I'm very relaxed. Probably *too* relaxed.

"I love this song," Joel whispers, lips pressed into my temple as we dance to *God Gave Me You* by Blake Shelton. "It makes me think of you."

"It does? Why?"

He lifts his lips from my head and leans back slightly so he can see my eyes.

"Because it's how you make me feel. Like I'm not alone. On my worst days, I know you'll be there for me, picking up my pieces."

I stare at him, unable to mask my surprise and confusion.

He feels that way about *me?* He does those things for me without a doubt. Do I really do the same for him? I don't feel like I give him half of what he gives me.

He slides one hand farther up my back, twisting it around the loose strands of hair that have fallen out of my bun.

"Do you not realize what you do for me? How you take care of me?" Heat rolls up my spine, and my body flushes. My heart is pounding as he moves closer, pushing his hardened muscle against my hip. "What you do *to* me?" he rumbles in my ear, then nips at my earlobe. "It's too bad there are other people around."

"Why?" I mutter, feeling lightheaded from his proximity to me, his grip on my waist.

"Because I'd love to kiss you right now."

I've always drawn a line about kissing in front of other people since we aren't technically together. We've kissed in front of our friends a couple of times, but that's it. They were fun, flirty little pecks. When he says he wants to kiss me now, I know what he means. I know what he wants. I want it too.

"What if I want you to kiss me?"

Again, he leans back and looks into my eyes. In this moment, I'm shameless. I'm full to the brim with desire, and I don't care about anything else. My eyes are begging, *kiss me.*

His breath hitches for a second, then that troublemaking smile crosses his lips and he slowly drags his tongue across his bottom lip.

"If you insist."

Then his lips are on mine, claiming me. Demanding more. I slant my mouth against his, opening for him, pleading for more. His tongue possessively sweeps my mouth, showing me I'm what he wants, what he needs, everything.

I wrap my arms around his neck and lean into him, not giving a fuck about who is around us. I've never wanted him more than I do right now.

"Joel," I whisper against his lips.

He pulls his lips from mine and locks eyes with me. For a moment, time stands still. It's just us looking into each other's souls, letting them exchange the words we're too afraid to say. *I'm* too afraid to say.

Joel looks at me tentatively and bites his lip.

I inhale sharply as a brief war occurs between my head and my heart. But my head doesn't stand a chance.

"Joel... take me home."

Joel

"Joel... take me home."

The words reverberate in my brain on the painstaking drive back to my house. Fourteen minutes. Eight hundred and forty seconds. In the overall span of life, it's nothing, right? Except right now, when it feels like a trip to fucking Mars.

My hand is gripping her thigh as she plays with the back of my hair and kisses my neck.

When we hit the stoplight at the end of the bridge leading back into town, I slam the car into park, then pull her to me again. We kiss fervently, the need for each other completely overwhelming us. She shifts in her seat and unbuttons my dress shirt until the car behind us blares their horn.

Fuck.

I rip my mouth from hers, put the car back into drive, then turn right. Onto my street. My gaze shifts sideways to her. I can't think about anything else. It's like I'm drunk on her. On us. I shouldn't be allowed to drive like this. I'm not coherent. All I smell is her perfume. All I feel is her touch. And all I want to look at is her. Fuck the road. I don't care that we're two minutes from my house. I'll pull over and let her have me right here.

She leans over, trailing her lips down my neck as her hand makes its way lower, brushing my bulge.

I'm so turned on I can barely keep my eyes open.

When I finally see my driveway, I flick my blinker on, pull in, park, whip my seatbelt off, and swing my door open. I climb out, slam the door shut again, then run around to open Sarah's. The second she gets out, I have her pressed against the car, grinding against her as I kiss her like the out of control, love-drunk sucker I am.

She hooks her leg around my thigh and moves with me until I can't take it anymore. I pull her from the side of the car and lift her up. She wraps her arms around my neck and her other leg around my waist, refusing to break our sloppy, reckless kiss as I carry her inside.

I nearly stumble walking in the front door, but it doesn't deter her. Her kisses are just as voracious, and it takes everything inside me not to moan into her mouth.

I navigate us up the stairs with one arm wrapped around her back and my fingers twisting in her soft strands.

When we get to my bedroom, I set her down outside the door, my brain overpowering my heart and my hormones for long enough to ask if I should be doing this.

Probably not, but I'm past giving a fuck.

Still, I need to make sure Sarah is okay. Kisses alone are not clear that she truly wants to do this. She's blurred lines in the past, tiptoed across others, but she's never gone barreling across them full force. I need to be sure she's not caught up in the moment. No matter where this ends up, I don't want her to regret it tomorrow.

"Sarah," I murmur, gently separating our lips.

Her big blue eyes focus on mine.

"Hm?"

"Do you want to do this?"

My stomach knots as I wait for her answer. I'm not asking if she's ready to be my girlfriend, to move forward in our relationship. Of course, I want that. I'm not naïve enough to believe it will happen because of this, though. I'm taking a risk and trusting that I'll be able to handle this, whatever the outcome is.

"Yes," she breathes. And my brain's time in charge is officially over.

I slant my mouth over hers again, owning her mouth with my tongue, showing her she's mine whether she's ready to admit it or not. Those blue eyes, that soft blonde hair, those gorgeous curves, her beautiful heart. All. Fucking. Mine.

I walk her backward into my room as she melts into me, pressing her mouth harder against mine and deepening our kiss.

She reaches for the button on my pants, and I groan as her fingers brush my crotch. I fumble with the zipper of her dress as she pulls my dress shirt off, then slides her hands along the edge of my undershirt.

I step back long enough to yank my shirt over my head, toe off my shoes, and drop my pants. When I step out of my pile of clothes on the floor, she's standing in front of me in nothing but pink underwear, pulling the last pin from her hair and letting the waves of blonde cascade around her shoulders.

I take her in for half a second, then wrap my arms around her, lift her up, and set her on the bed, immediately climbing over the top of her and dropping my lips to hers again.

She glides one hand up my back and into my hair, as the other moves down to my waist and tugs my boxer briefs down. I shudder as her hand wraps around my length.

After a deep breath, I pull my lips from hers, then move them lower, kissing across her collarbone as I bring one hand up to her perfectly proportioned breasts. I cup one and roll my thumb over her nipple, while pulling her other nipple between my lips and sucking gently. I swirl my tongue over it as she moans, stroking me hard.

"Joel... oh..."

"Protection," I mutter, in another brief bout of sanity.

"You know I'm on birth control," she musters between gasps. "Are you sure you're okay with that?"

"Yes," she breathes.

I inhale deeply, then run my other hand down her ribs, across her hipbone, and trace the line of her underwear. Then, in one fluid motion, I rip them off and slide my hand between her legs.

"Oh..."

"So wet..." I whisper in her ear.

Her heels dig into my butt as her hips roll forward, begging me to be inside her.

She wraps both arms around my neck and looks deep into my eyes. The vulnerability and desire in them undo me. I bury my face in her neck, then line myself up and slowly push inside her, inch by inch. She gasps when she feels me, and I could live off that noise.

I thread one hand in her hair as I push in farther and farther until I'm buried to the hilt and I can barely see. I don't know how I'm going to last. It's been too fucking long since I've had sex. A one-night stand right after we got to school *last year*. Then Sarah and I started kissing, and I was done for. A year later, and here we are.

I slowly pull back, then thrust in again, and I swear to God, this must be what heaven feels like. I'm not Miles. I haven't had that much sex. But nothing—*nothing*—has ever come close to this. To her.

She whimpers as I go deep again, and I'm lost to her.

We move together, bodies falling into the same rhythm, somehow anticipating the angle of each other's hips, the pace we keep, and the position we're in.

It's not fast and hard or slow and subtle. It's the perfect balance.

"Joel," she moans. "You feel so good."

She grabs my ass as her head drops back.

A chill rolls up my spine as I groan, and I slowly move my hand down between her legs, circling that swollen spot. Some women need that stimulation more than others, but I know Sarah well enough to know she'll never come without it. Not the way I want her to. I want to feel her shaking, trembling around me as she gasps for air.

I move slower as I explore, feeling the exact spot that lights her on fire. She presses into my fingers as I roll over it again and again.

Her walls tighten around me, and I'm hanging on by a thread.

"I'm so close," she whispers.

And I'm right there at the edge with her.

She moans again when I tweak her nipple with my other hand. "Harder, please."

I pull my hand from her nipple, grab her hand and extend it over her head, then intertwine our fingers. I move my other hand in a few more slow circles until she's writhing, and then, looking deep into those soulful blue eyes, I drive into her in hard punishing strokes, never stopping the movement of my fingers.

"Yes... yes." She chokes on a breath, then cries out my name as her walls clench around me. Her body tightens and trembles as she loses herself, and then I'm gone too.

"Fuck, Sarah!" I yell as I empty myself inside her. My body jerks and I'm blinded by ecstasy.

We're both panting, moaning, as we finish. She's still riding the last waves of her high as I collapse on top of her, sweeping her hair to the side and kissing her neck.

"Oh my god," she mumbles breathily.

Then she fists the back of my hair and shoves her lips against mine, pushing her tongue into my mouth—owning it like she's owned me for a long time now.

We roll onto our sides, never breaking our kiss, though it grows softer, gentler, until she pulls away and looks deep into my eyes.

"That was..." She bites her lip. "Thank you for taking care of me."

I run my nose up the side of her neck, then kiss her cheek. "You know I always will." I breathe out and say the words I hold back far too often. Words she knows. Words I can't hold back tonight. "I love you, Sarah."

I close my eyes and rest my head against the pillow, not expecting an answer. Not needing one.

"Joel?" she whispers, head resting on my shoulder.

"Hm?"

"I love you too."

My eyes flash open and I stare at her in disbelief.

"Sarah, you don't—"

"It's not because we had sex—though that sure heightened things. Wow," she says with a tiny smirk. "It's because I feel it every day, and no matter where we're at in our relationship or not-relationship, I feel it. And you deserve to know that. I love you."

I softly kiss her lips and say it again. "I love *you*. No matter what."

She leans into me, kisses my chest, and wraps her body around mine.

I hold her close as she drifts off to sleep, my tired mind wandering. And now wondering what this means for us. I said I wouldn't push her, and I won't. I'm not expecting us to move forward, but I fall asleep hoping we will, anyway.

Chapter Eight

Fallout

Sarah

THE IRRITATING NOISE OF my phone vibrating is the first thing I hear.

Then soft snoring.

I flash my eyes open and a smile immediately crosses my face. He's adorable. My phone vibrates again and my stomach knots up. We crossed a line last night. Scratch that. We blew it up. Bomb dropped.

One more vibration and I grab my phone in frustration.

Five missed texts. One from Rae early this morning saying she was about to board the plane. One from Mom. Two from Dad. One from Grandpa. Then I notice the time. *Crap.*

I flip through the texts.

Mom: Still meeting us for brunch? We're leaving the house in a few minutes.

Dad: I'm assuming you're alive but sleeping, however I'd love confirmation.

Dad: The family is ravenous. Get here soon or they're going to start without you.

Grandpa: Get your tiny butt to brunch, girly. Feel free to bring Joel with you.

Crap. Crap. Crap.

And how does Grandpa always know?

This is *not* how I wanted this morning to go. This is a delicate situation, and I wanted to handle it as such. Talk with him. Figure out what sleeping together meant to him. I know what it meant to me... everything. But that doesn't mean I'm ready to go beyond this.

My phone vibrates again.

Fuck!

I could wake Joel up and bring him with me, but we'd have no time to talk and that would send confusing messages to both him and my family.

Why couldn't my dumb ass have remembered to set an alarm?

Probably because that was the best orgasm of my life and I passed out in the comfort of Joel's arms three minutes later. After I told him I loved him.

My phone vibrates again and I drag my hand over my face.

I take a deep breath and force myself to do the only thing I can—the only thing that makes sense in this corner I've boxed myself into.

Easing out of bed, I sneak over to his closet, grab a pair of his sweats and a T-shirt. That'll get me home at least. Then I walk over to his desk and carefully open the top drawer. Finding paper and a pen, I quickly write out a note.

Joel,
This is not how I wanted to leave this morning, but my family is about to send a search party if I don't show up for brunch. Last night was so special to me. Let's talk either before we go back to the lake house or once we get there. Text me if you want to.
XO
Sarah

There's too much to say in a simple note, but hopefully that'll show I didn't want to leave and I don't regret what happened. Guilt courses through me as I think about the look in his eyes when he told me he loved me last night. He never pushed me to commit to more, but I know he wants that. I wish there were a switch I could flip inside me, but there's nothing. I want him. I love him. But there's a nagging feeling in my gut, still that deep uncertainty, telling me I'm not ready for this yet. Maybe I shouldn't have slept with him knowing that, but I think we were destined for this. It was incredible—the word really doesn't do it justice. And I don't regret it. I just hope he doesn't either.

Grabbing the note off the desk, I quietly walk back to the bed and watch him sleeping for a moment, more guilt and pain hitting me square in the chest. I never want to hurt him. I hope this isn't the thing that pushes him over the edge, makes him walk away from me.

Shaking my head, I try to remind myself of all the times he said he'd never do that—even if it is hard to believe.

I hesitate before slipping the note onto his bedside table, then kiss his head.

I collect my dress and walk toward the door, turning back to look at him one last time.

This is all wrong.

But we dropped the bomb.

Now it's time to deal with the fallout.

Joel

Groan.

First thing I do every morning. I hate waking up. Though I hate it less when Sarah's next to me.

Sarah.

I flash my eyes open and turn over, only to be met with an empty bed.

My heart sinks. I'm used to waking up next to her. That she'd leave after what happened last night... that hurts.

I roll back over, letting out a hefty sigh. Then I see a piece of paper on the bedside table. I grab it and read it. A small amount of relief hits me at knowing she didn't want to leave, but another part of me knows... I'm not getting what I want.

If Sarah had decided she wanted to be with me, she wouldn't have left a note. She would've woken me up and asked me to come with her.

I knew when we crossed the line last night it might end up like this. But then she said she loved me, and I let myself hope. Maybe that was a mistake.

Fuck.

I force myself out of bed, then get dressed and head to the bakery for a cup of coffee. Making my own is effort. On the way, I flip through my texts, seeing a couple from Aaron from early this morning before they got on the plane, and a couple from Jesse. Neither needs a return text, so I stuff my phone back in my pocket.

At the bakery, I grab a breakfast sandwich and a coffee, and am getting ready to leave when I hear Mackie's voice.

"Whoa. What happened to you?"

Shit. Do I look as shitty as I feel?

"I..."

She grabs my arm and drags me through the small corridor to what used to be a yoga studio. Her mom was never very consistent and only taught lessons when she had the time or energy. Once Deanna Barnes opened her studio downtown,

Mackie's mom was happy to let her studio go. This room has since been turned into a small seating area for the bakery. Her mom also rents it out to groups for meetings and things like that.

Mackie leads me to a table and gently pushes me into a chair.

"Talk," she says, grabbing my coffee and taking a swig.

She slides the coffee back to me and waits, but still no words come. I don't know what to say. Unlike Aaron and Rae, and I don't feel the need to let everyone see the complicated parts of my relationship or whatever the hell this is with Sarah.

Then again, I guess Aaron and Rae didn't want that either, but the tough stuff was so explosive it burned us all by proximity.

"I saw you leave with Sarah," Mackie says gently, giving me an opening.

"Yeah," I say, after a long drink of coffee. "We had an incredible night."

"Incredible?"

"If I say it was the best night of my life, will you mock me?"

"Mercilessly. So, what happened *after* the incredible night?"

"I woke up, and she was gone. I mean, she left a note. Had to meet her family for brunch. But I know what it meant."

"What did it mean?"

"That she's still not ready for this."

Mackie runs her hand over mine. "You don't know that. Maybe she wanted to talk to you about it in person."

I choke back a laugh. "Somehow, I doubt that. No, I made a choice to cross a line last night, one I knew would hurt today if she still wasn't ready. That's the nature of doing this with Sarah. She has my heart in a vise, and I just have to hope she doesn't crush it. This is the stupid part of *stupid-in-love*."

She smiles at that. "No. I don't think there's anything stupid about loving someone—and that's coming from someone who has had her heart shattered. Love is complicated. It doesn't always make sense. It fucks you up—that's all part of it. Give her time. Talk to her. See what happens."

"Yeah."

"Joel," she says with a sigh. "Look, I'm not saying you should get your hopes up, but you shouldn't assume the worst, either. Regardless of anything, you had an amazing night with her, right?"

"I did."

"So focus on that. Don't get caught up in any other worries until you have to. Enjoy what last night was and take everything else as it comes. Don't make yourself miserable if you don't need to. Life's too short for that shit."

I smile at that. "Yeah, maybe you're right. Thanks, Macks."

"What can I say? I'm brilliant." She smirks at me.

"Right," I say with a laugh. "So, anything happen with you and Hyla last night?" I ask, ready to think about something else for a little while.

She shakes her head. "No. We danced. Okay, we kissed. But I can't cross that line with her anymore. I love her, but she's still learning a lot about herself. How to be in a relationship. How to deal with the complicated things in her life that she allows to hold her back from that. Right now... I guess we're pulling an Aaron and Rae and being friends who kiss."

I chuckle at that. "There are worse places to be, I guess."

"Yeah. It hurts sometimes, but I can't turn off those feelings. And for the moment, I'm not interested in trying to move on, so I'm just doing the best I can."

"When did you become so wise?" I ask.

"Excuse me? I have *always* been the mature voice of reason. With a hint of snark."

"That is very true," I say with a laugh. "What are you up to this morning?"

"Helping my mom with some cookies, then heading back to the lake house. You?"

"Honestly, I think I'm going to go home and pack. A drive alone with a good podcast will hopefully take my mind off things. Plus, I don't want to risk having a conversation about Sarah and me with my brother."

"Oh yeah. If you tell him it was the best night of your life, he'll definitely mock you forever."

"Yep."

We both stand up, and I pull her into my arms. "Thanks."

"No problem. See you tonight. Pizza for dinner?"

"Sounds perfect. Later."

"Bye, buddy."

As she goes upstairs, I make my way outside, munching on my breakfast sandwich as I walk back to my house.

Once I get there, I pack up quickly, then wonder if I should wait for Sarah. If she wants me to wait for her.

Me: Hey, thanks for the note. Did you want me to wait for you to go back up?

I'm surprised when I get an immediate text back.

Sarah: As much as I'd like to see you beforehand, this has become the brunch that never ends, so you might as well go.

Sarah: We'll talk at the lake house?

Me: Of course.

Sarah: Okay... see you later.

Me: Please drive safe.

Sarah: I will. You too. [smiley face emoji]

I send the same emoji back, turn my phone screen off, grab my bags, and head out to my Tahoe.

I put on one of my favorite history podcasts—I'm a bit of a history nerd—and settle in for the two-hour drive back to the lake house.

Sarah

"Stupid son of a—you asshole!" I grunt as my bag falls out of my trunk, barely missing crushing my toes.

Is this karma?

"You okay?" Miles asks, looking both ways before jogging across the road to where I'm fighting with my bag.

I blow some hair off my face in frustration. Okay isn't the word I'd use to describe myself at this moment. I feel guilty. And like a jerk.

"I'm fine," I huff out.

I reach for the bag again, but Miles stops me, thoughtfully lifting it and maneuvering it into my trunk.

"How did you do that?"

He shrugs and grins at me. "I have skills."

I roll my eyes hard. "I miss my Durango," I mutter, sitting down on the curb. My first car baby bit the dust last year. It needed so many things fixed, it was cheaper to get a new car—well, new to me—so I did. And even though I like my Volkswagen Jetta just fine, I'm not used to driving a little sedan. I miss my big, boaty SUV.

Miles sits down next to me. "Somehow I doubt this is about you missing your Durango."

I side-eye him, then shake my head. "I thought you wanted to stay out of everyone's drama."

He chuckles. "No, I just grew tired of Aaron and Rae talking to everyone but each other. Maybe *I* was a little dramatic about that. But I'm still here for you, no matter what it's about."

"I slept with Joel."

He laughs again. "About time that happened. So why are you a big ball of chaos now?"

"Because I'm still not ready for... more. Not yet. And I feel like I owe him that. I feel selfish. I got what I wanted. He didn't."

"He got *something* he wanted."

I elbow him. "Yes. Of course, he wanted that. If it hadn't been a mutual feeling, we wouldn't have done it. But I know he wants the full relationship. And I... don't feel like I can give him that." I squirm a little. Miles is right. I am a ball of chaos right now. I feel it coursing through my veins. I'm mad at myself. But I also loved what we did last night. I wish I could've talked to him this morning. My brain flits from one emotion to the next, and I'm starting to feel a little crazy.

"You two haven't talked yet?"

"No. I had to leave early to meet my family for brunch. I left a note. I don't regret it. Not what we shared. If I hurt him... I regret that. You probably think I'm ridiculous and should just be in a relationship with him."

He drapes an arm over my shoulders. "Actually, I don't. Well... I think you should do what feels right, what you feel ready for. As long as you aren't leading him on."

"I'm not," I say quickly. "I'm just not ready for that yet." I look down and he presses his fingers into my arms.

"Hey, no judgment here. You know what I was doing after the wedding last night?"

"Hm?"

"Sleeping with some girl I met on Tinder. One who I knew nothing would ever happen with. Sex. Nothing more. And it fulfilled the physical needs, but there's another need I have that has never been filled. Not romantically. It's the emotional need. And the reason for that is love is complicated. It's confusing. It changes everything. You have to learn how to continue being yourself while building a relationship with someone else. I don't want to half-ass that. One day, I'll meet the right girl and it'll probably be some star-crossed, can't take our eyes off each other, everything changes with a touch, Aaron and Rae shit. But until then, I'm not interested in dating. I don't want to do it unless I'm going to do it right. That's what you want too, right?"

I nod slowly. "Totally different reasons," I laugh, "but yes. I want to get it right. And I still don't feel like I'm in a place to take care of myself, do what I need to do for school, and give him enough, too. I want him. But—"

"You don't want to half-ass it."

"Exactly."

"Then tell him that. I know you've had people leave you, but I want you to remember everyone who stayed. All of our names are on that list, but Joel is right at the top. You've screamed at him and told him you hated him while you were drunk. He's seen you in most of your worst moments and they didn't faze him. He's taken care of you while giving you the space to figure out what you need to do for yourself and to be ready to be with him. He's not just going to stop. Trust him. And at some point, try to trust yourself, too."

I chuckle at that. "Trev gave me similar advice."

He bumps his leg against mine. "It's almost like we know you or something. Joel does too."

He leans over and kisses the side of my head before standing up. Offering me his hands, he pulls me up, too.

"I've gotta finish packing, but I'll see you back at the lake house, okay?" he says.

"Yeah. Thanks, Miles."

He winks at me. "Always, Sarbear. Drive safe. Love ya."

"Love you too."

I wave as he turns and walks back across the street. I glare at my bag sitting perfectly in the trunk, then close the trunk. After brunch, my parents went up to my grandparents' house for more family time. I said goodbye to everyone as we left brunch.

Guess there's nothing to it but to do it. I climb into the front seat of my car and put on one of my favorite podcasts, trying to take my mind off everything and focus on the drive back to the lake house and *not* on hyperanalyzing everything related to Joel and me. Easier said than done.

When I get back to the lake house, Mackie, Joel, and Amanda are already there. Trev is probably at Chelsea's apartment.

I make my way inside and find the living room and kitchen empty. Glancing at the stairs, the rush of terrible emotions comes back. But Miles was right. All I can do now is talk to him. *And trust him.* Easier than trusting myself. And that's really where the problem comes in. I don't trust this will be okay. I don't trust that I've handled it right. I don't trust that I haven't hurt him.

At the top of the stairs, my steps slow. The master is the first bedroom.

I glance through the doorway before entering and see Joel unpacking.

"Hi," I say softly, walking into the master and setting my bag down.

Joel stops halfway between the bed and the dresser and looks at me. "Hi. Sorry I left before you got back."

"It's fine. I'm sorry I had to leave before you woke up this morning. I... wanted to lay in bed with you. Talk." That word is choked coming out. *I shouldn't have done this. Maybe Trevor was right. Maybe it's a self-fulfilling prophecy. Or maybe I'm*

*just selfish. I wanted to have us, feel us, when I knew I wasn't
ready for it.*

"I do wish I could've woken up with you in my arms."

"Joel," I whisper, closing the door behind me. "I..."

Hurt fills his eyes, though he quickly pushes it away.

I'm the worst.

"Sarah, you don't—"

"I do," I say, tears clogging my throat. I walk over to him and
take his hands. "There's a lot I need to say. First, I'm sorry—I
shouldn't have—"

"Do you regret it?" he asks, looking more vulnerable than
he's ever been before.

"No," I breathe. If he takes only one thing away from this,
I want him to know I don't regret it. "I loved every second of
last night. It meant so much to me. I only regret it if I hurt
you by doing it. Hurting you is the last thing I want to do. It's
why..." Tears roll down my cheeks, but I quickly wipe them
away.

He steps to the bed and pulls me down onto the edge with
him, squeezing my hands tightly as he looks into my eyes.
"Tell me. Whatever it is."

I nod, sniffing more tears away. "Last night was beautiful.
No one in the world has ever made me feel as special and
cherished as you. I don't know if I'm any good at showing
you that in return. That's a part of all this. I want to fall into
your arms, let you kiss me and give in to all of this. But I'm
not ready yet. I wish I could explain it more than that. I wish
there were words that would make this feeling deep in my
soul make sense, but I'm not sure there are. Just know it's
not about you. You're amazing. Too good for me—"

"Stop. Don't talk about yourself like that. You are incredible.
Strong. Loving." He lets out a shaky breath, sliding a hand into
my hair. "I knew what I was getting into last night. You didn't

make any promises. I knew you might not be ready. And I made the choice to keep going, anyway."

"Do *you* regret it?" I ask.

"Never," he answers, before I've gotten the full sentence out.

"I want to be sure I'm ready. I want to get this right."

He drops his forehead against mine, his eyes drifting closed. "I can wait, Sarah, as long as you keep being honest with me. Do you still see us in your future?"

"Yes," I exhale, my lips just centimeters from his. He's always my future. No matter what other variables change, he's my future. But in that future, I feel comfortable, confident, no uncertainty about my emotional and mental health, no concern about how busy or stressed I am. And maybe that's a fantasy, but it's what I'm aiming for. Being the best, most balanced version of myself before I do this with him.

"Then we're fine."

"Promise?" I ask, sniffling.

He slowly pulls back, then kisses my forehead. "Promise."

He squeezes my hands, then lets them go and stands up. I stand as well and watch as he grabs a couple of things from his duffel bag.

"I was about to go for a run. I wanted to get one in before dinner."

"Okay," I say, wondering if it's me he wants to run away from.

"Hey," he says, looking at me and somehow reading my mind. He steps over to me and pulls me into his arms. "I promise, we're okay. I'm going to go for a run, then we're all going to have pizza. Maybe after that we can watch the next *James Bond* in bed?"

I nod as I step away, trying to push away my tears. "Yeah. Sounds good."

He kisses my cheek, then goes into the bathroom to change. I wipe my eyes, then start unpacking.

Joel

One foot in front of the other. It's colder than I remember it being when we got back to the lake house. Of course, the sun is slowly dropping in the sky. I should've worn my thicker leggings. They might not look particularly cool, but athletic leggings with exercise shorts over them is the proper gear for running. Wearing sweatpants is a great way to overheat yourself, then soak yourself with sweat that hangs in the sweatpants. It'll make you colder eventually and create a stink that's next to impossible to get out.

My face heats more with each step I take, and the warmer my muscles feel, the harder I push myself. Outrunning my emotions isn't an option, but I have to get them out before I get back to the lake house.

I don't blame Sarah. I knew what I was getting into, but that doesn't mean it doesn't hurt.

Of course I wanted her to tell me she was ready. I wanted her to fall into my arms and let me love her as fully as she deserves to be loved.

Tears crest in my eyes, and I run faster through the blur before bringing one arm up and wiping them away, though they're quickly replaced by more.

By the time I get to a bench overlooking the lake, tears are steadily streaming down my cheeks and my heart is pounding.

I drop onto the bench, forcing a few big breaths of air into my lungs.

As I stare out at the lake, emotion hits full force.

I just want her to let me in. To stop being afraid. Why won't she let herself love me? What if she never does?

My head drops into my hands as I sob, the kind of sobs that make my body shake.

Leaves crunch behind me, then the bench shifts slightly, and an arm wraps around my back.

"Come here," Mackie whispers.

She pulls me toward her and I rest my head against her shoulder. She wraps her other arm around me and hugs me tightly as I cry.

"She'll get there," Mackie says softly. "You mean everything to her."

"It's hard some days, Macks. I've been doing this with her for a year now. Being committed to a *someday* future with her. We sleep in the same bed. Sometimes we do sexual stuff. Or we launch over that line like we did last night. In some ways, we make progress, but in other ways, it feels like we've barely progressed at all, and that hurts. I promised her I wouldn't push as long as she was honest with me about wanting to be with me and working toward that. Sometimes I get scared she's using it as an excuse. I'm scared one day she'll wake up and change her mind."

Mackie squeezes me tighter. "If there's one thing I know about Sarah, it's that she doesn't want to mess up what she has with you. Even if she is using it as an excuse to hold back, I doubt it's because she's going to change her mind. It's because she's still working through her own stuff. She's still figuring out how to love you. And maybe how to love herself."

Those words hit right at my gut. *How to love herself.* There's a part of me that knows she's critical of herself, but I never considered that she's still learning to truly love herself as she is, but it makes a lot of sense. People say you won't find love until you love yourself. Personally, I think that's bullshit. Love doesn't work that way. You fall for someone, messes and all, and you love each other through it. That's how it works. But if Sarah doesn't feel she deserves my love, or hasn't earned it... it makes more sense. It makes sense she can tell me she loves me, but be afraid to be with me. I just wish she understood that her love is all I need. I wish she'd let me love her so fully that she feels safe to process her own feelings and learn to love herself.

Waiting for her to be ready is gut-wrenching some days, but I'll keep doing it. If there's one thing I'm sure of, it's that she's my future. I hope she's being honest with me when she says she wants the same.

My tears subside and the storm in my stomach calms.

"Come on," Mackie says. "We've got pizza to pick up. I left a little early since I saw you go out for a run. Thought you might need to talk."

I let out a wry laugh as we walk to her car. There's never been much hidden between the six of us.

Mackie and I pick up the pizza and head back to the lake house. By the time we get there, I'm feeling better. I'm still going to feel rough for a couple of days, but I can handle it. And when Sarah smiles brightly as I walk in, I remember exactly *why* I can handle it. She's worth it. Even if nothing worth it ever comes easily.

Chapter Nine

Spiral Up

Sarah

"PUPPY CHOW!" AMANDA EXCLAIMS as I set the bowl of peanut butter and chocolate Chex Mix in front of her on Rae's bed.

"You're like a little kid," Mackie laughs.

"Sorry, not sorry. This stuff is delicious."

"I wanted something fun for girls' night. Take out sushi is the meal. We need snacky dessert stuff," I say.

"Speaking of sushi," Mackie says, "where is Rae?"

"Right here," she says, stepping into her and Aaron's room and smiling brightly.

We all squeal and run over to her. She and Aaron got back from their honeymoon a couple of days ago, but extended it by staying at their apartment in Ida until this morning when they drove back up just in time for their classes. It may have been a little crazy for them to get married and take a honeymoon mid-semester, but they planned ahead and worked with their professors so it wasn't a problem.

Rae only had a half day of classes, then was at Promise for the afternoon, so none of us have seen her since the wedding.

As Mackie and Amanda pull the bags of food from her hands, I wrap my arms around her. Even with her living in a different apartment back home, it's rare we go a day without seeing each other, let alone talking.

"God, you look beautiful!" Mackie says as I step away from Rae. She does. She's tan and absolutely beaming with happiness.

"Thank you." She does a little shimmy and laughs. "I feel good too."

"A week of vacation and good sex will do that," Amanda teases.

"Mm, yes it will," Rae says as we all get comfy on her bed.

Once we've filled our plates with sushi, Amanda looks at Rae. "Details."

Rae laughs. "Oh my gosh. It was—seriously, Mands, you did amazing setting that up for us. It was the *perfect* honeymoon. Equal parts having fun exploring and having phenomenal sex."

"I'm surprised you had time for exploring outside the bedroom," Mackie says.

Rae elbows her and she laughs.

"It was Spain! We had to go sightseeing and enjoy some beaches. And the food! We had a pretty consistent schedule, though. The morning was spent sleeping in and *relaxing* in bed. Then we'd have breakfast, go explore, come back to the hotel for a siesta—which usually involved very little actual sleep—then go explore some more, have dinner, then the rest of the night was ours. We even laid out and watched the stars on the beach one night. Of course, a couple of days we were traveling by train, so we might've had to fulfill a few needs in the bathroom."

We all screech with laughter.

"Anyway, we'll show you guys pictures during dinner tomorrow. Now, I want to hear what happened here!"

Mackie and Amanda's eyes land on me. *Of course.*

"Oh boy. What did I miss?" Rae asks.

"Just know it's not some big dramatic thing, but... I might've... slept with Joel. The night of your wedding."

Rae's mouth falls open, her eyes huge.

"You... and Joel... oh my god! Details!" she screams. "You know, except the ones I don't want to hear."

"Finally! She refused to tell us anything until you got back," Amanda says.

"Well... I know some of it," Mackie says quietly.

"Joel told you?" I ask.

She nods. No wonder she didn't have a big reaction when I mentioned it.

"He was..." she pauses, choosing her words carefully. "He was worried about how you were feeling."

I look down, feeling guilty all over again.

"Are you guys okay? I'm assuming you aren't together, or you'd have led with that," Rae says.

"We're good, but no, we're not together."

"Okay, start from the beginning. How did this happen?" my sister asks.

After a week of keeping it to myself, I finally tell them everything, skirting around any descriptive dirty details for Rae's sake.

"Wow," she says when I'm finished.

"Are you mad at me?" I ask.

"What? Why would I ever be mad at you for that?"

I shrug one shoulder. "I don't know. If you thought I hurt him."

"Do you feel like you hurt him?"

I nod quickly and look down. "He'd never say it, but I think I probably did."

Rae grabs my hand. "I love Joel and I'll always be here to support him, but you're my sister. You know I'm always on your side. Even when there are no sides. Sister privilege."

"Love you, Rae baby."

"Love you too. For the record, I think I speak for everyone in here when I say that even if you two were fighting, there still would only be one team. Team Sarah and Joel. Just like you guys were always Team Aaron and Rae."

Amanda laughs. "I think I might've been Team Rae when I first met you."

"You didn't know the whole story then."

"True. And clearly Team Aaron and Rae was the place to be."

Rae smiles and looks down at her rings. "Absolutely."

We take a break from heavy conversation and devour most of our sushi.

After we've finished, Amanda looks at me, surprisingly serious. "Can I ask you a question?"

"Of course."

"Why do you think you're not ready to be with Joel? I'm not doubting you, but I don't really understand what's holding you back. Sometimes you two seem like a couple, and I know he makes you happy. I guess I'm wondering what more you're waiting for."

I nod slowly, then glance at Rae, who gives me a reassuring smile. She doesn't have to ask. She knows it all.

"On the surface, it looks simple. Be with someone you care about, who cares about you. But it's more complicated than that. Especially for me. Despite what it feels like most of the time, you haven't known me that long. You've known a more put-together, healthy version of me. But I've been known to be messy. Drinking to deal with my problems, testing the people I love to see if they'll stick around, and dealing with some pretty rough mental health stuff. Because of that, I try to be acutely aware of where my mental health is and what I need—what I can give someone else. It's not that I'm in a bad place right now—I'm not. But I don't feel like I have enough to give him right now. So, I'm trying to balance waiting until I'm ready with not waiting so long that I let it become an excuse. If I'm honest, I feel like I'm teetering on the edge of that now."

"Wow. That's way more mature than me," Amanda says with a laugh.

"No way. You've been supporting Jamie through starting a career in professional baseball, all while having a long-distance relationship. We're all mature and strong and we've grown a hell of a lot. Which is pretty cool to watch."

"Agreed," Rae says. "The last couple of years have seen so much growth. It's a strange feeling to see how far I've come, but it feels good."

"That's so true," Mackie agrees. "Despite what I may have projected, I had pretty poor self-worth, especially when I was dating Hyla. I was insecure all the time. Not that my concerns were unfounded, but the way I handled them was. I could be clingy and dismissive of red flags. I'm calmer now, more confident, and I know my worth and what I'm willing to compromise on."

I laugh as I think back to the beginning of senior year. "A few years ago, I was still battling cutting my biological mother out of my life. I got drunk at a party, told Joel I hated him several times when he saved me from a guy with bad intentions. But I talked to my parents, went back to therapy, and it helped me. I'm far from perfect, but each time I hit the bottom, I spiraled up."

"Oh! I love that," Amanda says. "I suppose I've been through my own growth. I was also very insecure, especially when I met you guys. You all helped me be more comfortable with who I am and embracing every side of myself. I always used to feel like I needed to apologize for being the boss bitch I am."

"Never," I tell her. "You should never apologize for being your amazing self."

Mackie and Rae nod in agreement.

"Here's to always spiraling up and having each other's backs whenever we do," Amanda says.

"Hell yes!" Mackie agrees.

We all grab our water bottles and tap them together, laughing as we take a drink.

"Here's to that," Rae says.

"Now, how about we dig into the puppy chow and watch a movie?" I say.

"Sounds perfect," Amanda says.

We all crawl under the covers, then grab the puppy chow and munch while watching the newest Netflix romcom.

Joel

"So the honeymoon was good then?" Miles says with a grin as Aaron finishes telling us some general details about their trip. The amount of times he alluded to having sex says that he *definitely* had a good trip. Not that I was expecting less. He and Rae can barely keep their hands off each other on an average day, let alone when they're alone for a week on their honeymoon.

"It was," he says with a coy smile. "But we had a lot of fun too. We figured we'd show you all the pictures tomorrow during dinner. Don't worry, we didn't take any dirty ones. How were things here?" He glances at me. Though he hadn't seen Miles or Trev until he got back tonight, the two of us grabbed coffee today, and I told him *my* dirty details. "Besides the Joel and Sarah fun."

Trev chuckles at that. "Well, I had fun spending the weekend with my girl."

Trevor and Chelsea started dating two months ago, about three days after they met. He's obsessed with her. It's sweet and incredibly nauseating.

"A hotel room alone with your girl is *always* fun," Miles says with a laugh.

Trev clears his throat. "Not that it's any of your business, but... we haven't done that yet."

My eyebrows shoot up. Trev isn't the kind of guy who thinks with his dick—most of the time—but he's never been shy about his enjoyment of sex and female bodies.

"She waiting for marriage or something?" Miles asks, half serious.

"Fuck off. It's none of your business why she wants to wait, but she does, and I respect her. If she doesn't want to cross that line, we won't. We do some things. I mean, it's not always easy. In fact, sometimes, it's very *hard* because she is legitimately my dream girl—and not just physically."

I laugh at that. "Sarah told me you thanked her for dumping you after your first date with Chelsea."

Trev shrugs. "I'm fucking glad now. I loved Sarah, but this shit is different."

"You're in love with her?"

"Definitely. She's sweet, kind, but she has this funny, raunchy side. She loves my dumbass dirty jokes. We want the same things out of life. And yes, she is ten out of ten what I imagined my dream girl would look like. Plus, she respects the fact that I'm waiting for her to be ready for sex, and she hates thinking she's giving me blue balls, so she bought me one of those sex toys for guys."

"Which one?" Aaron asks like we're all idiots. Maybe fair, because I've never used a sex toy for a guy. I used a vibrator on a girl once. That's it. And now I want to gag because I do not want to think of my best friends using sex toys.

Trev cocks an eyebrow and smirks, clearly amused by this admission about Aaron's sex life.

"You can't possibly be surprised that Rae and I would use stuff."

"Guess we shouldn't be," Trev says. "Anyway, it's one of those that you slide over your dick and... holy fuck."

"Yeah, they make you," Aaron coughs, "super fast."

I feel like an inexperienced idiot now.

Then I look over at Miles, who is tapping away at his phone.

"What are you doing?" I ask.

He looks up from his phone and grins. "Ordering some things."

I shake my head. "I need to order some noise canceling headphones." *And maybe some other things. Sarah would probably love using toys together. Shit. Don't think about that.*

"Nice," Trev says, fist bumping Miles. Then he gets serious and looks at Aaron. "How are you feeling about this week?"

Aaron blows out a breath. "Nervous. The wedding and honeymoon were excellent distractions. Now? I'm so fucking nervous. I've never even had surgery before. This is surgery that can affect not only my ability to play baseball, but also my quality of life. So, any distraction you guys would like to give me would be welcome at this point."

"How about we start with wings and a shitty action comedy movie?" Miles says.

"Only if we can openly mock it," Aaron says.

"That's a requirement," I say, flipping open the boxes of wings so we can all dig in.

I come back downstairs from using the bathroom—I always use the master bath if I can. I'm over communal toilets at this point—and see Miles and Trevor hyper focused on some video game. Looking around, I spot Aaron on the back deck and head outside.

"Hey, you hiding out here?"

He chuckles. "No. Just thinking."

I walk over and stand next to him, leaning against the railing on my elbows.

"Thinking about surgery?"

He nods. "I'm scared. Scared to want to be able to pitch. Scared to lose it all over again."

I hear what he doesn't say.

I bump my arm against his. "No matter what happens, you're never going to be that guy again. You know that, right?"

He sighs and shoves a hand through his hair. "Honestly? I keep trying to tell myself that, but it worries me."

"You are so much stronger than you were back then. Plus, you've learned how to open up, especially to Rae. And we all know how to handle it better than we did back then. Most importantly, Rae knows. So do I," I say quietly.

He turns to me and takes me in, then stands up straight and folds his arms over his chest.

"Tell me you're not still beating yourself up. We talked about this. We're good."

I huff out a sigh and spin around, leaning against the railing as I look at him.

"You forgave me. Which I appreciate. But it doesn't mean I let it go. I know we all say we're best friends. Rae is like my sister. But you're my *best* friend—like best man at my wedding kind of thing—and I was a shitty friend to you, which is the last thing I ever want to be."

He laughs at that. "Do you really think you're a shitty friend? Because that's the last thing any of us would ever describe you as. Yes, you're a pain in the ass sometimes..." He smirks. "But you're always here for all of us. You know, you guys tease me that I take the blame for stuff I shouldn't, but you have a hard time letting go of things." He frowns and furrows his brow, taking me in. "But you're right, we *are* best friends. There's a reason why you were the best man at *my* wedding. If this is something that's staying with you, that worries me. And if you're constantly feeling guilty about more than this, we should be talking about that."

God damn him. Now I want to cry.

I gesture to the nearby bench and sit down. He sits down next to me and looks at me with concern.

"You know Sarah hates being alone. I'm the same way, I just show it differently. Feeling alone or isolated sucks. It hurts. I never want the people I love to feel that way. That's why I feel so terrible about how I handled things with you. I put you in a position that would've emotionally destroyed me. It's impossible for me not to feel bad about that. But there's another selfish piece to all of this... I want to be the most likable one in the room. I want to be the upbeat person that everyone wants to be around. Because I'm scared of being alone, and if I'm not the best version of myself or I let you down, I get scared people won't want to be around me as much. It's part of why doing what I've been doing with Sarah is so fucking terrifying. I'm afraid one day she'll leave me. Decide I'm not actually what she wants or needs. I won't be enough to keep her."

Aaron blinks a few times, taking it all in, then he leans back against the bench.

"First of all, I'm calling bullshit on the idea that we would ever care less or want to be around you less. You need to hear me when I say this. We love you. We love you on your shittiest days and your best ones. You're more than the life of the party. You're kind and thoughtful and honest. You're also imperfect, just like the rest of us, and you know what? You're not supposed to be perfect. We know you're here for us and we're always here for you. *I* am always here for you. And I know you've got my back, too. I know I teased you about it initially, but I'm glad you're going to be there when I have surgery. Not only for Rae's sake, but mine too. You always know how to cheer me up and take my mind off the hard stuff." He pauses, then says, "I'm sorry if your parents ever made you feel like you're not enough or not worth it. I know your relationship with them is tricky, but know that's a reflection of them, not you. As for Sarah... I understand your fears. Believe me, I get it. But Sarah loves the same way you do, and I don't believe there's anyone she loves more than you. You don't give up on her, she's never giving up on you either. Do your best to trust in that."

His large hand clamps on my shoulder and gives it a firm squeeze as I wipe my eyes, emotions pouring out of me.

"Let the guilt go," he says, pulling me into a hug.

"Thanks, A," I say quietly as I pull away.

"Always. *This* is what we do for each other, got it?"

"Got it."

"Good." He smacks my back and stands up. "Now, let's go kick Miles's and Trev's asses at video games."

He extends his fist and I bump it.

"Hell yes. Let's go."

We walk back inside, and some of the weight on my shoulders washes away. I like to pretend I have it all perfectly together. It's the face I put on most of the time. But Aaron is right. We're all messy in our own ways, and maybe it's time for me to be a little more open about that instead of trying to deal with it by myself.

I choke back a laugh as I think that.

Jesus Christ. I'm more like Rae than even I realized.

Learn something new every day.

Chapter Ten

The Buildup

Joel

"YEAH, THEN YOU SHOWED up at my house all terrified, looking like you got hit by a bus."

Rae and I are laughing as Aaron smacks my arm. He's wearing a hospital gown and covered in about six blankets because it's freezing here in the pre-op area.

"Shut up. Aren't you supposed to be putting me in a good mood, not giving me shit?"

Rae runs her fingers through his hair. "What? You don't think how unbelievably dumb we were was funny? We should've made out that night and asked questions later. I sat on the edge of my bed like an idiot, touching my lips and squealing to Sarah, who was so frustrated because I couldn't make any words to tell her what happened."

"I'm just happy I was right all along," I say.

"Everyone could see it," Aaron says. "Except us." He runs his thumb over Rae's hand and laughs.

"Well, it's hard to see things when you've got blinders on. But in fairness, Joel was the very first person to actually help me see what we were doing. The girls would give me shit. The boys would give you shit. But we had some real talk. Do you remember what you said to me?" she asks.

My mind drifts back, and then I smile.

"Something along the lines of you two not being a couple but also being more than friends."

She smirks and puts on a voice like mine. *"At some point, you have to figure out what you want. Because you two have never been just friends, but you've never been a couple, either. And that makes things complicated.'* Or something like that." She winks at me, then looks at Aaron. "Then you picked on me when I said we needed to be careful with our friendship."

He leans forward in the bed and kisses her.

"Being *just friends* with you would've been no fun at all."

Rae is swooning over him now, and I can't help but roll my eyes.

"You guys go from fun to nauseating way too fast."

"Knock, knock," a voice says from behind the curtain that's blocking us from the hallway.

It slides open and we see two nurses and the anesthesiologist who came in earlier. Aaron's parents are out in the waiting room. His mom thought I'd be able to keep his mind off things better than she would, and of course Rae would be back here. She's his wife—and he's happily told that to everyone he possibly could today.

"It's time to get this show on the road," one nurse says with a smile.

Rae and Aaron exchange a quick glance and the second nurse says, "I know Doctor McCarthy spoke with you already, and he thinks it'll take between forty-five minutes and an hour and a half. He'll be out to speak with you as soon as he's done, and once your husband is moved to recovery, they'll call you back."

Rae nods, projecting strength even though I know she feels anything but strong right now.

"And you have the easy job," the anesthesiologist says to Aaron. "You get to take a nap."

Everyone chuckles, then I turn to Aaron and hold out my fist. "You've got this, A." He bumps my fist, then I lean down and whisper, "And I've got her. No worries."

"Thanks, man."

I step out of the way, then watch as Rae leans over, wraps her arms around him, and gives him a kiss.

"Love you, Ace," she whispers. Then she takes his hand and slides his wedding band off—you're not allowed to wear them during surgery, but he wanted to keep it until he went back—and says, "I'm gonna borrow this."

Aaron kisses her one last time and says, "Love you, Beautiful. See you soon."

He's putting on a calm face, but I can see the worry in his eyes. I know Rae can too.

Rae moves out of the way, and we both wave as they push him down the hall.

Once they're gone, I drape my arm over Rae's shoulders and guide her out of the pre-op area and down the long hallway toward the waiting room. Halfway there, she sniffles.

I stop and pull her into a hug, letting her cry on my shoulder.

"This is so dumb. I know it's just a short procedure, but I can't help it. I hate seeing him like that. I hate seeing the fear in his eyes. Then I start blaming myself..."

I step back and look at her.

"What?"

"It all goes back to one night, Joel. And logically, I know it isn't my fault. But the fact is, I could've walked off that dance floor with him, but I was stubborn and sassy and I didn't do it. That choice has affected us individually and our relationship ever since. Most of the time, it doesn't get to me, but every so often, especially when this stuff comes up, those feelings of guilt—whether it's right to have them or not—trickle in."

I hug her tightly again.

"It's not your fault. You both could have done things differently or handled things better. At the end of the day, you made your way through it all. You figured it out. And you're stronger because of the struggles you had. I hold on to the guilt, too. Big shock that we're similar..." She laughs at that. "But you've gotta let it go. Focus on where you are right now and how you can support him when the procedure is done. That's what matters. We don't get to change the past, but we get to change and grow and become the best versions of ourselves. You've done that and so has he. Now you have the chance to make your future even more beautiful. Take a breath, let the bad stuff go."

"Thanks, Joelskies," she says, stepping back and wiping her eyes. "Okay, I don't want Aaron's parents to see me cry. Can we go grab some coffee?"

"Absolutely. I already looked up where the best place in the hospital for coffee is. I'll text his mom and see if they want anything."

She loops her elbow through mine and rests her head on my shoulder. "You're the best. I'm glad you're here."

"I'm glad I am, too. Love ya, Rae Rae." I pop a kiss on her head.

"Love you too, Joelskies. Let's get some caffeine."

It's been just under an hour since Aaron went back. With some coffee and one of her favorite books, Rae is calmer now, though I notice her eyes frequently flit up to the clock. I've been keeping everyone updated via group chat, but there's nothing new to report. Rather than scrolling Instagram for the hundredth time today, I open my texts with Sarah and type the words that have been running through my brain for days.

Me: I miss you.

Little dots appear immediately, quickly followed by a text.

Sarah: I miss you too.

Me: Whoa. Wasn't expecting a response that fast. Figured you'd be too busy.

Sarah: Lol. Usually. My clinicals are at a state facility today, and because of that, we get government sanctioned fifteen-minute breaks.

Me: Nice. So, how far into your break are you?

Sarah: I have eleven-and-a-half minutes left.

Me: Up for a phone call?

Rather than a text back, my phone rings a few seconds later. I motion to Rae that I'm going to step into the hall to take it.

"Hey," I say as I walk down the hall. Finding a secluded spot, I lean against the wall.

"Hi. So, you miss me, huh?"

"Yeah. I feel like I've barely seen you lately. We sleep in the same bed, but you're gone before I get up most days and half the time you come in after I go to bed or are so exhausted you fall asleep in minutes." I clear my throat. "I'm not gonna lie. I've been a little worried you were avoiding me after... everything."

"Oh my gosh. No. I would never. I... that night was amazing, Joel. Just because I'm not ready to be in a relationship yet doesn't mean I don't want to be around you. I've just been crazy busy with studying and preparing for midterms. I've missed you too. I miss spending time with you. I miss us."

"Me too. Any chance you have a free night so we could spend some time together? Maybe go on a date?" *Shit. Is that too much of a relationship thing?* "We don't have to call it that."

She laughs a little and I can feel her smile through the phone. "How about tomorrow night? I have a test in the morning, then clinicals in the afternoon. After that, I'll be more than ready to unwind. With you."

"Sounds perfect. I'll start planning."

"Can't wait."

It's quiet for a moment, but not in an awkward way. It's comfortable, easy.

"I should get back. Hopefully, the surgeon will be out soon."

"Definitely. Go. Give my sister a hug for me, okay?"

"Will do. See you tonight."

"Tonight. Bye, Joel."

"Bye, Sarah."

I hang up and rest my head against the wall for a moment. My heart is pounding and my body temperature feels several degrees higher than it was before I answered my phone. How does a simple phone call with her have that power over me?

Or maybe it's that she agreed to let me take her on a date.

Sometimes it feels like we're stuck in place, but when I look closely, I see the tiny shifts and forward motion, like she's inching closer to being ready. She just needs to convince herself.

Heading back into the waiting room, I drop down into my seat between Rae and Aaron's mom, who has been focused on a crossword puzzle book. Rae is fidgeting while staring at her Kindle, but not reading anything off the page it's open to.

"Hey. Sarah says hi. And to give you a hug. But you're kind of spazzing right now."

She smiles and elbows me. "Have I ever been a patient person?"

"Not usually," I say with a laugh. "In fact, I have a strong memory of you yelling at me to hurry up whenever I wasn't going fast enough in the bathroom when we were in kindergarten."

"Oh my gosh. You used to take forever."

"I liked the hand dryer."

We both laugh at that.

"In fairness, I used to wait until the last possible second to go to the bathroom. It's a miracle I didn't pee my pants."

I laugh hysterically. "You mean it's a miracle you didn't pee them more often."

Her eyes flare. "What?"

"Do you not remember you used to pee your pants all the time in pre-K and kindergarten?"

"No, I didn't—oh my gosh!" She covers her mouth, then drops her head against my shoulder as she laughs. "I completely blocked that out. Oh! Aaron used to cover for me and say he accidentally spilled water or juice on me. Oh my gosh..."

When she lifts her head, she's laughing so hard tears are coming down her cheeks.

"I know he used to cover for you. But Mackie and I always knew."

She wipes her eyes and takes a deep breath. "Thank you for not holding that over my head and using it against me more."

"Missed opportunity. Clearly."

She shoves my arm, and we both laugh again.

"Thanks for that," she says quietly after a few deep breaths.

I shoot her a wink and she goes back to her Kindle, actually reading the words this time.

She's settled in well when we hear, "Mrs. Cooper?"

Rae shoots out of her chair, and Aaron's mom stands up too, while his dad and I both listen as Doctor McCarthy—or Doctor Max as Rae and Aaron have been calling him—gives an update.

"We're all finished. Everything went really well. Thankfully, we didn't need to cut away any bone. As anticipated, we broke and realigned a few areas in his fingers and hand, but they came back together very smoothly, and I really think Aaron will see great improvement from this."

"Thank you so much," Rae says.

"Of course. Once he's awake, I'll be in to speak with him as well and answer any questions. Usually we have a nurse come out and let you know when he's in recovery, but he's settled in back there already, so I can lead you back."

"Perfect," Rae says. I quickly put her water bottle and Kindle in her bag and hand it to her. *Thanks,* she mouths. Then she gives Cathy's arm a squeeze. "I'll have him text you when he's awake."

"Thank you, honey."

As Cathy sits back down next to Aaron's dad, I watch Rae go, relief hitting me as well. I hope this surgery is healing for him in more ways than one.

Aaron

I should've said no to coming to this stupid party.

Actually, in the realm of things I should have done differently, I should have talked to Rae after the game. After I kissed her. God, I want to kiss her again. But right now, she's in the middle of the dance floor, dancing with Trevor, and my jealousy levels are off the charts. He's not even touching her, and I'm jealous.

I should go out there and dance with her, but I feel stupidly nervous about all of this, too. What if she doesn't feel the same? *What if you just talked to her?*

When I look at her again, I see she's walking across the dance floor to me. And I'm still standing here with my arms folded over my chest, acting like some possessive asshole.

"Hey," she says when she gets to me, "what's wrong?"

"What are you doing?" I ask, my voice conveying the same asshole tone as my posture.

"Um, dancing. Why?"

"You're acting ridiculous."

What am I even fucking saying?

"I'm acting ridiculous?"

Okay, it's unlike her to dance in a group of people. Maybe ridiculous is the wrong word.

"This isn't you," I say, leaning in toward her, "this isn't who you are."

"What? I'm not normally fun? Because dancing like that was fun," she says, full of attitude. Ugh. I forgot how sassy she can get when someone crosses her. But that's also definitely *not* what I'm saying.

I shake my head. "That's not what I meant. You're always fun." I give her a sweet smile. "I want you to enjoy yourself, but I also want you to be yourself. You're awesome. I don't get why you're trying to change."

"I'm not trying to change. I just wanted to let off a little steam. It's not like I'm drunk." Her voice is calmer, but there's still an edge. I fucking hate this. I'm frustrated and nervous and still jealous, even though there's nothing to be jealous of. So naturally, I have no filter.

"But you're dancing with random guys."

"No, I danced with Trevor. But even if I had been dancing with other guys, so what?" She locks eyes with me, and I know she's trying to push my buttons. Probably fair, because they need to be pushed. "You were talking to Caity."

"Yeah, so? We've become friends. That was nothing."

"Just like me dancing with Trev was nothing." She sighs, then her voice softens. "I'd rather have been dancing with you. Why don't we go dance?"

I look into those gorgeous eyes and even though part of me is screaming to get her out of here and off the dance floor and finally fucking talk to her, I know trying to push her right now won't help. My gut reaction is to go all caveman and throw her over my shoulder and drag her out of here. Also, not the right call. She's stubborn. The absolute last thing I want is to push her away, so I shove every other feeling and uncertainty away, and smile back. My stomach warms.

Yes, lean into flirting. We're good at this.

I drop my lips next to her ear and say, "Only if you promise to go for a walk with me after."

Her eyes widen slightly, but the smile grows. "Sounds perfect. Come on, Ace."

She grabs my arm and leads me back onto the dance floor. We dance close together, facing each other, then she turns around and leans back, dancing against me.

Fuck. Dancing was such a good idea.

I wrap an arm around her waist and move with her.

Until I can't anymore. Because a certain area is about to be rock hard.

Instead, I lean down and rumble in her ear, "How about we go for that walk now?"

She spins around, eyes wide and filled with excitement.

"Yes. Let's go."

I take her hand and lead her off the dance floor and out of the house, making our way to the backyard where it hits the woods.

"Dancing was fun," she says softly as I lead her down a wooded trail.

"It was. But I wanted to talk to you, too."

"Oh? About what?" she asks, playing coy.

"I think you know," I say, spinning her around and walking her backward until she's against a tree. Bracing one hand next to her head, I lean down and brush my lips over hers. "I want to talk about your lips on my lips."

"What about that?" she asks breathily.

"I'd like to do that a lot more."

"Yeah?"

"Mhm. But only if you agree to be my girlfriend."

Her smile is radiant as she says, "Really?"

"Fuck yes," I answer. "It's always been us. I'm done pretending otherwise."

She throws her arms around my neck and leaps into my arms. "Hell yes, Ace. Hell yes."

She kisses me passionately, but then I hear...

Ace.

Ace.

You in there? Wake up, babe.

My eyes flutter open and I see my girl's beautiful face. Before I make sense of where I am or what's happening, I reach up and pull her to my lips.

"Easy, killer," she says with a smile. "Having a good dream?"

I blink a couple of times as I make sense of everything. Hospital. Surgery. That dream. The way I wish that night at the party would've gone.

I shake my head slowly and look down at my arm in a cast, the mix of what I wish would've happened and where we are now settling on me.

"You okay?" she asks. "Any pain?"

I shake my head and scoot over in the bed so she can sit next to me.

"No pain. But I was dreaming of the night..." I glance down at my hand, wrapped in a cast.

"Oh."

"I was dreaming of how it could have gone."

"Oh? What happened in the dream?"

"I danced with you, took you outside, told you I wanted to kiss you more... if you'd be my girlfriend."

"That would have been pretty sexy," she says, ruffling my hair. "But it wouldn't have been honest for where we were at. We had a lot to learn."

"We definitely did."

"But..." She holds up her hand, taking in the beautiful engagement ring from her grandmother and the delicate floral wedding band I had made to match it. "Who knows if we'd be here right now. I love here."

"Me too," I say softly. Then I wince. I guess there is some pain.

"Want me to call the nurse?"

"In a few minutes."

I wrap my non-casted arm around her and pull her close.

"How much did you cry?" I whisper.

She chuckles. "Only a little bit. Joel mopped up my tears. Don't worry."

I kiss her cheek and rest my head against hers.

"Hello, hello," Doctor Max says, walking around the curtain. He smiles when he sees us. "How are you feeling?"

"Still a little groggy. Starting to feel some pain."

"Okay. I'll let the nurse know. We'll be sending you home with a prescription for an increased dosage of ibuprofen. They can give you some here before we discharge you." He grabs a nearby rolling stool and sits down on it. "I already spoke to your wife, but I wanted to tell you also. Everything went really well." He explains that it was what they expected, and he thinks it will heal up well from here. "Any questions for me?"

"No. I don't think so. Other than when I get to start using my hand again."

He laughs. "First and foremost, you had surgery, and that takes a toll. Rest for at least a week. No strenuous activity. If you're feeling up to it, you can return to classes next week, but if not, just call the office and we'll write a note. As for physical activity, I'd prefer you wait until after your follow up next Friday. We'll take a look at things and adjust your cast if we need to based on how much the swelling goes down. The nurse will go over all the care instructions before you leave and give you access to a twenty-four-hour nurse hotline we utilize for any basic questions when you can't reach the office. After your six-week follow up, we'll get you set up with physical and occupational therapy again. After next week, you can add in some lower body exercise and cardio, but keep resting that hand as much as possible."

"Okay, thanks. I really appreciate this."

He gives me a small smile. "Absolutely. We'll see you both soon, okay? Don't hesitate to call with any questions. Take care."

"Thanks, you too," Rae says as he leaves.

Her gaze shifts back to me, and a look of pure emotion passes between us.

My stomach swells with anticipation. After all these years, I might finally have some relief, not to mention the ability to pitch well again.

I'm still scared to get my hopes up, but I'm excited too. And right now, I'm ready to get back to the lake house, rest, and let Rae take care of me like only she can.

Sarah

It's been a long ass week. I was up early every day for the last two weeks to meet up for a study group for midterms. Today, I had my last one. Between that and clinicals, I'm exhausted, but

I have no intention of showing that, because tonight is my date with Joel. And I look *gorgeous*. You know, if I do say so myself.

Rae took a break from waiting on Aaron hand and foot—and desperately trying to get him to rest, which is like trying to tell a husky not to run—and helped me get ready. Joel went downstairs to get ready in Miles's room so he could pick me up, and I'm having a hard time not squealing over how freaking cute he is.

I'm thinking we've done this whole thing—whatever we're doing—wrong. When we first moved in here, Trev told me to have fun and enjoy this because it's the buildup to our relationship. It's us falling in love.

We've done sexual stuff, we sleep in the same bed, we spend time together, but we haven't done a typical thing people do leading up to a relationship. We haven't dated. We've crossed lines and avoided others, but I'm realizing how backward it all seems now. I'm still not ready for the commitment of a boyfriend—more than that because I know once we cross that line it's going to be *everything* very fast—but I love the idea of dating him. That's the exact slow buildup I've been wanting. How did I miss that? Probably because big feelings have been involved with us for a while. And maybe it feels a little weird to date your best friend. But I want to. I'm ready for that much.

There's a knock on the bedroom door—five minutes early, as expected—and I check my reflection in the mirror one last time, then smile. I'm wearing a silver sequined T-shirt dress that cuts at my mid-thigh and four-inch silver heels. My legs are going to freeze, but it's worth it for how perfect I look. I grab my wool coat and my clutch and swing the door open.

Joel is standing there with a bouquet of light pink tea roses and smiling brightly.

My mouth drops slightly as I realize he didn't just get ready in Miles's room. He went and got me flowers too.

Damn it. He's adorable.

I'm swooning.

And giddy.

Oh my gosh. This is what I've been missing. The rush. The anticipation. The buildup. We've been teetering on the edge of this massive line, but we blew past so many of the fun things. I want more of this.

Then I notice his outfit.

He's wearing a white button down, untucked, with a heather gray sweater over it. He's got on tight, light wash jeans, and cream-colored boots, and his hair is slightly mussed. *Good Lord.*

Romance books love to describe a guy as devastatingly handsome. Whenever I read that, part of me wonders what the hell they're talking about, and the other part intrinsically knows—and it's this. It's this pure perfection. That troublemaking grin. The outfit. Those piercing eyes. He makes my stomach flip and whirl like I'm on a roller coaster. I can't take my eyes off him. *He* is devastatingly handsome. The kind of handsome, hot, sexy that makes me want to pant and fan myself. Add in that swagger and charm. *I'm a freaking puddle.*

"Hi. You look so handsome," I finally muster, taking the flowers—which are already in a vase—from him.

"And you look stunning. Dazzling, magnificent. There aren't enough words for how gorgeous you are."

Heat creeps into my cheeks and he bites his lip.

Maybe this is why I've held off on dating him. I want to jump him.

"Ready to go?" he asks.

"Absolutely." I set the flowers on the dresser and take his extended elbow, my stomach fluttering like there are some drunken butterflies in it that keep bouncing off the walls.

"This is really beautiful," I say, looking around the nice Italian restaurant we're sitting in. It's not crazy fancy like our Valentine's date was, but it's still upscale with a romantic ambience. "How did you swing reservations here on such short notice?"

I get the trademark charming smile.

"I can be very persuasive."

"True."

He reaches over the table and rests his hand on top of mine, gently brushing his thumb over my skin as we both look over our menus. That tiny touch sends a magical feeling coursing through my body.

We order and then chat about how our weeks have been and how Aaron and Rae did yesterday. It's simple, on the cusp of small talk, but every time I speak, his eyes are trained on me as he listens intently to every word.

I'd forgotten what it was like to go on a date with him. To feel like the only girl in the world. To feel adored.

After eating an appetizer of eggplant rollatini and some fancy, fresh Italian bread, I find myself silently staring at him, taking in every detail of his face. The small mole on his left cheek. The smattering of barely visible freckles over his cheeks. The way his cheeks scrunch up to his eyes when he smiles—not the charming grin, but the full-fledged Joel smile, which has a childlike happiness to it.

Brushing his thumb over my hand again, my gaze is drawn to those hazel eyes glimmering under the soft yellow light above us.

Then, in a low voice, he says, "Tell me a secret."

My eyes flare slightly at the use of my special phrase. The one I say when I'm ready to be vulnerable, but I need someone else to go first. Or when I need to get someone I love to tell me the truth about something. Either way, Joel knows the power those words hold for me. What he's asking me right now is to be vulnerable with him.

And I give in. It's impossible not to with his piercing eyes locked on mine and a soft smile on his face.

"Okay... I really like this. That sounds silly when I say it out loud, but I like... dating you. And I'd like to do this more."

The smile I get at those words is downright blazing. Smoldering. Hot as sin, matching the desire in his eyes.

He lifts my hand and softly kisses it.

Oh. My. God.

"I would love to do more of this," he says in a low rumble. "I'd love to date you, if you'll let me."

All those butterflies in my stomach are acting more like crazed fangirls now. Jumping up and down. Bouncing around. Probably screaming.

I bite my lip. I do want that. And I can commit to a night like this once a week. A night for us to connect. Build our foundation.

"I'm not ready for the words boyfriend or girlfriend yet. And my availability will change by the week, but... I'd love to date you, Joel."

His smile grows, lighting up his entire face. Then he squeezes my hand, leans over the table, and kisses me. It's soft, simple, but the kind of kiss I could get lost in. If we weren't in the middle of a restaurant, I'd happily let myself melt into him and forget everything else exists.

He must be as acutely aware as I am that we're right on the edge, because he carefully pulls his lips off mine, smiling at me, though his eyes are dark, as he sits down.

A moment later, our waiter sets our food down, and the rest of the meal is spent talking and sneaking glances at each other as we enjoy our food.

I'm on fire. Hot as hell, burning up for him.

His hands settle on my waist as our tongues twist together and my hands thread his soft brown hair.

We're like two horny teenagers as we make out in the front seat of his Tahoe, me on his lap, pouring everything inside me into this kiss.

He slides one hand up my waist, then into my hair, his fingers twirling around the strands as his tongue dances with mine.

He presses his lips harder into mine, his kissing growing more forceful for a moment before he slowly pulls away, panting.

"Sorry. I, um—" He looks down.

I follow his gaze and look down at his crotch. I was doing my best not to grind against him, but we were getting pretty hot and heavy.

"It's okay," I say softly, then kiss his cheek before climbing off him. "Let's head home."

We buckle up, then he starts the car. Before he pulls out of the parking lot, he takes my hand.

And he doesn't let it go the entire drive home.

Once we get to the lake house, he finally unfurls our fingers, then climbs out and hurries around to open my door. I'm not sure what kind of magic he worked, but no one is downstairs when we get back, so there are no prying eyes as we make our way up to the master bedroom.

He stops outside the door and says, "If I were dropping you off, I'd do this." Then he gives me a slow, sexy kiss. No tongue, but still full of desire. "But since I'm not..." He swings the door open, takes my hand again, and leads me through it, shutting it behind me.

We slip our shoes and coats off and then we're lying on the bed, making out again like we were in the car. This time he leans into me, grinding against me. I wrap one of my legs around his and deepen our kiss.

I've always loved kissing.

I've always loved kissing? That sounds unbelievably dumb.

It's true, though. One of the best parts of falling for someone, even being in a relationship, is the kissing. Making out is sexy and fun and a great way to connect with your partner. Anyone who thinks it's just for teenagers or people in a new relationship... well, they need to pull the stick out of their butt and probably get kissed so they can relax a bit.

Even though this make-out session is rolling way past relaxing now and into frantic, messy, hookup territory. Don't get me wrong, any time I've done anything sexual with Joel, it's been amazing, but I don't know if that's what tonight is supposed to be, if that's what I want it to be, or if he'd even be comfortable going further.

Maybe a little more.

But then I feel his hard-on poking into my hip, and I reluctantly pull away.

"Shouldn't we stop?" I ask, trying to catch my breath.

"We don't have to. We can touch ourselves. Or each other. It depends on what you want."

The throbbing between my legs is clear about one thing I want.

"I want a lot of things, Joel." I look into his eyes and know what I really want. "But it's been a long week. I've missed you. Can we just lay together?" I smile at him. "Snuggle me?"

He grins and laughs a little, then quickly stands up. "Get changed, go to the bathroom because once you get in this bed, I'm not letting you go till morning."

There's that giddiness again. That feeling of falling in the best way. A free fall where the ground never comes—hopefully.

We both quickly change and use the bathroom, then crawl back into bed.

He wraps his arms around me and pulls the blanket over us, then kisses my forehead.

"Goodnight, Sarah."

"Night, Joel," I whisper as I melt into him, safety and happiness washing over me and lulling me to sleep.

Chapter Eleven

You

Joel

I DIG MY PHONE out of my pocket as I walk through the door of the lake house. "I'm going," I say, like the vibrations of my phone will understand me. I extricate it from my pocket and shove it against my ear. "Hey, Mom."

"Hi, honey. Oh, Dad's going to get the car, but he wanted to say hi."

Dad's voice comes on the line. "Hey, bud. How are ya?"

"I'm good, Dad. Just finished up my last class before break. Ready to relax. How are you and Mom?"

"We're good. I'll pass you over to her for the specifics."

"Okay. See you soon, Dad."

He mumbles some kind of goodbye, then my mother comes back on the line.

"How have the last couple of weeks been?" Mom asks.

"Pretty good. Everyone has hit the point of being over school for the semester. I'm excited for break. When did you say you and Dad would be back home? Jesse isn't leaving for his guys' trip until Wednesday night."

"Well, I actually wanted to talk to you about that. I know it was supposed to be you, Jonathan, and us for Thanksgiving, but we had some friends invite us to spend Thanksgiving with them down in Florida." My stomach sinks. *Seriously?*

"And you're going?" I ask calmly. "What about Jonathan and me?"

"Oh, Jon had already called to say he'd been invited to his girlfriend's house. It seemed silly to make a whole dinner for just the three of us, so we figured we could all branch off and do our own things. Don't worry, though, I already spoke to Jared, and he's happy to have you for Thanksgiving."

My shoulders slump. I should've been expecting it. Shouldn't have gotten excited. I was looking forward to reconnecting with my parents, especially since it would be such a small group. I've been texting more with Jonathan and we're getting along better—not like Jesse and me, but it's something. I was actually looking forward to a small Thanksgiving with them this year.

Now my options are spending it alone or with Jared? I'll stick with alone, thanks.

"Okay. That's fine. A few of us might actually hang around the lake house," I lie.

"Oh, that's perfect, then. If you change your mind, let your brother know. Looks like your father is here with the car. We'll call soon. Love you, honey! Happy Thanksgiving!"

"Happy Thanksgiving, Mom," I say flatly, then the line disconnects.

I toss my phone onto the counter and drop my head into my hands as tears crest in my eyes.

I shouldn't have gotten my hopes up. I mean, why would my parents actually want to spend the holiday with me? There are always more exciting things. I would've loved to have a small holiday with just my parents. Why is it that I'm not enough of a reason to come home? To spend time with? Pain floods my body as the answer floats through my brain—one I've known intrinsically since I was young.

They would never say it. Never admit to it. In some ways, I doubt they even realize it, but it's the truth. I will always be the kid they were stuck with, not the kid they wanted.

Sarah

I'm in a good freaking mood. School is done for Thanksgiving break. Tomorrow we head up north to our family's week-long Thanksgiving shenanigans. I got my midterm grades back, and I did amazing. Joel and I went on another sweet date last night. To top it all off, there's a light snow swirling in the air. It's a perfect day. I think this calls for some hot chocolate.

Only Joel's car and Amanda's car are here as I walk into the lake house. Amanda had a huge test today and was up all night studying, so she's probably sleeping right now.

The house is quiet when I walk in, so I take my stuff off and head upstairs to find Joel. When I swing the door to the bedroom open, everything is dark except for a light in the bathroom. That's when I hear sniffling. I drop my purse on the love seat and run into the bathroom where Joel is sitting on the floor, still wearing his coat and shoes, sobbing. A moment of panic rushes through me until I rationalize that if something had happened to someone, he would've called.

I slide onto the floor and crawl over so I'm sitting next to him, then I wrap my arm around his back and pull him against me.

"What happened?" I whisper.

He wipes his eyes with the back of his hand. "Nothing. It's stupid."

"If you're upset, it's not nothing. It's not stupid."

"I shouldn't be upset. I should've been expecting it."

"Tell me," I breathe, gently twisting my fingers through his short hair as my head rests against his.

"My parents ditched me for Thanksgiving. It's so dumb that I was actually looking forward to it, that I believed it would happen," he sniffs.

Joel's parents suck.

As he tells me what happened, I carefully slide my phone out of my sweatshirt pocket with one hand and send a text.

"But don't worry. I can go to Jared's."

"No way," I say as my phone vibrates. I glance at it, then smile.

"I'll just be alone, I guess."

"You'll be with me."

"What?"

"I just texted Grandpa. It's a done deal."

"Sarah, you don't have to."

I turn and sit up on my knees, looking into his eyes. "I don't know why you think I'm doing this because I *have* to. I'm doing this because I want to. I'd never ever let you be alone for Thanksgiving, but more importantly, I would love to spend Thanksgiving with you. I thought about asking you to come with us, but you were excited to see your parents." I gently rub my hand over his cheek. "I'm sorry they suck, but now you get to spend Thanksgiving with me. And Aaron and Rae. We'll have an amazing time."

He cracks a small smile for the first time.

"Thank you," he whispers, wiping the last of his tears away.

I lean forward and softly brush my lips over his. "You never need to thank me. No matter what I'm ready for or where we're at... I love you. And I want to see you happy." I stand up quickly and hold out my hands. "Come on."

He takes my hands, a soft smile growing on his face.

I lead him back into the bedroom to the edge of the bed and slide his coat off.

"Sit."

He plops down on the edge of the bed, and I squat in front of him and pull his shoes off, then stand up again. With a little smirk, I push him backward on the bed, then grab his feet and lift them up, pushing them so they're on the bed as well.

"What are you doing?" he asks with a laugh.

"Cheering you up."

He raises an eyebrow, then gives me a tiny hint of that cheeky grin and my heart warms.

I climb onto the end of the bed, take one of his feet in my hands, and start massaging. I work on that one for a few minutes, then switch to the other foot before making my way up his leg. I massage one, then the other as he melts into the bed.

"You're good at the cheering up thing," he mumbles, then yawns.

"Flip over," I say softly.

I get the smile again. Then he rolls onto his stomach.

He inhales sharply as I straddle him, and it takes everything inside me to focus on the task at hand. This isn't supposed to be sexual. It's about relaxation. Helping him feel better.

With my mind out of the gutter, I bring my thumbs along the edge of his spine and slowly massage up to his shoulders. When I reach his neck, I run my hands down his back and start at the bottom again, moving my thumbs outward slightly. I repeat that until I've gone over his whole back, then focus on working my thumbs and palms in soft circles over his shoulders and neck.

He sighs softly, and I feel the weight lifting off him, which is exactly why I did this. I can't fix the pain he's feeling, but if I can take any of it from him, I will do whatever I can to make that happen. I don't like seeing any of my friends sad, but seeing Joel hurt pricks at my heart and makes me ache, too.

He's almost snoring by the time I finish. I end with a scalp massage before telling him to sit up.

He looks at me, starry-eyed and content.

"Get cozy," I whisper as I pull the covers back.

He slides under them, then I tuck them back over him and kiss his cheek. Grabbing the remote, I hand it to him.

"You pick a movie. Whatever you want. I'm going downstairs to make us hot chocolate and popcorn, then we're going to cuddle in bed and watch whatever movie you pick—I won't complain if it's something Christmassy."

He looks at me in awe, then grabs my arm and pulls me to him.

He slides a hand into my hair and kisses me. "You're amazing," he breathes as he pulls away.

I shake my head, flushing slightly. "No. I just need you to know how loved you are." Wrapping my arms around his neck, I hug him tightly.

He squeezes me back, then kisses my cheek as he lets me go. "Make me hot chocolate," he says adorably.

"With extra whipped cream." I wink and hop off the bed, smiling to myself as I walk out of the room.

I love being the person who takes care of him, the one he relies on.

Oh.

That's what a girlfriend would do, isn't it?

I'm still not sure I'm ready for that yet, but for the first time, I feel like I can handle it. *That's something.*

Joel

I'm looking out the window of the backseat of Rae's Corolla as we make our way up north for the week. Sarah is snuggled against me with a blanket pulled over her and her Kindle in her lap. Rae and Aaron are chatting as Aaron drives through softly swirling snow, Christmas music playing quietly through the speakers.

My heart feels so full.

I was bummed after the phone call with my mother yesterday, but then Sarah swooped in and took care of me both physically and emotionally. I know she doesn't always realize how much she does for me—gives me—but yesterday, I think she saw it, too.

Between that and our newly regular dates, I feel hopeful about the direction we're moving in. Maybe my patience is finally paying off. Either way, I'm excited to be spending the week with her, Rae, and Aaron—not to mention most of Rae and Sarah's family—for an all-out Abbott family Thanksgiving.

"So, what do we have to look forward to this week?" I ask.

"Shenanigans," Rae says, looking back at me with a smile.

Sarah laughs and puts her Kindle to the side.

"Oh boy," Aaron says. "I've been hearing about this for months now. And yet, I've gotten no specifics."

"Well, you're both lucky that they all know you to some degree already," Sarah says.

"Yes, you may be Abbott family Thanksgiving virgins, but you're not new to our family as a whole. That'll help when the sarcasm starts and Gram and Grandpa have a little bit of alcohol and the inquisition begins," Rae says.

"Inquisition?" I ask with raised eyebrows.

"Oh, not just you two," Sarah says. "No one is excluded from the questioning. It's equal opportunity."

"Yep. Could be as simple as whether someone is getting a raise at work or as complicated as when someone is going to find the love of their life. As if that's predictable."

Aaron chuckles. "Might've been for some people."

He wraps his hand around Rae's.

"Well, as long as I'm not stuck at my brother's house with his bratty toddler and, well, *him.* I'm happy. Even happier that I'm with you guys."

"I'm happy you're with us, too," Sarah whispers. Then she nestles into me again and continues reading.

"Gram! Grandpa!" Rae yells as she jumps out of the car. Sarah is right behind her as they run over to their grandparents and maul them with hugs.

Aaron and I climb out and watch our girls for a moment.

Whoa. Our girls? What is my brain doing? We might be dating, *but Sarah and I aren't together. Even if, in my heart, she is my girl, no matter what.*

Fuck, I'm pathetic.

"Well, well, Aaron Cooper and Joel Wilkinson. Get over here," Pete says.

Leaving the bags in the trunk, we make our way over to Pete and Bea, shaking hands with Pete and hugging Bea.

"About time we officially indoctrinated you into our clan," Pete says with a wily smile.

"Oh boy, starting trouble already?" Bea asks.

Pete winks at her, then kisses her cheek. I stifle a laugh when she looks up at him the *exact* same way Rae looks at Aaron.

"I just want them to know we're happy to have them," Pete says, a troublemaking look in his eyes.

"How about we show them the house, then?" Bea says, ever the voice of reason.

"Grab those bags, boys, and we'll show you around."

Aaron and I grab the bags from the trunk and follow them inside.

"This here is what we call the small house," Pete says. "Four bedrooms and two bathrooms. There's a little trail through the woods that leads up to the big house. That one belongs to Chris, our oldest. He owns all of this property, and we had this house built as overflow for when the whole family is visiting. On the other side of the property is Chris's younger brother's house—that's Darren. He's the youngest boy, just two years older than Kara. Our second oldest, Sylvia, and her family always stay with Chris, while the two of us, Kara and Charlie, and the girls stay here, though you'll find most meals and down time are spent at Chris's house. It's an open-door policy around here. Except the bedrooms." Pete winks at us.

For a "small" house, this one is spacious enough. There's a medium-sized kitchen open to the living area, a small dining room, a bathroom, and a large bedroom—where Pete and Bea sleep—on the first floor. They lead us upstairs, pointing out which bedroom will be Kara and Charlie's when they get here tomorrow. Next is Aaron and Rae's room. Aaron drops the bags and they head inside to "get settled." *Sure.*

Finally, we end up at a cozy bedroom, and for the first time, I realize we'll be sharing a bedroom and a bed.

Seeing the look on my face and clearly reading my mind, Pete chuckles and slaps my shoulder.

"Whatever you two are doing or not doing, don't insult my intelligence by pretending you don't share a bed."

"Peter Abbott," Bea hisses.

He chuckles and kisses her cheek. "We'll be downstairs if you need us. Take your time!" he calls as they walk away.

Sarah laughs and leads the way into the room. It's small, but has two closets, a dresser, and a TV, along with a queen-sized bed.

"Your grandparents are crazy," I say, setting the bags down, then dropping onto the edge of the bed.

She shuts the door, then walks over to me and climbs onto my lap, straddling me.

My body heats up instantly, and I find myself wanting to pull at the collar of my shirt.

"They are. In the best way."

She looks into my eyes as I wrap my arms around her back.

We sit in silence for a moment as her blue eyes dive deep into my soul.

Finally, she rests her head against mine and whispers, "I'm glad you're here." Then her lips brush mine and I'm a goner. I pull her backward onto the bed with me, deepening our kiss, losing myself in her as we make out like we have after each date, so far.

The concept of time fades away as our swollen lips crush together, tongues teasing each other, hands roaming. God, I love the feel of her body against mine.

"I'm glad I'm here, too," I mutter against her lips.

She pulls back slightly and smiles. It's vibrant and full of happiness. I love when she's happy like this. Not just content. Not just comfortable. But completely, joyfully happy.

She sits up and takes my hand. "Come on. I can't wait to show you everything."

Her blue eyes dance, and it reminds me of when she'd get excited about something as a kid. She'd be bouncing in place, excited to show or tell us all something. She's adorable. And I'm a sucker for her, like always.

Sarah

"Now is the time to fight! We've got them outnumbered. And even if we didn't, by nature, we have them outsmarted."

"Hell yes, baby," Rae says, her cheeks rosy in the cold.

We're sitting behind the shed with our cousins—Uncle Darren's oldest, Cassie, who is twelve, Aunt Sylvia's daughters Dani and Olivia, who are twenty-three and twenty-one, and Uncle Chris's youngest daughter, Andrea, who is twenty-four.

This is our home base for the epic snowball fight we're having against the boys—Joel, Aaron, Uncle Darren's son Lincoln, who is ten, Aunt Sylvia's oldest, Weston, who is twenty-five, and Uncle Chris's son Cole, who is twenty-six. We'd have his wife, Justine, on our team too, but she's pregnant with their first, so snowball fights are not the place for her. Especially in the Abbott family. We. Play. Hard.

It snowed on Sunday night, and on Monday we all made snowmen. Yesterday we lounged around the house, then last night it snowed again. Today we decided on a snowball fight, and sledding later tonight so the few younger kids can participate.

Dani peeks out from the side of the shed, spotting the boys over by the large tree that is their home base.

"I say we go around to the right, use the tree line as cover," Dani says, crouching next to me.

"You, Dani, and Andrea, take Cassie," Rae says. "Olivia and I can cover you from the front of the shed."

Olivia fist bumps Rae, and we all put our hands in a pile.

"Who runs the world?" I ask.

"GIRLS!" we all shout, then break off in separate directions.

As Rae and Olivia set up a barrier of old pallets from the shed, Dani, Andrea, Cassie, and me sneak into the woods. We move slowly, trying to disguise the sounds of our footsteps, and once we're concealed by the trees, we split up. Dani runs farther ahead, Andrea stays behind, while Cassie sticks with me and we take a position behind a tree in the center.

The goal of the game is to either capture the other team's base—which requires two people unless both teams are down to one or two people each—or to get everyone on the other team out. To get someone out, you have to hit them center mass between the hips and the shoulders. It can be from the front, back, or side, but anywhere else doesn't count.

We watch carefully as the boys break apart. Joel and Lincoln stay near the tree while Aaron and Weston push up the center using old garbage can tops as shields. Since his right wrist is still in a cast, he's using his right hand to hold the shield and making and throwing snowballs with his left hand. Cole is patrolling along the tree line.

Rae lobs a snowball into the center of the field signaling the beginning of the game, and we all start making and throwing snowballs.

Dani is the first to land a hit, nailing Weston right in the ribs and taking him out. She sticks her tongue out at her brother, who per tradition of the game, lies down in his spot on the field.

Though Cassie is aching for action, I tell her to stay hidden with me behind the tree. The longer we stay out of sight, the more we build the element of surprise.

Cole strays away from the trees as Weston goes down, giving Andrea a chance to sneak a throw at him, but he turns slightly at just the wrong time, and the snowball hits him in the arm.

Fast on his feet, Cole scoops up some snow, quickly forms a ball, and nails Andrea right in the boob. Cole laughs boisterously at the pissed off look on his sister's face. But mocking your siblings will always come back to haunt you, because Olivia takes the moment to hit Cole right in the belly button with a snowball.

She winks at him, but misses Lincoln bolting away from the tree, ready to avenge Cole. Dani tries to warn her, but Lincoln is fast as hell, scooping up snow as he runs. He slams a snowball right into Olivia's chest.

"Shit," she mutters.

"You have to put a dollar in the swear jar!" Lincoln yells.

"Put a dollar in this!" Dani yells, running down the field, then chucking a snowball at Lincoln.

"Aw, man." He dramatically flops into the snow as Dani dives behind the barrier next to Rae.

Rae sticks her head up. "You coming for me, Ace?"

"Depends. You like it when I come for you, Beautiful?"

"Gross! There are children present," Joel yells. Still crouching behind a tree, Cassie and I stifle laughter.

"Cover me," Rae tells Dani, then grabs a sled and holds it in front of her as she stands, ready to meet her husband in battle.

Dani forms a ton of snowballs, then chucks them as Rae walks out onto the field.

Dani lays decent cover, though Rae and Aaron occasionally make and throw snowballs, hitting each other's shields every time. Dani catches pieces of Aaron, but never enough.

Then, Rae scoops up some snow, forming a few balls, and charges at Aaron, chucking the snowballs as she goes. Before she can throw the last one, though, she slips and lands hard on her back.

At that moment, Aaron throws down his shield and runs for Rae as Joel goes sprinting down the field, yelling at Aaron. Cassie and I are watching raptly to see how this plays out—I have a feeling I know what will happen first.

And it does. As Aaron gets to Rae, she chucks the last snowball at his chest.

"Gotcha."

But Joel saw it coming too, and he spikes a snowball down into Rae's chest.

Aaron collapses half on top of her, both of them laughing, and I can't help but think that's exactly what she wanted.

"Come on," I say to Cassie, grabbing her hand and leading her out of the trees toward the boys' unguarded base.

Dani chucks a snowball at Joel, but he ducks, then grabs Aaron's shield and hurries back toward their base, but then catches sight of us zigzagging across the field.

When running in a battle, *always strafe.*

He throws a few snowballs at us, but misses as we take cover behind the slide on the swing set.

But Joel isn't giving up. He moves closer and closer, so I finally tell Cassie to make a run for it.

Joel tries to hit her, but I stand up and distract him. He grabs a snowball and aims for me, but then quickly whips around and hits Dani—who was running up the field toward him, snowball in hand—right in the stomach.

She falls to the ground as Joel turns back to me, just in time to be hit smack in the chest.

He gives me a troublemaking glare as he falls to the snow.

I throw my arms over my head and am about to declare victory when a snowball hits right below my collarbone.

What the hell?

"Nice try, cuz." My professional-football playing cousin, Mark—Uncle Chris's youngest at twenty-three—grins at me. He had a game on Monday night, and practice yesterday. I knew he was coming home today, but didn't even notice he had pulled into the driveway.

Damn him.

Ignoring my excitement at seeing him, I shout, "You jackass!" Then I reluctantly fall into the snow.

But not before I catch Cassie out of the corner of my eye. She barrels at him, like she always does, and jumps at him, wrapping her arms around his neck from behind and tackling him. Once he's on the ground, she grabs a pile of snow and slams it into the center of his back.

Then she jumps up and down shouting, "Girls win! Girls win!"

Everyone slowly gets up and comes to the center of the field. Hugs are exchanged, and then the girls rub our victory in the boys' faces.

Aaron teases Mark. "Couldn't handle one little girl? Isn't it your job not to get tackled?"

Mark rolls his eyes. "Shut the fuck up. Not my fault all the linemen were down."

"Ooh, you have to put some money in the swear jar!" Cassie says.

Mark grabs her and tickles her until she's laughing too hard to pick on him anymore. Then he looks at Aaron and Joel. "You know, if you two think you're so good at football, maybe we should play a game."

"No!" Rae, Aaron, Joel, and I all yell simultaneously.

Never ever again.

Laughing, we all make our way back inside to warm up with some hot cocoa around the fire.

I love my family.

Rae, Dani, and I are in the kitchen of the big house making hot cocoa while Mark and Olivia entertain the younger kids. Cassie is dancing in and out of the kitchen. She's growing up fast, but I love that she still has her childhood joy. I hope her incoming teen years don't rip it from her.

191

Gosh. When the hell did I become old and nihilistic? I'm only twenty.

Dani hops onto the counter as the milk and chocolate simmer together on the stove. "So, how would you feel about me moving to Ida?"

"Wait, seriously? You're thinking about it?" I ask happily.

She bites her lip and smiles. "Not just thinking about it. I'm heading back this weekend. I'm staying with Grandma and Grandpa."

"Really? That's so exciting! I mean, we aren't there all the time, but hopefully after college..." Rae trails off. "I mean, we don't know for sure yet, but Aaron and I plan on moving back after college," she says. "Why the move, though?"

It's not surprising that Dani would end up somewhere like Ida. She's always been more of a small-town girl. As long as I can remember, she's complained about living in the suburbs and how she'd much rather have grown up on Grandma and Grandpa's farm.

"Well, me nannying for Mason and Taylor was always temporary until they could find someone new." After her engagement broke off in the late spring, Dani moved up from down south where she's lived her whole life to help our cousin Mason out when he and his wife Taylor were in between nannies. "Grandpa set me up with someone he knows down in Ida who was looking to hire an interior designer full time. We had a video interview on Friday and he offered me the job."

"Who?" Rae asks excitedly.

"Leo Barone. He owns a construction company."

Rae and I both laugh.

"AB Construction," I supply.

"Yeah! You know him? Never mind. Small town. Of course you do. Is he nice?"

"He's great. Dad could tell you all about him," I say.

"And you've actually met his daughters," Rae says. "When you were visiting Grandma and Grandpa over the summer and at all my wedding shenanigans. Maia and Jenna. And his business partner, Noah, is Nick and Vince's dad."

"Oh. Damn. I can't believe I didn't put all that together. Now I'm even more excited. And I'm looking forward to building a home for myself. I haven't had that since I moved."

"Selfishly, I'm glad it'll be in Ida. Spending more time with you sounds perfect. Plus, you'll have built-in friends whenever we're around." I refrain from pointing out that Jesse—who she seems to have a love-hate relationship with—also lives in Ida.

Dani hops off the counter and throws an arm around each of us. "The best part."

Seriously. I love my family.

Joel

I wake up to the sound of knocking. Though I try to ignore it, it gets louder. Sarah, sleeping like the dead as usual, doesn't notice. Am I the only one who hears it? Is it like the *Polar Express* train whistle? Or bell? Or whatever the hell it is. When I stumble out of the bedroom, I see Aaron in the hallway, looking as confused as I am.

We make our way downstairs as the knocking continues.

We walk over to the door, then I look at Aaron, who shrugs.

Pulling the door open, we're greeted with Mark's face.

"About time. I was wondering if you two were ever going to drag your asses out of bed. Come on. We're going for a run."

Aaron squints at him. "You ever hear of text? Or normal waking hours?"

"A run is the best way to wake up." Mark smacks Aaron's shoulder. "Get dressed. Meet me back down here."

"Fine," Aaron complains. "You're lucky it's one of the few exercises I'm allowed to do with this cast."

Aaron turns back to the stairs. I give Mark a nod and follow Aaron. I agree with Mark. A run is a great way to wake up. Usually, no one in my life agrees, though. Maybe this will be fun.

After quickly stretching and warming up our muscles, we set out in the frigid weather for our run. Though Aaron was grumbling initially, he's in a better mood now. With the potential for playing this season, he's been working out more often and adding more cardio back in. I've always been a runner, unlike everyone else in my life except for Jesse and my dad. It's nice to have someone to run with who isn't complaining.

"So, what exactly are your intentions with Sarah?"

Scratch my previous comment about fun. This was a trap.

Aaron snickers at Mark's words and I reach over and smack his good arm.

"Hey, it's my duty as the closest thing they have to an older brother to question the men they bring home."

I'd like to tell him that Miles, Aaron, and I have always been the closest thing the girls have had to brothers—besides Mackie who has actual brothers, though she's not that close to them—maybe not for all of them, but I've always been like a brother to Rae and so has Miles. Like Aaron and Miles always have been for Sarah. And we've all been that way for Mackie. We definitely know the girls better than he does, but I figure I don't need to pick a fight.

"Really? Did you question him?" I throw my thumb out in Aaron's direction.

Mark chuckles. "It's unnecessary when he proclaims his intentions in elementary school."

"He did attempt to scare me after Rae and I got back together. Luckily, he's all bark and not much bite."

"You're an asshole, you know that?" Mark says.

Aaron shrugs and smirks. "Not like you'd have been able to change my girl's mind about anything, ever. She's got that big stubborn McKinley energy."

I laugh at that. "Accurate. Sarah's got some of that too. She's just quieter about it."

Mark looks over at me, sizing me up. "Again, I ask, what are your intentions with Sarah? She's bringing you home for Thanksgiving, but you're not officially a couple. What the hell is that shit?"

Aaron's eyebrows shoot up because he knows Mark pushed the wrong button.

"I'd tell you to ask Sarah about that, but it's not actually any of your business. Since you won't let me run in peace if I don't say something, I'll tell you this. I love Sarah, and I've loved her for a long time. Long term, my intention is to be with her forever. Short term, my intention is to be there for her. Support her. Take care of her. Be steadfast until *she* is ready for more."

He slows his pace until he's running in place and stares me down. Then he nods, smacks my arm, and says, "Okay. You pass."

"Woohoo," I say flatly. "Can we continue our run now?"

"Sure. Care to make it interesting?"

Aaron groans.

"C'mon. I need someone to push me," Mark says.

"Fine, I'm in. What are we making interesting?" I ask.

"If I beat you back, you have to learn everything there is to know about football before Christmas time. And I *will* be giving you a quiz."

I sigh. "Fine. But what do I get if I win?"

"I'll learn everything Grandpa never managed to teach me about baseball."

"All right, you're on."

We quickly shake on it, then look at Aaron.

"Oh no. Fuck all of that. I've hit my three miles for the day. I'm calling Rae to come get me and then I'm crawling back in bed with her," he says, slowing his pace.

"Have fun with your second round of cardio!" I call as Mark and I continue on.

"Nice," Mark says, fist bumping me. Then he smirks. "Three, two, one!"

We both pick up our pace, ready to challenge ourselves for the last two miles on the loop back to the house.

The Thanksgiving table is beautifully set. I'm sitting between Sarah and Aaron, who is frustrated with his inability to use a knife.

"If you need me to cut something for you, I can. That's what I'm here for, Ace," Rae says.

Aaron grumbles at this.

"I thought you liked it when I waited on you," Rae says with a fake pout.

"It was fun at first. Now I'm annoyed I can't do things."

"Just a few more weeks," Rae says soothingly, rubbing his arm. He softens immediately and I smile at that. After all their drama and inability to communicate, they've come so far.

Pete sits down at the same time Chris places the turkey on the table.

"All right everyone. As you all might have noticed, we're not much for religion in this family, but we do believe in blessings—we've all had many. As is tradition on Thanksgiving, we're going to go around the table and each say one thing we're thankful for."

He nods to Chris, who is sitting to his left to start.

"This year, I'm thankful for my family, as always. And that Mark won his game on Tuesday night, so we didn't have to spend Thanksgiving shit-talking him."

"Thanks, Dad," Mark says flatly from across the table as Chris's wife says, "Swear jar. Make it two dollars for swearing during your thanks on Thanksgiving."

There's stifled laughter from around the table before the next person says their thanks.

When it gets to me, I look around the table, then at Sarah, feeling emotional.

"I'm thankful you all have welcomed me to a week of fun and crazy celebrating. I'm thankful for Sarah..." I clear my throat. "For inviting me." Then, trying to squash the emotions I'm feeling, I say, "And I'm grateful I don't have to learn all about football." I smirk at Mark.

"Yeah, yeah. You won by three steps because you sprinted harder than you had the whole run once we got to the driveway."

Sarah laughs at that. "I'm thankful I don't have to try to teach you football. I'm also thankful that you're here with me. And that I get to celebrate with all of you crazies this year."

The thanks continue, but I don't hear any of it because Sarah reaches down, threads her fingers through mine, and squeezes my hand. My heart hammers as I look at her. Her eyes shimmer with vulnerability as she whispers. "I'm so happy you're here."

Me too.

⎯⎯ ♥ ⎯⎯

When I walk into the bedroom after using the bathroom, Sarah is sitting up in bed, scrolling on her tablet.

"What are you doing?" I ask as I slide into bed with her.

"Getting a head start on my Christmas shopping. I always feel inspired about what to get my cousins after I've been with them. What about you? What do you want for Christmas?"

Her.

It's the first thing that comes to mind. The perk of having rich parents—even if they aren't always around—is that you can buy yourself whatever you want. There's nothing I specifically want. I have everything I need. Everything except her.

She raises her eyebrows in question, but I'm not sure I should say that. I promised I'd never push her. But the longer this goes on, I wonder if she needs that gentle push, or to hear how I feel about her. But uncertainty hits before I can find the right words.

Instead, I tell her, "I don't know. I guess I'll have to think about that."

"Do that," she says with a smile, setting her tablet to the side. "Because I want to give you something special."

She snuggles under the covers and flips off the lamp, so I slide down too, extending my arm out. She rolls against me, splaying her arm over my chest and resting her head on my shoulder.

This is what I want. For this to be real. This last week with her has been incredible, but I wish I were here as her boyfriend. What I really want is for her to trust herself enough to finally let our relationship grow.

Sarah

I dramatically flop onto the bed in the master bedroom of the lake house. This week was tons of fun, but I'm exhausted. Since it was our last night there, Cassie kept Dani, Rae, Olivia, and I up late talking and playing card games. Rae won the first game of nickels, but Cassie—who we've taught well—won the second. It was amazing, but we stayed up until two in the morning. Then we got up early for a family breakfast before heading home. Energized by that, I didn't sleep at all in the car, but now I'm ready to pass out. I close my eyes and let my arms rest at my sides, my legs dangling off the end of the bed.

After a moment, the bed shifts, and I can feel Joel's presence above me.

Slowly, his lips press into mine, in an upside-down *Spider-Man*-style kiss. My heart flutters as his lips move over mine, calming me while infusing me with desire.

When he pulls away, he whispers, "You."

I flash my eyes open and look at him. "What?"

"You asked me what I want for Christmas. The answer is you. You're what I want. The only thing I don't have."

My heart pounds at his words. This is the first time he's ever asked for it. Ever even fully alluded to it. He's always left the ball sitting there, waiting for me to pick it up and start playing. Now he's lobbed it into my court. It's my move. *Shit.*

Trying to calm my thumping heart, I sit up and look at him. He's got a sweet smile on his face, but it's undercut by the devilish look in his eyes.

"I'll take that under advisement," I say smoothly.

"Good." He kisses my cheek, then hops off the bed, winking at me as he heads out of the room.

The moment he's gone, I flop back on the bed again and run my hands over my face.

I have got to figure out what the hell I'm doing.

Chapter Twelve

Merry Christmas

Sarah

I BRUSH MY LIPS across Joel's cheek as I slip under his covers. "Merry Christmas."

He turns over and smiles brightly at me. "Merry Christmas. How was your day?"

"Long, crazy, but nice. I missed you, though."

He kisses my forehead. "I missed you too."

"How was your day?"

"Oh, you know... Christmas with the Wilkinson's. Lots of presents, a catered meal, and some good alcohol. It was nice actually spending time with my parents, but it's just Jesse and me tonight. My parents left this evening to go to Jared's, and Jonathan left after we ate to go to his girlfriend's house."

"I guess it's a good thing I'm here to keep you cozy and make you breakfast tomorrow."

He chuckles at that. "Maybe one day I'll find something I can cook without burning it."

"Between Miles and me, I bet we could teach you. Either way, I like cooking breakfast. I'm not a great cook either, but I've mastered breakfast foods."

"My favorite meal," he says, kissing my neck, and I don't know if he's talking about breakfast or me.

Though his lips on my skin feel incredible, I stop him before I get too wrapped up. I push down the anxiety trying to take hold of my body so I can tell him this. I promised him honesty, even when it's hard. He deserves that much. He's been honest and understanding with me—far more than I ever could have expected.

"Joel," I whisper.

"Hmm?"

"I, um... I talked to Santa. And that thing you wanted for Christmas... he says it's going to be a little late."

I bite my lip as I look at him. His eyes flit over my face, taking me in, then he nods.

"Okay. As long as Santa promises it'll be here... soon."

I swallow hard and nod. "He promised."

"Okay then," he says softly. Then he wraps his arms around me and holds me close. "You smell like Christmas cookies."

I laugh at that. "All my cousins wanted to do at Gram and Grandpa's was make and decorate cookies. There's a plate full in the kitchen."

"Mm. Perfect. We can sleep in and eat cookies for breakfast."

"Guess I'll have to save my *incredible* cooking skills for lunch. I can make grilled cheese."

He nuzzles his face into my neck and I melt into a puddle. Why is he the sweetest, most adorable human on earth? He makes my heart feel like it's going to burst in the best way.

"My favorite." He kisses the spot on my jaw right below my ear, and anything that was left of me dissolves. He's fucking perfect. I just hope he's okay with the fact that I'm not. I might never be perfect enough for him, but I will take care of him however I can. *When I get there.*

Although lately, it seems like I've been driving around the block over and over to avoid pulling into the driveway.

As his warmth wraps around me and his tongue glides into my mouth, all those thoughts fade away. *At least I'm good at this.*

After a breakfast of Christmas cookies, coffee, and breakfast sausage, Joel and I went for a walk, enjoying the light snow in the air and the lingering Christmas vibes. Then, as promised, we had grilled cheese sandwiches, and Joel warmed up some tomato soup. It reminded me of snow days as a kid. Mom would always get out her electric griddle and make grilled cheese for all of us with plenty of tomato soup. In our house, we would actually pour a ladle full of soup over the top of our sandwiches. Judge if you want to, but I still think it's way better like that.

Rae, Aaron, Miles, and Mackie came over and we spent the afternoon setting up for the annual friends' Christmas party, which I swear grows a little bigger each year.

I had Rae bring over my dress and makeup so I could get ready here. Looking in the mirror, I make sure my makeup is just right and do one last twirl in this dress.

I *love* this dress. It's a shimmery red sequin bodycon dress that fits like a damn dream. Hem falls in the right place on my mid-thigh. It stays put so I'm not pulling it down constantly. And it is giving all the romantic vibes I want. Paired with a matching bright red lipstick, I feel ready to take on the world. And hopefully wow Joel. With Christmas this week, we didn't get to go out on our weekly date, so I'm doing my best to make the party a reasonable substitute for that.

The party is in full swing as I descend the stairs. Christmas music is playing from speakers in the living room, and alcohol is flowing freely. People are laughing and chatting and munching on the massive variety of appetizers and food we have every year.

My medium-length hair is done in soft waves, and I feel gorgeous.

I know the moment Joel's gaze lands on me. It's like a tractor beam, holding me in place, guiding me toward him.

When I look at him, I see a devilish smile on his face, eyes laced with heat, and one eyebrow slightly lifted. Joel looks scrumptious dressed in loafers, jeans, and a red sweater with a holiday pattern across the chest, but it's clear my outfit is achieving *exactly* what I wanted it to.

He strolls up to me, eyes dark and intense. "Are you trying to kill me?" he asks, pulling me close to him, his fingers brushing my ass. His voice is low and growly. "Do you have any idea how badly seeing you in this dress makes me want to see you *out* of it?"

My cheeks heat, but I smile.

"Maybe that was my intention."

I kiss his cheek and walk toward the kitchen, leaving him staring at me, stunned.

Maybe I shouldn't be pushing it this far, but I'm insanely hot for him tonight.

"You look sexy, baby," Rae says, stopping next to me and grabbing a plate. She hands me one, too, and we stare at the massive spread of food.

"Thank you. You look adorable in that outfit." She's wearing black pants with a red bandeau top that twists into a bow at the front. "How's Aaron holding up? He ready to unwrap his present?" I flip at the bow as she smiles.

"Mm, he definitely is. Of course, he's also loving having his cast off so he can..." she clears her throat, "fully enjoy all his gifts."

We both laugh at that.

"How's his hand doing?"

"Good," she says as we make our way down the table, adding food to our plates. "Still some pain, but it already seems better than it was and PT and OT are helping, though his muscles in that hand fatigue easily."

"I bet he loves that."

"Yeah, you know him. Doesn't love to rest. Luckily, I have my ways. Even if I have to use my feminine wiles on occasion."

We both giggle again.

"What are you two laughing about?"

We turn to see Joel and Aaron standing together, blatantly checking us out.

"Nothing," Rae says innocently to Aaron.

"I doubt that," Aaron growls.

Joel rolls his eyes, but Rae gives him a menacing look before walking away with Aaron.

I turn back to the table, adding one more thing to my plate, but then Joel's arm wraps around my waist. "I meant what I said before." He kisses my neck. "This dress is torture."

Then he turns and walks away like he didn't just set me on fire.

It's going to be a long night.

Joel and I have been flirting all night. As much as I wanted this dress to drive him nuts, he's turning it back on me and teasing me.

"I've missed you," I hear as I exit the bathroom. Down the hall between the bathroom and the kitchen, I see Mackie and Hyla.

"I know. I've missed you too," Mackie says.

I pause, not sure where to go other than to hide in the laundry room, which seems ridiculous.

"Can we try again? Please?" Hyla's voice is pleading, but I also notice her slurring a little.

"Hyla, I—"

"I love you, Mackie."

Oof. She's definitely been drinking.

"I love you too, Hyla. But I can't start this again when nothing has changed. Until you're ready to fully commit to me, to stop letting your parents control your life, I can't go down this road again. I'll always be here, and I'll help you and support you however I can as you figure things out, but I have to take care of myself, too." She squeezes Hyla's hand, then kisses her cheek and walks away.

Hyla sniffs and wipes away a couple of tears.

"Hey," I say softly.

She looks up. "Great. Someone else saw that."

"If anyone is going to see it, I'm a pretty good person." I wipe a tear off her cheek and take her hand. "Come here."

I lead her to the office at the other end of the hall and we sit down on the couch together.

"Do you want to talk about it?" I ask.

She sniffs. "I just feel like a mess. And Mackie's right. I haven't changed anything. No wonder she doesn't want to be with me."

"You know it's not that."

"No. It's my stupid behavior and my shitty parents. Every time I try to stand up to them, I end up giving up. I have no backbone. The strongest thing I did was leave school and move home. I couldn't keep studying business and politics. I hated it. Now I have no idea what I want to do with my life."

"At least you're living it," I say softly. "You have your own apartment. You're teaching yoga. Do you like that?"

"Yeah. I don't see it as a career, but I like it for now."

"That's something," I say softly.

"Sure. It's something to be berated about by my parents, because I just can't quit. I can't stop trying to change them. Begging them to love me. I go to dinner every week and let them insult me and treat me like trash. And I can't seem to tell them to fuck off. Or that I'm—I'm... bisexual. Or maybe a lesbian. I don't even know. I don't know how I feel. That's ridiculous! There's something wrong with me."

She drops her face into her hands and cries.

"There's nothing wrong with you," I say firmly, wrapping an arm around her back.

"Nope. There's something wrong with them," Trev says, strolling into the room. "Mackie thought you might need me."

Hyla looks up at him and hope fills her eyes. Mackie is strong to recognize what she needs to do to take care of herself, but still care for Hyla like she does.

"I'll let you guys have a minute," I say softly, then lean over and kiss Hyla on the cheek. As I rise from the couch, Trevor gives me a thankful smile.

I nod in return, then look at Hyla.

"You don't have to have it all figured out right now. Take care of yourself and your heart."

I make my way out of the room, heart hurting for Hyla, but I get it. Though we handle it in different ways, we both recognize our own messiness. While Hyla holds on tightly out of fear of losing people, I keep them at arm's length. I'm not sure either of us is right, but if it keeps the people I love from hurting the way Mackie is right now, then hopefully I'm doing something right.

Then I think of how it felt to tell Joel I'm still not ready yet last night, and I can't help but wonder if I'm hurting him by doing it my way.

Joel

Mackenzie Montoya is the quiet kind of fierce. She listens, thinks before she speaks, and is kind and objective with any words of advice she gives. She's also funny as hell and doesn't take herself too seriously. An odd combination, but that's Mackie. The Mackie I fell for—in a platonic way—the first time I met her. She's the kind of person you can easily spill your darkest secrets to and know that they're safe once she hears them. Of the girls, she is by far the most stoic and even-tempered.

So when I see tears cresting in her eyes—tears almost anyone else might miss—I follow her upstairs and find her in my bedroom.

"Macks," I whisper as I sit down next to her. She snuffles and presses the heels of her palms against her eyes. "Come here." I wrap an arm around her back and pull her close.

"I hate seeing her like that," she sniffs.

"Hyla?"

She nods, dropping her hands away from her eyes. "She's struggling, and I don't know how to help her. She wants me back, but I can't do that. Not like this. Take how things were between Aaron and Rae when he was at rock bottom and amplify that by ten. Only instead of ragey anger and guilt, Hyla has a hefty dose raw pain and self-loathing. She's still chasing down the love of her parents like it's some 90s feel good TV show and they'll eventually come around. They aren't going to. And instead of taking care of herself and learning to stand up stronger, she's giving in to the negativity. Getting drunk and then feeling worse. I've tried to talk to her, but she puts on that chipper voice and a big smile and says she's fine. She's not, though. And it kills me.

I wanted to say yes to her tonight, but I know I would've ended up with a broken heart all over again. I hate this."

"I'm sorry. But for the record, I admire your strength. Telling her no, even when it's hard."

She nods, resting her head against my shoulder.

After a few silent moments, she says, "I think you're strong, too. What you're doing with Sarah. Being patient, showing up for her, not pushing her."

I blow out a breath, my gaze landing on Sarah's T-shirt on my bedroom floor. "It's hard sometimes. Especially not pushing her. But I love her, and if this is what it takes, I'll do it."

She smiles and kisses my cheek. "You're a good man, Joel Wilkinson."

I chuckle at that and stand up, extending my hand to her. "So are you, Mackie."

"Hey," Miles says, standing in the doorway. "You okay?"

"Yeah. I will be." She walks over to him. "But I could still use a hug. And maybe some fresh air."

Miles hugs her tightly, saying, "We'll go for a walk."

He shifts her out of the way, so I can walk through the doorway.

"Thanks, Joel," she calls after me.

"Always. It's what we do for each other."

I make my way back downstairs and my eyes are instantly drawn to Sarah. She's standing by the Christmas tree talking with Amanda and Jamie. When she feels my gaze, she turns toward me, smiles, and scrunches up her nose.

My heart flares. Then, out of the corner of my eye, I see Hyla walking out from the hallway with Trev. Hyla is wiping her eyes as Chelsea walks over to them and gives Hyla a hug.

Sometimes I don't understand exactly why Sarah is holding back from me, but looking at Hyla, I understand, at least a little bit. She doesn't want to be where Hyla is, hurting the people she loves because she's struggling. I'm not sure it's the same thing, but I think that's how Sarah sees it.

This is where it's easy for me to stay the course. Even though it hurts sometimes, it's worth it. To me, it'll always be worth it to make sure Sarah feels loved and supported. She does the same for me, and I'm hoping once she realizes that, she'll be less afraid to cross the line we've been walking along the edge of.

The party, as usual, was a success. Of course there was drama, but it wouldn't be a bunch of twenty-year-olds in a small town if there wasn't any drama.

Hyla seemed better for the second half of the party, and after a walk with Miles, Mackie was in better spirits as well.

Though I'm not planning on doing a big clean until tomorrow when Miles, Mackie, Aaron, and Rae will be over to help, I've put all the food away and am in the process of dumping all the plates and cups I can find.

And maybe getting distracted every time Sarah squats down in that dress, her black high heels making her leg muscles look even more toned than usual.

She stands up, turns around, catches me staring, and gives me a sexy smile, lifting one eyebrow to let me know she's aware of the effect she has on me.

That fucking dress.

Christmas music is still playing in the background as we finish, and Sarah is leaning against the counter, sexily drinking from a bottle of water. Or maybe it's just that her head is tipped back and her gorgeous neck is on full display, and I can't stop myself from thinking about running my lips across her skin, then dragging it between my teeth.

Great, a boner is just what I need right now.

As a new song starts, Sarah stops drinking and listens, then she smiles. She walks over and turns up the music, mouthing the words.

I set down the cups in my hands and focus on her.

"I love this song," she says softly. "Mom and Gram would listen to Vanessa Williams's Christmas CD every year. Rae always loved *I'll Be Home for Christmas,* but my favorite is this one."

"You like *Baby It's Cold Outside,* huh?"

She nods. "I know some people think it's about a guy trying to coerce a girl, but it isn't. It's two people caught in a dance. She wants to stay, but is worried what people will think. He just wants to be with his girl. Certain versions of it you can hear the way they tease each other. And Gram explained that the phrase 'say what's in this drink?' was actually related to people thinking a drink wasn't strong enough. Of course, I always took it as the girl asking what kind of mixed drink it was."

I laugh a little. "Didn't realize it was so nuanced."

She shrugs.

"Come here." My voice comes out huskier than I intended, but I can't help it. She looks stunning in that dress, and it's been driving me nuts all night.

Her eyes lock on mine, a little wide, but filled with desire—like I am for her.

She strolls over to me and I take her hands, pulling her in to dance.

"I like this song, too," I breathe after a moment.

Her body is molded against mine, and I can't hide how fast my heart is beating, but neither can she.

Her breaths grow heavy as the song goes on.

"Joel," she breathes, looking up at me, heat pouring from her eyes.

I smash my lips against hers, claiming her mouth, wishing she was ready for me to claim her heart—all of her.

She moans against my mouth and I'm done.

With a growl, I pull away and grab her hand, leading her toward the stairs, but we don't make it far before we're kissing again. Stumbling backward up the stairs, not wanting to tear our lips apart.

By the time we make it upstairs, we're both panting.

We crash through my bedroom door and I shove it shut behind me, then spin her around and walk her backward until she's pressed against the wall.

She hooks one leg around mine and realization slams into me. We've been here before, and I remember how I felt after. It was more than I ever could've imagined it would be... until the next morning when I was left hurt. I don't want to feel that again.

Fuck my life. I can't believe I'm about to stop this.

I allow myself one last decadent kiss. Then I prop my hands on the wall on either side of her head and pull my lips away.

"Sarah, we need to stop."

Her eyes flash open, cutting right to my soul as she stares at me, a mixture of sadness and confusion in her eyes.

"What?"

I push off the wall and throw my head back, pinching the bridge of my nose as I try to find the right words.

When I look back at her, her eyes are glassy and she has her arms wrapped around herself.

"As much as I want you, I can't do this if we aren't together."

I'm not sure those were quite the right words, but they'll have to do.

Her arms drop to her sides, and she mashes her lips together. "Oh. I understand."

The hurt in her eyes could rip me to shreds.

Her gaze drifts downward as she shifts her body away from mine. "If you want me to start sleeping on the loveseat at the lake house—or with one of the other girls—"

I step to her and cup her cheek in my hand, then slide my fingers up, gently threading her hair.

"That's not what I want. I want you. Every piece of you. I want you in my arms every night, but I want your days, too. I want the smallest moments and all your fears. I want *everything* with you. I don't want to stop what we're doing, but I can't cross *this* line again until you're ready for everything, too. Does that make sense?"

She nods, her cheek brushing my palm as she does. Her eyes close and a few tears leak out, streaming down her face.

I rest my forehead against hers, wanting nothing more than to take her pain away.

"Please don't cry."

She flickers her eyes open. "I'm sorry I hurt you before. When we—"

I press my lips against hers in a soft, reassuring kiss.

"We're fine, babe. I promise. I love you."

I pull her tight to me and kiss her forehead. She nods against my chest, not saying the words I can feel radiating off her.

"Come on." I step back, grab some sweats from my dresser, then turn to her again.

Her cheeks are still streaked with tears, and as much as I want to kiss them away, that isn't the answer right now. She needs to know I'm not walking away from her. And I've learned well enough by now, that telling Sarah something helps, but showing her is how she believes it.

"Turn around," I whisper.

She looks uncertain for a moment, then does it.

I unzip that sinful dress—one I'll have to beg her to wear again some day in the future, when we *will* be taking things further.

Running my hands up her back, I massage her shoulders a few times, then glide my hands across her shoulders, pushing the sleeves down her arms. As the dress falls to the floor, I slip her bra straps off her shoulders, then lift her arms out of them. After that, I spin her back around and grab one of the shirts I got out. I carefully pull it over her head, and she puts her arms through the sleeves. Then I reach up the back, unhook her bra, and pull it off, dropping it on top of her dress.

She looks up at me, those cerulean eyes filled with adoration, tears now fading away, and a content smile on her face.

I scoop her into my arms, then carry her over to the bed and tuck her in.

Before I get changed into my T-shirt and sweats, I press my lips to her cheek, letting them linger for an extra moment before slowly lifting them away.

After quickly changing, I lie down next to her and pull her close. She nestles against me, her soft exhale letting me know how relaxed she feels. I hold her tight, hoping that with each passing day, she feels more certain of my dedication to her, to the future I see with her.

As she drifts off to sleep, the weight of her body growing heavy against mine, I also hope that with each day, she'll let her guard down more, until there's nothing left to hold back and she finally lets me all the way in.

Chapter Thirteen

Every Part

Sarah

I NEED TO WORK on saying no. Today was supposed to be my day off, but what did I do? I agreed to come in and work for a few hours this morning because someone else had an appointment. I love what I do, but I've got to find my off switch because I can feel myself starting to burn out, and it's supposed to be winter break. I haven't taken much of a break at all, which is why today is all about that. At least, from here on out. First, I'm headed to Rae's for some sister time, which we haven't had much of lately. Then the girls—minus Dani because she has to work—are coming over to hang out. I'm hoping that will be good for Hyla, too. Trevor told me she decided to come out to her parents. Supposedly she was going to do it at dinner with them last night—Trev was planning to go with her—but I don't know if it happened. I texted Hyla last night to ask how it went, but I didn't get an answer.

As I pull my car door open and sit down in the driver's seat, I dig my phone out of my bag and check my texts. Still nothing. I texted her a second time this morning as well. A flare of concern wells in my gut, but I take a deep breath and push it away. I'm a little worried Hyla wasn't ready to tell them—that she was doing it to prove something to herself. Opening my conversation with Trevor, I send him a text asking how it went. Not expecting an immediate response, I drop my phone on the passenger seat and settle in for the twenty-minute drive to Rae's.

I pull up to the curb beyond the bakery and flip my mirror down to make sure I don't look like complete trash. Not that my sister will care, but I'd rather not look like hell if I can avoid it.

My stomach growls as I put the mirror back up, and I decide to grab something from the bakery before heading up to Rae's apartment. Mackie's mom makes the best homemade bagels.

I grab all my stuff and swing my door open. As soon as I've closed it behind me, my phone rings. Digging it out of my bag again, that little flare of concern I had earlier grows into a fire.

Trevor.

Trev never calls me. Maybe once or twice since we dated. Sure, we text all the time, but phone calls? Not so much.

Pushing down the feeling in my stomach, I shove my phone to my ear.

"Hey, Trev."

What I hear makes the concern in my gut burn even hotter.

No words. Just sobbing. Ugly, gut-wrenching sobs.

"Trevor? What's going on?"

"Hyla..." he chokes out, and I get a very bad feeling about where this sentence is going. "Hyla tried to kill herself."

I brace my hand against the back of my car, trying to stabilize my shaking body.

"Wha—what? When? Where are you?" I gasp out.

"At the hospital. It happened early this morning. Last night—she came out to her parents—it went horribly. They said awful things. Basically disowned her. I stood up for her, got her out of there, then went home with her. I didn't want to leave her alone. I made sure she fell asleep first, but I woke up this morning to clattering in the bathroom. And I found her." His voice breaks again and tears stream down my cheeks. The pain she must have been feeling. And now Trevor has to deal with all of this.

"Trev is she..."

"Going to be okay? She's alive, and that's about all I know at this point." He chokes back a sob. "I had to call my mom and tell her. I called Chelsea. I don't want to say it again. Fuck," he sobs, "I don't want it to be real. Can you tell everyone else? Will you come?"

"Of course. You want me or everyone?"

"Everyone. I need you guys. Hyla needs you. Please." His voice cracks again.

Steeling myself, I take a deep breath and say, "Text me where. I'll handle everything else."

"Thank you."

"We'll be there soon. I love you, Trev."

"Yeah. I love you too. Bye."

"Bye," I whisper, then hang up. I lean against my car, staring at my phone and shaking. Then I realize what I agreed to. I have to tell everyone. *Shit. Mackie.*

I turn my phone screen on again and open my messages.

The way Joel handled my fears and pain at the Christmas party made me feel even more connected to him, and I'm trying to quiet the voice of fear deep inside me and let myself rely on him, let him in more. And right now, I need him. I want him by my side through whatever this is and whatever pain it brings out in me.

I type out a text, holding nothing back.

Me: I NEED YOU. Bakery.

Then I close my eyes and hold my phone to my chest while praying to any god who will listen that Hyla will be okay.

My stomach twists and I flash my eyes open as a memory hits of me standing alone in the bathroom crying, feeling like everything inside me was broken. *I can't go down that road right now.*

Out of the corner of my eye, I see movement on the other side of the street. A car passes, then Joel bolts across the road, stopping in front of me. He's in a T-shirt and jeans despite it being the middle of January.

"What's wrong, babe? You okay?"

I look up at him and want to shatter, but I've got to hold it together. I manage to tell him, and he pulls me into his arms.

"I'll text everyone to meet us at Rae's. Aaron should still be there. When we get upstairs, I'll call Nick," Joel says.

"Thank you. Just... thank you."

He pulls me tight to him and kisses my head. "Of course. Come on."

He leads me to the door and up the stairs, then guides me to Rae and Aaron's apartment. Rae swings the door open as we get to it.

"What's going on?" she asks with wild eyes. Aaron is standing behind her, looking concerned.

I nod toward the apartment, not wanting to say this in the hall. Rae steps out of the way and we walk in, my stomach churning. Mackie needs to know.

Even if things were complicated with them, if it were someone I love or loved, I'd want to know.

"Miles is on the way with Mackie," Joel says.

I nod. I'm not going to say it twice. Well, I guess I'll have to tell Amanda, but I can't—

"Hey, what's going on?" Mackie asks, walking into the apartment with Miles on her heels.

I walk to Mackie and take her hands as everyone moves closer, looking at me in uncertainty. After a breath, I force the words out, giving the essential information all at once.

There isn't much worse in life than having to give someone bad news. Watching Mackie's reaction tears at my heart.

Her hands drop from mine as her knees buckle and she screams and cries. Miles wraps his arms around her.

"Give me your keys," Aaron says to Joel. "I'll go get your Tahoe. Get everyone ready to go."

Joel nods and hands him the keys. "I need to call Nick, too."

"I'll call Amanda," Rae says, squeezing my hand.

Thank you, I mouth. Then I turn to Aaron. "I'll come with you." I'm stress sweating and in desperate need of fresh air.

"Sure," he says, grabbing his coat.

We walk downstairs, both a little shell-shocked. Maybe I shouldn't be. Maybe I should've seen signs. This isn't the first time Hyla has tried. I don't think anyone knows that besides me, Trevor, Greg, Jenny, Trevor's mom, and Hyla's parents. It was during senior year. Hyla was struggling with who she is and what she wanted—especially those things being at odds with her parents' wishes for her. She took a handful of sleeping pills. Thankfully, her parents were home and discovered her while she was still conscious. Of course, they handled it like shit, trying to act like nothing happened. Trev's mom took her and Trevor out of town for a few days to get Hyla away from the situation, then helped her get set up with therapy when they got back. I don't think she went for long before she decided she was better—and maybe she felt that way, but mental health ebbs and flows.

The last few times we were together, I noticed her drinking more than normal. I should've talked to her about it. She might've opened up to me.

As we hurry down my driveway and across the backyard, I notice Aaron's hands shaking.

"You okay? Actually, that's a really dumb question."

"Yeah, I—" He blows out a breath. "I don't know. Somehow, we made it this long without any of our friends—without this happening." He swallows hard. "Braden had his shit to work through. I struggled and so did Rae, but none of us ever... I don't know what to say. Or do. Or how to support Trevor or Hyla."

We stop in front of the Tahoe and I squeeze his hand. "You show up. Listen. That's all you can really do."

My stomach is in knots as we get in the car. *Rae never told him.* That truly shocks me. Not much has ever been left unsaid between them. Other than their feelings for each other. But the serious stuff. Aaron has always been the one she leaned on. The fact that she never told him?

"How do you know how to handle it?" he asks, backing the car out of Joel's driveway.

"Uh... well... Hyla tried once before."

His eyes widen.

"Seriously?"

"Yeah. Senior year. I was one of the few people Trevor told."

"Wow," Aaron breathes.

"Yeah," I mutter, trying to shake off the intensity of all this, but it's impossible. Not only am I worried about Hyla, but it brings my own mental health front and center. *It could be me.* I try to take care of my mental health, take care of myself, but... if I slip, I know where I could end up.

Stop thinking about that right now.

We pull up in front of the bakery, and everyone comes out the door leading to the apartments. I climb out and help Miles get Mackie—who is crying hysterically—into the back of the Tahoe. Rae climbs up front with Aaron, and Joel climbs in the back, sitting in one of the seats in the middle row.

"Nick and Amanda will both meet us there," he says as Miles and I sit down on either side of Mackie.

"I—I..." she blubbers.

"Macks," I whisper, wrapping an arm around her and kissing the side of her head.

"She called me last night. I didn't answer. I didn't—" She chokes on tears and my heart aches for her. "She's been off lately. I didn't know she was going to talk to them. But I'd have gone with her. I would have—I would've answered my phone!" she screams. "Maybe if I'd answered, she wouldn't have—"

"Mackie," I say sternly, "this is *not* your fault. Trevor was there with her all night. Even if you had answered, that's no guarantee it would've helped anything. Stuff like this isn't rational. It's pain and extreme mental health issues combining to create something so toxic that you think the world is better off without you in it. It's not on you. Hyla needs help. And hopefully she's going to get it now."

"I told her we couldn't be together if she wasn't honest with her parents. What if she was doing it for me—what if..." She trails off, crying so hard she can't speak.

I wrap my arms around her and hold her close, tears springing to my eyes.

"She knows you love her, Macks. She knows. It's not your fault. She's going to need you now."

She sniffs on tears. "I don't know... how to help her."

"Just be there," I whisper. "Just be there."

I look toward the front of the car and see Rae staring back at me. Our eyes meet and a silent understanding is exchanged. I'm so thankful I had her and my parents in my worst moments. Without a doubt, they saved my life.

By the time we get to the hospital, Mackie is calmer, though it's evident she's been crying. Hyla is on the mental health floor, thankfully, so we make our way up there. When the elevator doors open, Trevor is the first thing I see. I rush over to him and pull him into my arms.

He sniffs, but overall seems better than when he called me.

"How are you doing? How is she?"

He steps back and looks at me, then at the entire group. "She's alive." He sounds exhausted. "Safe to say today has been the worst day of my life. And yes, I'm including the day I crashed snowboarding. At least I was unconscious for most of that." He shakes his head. "Her parents. Thank fuck she's twenty-one and on her own insurance now so we don't have to call them. Because—they might not have caused it, but they are part of the reason she felt so fucking hopeless. I should've brought her to the mental health emergency unit last night. I knew she was in a bad place, but I thought if I stayed with her..." He clears his throat. "Woke up this morning to clattering and found her unconscious on the bathroom floor. She slit her wrists." His voice breaks and he forces back a sob.

A hand clamps down on Trevor's shoulder, and I realize Nick must've walked in at some point. I turn around and see Amanda is here as well and hugging Mackie.

"We're all here for you both. Whatever you need," Nick says.

"I know. I appreciate all of you."

Nausea is rampant in my stomach, and I feel a little dizzy. The pain, desperation, and hopelessness it takes to get to that place. The awful inner monologue that happens. *Fuck*. My hands are trembling, and I want to cry.

The elevator dings, then the doors open and Trevor freezes. Chelsea blows past everyone else and throws her arms around Trevor. He melts into her and starts crying again.

I take a few steps back and turn to Joel. He wraps his arms around me and I try to breathe deep, but my chest feels so tight it's nearly impossible.

I hate this.

We've been here for about an hour when Trevor walks back into the waiting area after seeing Hyla. He looks emotional, but less stressed when he drops into the chair between Chelsea and me.

"A year ago, I was in this hospital completely broken physically. Somehow that seems like a much easier thing to deal with." He sighs and rubs his hands down his face.

"How was she?" I ask, tightly holding Mackie's hand. She's next to me with Joel on her other side.

"Okay. You know the last time—"

"The last time?" Mackie asks, horrified.

Trevor and I exchange a glance.

"Fuck. I forgot the rest of you didn't know. Guess it doesn't really matter. She took sleeping pills during senior year after a particularly bad fight with her parents. It was October or November, I think. Either way, it was so different. And she barely had time to process what she'd done before her parents were there, judging her and treating her like shit. She had to stand strong and fight them immediately. After the fact, she told me she didn't really want to die, she just didn't care anymore. She needed the pain to stop."

I get that.

"This was different. She admitted that. She said that this morning, she believed most people didn't love her or want her and the few who did would be better off without her. I told her that was absolutely not fucking true because if I lost her, I'd never recover." He sniffs. "And it's true. It may not be biological, but she's been my sister for as long as I can remember. If she could have, my mom would've adopted her. Taken her away from all that bullshit. Whatever. She's clearly embarrassed and ashamed, and she said it was sobering—she knows how much she wants to live right now—even if she still feels a lot of negative things about herself and life. She asked them to admit her to the inpatient psych unit for a few days. She wants to be here. She wants to get better. I'm fucking thankful for that. And right now, she really needs our support." He looks at Mackie and me. "She specifically asked to see the two of you, if you're willing."

I turn to Mackie and grab her hand. "We can go in together if you want."

She looks at me, then slowly shakes her head. "I appreciate that, but I need a few more minutes to prepare myself. Will you go in first?"

I squeeze her hand. "Of course."

Even though my heart is pounding and I'm shaking, I push it all away. *This* is something I'm good at, staying calm in a crisis. It's a skill set I learned working in the medical field and training to be a nurse. I can break later. Right now, I'll be the calm, supportive one.

Letting go of Mackie's hand, I stand up and walk down the hallway toward Hyla's room.

I've been in this psych unit before. Three long—but necessary—days. I remember all the staff going in and out and Rae hanging out in my room, refusing to leave me unless our parents forced her to.

When I walk into her room, Hyla is looking out the window.

"Hey," I say softly.

She turns to me, and I can see a flash of disappointment in her eyes.

"Mackie's here. She'll be in after me," I say as I sit down, wanting to reassure her. I don't know if Trevor told her all of us are here.

Hyla nods slowly. "Thanks for coming in."

"Of course." I gently push a few tendrils of hair from her face and smile softly. "This might sound silly right now, but you look beautiful. Your hair is perfect," I say with a laugh.

"Well, that's one thing."

"You know you can tell me anything, right? We don't hold back from each other."

She sniffs. "I did something dumb, horrible, and hurtful. Now I have to live with it."

"Or," I say softly, "you were crumbling under the weight of severe mental health struggles and a whole lot of pain. No one is blaming you or judging you. We're here to support you."

She wipes a hand across her eyes. "I don't feel like I deserve that."

"I get that," I whisper, taking her hand. "But you do. You deserve all the love in the world. And if you could see that waiting room—well, I hope you'd feel all of that love. You're worthy of that."

She sniffs again and squeezes my hand back. "Thank you for being here. Can we... talk about something else now?" She looks down at her bandaged wrists. "For a little while, I really need a distraction."

"Deal."

I lean back in the chair, but keep hold of her hand, and start telling her any random, funny stories I can think of.

Joel

Mackie drops back into the chair next to me after pacing back and forth several times.

"I don't know how to do this," she says. "I don't know what to say. I'm upset and scared and angry. Then I feel guilty for feeling angry."

I glance across the room at Rae, who is leaning against Aaron with her eyes closed.

"You're allowed to feel however you feel, but do your best not to put that on her. Think about Rae. How she doesn't like to tell us when she's hurting because our reactions would be too much. When you're supporting Hyla, focus on being there for her. We can talk it through with you after. Go in there, let her talk, be there for her. I think that's really all you can do. I don't know for sure, but I guess that's what I'd do."

I watch as Sarah exits Hyla's room and leans against the wall.

It's what I do with her. Listen. Support. Make sure she feels safe.

Mackie exhales softly and nods. "I think I can do that."

"Good. Because it looks like it's your turn." I squeeze her leg and nod toward the hall where Sarah is standing.

"Okay." She nods again and stands up, taking a long, deep breath as she does. Then, with determination, she walks down the hall, stopping only to give Sarah a hug on the way.

As Mackie walks into Hyla's room, Sarah turns and walks down a different hallway. She's been strong all morning, even though I could see the pain deep in her eyes.

I stand up and walk in the direction she went, weaving down corridors until I end up in front of the hospital chapel.

Though none of us are much for religion, there's something about the solitude of a hospital chapel that's comforting, or at the very least, quiet.

Sarah is sitting alone in a pew, crying. I walk over and sit down next to her, wrapping my arm around her. She leans into me.

I softly kiss her temple. "I know it's scary, but Hyla is where she needs to be. And Liz is going to make sure she gets the help she needs."

"I know," Sarah sniffs. "That's not... that's not the only thing though..." She shakes her head.

"What do you mean?"

She looks at me, eyes red and puffy from crying. "You say you want me no matter what. Even if this is part of it?"

My eyes widen and my stomach lurches. Sarah's battled her fair share of mental health stuff, but I've never known her to be suicidal. Then again, we aren't like Aaron and Rae where we know every second of each other's histories.

"Why do you say that?"

"Because I've been where Hyla is."

"You've tried to—"

"Not right where she is, but where she was. When she did this. I... almost tried once. Had the bottle of pills in my hand."

Shock hits me. And then pain. I pull her closer. The mere thought that I could've lost her is enough to destroy me.

"What happened?" I whisper.

"I don't really know what happened or where it started. Obviously, Vanessa is a big trigger for me, but she had nothing to do with it. Not directly, at least. After the fact, my therapist said it was probably a combination of some past trauma hitting me and all the hormonal and brain chemistry changes your body goes through in your pre-teen and early teen years. Anyway, I was twelve. It was late August. I had picked a fight with Rae over nothing—something I hadn't done in years. Everything inside of me felt wrong. I don't remember what I fought with her about, but I remember yelling that I didn't want to be here anymore. She offered to go somewhere with me, something, anything. Then I screamed that I didn't want to be alive anymore, which surprised me a little when it came out. And it scared me. Until then, I hadn't been able to find words for any of the things I'd felt."

She stops and looks at me. The eerie calm in her voice as she tells this story makes it all the more unsettling.

"It's okay," I say softly, wanting her to know it's safe for her to say whatever she needs to.

She nods, takes a deep breath, and keeps going.

"I ran to the bathroom and slammed the door shut. Locked it. Then I grabbed some Tylenol from the medicine cabinet. I'd heard enough stories in middle school to know that taking a bunch was how to do it." *Jesus fucking Christ.* "I had the bottle in my hands. I flipped it open and closed several times, crying hysterically, thinking there was something wrong with me, that I didn't belong there. Like I didn't deserve my parents' love. I don't know what stopped me. It was like I saw some sort of flash of what would happen if I was gone, and I had the tiniest moment of clarity in it all. After another minute, I put the bottle back and went downstairs to my parents. I was still crying, and I broke down in my mom's arms, saying that I needed help. They obviously couldn't give me what I needed on their own, so they brought me to the mental health emergency unit here. I was here for a few days. I don't know if you remember when I was 'sick' in the hospital, but you guys weren't allowed to visit me."

My stomach churns. I remember. I remember being worried, but I had no understanding of what was truly happening. And Rae hid it fucking well. Even back then, she was a master at burying shit and saying she was fine. *Son of bitch.*

"I remember," I mutter, my heart feeling like it's in a vise. I hold her tighter, burying my face in her hair. "I'm so glad you're still here."

"Me too," she whispers. "Those few days in the hospital were hard, but they were necessary. Then I started going to therapy again, and it helped a lot. I got through it. But that day stayed with me, and for a long time after that, I'd think about what would've happened if I made a different choice. I actually said that to Rae years later, and she told me for the first time, that she had run downstairs and told Mom and Dad, and they were about to go up to the bathroom when they heard the door open and me coming down the stairs. Rae ran back up. She pretended not to know just so I could process it all how I needed to..." She chokes up as she says those words. "Besides my family, the only person I ever told was Trevor. Which is why he told me when Hyla tried the first time. She and I talked a lot about it all. They're the only ones that knew." She sniffs and wipes her eyes. "Telling you this..." She trails off, trying to hold back tears. "It's really hard for me. Part of me doesn't want you to know this piece of me. But I also know you have to. Because I can't promise I'll never feel that way again. If you really want to be with me... this is what you could be getting into. I'm a mess. I'm not easy to love."

Fuck that.

I lift my head off hers and palm her cheek, looking deep into her eyes. I need her to feel these words in her soul. To know I mean them with everything inside of me.

"I don't know why you think that, but it's not true. It's not a burden to love you. Loving you isn't hard. It's the easiest thing I've ever done. Maybe that's what you don't understand. I already love you. It doesn't matter if you choose to let me. I love you. Right now, just like this, I love you. Us being together isn't about me loving you or you loving me. It's about whether you're ready to trust in us, to trust that love to make it through whatever life brings our way. I already believe in that, Sarah. You have to believe in it, too. When you're ready, I'll be here. I don't care if it's messy or hard. I only care about us doing it together. Until you're ready, I'm going to be right next to you, showing you I mean it. I love you."

I pull her tight to me, holding her close as she cries. I don't need her to say anything else. I just need her to know I'm here, and I always will be. No matter what.

Sarah

I wasn't expecting to have a full-on meltdown in the chapel, but telling Joel all of that brought many complicated feelings to the surface. Yet, even in the midst of those murky feelings, I felt safe. I knew I could tell him anything. And after all these years, I'm glad I finally did. Being honest with him about the darker pieces of myself is part of moving forward. He's seen a glimpse, and I have to trust that as I reveal more, he'll continue to stand steadfast next to me. It's not easy for me, but he's never given me even the slightest reason to doubt that.

"I think I need some air," I say softly as we walk back toward the waiting room.

"There's a courtyard downstairs. It's freezing, but we can get some air," he says.

"Yeah. That sounds good. Let's grab our coats."

But as we get back to the waiting area, I see two familiar faces at the nearby desk.

"Give me a few minutes?" I ask Joel.

He nods, then kisses my cheek. "Text me when you're ready for me."

"Will do."

Rae shoots me a wink as I walk over to the nurses' station.

"What are you two doing here?" I ask.

Gram and Grandpa turn to face me.

"There's our other girl," Gram says, taking my hand.

"We brought some food for everyone. We've known Trevor's family a long time. As far as I'm concerned, Hyla is one of them. They all need some support right now, so we figured some food might help. There's plenty to go around."

"You guys are the best," I say, throwing my arms around them.

"Oh, honey," Gram says as I step back.

"Do you two have a few minutes? I was just going to get some fresh air. Want to join me?"

"Sure thing, girly. Lead the way."

We head for the elevator, taking it down to the first floor. When we get to the courtyard, we end up on a bench with me sandwiched between the two of them.

"How are you doing, honey?" Gram asks.

"Okay. This brings up some... painful memories."

"You made it through all right, though," Grandpa says.

"Yeah. I know. Thanks to you two, my parents, Rae. I wouldn't be here if I didn't have your love."

"Now don't make this old man cry, girly," Grandpa says.

Gram and I chuckle at that.

"I told Joel," I say softly. "I thought he should know... if he really wants to be with me."

"Do you doubt his feelings for you?" Grandma asks.

"No. Not really. I think I'll always have a gut reaction of not trusting whether someone will stick around long-term, but Joel has proven it over and over again. I know he's telling me the truth and I don't think he'd ever walk away from me."

"Then why are you holding back?" Grandpa asks. "Didn't learn your lesson from watching your sister?"

I laugh at that. "No. It's not that. I'm not hiding my heart. I'm protecting his. I want to be sure I'm ready to love him the way he deserves to be loved."

Grandpa's brow furrows, but Grandma speaks before he can. "Honey, no one is ever really ready. It doesn't work that way. Life is a constant ebb and flow, and with it, relationships change and evolve and grow. You're never truly ready because there's always a new learning curve—whether it's about yourself, your partner, or your relationship. The only thing you have to be ready for is commitment, and it seems to me you've already committed yourself to him—in some small way, at least."

Her words settle firmly in my gut. Have I been hiding behind the idea of readiness? Or perfection?

"What do you want, girly?"

"Huh?" I ask, looking at Grandpa.

"You either want to be with him or you don't. If you do, the only thing holding you back is yourself. If you don't, then you might as well let him go right now."

"I want him," I choke out, then look between them. "Of course, I want to be with him."

Grandpa wraps his arm around me and gently squeezes my shoulder. "Then stop holding back out of fear. Life's too short for all that. Don't waste your minutes. You never know how many you're going to get."

As the cold air seeps into my bones, so do Grandpa's words and their undeniable truth. Nothing is promised. Is this really the way I want things to be with Joel?

By the time I crash into my bed, I'm utterly exhausted. We spent most of the day at the hospital, and the final few hours of the evening together at Rae and Aaron's apartment.

I'm halfway to sleep when Joel sits down next to me and rubs my back.

"Sarah?" he whispers.

I roll onto my back and look up at him. His tone is serious, and his eyes are filled with emotion.

"Hmm?"

He sighs and lies down, settling on his side. His eyes scan my face, then he rolls on top of me and looks deep into my eyes.

"Thank you for being open with me today. It means everything to me," he says softly, tucking some hair behind my ear. "I know it's not easy for you to be vulnerable, but I appreciate it."

"Thank you for listening. Supporting me."

"You don't have to thank me for that. I'll be honest, it was hard to hear, mostly because the thought of losing you..." he trails off, blinking back tears. "That would destroy me, Sarah. So, I need to tell you something."

"Okay," I whisper, my chest feeling tight again as the fear that it's all too much for him hits me square in the gut. But then his gaze softens. He looks at me reverently, a whisper of a smile on this face.

"I love you. I will always love you. I will be the one holding your hand and cheering you on through the best things, and I'll be there to support you and hold you up through the hardest times and the darkest moments. No matter what those might be. If that means I need to learn more about a mental health condition I don't understand, then I'll do that. I'll do whatever I need to do. And I don't need you to say anything back right now. I just need you to hear it and know how much I love you, and that I will be there to walk every road with you, no matter how rough. I will love you through everything. I promise." He brushes his lips over mine and whispers again, "I promise."

Then he rolls onto his side and pulls me close to him.

The weight of the day washes over me. The memories of my past. Hyla. Joel's words. My grandparents' words. All of it. And then a surprising feeling in the center of it all.

My heart pounds as I lie against his chest, feeling his gentle inhale and exhale, and I realize there are no more excuses. I've been afraid of what I could give him, what I could commit to, but all he really wants is me. All he needs me to give him is my love. The only commitment he wants is for us to be honest with each other. Handle things together. Everything we've already been doing.

That's it.

I can't hold back anymore.

And for the first time, I don't want to.

Chapter Fourteen

Magic Dick

Joel

THE SMELL OF CHOCOLATE fills my nostrils. Blinking my eyes open, I focus on a steaming mug of hot cocoa on the bedside table, topped with a ridiculous amount of whipped cream. In front of the mug is a note.

Joel,
Happy Valentine's week. I hope you're ready to be spoiled. Most importantly, I hope you don't have any plans for Valentine's Day because I do. And you're the center of all of them. Enjoy the hot chocolate and any other special surprises that might come your way this week.
XO
Your secret admirer

My heart thunders in my chest as I hold the note to my nose and sniff Sarah's perfume. Last year, I planned something special for her. Something I think started all this. Seems like she wants to build on that this year. We both agreed our date this week would be on Valentine's Day, and I had some ideas, but it sounds like she wants to take the lead this year. I'm choosing not to read too much into that, though I will enjoy her spoiling me this week. Of course, I'm still going to spoil her too.

Climbing out of bed, I slide on my slippers and grab the hot cocoa before heading downstairs.

I find Sarah alone in the kitchen. She has a week off from clinicals and her classes are lighter this week as they are doing practice exams for the RN exam instead of typical lessons. Sarah has had an RN exam practice guide since freshman year, so she's been studying in chunks for months. I've been testing her, and she's been doing fantastic. It's good to see her feeling relaxed and confident about it. Sarah is cool under pressure, so I know she'll nail hers.

"Good morning," I say, strolling over to her.

She turns from the stove and looks at my hot cocoa.

"Where'd you get that?" she asks, one eyebrow cocked.

"This?" I shrug. "Secret admirer."

"A secret admirer. Should I be jealous?"

She pulls some hash browns off the heat and sets them to the side before flicking the burner off and looking back at me.

Setting my hot cocoa down, I wrap one arm around her waist.

"Very jealous. I hear she has plans for me on Valentine's Day."

"Oh really? Guess I'll have to fight her."

I shift closer, sweeping my other hand up the side of her neck and into her hair.

"Mm. Guess so."

I capture her lips in a fiery kiss. It's a little sloppy, but powerful, and riles me up in about two seconds.

Our bodies melt together as our tongues twist.

When I hear footsteps on the stairs, I try to pull away—we don't do this in front of other people—but to my surprise, she doesn't let me.

She fists the back of my shirt with both hands, keeping me close, not allowing my tongue to separate from hers despite the footsteps growing closer. For the first time it feels like *she* is claiming *me*. And I can't deny that I fucking love it. Except I'm about to start groaning and we don't need an audience for that.

A throat clears. I can tell by the deep resonance that it's Miles. Then there's a chuckle. *Aaron.*

Slowly, Sarah untangles her tongue from mine and our lips part. She looks up at me, starry-eyed, then smiles and pinches my butt.

What the hell?

She pops a kiss on my cheek and whispers, "See you later, sexy. I'll tell your secret admirer you said thanks for the hot chocolate. And the kisses." She winks at me and walks over to Rae, looping her elbow around Rae's.

"Ready to go, Rae baby?"

"Yes, ma'am. See you later, boys!"

Out of the corner of my eye, I see Rae give Aaron a kiss, then she and Sarah head out. I'm still standing slack-jawed that Sarah gave such a public display of affection.

I feel like a seventh grade girl standing here fawning and wondering what the hell it means.

Then I look down and feel like a seventh grade boy.

Shit.

I quickly turn and face the counter, my erection pressing into the cabinet underneath.

Though I'm trying to think of anything else, it's not working. All I can think about is her. Her lips on mine. How possessive she was.

Fuck.

I busy myself grabbing plates from the cabinet above me, then scooping hash browns onto them while wishing I were closer to the fridge, so I could grab an ice cube and stick it down my pants.

I'm pathetic. As usual.

A hand smacks my back, and I look over my shoulder to see Aaron.

"Okay over here?" he asks with a grin like he's never been the one hiding his boner.

"Fine," I say, but my voice cracks on the end of the word.

Miles laughs. "Dude, we can handle it if you have some," he clears his throat, "wood. We've all been there. Especially A."

I turn slightly and see Miles smirking at Aaron.

"No idea what you're talking about," Aaron says, attempting to keep a straight face, though his eyes are dancing.

"Really? You don't remember the morning after homecoming when I found you moaning like a porn star in Joel's basement?"

My eyes go wide and finally my dick relents.

"Seriously?" I ask with a laugh.

Though his cheeks are a little pink, he doesn't deny it, shrugging instead.

"I can't control the dirty dreams I have about my girl. I do remember you chucking that pillow at me, though."

Miles points a finger at Aaron. "You were a dumbass that morning."

Aaron shrugs, then glances down at his left hand before holding it up and wiggling his ring finger. "Worked out okay."

"Talking about hands... are you ready for today?" I ask, taking a drink of my hot cocoa, which is delicious, but I need to add some coffee to it.

Aaron inhales deeply, then nods.

Today is his first day attempting to pitch again since his surgery.

After getting his cast off, he started PT/OT focused on regaining regular movement and strength. It's been a massive improvement for him, and he doesn't have pain when writing or doing other daily tasks anymore. For the last few weeks, he's focused on restrengthening his arm and hand for pitching. It'll still take some time for him to get back to pitching as fast and accurately as he used to, but it's time for him to get a ball in his hand and start practicing again.

He nods slowly. "I am. A little nervous, but honestly, super excited. And grateful you guys will be there with me." He looks at Miles. "Glad your glove will be what I'm pitching to."

After the offer to join the team, Miles went to Coach's office and told him it was a yes, as long as it was permanent, because he wouldn't want to stop once he started playing with us again. Though Coach didn't show it outwardly, he was very excited about that.

Miles puts a hand on Aaron's shoulder. "Me too. Can't wait to see you pitching like an *ace* again." He winks at Aaron, takes a sip of his coffee, grabs a plate, and sits down at the kitchen counter.

"I'll take being able to make it over the plate for now," Aaron says. I hand him a plate of hash browns, then he opens the oven and pulls a tray of mini-quiches out. Off my raised eyebrows, he says, "Your girl was busy this morning."

He puts four on his plate, then walks over to the island and sits down next to Miles, sliding two onto his plate. They clink their coffee mugs together.

My girl?

Wouldn't that be fucking incredible?

I load up my plate, add some coffee to my hot cocoa, and join them at the island.

"I don't know if she's *my* girl."

Both Miles and Aaron stop with their forks midway to their mouths. But it's Trevor who says, "Dude, you're an idiot."

He smacks me on the back and walks past us into the kitchen, pouring himself some coffee and piling food onto a plate before coming back to the island. Instead of walking around to our side, he sets his plate down and stands across the island from us.

"We're not officially together," I argue weakly. Because we're not. Even if we sort of are and just don't admit to that.

"It looked official this morning," Aaron says.

"Yeah, and you and Rae looked official plenty of times before you actually were."

At that, he laughs. "Except you all told us over and over and *over* that we were, in fact, always in love and essentially always together, even when we didn't want to admit it to ourselves."

He clinks his mug against Trevor's as Miles chuckles.

"You know, I understand why you don't want to say you're together—why she doesn't—but that doesn't mean there isn't something special there. For the first time, it seems like she wants the world to know that. Revel in that shit. And the fact that you won't be a lonely son of a bitch on Valentine's Day like I will be," Miles says.

"You can't get a girl for Valentine's Day? Losing your touch?" Trev teases.

"No, asshole. I know what most girls expect from Valentine's Day—love. And that's not going to be what happens, so I'll happily enjoy some alone time and some takeout. With noise canceling headphones so I can't hear the rest of you getting laid."

Trev puts his hands up.

"I'll be at Chelsea's, thank you." He shakes his head. "Now, for a conversation that doesn't involve our dicks, what time are we meeting at the field today?"

Aaron lifts his head. "You're coming?"

"Of course. There's no way in hell I'm missing out on seeing you pitch again."

"Thanks, man."

"No thanks needed. This is family."

A moment of acknowledgment passes between the four of us. We've come a long way in the last few years, but our friendships have only grown. That's pretty fucking cool.

Sarah

I am in a ridiculously good mood. Kissing Joel this morning was a better high than any drug—or my personal vice, caffeine—could ever be. That and how excited I am for this week in general. I've been planning it for almost a month and I'm ready. Finally, I'm so fucking ready to make things official with him.

Ever since I had that realization, I've been holding that feeling in my heart, letting it grow, letting him a little deeper into my heart every day. And it has me in my feelings—naughty feelings, romantic feelings, all the feelings. Most surprising is how often I think the words, "I fucking love him." Which is *a lot.* He's on my mind constantly.

I'm so glad I did my practice exam this morning. Now, other than showing up for a few study groups to help other students prep, I'm free for the week. Free to focus on Joel. And I definitely have some surprises up my sleeve.

"Hey, baby," Rae says, sitting down next to me in the cafeteria. We've both been busy and our schedules haven't lined up much this school year. "I'm so glad we get to have lunch together today. All four of us." She smiles happily.

"Me too."

A few minutes later, Mackie and Amanda join us and we all end up chatting about our plans for the week.

"I'm glad you're going to spend some time with Hyla," I say to Mackie, who is going to spend Valentine's Day and then a long weekend back home with her.

"Anything romantic between us is way on the back burner. I just want to be there for her," Mackie says. "She needs me."

Rae reaches across the table and squeezes her hand. "I understand. I really do. When you care about someone and they need you, the other stuff fades away."

"Exactly. And Trev's mom is creating an epic girls' weekend for us."

"What exactly ended up happening with Hyla's parents?" Amanda asks. "I've been afraid to bring that up. Did they ever find out?"

I nod slowly. "Yeah. Liz called them eventually and told them. Then she told them she was done with them and they're horrible people and they weren't allowed to see Hyla anymore. Trev said Hyla blocked their numbers. Plus, she let her apartment go and is living with Liz now, and Liz has a fully fenced in property with a driveway gate that requires a passcode to enter. They aren't getting near her." I roll my eyes. "Her dad was upset, and it actually made Liz question her decision for a moment until she realized he was upset he couldn't use Hyla to make it look like he had a perfect family in his upcoming senate campaign."

Amanda blinks a couple of times. "You know, there's a word for people like that, but I'm enough of a lady that I'm not going to use it. But it starts with a c and ends with a t, so..."

"Yeah, no shit," Mackie says bitterly.

I know Mackie still harbors some guilt and pain over the way things happened with Hyla, but seeing how atrocious Hyla's parents have been and talking with her more about her headspace when she did that has helped a lot.

"Hey, ladies," Chelsea says, dropping into a chair at the end of the table.

"Hey! I thought you said you couldn't come," Rae says.

"My class ended early. Figured I'd stop by and see you guys for a few minutes."

"Before you go make out with Trevor?" I ask with a smirk.

She flushes slightly but laughs. I love seeing Trevor so happy. Chelsea is one hundred percent the right girl for him. After their first date, he showed up in my bedroom and in a conversation that was equal parts emotional and funny, thanked me for breaking up with him—for recognizing things weren't right and not holding on when I could have. Ultimately, we ended up on the right paths. With the right people.

And my mind turns to Joel again. Sweet, sexy, and possibly the most patient person I've ever known. I have so many glorious plans for spoiling him this week.

"What are you and Aaron doing for Valentine's Day?" Chelsea asks, and I realize I've completely zoned out of the conversation. Snapping back to it, I look at my sister, who is smiling coyly.

"A sweet date, a spicy night... you know. Obviously, we prioritize our relationship every day, so Valentine's Day is just an extra special day to celebrate our love. We don't go too crazy. Though we do exchange little notes throughout the week. We're doing things more simply this year. After paying for a wedding, we're a little strapped for cash. But honestly, you don't need cash for an incredible night. Just time together and music to drown out the moans." She takes a sip of her drink as the rest of us laugh. "How are your plans for Joel going?" she asks.

Of course, Rae was the first person I told about my plan for this week. He made everything special last year, and much like Aaron and Rae who didn't actually start dating on their anniversary, but crossed a small line and everything changed, I wanted to do the same. I wanted to honor where we started and how far we've come.

"I just started this morning, but kissing him in the kitchen felt so good. Not to mention the surprised look on his face when I turned away. I think the hardest part will be avoiding doing anything *too* sexual with him until I make it official."

Mackie smiles brightly. "You two are adorable. He doesn't have a clue, does he?"

I shake my head. "No. I don't think he does. A place where my ability to drag my feet has paid off because I can actually surprise him."

"I don't think you were dragging your feet. I thought you handled it well. You didn't jump in feeling uncertain. You waited until you were truly ready. That shows respect for yourself and for him. It also—oh my god!" Amanda shrieks and jumps up from her chair.

I spin around and see Jamie walking toward her with a bouquet of white and red roses in his hand.

I turn to my sister, who is not the least bit surprised.

"Did you have something to do with that?" I ask.

"Sort of. He was planning on coming up on Valentine's Day, but I told him Aaron was going to try pitching some today because I thought he might want to be here. Win-win."

"You're a good wife," I say, bumping my arm against hers.

She chuckles and leans toward me. "And you're an amazing girlfriend, whether or not it's official yet." She wipes her mouth, then takes a drink of water and says, "I gotta go. I'll see you ladies later."

She kisses my cheek as she stands up.

"Bye, Rae baby. Have fun at work."

"I should get going, too. I'm going to kiss Trevor's face off till I have to go. See you there, Rae," Chelsea says.

"Bye," Rae calls, waving as she goes.

Chelsea waves as she leaves.

"Yeah, I should head to class. I need caffeine first. I'll see you at home," Mackie says. Then she glances at Amanda and Jamie, who are full-on making out in the middle of the cafeteria. "Guess I'll leave them to it."

"Probably for the best. Later, Macks."

I pull my phone out of my bag and click on my messages. I don't have to scroll to see Joel's name. A little flutter hits my stomach as I click the edit contact info and change his name to *Boyfriend* with a ridiculously cheesy little heart next to it.

As I'm returning to our conversation, the little bubbles next to his name pop up and I wait with anticipation for his text.

I'd forgotten what this was like. Getting caught up in falling for someone—even if I already fell—it's the whirlwind of romance.

Boyfriend: Hey, whatcha doing? Want to grab some coffee?

Me: Definitely. I'll meet you there.

Boyfriend: Where are you?

Me: The Whitman dorm dining hall.

Boyfriend: I'll walk with you. Meet me downstairs in 5.

Me: Okay, see you then.

With a fluttering heart, I throw my stuff away, make my way past Amanda and Jamie, and head downstairs to meet up with Joel.

I thought not getting too *dirty* with him this week would be the hard part. Now I realize the hardest part will be not blurting out how much I love him before our date.

I'm so damn ready for it to be Valentine's Day.

Joel

Aaron is doing some last stretches by home plate before taking the mound. I can sense his nerves, but I know once he throws a few balls, he'll ease back into it.

Trevor strolls out onto the field. "You ready to do this?"

Aaron inhales deeply. "Yeah, I think so."

"You got this, A," Miles says, clapping a hand on his shoulder. "I agree."

Aaron spins around in shock as Jamie strolls over from the dugout.

"What are you doing here?" Aaron asks.

Jamie smiles brightly. "Rae told me you were planning on pitching again today. No way in hell I was going to miss that."

He extends his fist and Aaron bumps it.

"Come on," Jamie says, slipping on his glove. "Let's warm up that arm."

They throw the ball back and forth a bit, Aaron getting used to the feel of throwing again. Every few throws, Jamie moves back several steps and they continue.

"Okay," Aaron says, holding up his gloved hand with the ball in it. Then he drops the ball into his right hand and quickly spins, whipping it at Miles, who, of course, catches it like it's nothing. "I'm ready."

Jamie, Trevor, and I stand along the first base line as Miles gets in position. He throws the ball back to Aaron, who shakes out his neck and arms, settling into his stance on the mound.

"Hey," Jamie calls.

Aaron glances at him. "Yeah?"

"Don't try to throw the way you used to. Find what feels good now and lean into it."

Aaron cracks a smile. "That's good advice. When did you become the coach?"

"Oh, I'm not. But I had a damn good one." Jamie gives a little nod, and Aaron faces Miles again.

After a long moment, Aaron takes a deep breath, and with his usual perfect form, throws the ball.

It lands a little low, but some umps would probably still call it a strike.

Trev and I both whistle as Jamie claps.

"Keep your pants on," Aaron yells. "It was only the first pitch."

And his words ring true as he repeats it, making the smallest adjustment—one I can't even see, but I know him well enough to know he made—and nails it.

Though not every pitch lands perfectly, he takes his time, enjoying each throw and getting into the feel of it all again. I've always loved watching him pitch. It's like a masterclass. But the best part is seeing the smile on my best friend's face, getting to see something he's always loved come back to him.

When Miles says he needs a little break, I jog over to the mound.

"You're killing it."

"I don't know about that."

"I do. And you know how long you've been throwing for?"

He shrugs.

"An hour. Do you have any pain?"

His eyes widen and he looks down at his hand. "I've had a few small twinges here and there, but no. No stiffness, either. Fuck," he breathes out, emotion filling his eyes. "I can't believe this is really happening. That I get to do this again."

I squeeze his shoulder as I look at him. "I can. And you deserve it. Now, what do you say to closing out this pitching practice with some flair?"

He laughs, knowing exactly what I'm thinking.

"Fuck yes."

I give him a nod, then head back over to where Jamie and Trevor are standing. With Miles back in position, Aaron throws a few more pitches, then reaches up and slightly adjusts his cap. With the hint of a smirk on his face, he takes his position again, and then, like the pro he's always fucking been, pitches an utterly perfect screwball.

Miles catches it, stands up, and jogs up to him as Jamie, Trevor, and I walk over to the mound.

"Looks like Aaron freaking Cooper is back," Jamie says with a laugh.

Aaron rolls his eyes but smiles. "I've got a lot of practicing and fine tuning to do, but it feels good." He looks down at his hand. "It feels really damn good."

❤

When we get back to the house, we're all still talking about how pitching went. As soon as the door closes behind us, Rae appears at the top of the stairs. She locks eyes with Aaron, who smiles. Then she runs down the stairs and across the room, stopping in front of him.

"How'd it go?" she asks, voice thick with emotion.

"I pitched for an hour. Hardly any pain. No stiffness. And I threw a screwball."

Rae jumps into his arms. "I'm so proud of you." She sniffles as she wraps her legs around his waist and holds him tightly. She kisses him a few times, then buries her head in his shoulder as she cries. "After everything..." she mumbles.

"I know," he sniffs. "Thank you for supporting me through it all."

She lifts her head and looks into his eyes. "I love you, Ace."

"I love you too, Beautiful."

Then they kiss again, and the cute moment turns gross. Luckily, my phone lights up with a text.

Sarah: Come upstairs.

Rather than waste time responding, I haul ass up the stairs and swing open the door to the master. I stop in my tracks when I see candles lit and rose petals on the floor leading to the bathroom. After locking the door, I toe off my shoes and slip off my coat, then head for the bathroom.

When I step inside, I see a bath drawn, rose petals floating on top, and Sarah standing there in a silk robe, looking like a fantasy come to life.

Sarah

His widened eyes and cheeky grin are *everything*.

"Hi," I say softly.

"Hi." He walks over and looks down at me, draping his hands on my waist. "What's all this?"

I shrug. "Dunno. Your secret admirer just left. I guess she must have set that all up."

"Oh really?" He playfully looks around me, glancing at the window, then smiles. "Too bad. I guess that means we'll have to use it."

"I guess so." I wrap my arms around his neck.

Leaning down, he kisses me softly, then pulls on the tie of my robe, undoing it. He pushes the fabric off my shoulders, letting it fall in a heap on the floor.

My stomach tightens and my core clenches as I try to control the intense desire I feel for him.

He drags a finger across my collarbone, eliciting a sharp inhale from me. A laugh bubbles in his throat and he smirks at me, my response urging him to continue.

That finger trails down my chest, between my breasts, then he kisses me again as he wraps one hand around each of my breasts, palming them, squeezing them, and then teasing my nipples with his thumbs. I gasp as he leans into me, letting me feel how badly he wants me.

My breaths grow heavier as he wraps one arm around my back while letting his finger continue its journey. Down my stomach, to my pelvis, and then...

"Joel," I breathe as that finger drops between my legs, lightly swirling, exploring, before darting inside me for a moment. My knees nearly buckle as he pumps it in and out several times before pulling it out and dragging it back to a certain swollen spot.

I knew I wanted to do something special with him tonight, but I was not expecting *this*. And as much as I'm enjoying it, I want to take it slower.

I press my hands against his chest, and he pulls his finger away, leaving me longing for more—though I push past it and focus on the defined pecs under my palms. Gliding my hands down his stomach, I slip my hands under his shirt and push it up, enjoying the heat of his skin against mine. Finally, I pull it off him and drop it on the floor with my robe, then tease him the way he teased me, slowly gliding one finger along the top of his waistband. His abs tighten and his breath hitches, and it takes everything inside me to keep from dropping to my knees as I think about our date a year ago, and how incredible it felt to own his body like that.

I close my eyes for just a second and reorient myself, then continue undressing him. When he's down to those sinfully tight boxer briefs, I carefully slide them off, trying not to look directly at the hard muscle that breaks free. I'm scared it might put some kind of spell on me and I'll forget what I'm doing—trying to go slow—and get a little wild.

Jesus Sarah, that gives a whole new meaning to the idea of magic dick.

"Come here." I take Joel's hand while silently telling my brain to shut up and lead him to the tub.

He climbs in first, then offers me his hand.

I climb in too, but rather than settle against the opposite side of the tub from him, I turn around and sit down, letting my back rest against his chest.

His sharp inhale fans the flames of desire inside me, but I take a calming breath. I'm going to enjoy every second of this.

"How was your day?" he asks softly, massaging my scalp with his fingers and twisting them through my hair.

"Good. Relaxed. I wish I could have more days like this. It was nice having lunch with the girls. Seeing Amanda's face light up when she saw Jamie. I'm proud of how hard I've worked, especially over the last year as my classes and clinicals really ramped up, but I've missed this stuff. I've missed seeing you on campus, too."

He kisses my neck and I think I black out for a second. I feel like I'm going to spontaneously combust being this close to him, but if I move away, I'm afraid I won't be able to breathe anymore.

"I'm glad we have our coffee dates. And our weekly dates. Any idea what my secret admirer might be planning for Valentine's Day?"

I smile at that. "Oh, she has many plans, but you'll have to wait to find out about them."

"Really?" he rumbles in my ear. "I can't convince you to share... anything?"

He rolls my nipple between his thumb and forefinger, and I'm a breath away from coming undone. Going insane. Throwing myself at him and begging him to fuck me on the floor, love me forever, marry me, build me a house, make babies with me. *Oh my god.*

The moan that falls from my mouth is loud and unladylike, but I cannot hold back another second.

Whimpering, I spin around and straddle him, letting my wet center glide across his hard muscle and pushing the line between having sex and not. If I leaned back and he tilted his hips up, he'd be inside me, but I won't go that far. I may be ready to give him everything, but I'm not crossing that line until I officially tell him. Instead, we grind against each other, letting the friction take us to incredible highs before floating slowly down again.

I let the weight of my body rest against him as our chests heave and hearts pound.

He fists my hair and looks deep into my eyes. "Sarah—"

I kiss him intensely, letting my lips do the talking, showing him exactly how much he means to me. Then, as I pull away, I whisper the words I've only said out loud to him a handful of times.

"I love you, Joel."

He searches my face like he's looking for clues. Trying to understand what changed in the last few weeks. But the answer isn't concrete. It's nothing, and it's everything.

"I love you too," he whispers back, quickly kissing my lips, then my nose.

I spin back around, nestling against him again, and we soak in the tub, chatting, until the water gets cold and we're both shivering.

Once we're out of the tub and dried off, we put on comfy clothes and eat leftovers in bed while watching a movie. As I snuggle against him, my heartbeat ticks up yet again. I'm so freaking lucky he's been so steadfast, had so much faith in me and our future. I hope I'll do a good enough job of returning that.

Chapter Fifteen

Ready to be Mine

Joel

"Stop primping, you look fine," Miles says.

"Primping? Who says that?" Aaron asks, then looks at me. "But he's right. You look fine."

I drop my hands and step away from the mirror. The mussed hair look is harder to achieve than girls think. Because it has to be sexily mussed. Not I-just-rolled-out-of-bed-and-one-side-of-my-hair-is-sticking-up mussed.

"I want to look better than fine," I say, glancing at the mirror again and adjusting the unbuttoned collar of my white long sleeve button down with the sleeves loosely rolled up to my elbows. I'm wearing it untucked with medium wash jeans and black lace-up boots. Sarah said our date won't be quite as upscale as last year, but I still want to look good for her.

Aaron smacks my arm, and I turn to look at him. "You look great. I promise."

I nod. "Thanks."

He gestures to himself and I roll my eyes, robotically saying, "You look good, too."

Even though he does. Aaron is a master of the sweater and jeans combo, and of course, he ran his hands through his hair twice and ended up with that perfectly-mussed look. *Jackass.*

Why do I keep saying mussed?

It's possible I'm a little nervous. After how Sarah has been acting this week—like we're a couple—and all the sweet things she's done to spoil me from coffee to love notes to making me breakfast every day, it's hard to know what to expect tonight. If I've learned anything, it's to level set my expectations with her, so I don't end up bummed out, but I have no idea where to set those levels tonight.

"Dude, you need to chill and enjoy this night with your girl," Miles says.

With a deep breath, I nod and grab the chocolates I bought.

"Ready, A?"

"Let's go get our girls."

"Enjoy your night. If you need me, text me. I will have noise canceling headphones on *all night.*"

"We're going to be gone for a while, you know that, right?" Aaron says.

"I don't trust any of you to be able to keep your hands off each other very long," Miles says with a smirk. "Seriously, have a great night."

"Thanks, man," I say, and Aaron and I head upstairs to the master, where Rae and Sarah are getting ready. Mackie left this afternoon to go back to Ida, Trevor is staying at Chelsea's tonight, and Amanda and Jamie left earlier this evening to get their date started.

I knock on the master bedroom door, and it swings open almost immediately. Rae appears in the doorway first, looking beautiful in a dark gray sweater dress and knee-high boots. "Hey, Joelskies. Hi, Ace." They eye-fuck each other for a second before Aaron hands her a bouquet, then kisses her.

"Ready to go, Beautiful?"

"Definitely."

She turns and I finally get a glimpse of Sarah wearing *that* red dress. The one she wore to the Christmas party. The one I told her I wanted to take off her—which I did, just not the way either of us hoped.

She smiles brightly when her blue eyes land on me.

Rae and Sarah share a quick kiss on the cheek, then Sarah whispers something to Rae that makes her giggle.

"Bye, baby," Rae calls to Sarah. Then she winks at me and pats my chest. "You look good, Joelskies. Have fun!"

She loops her arm through Aaron's and they walk downstairs.

Finally, I turn and get a good look at Sarah. The red shimmery dress paired with suede black booties. Her hair is straightened, and she has on bright red lipstick and smokey eye makeup.

"You look fucking incredible," I say. "Radiant. Gorgeous. Damn."

She laughs lightly and grabs her clutch. "Thank you." She tugs on the collar of my shirt, then kisses my cheek. "You look very handsome. Good thing you're wearing an undershirt or I'd be able to see your abs through that shirt." She pokes my stomach. "Although maybe that wouldn't be a bad thing."

Her eyes dance, and I want to pull her into my arms and kiss her like the lovesick idiot I feel like, but since we're just getting this date started, I hold out the chocolates I got for her.

"Since I've been doing flowers for our other dates, I thought I'd mix it up."

She takes the heart-shaped box and looks at it.

"All dark chocolate. You know me well."

"Yes, I do," I say huskily. Too huskily. Jesus, we'll never make it to the car at this rate.

She smirks at me as she sets the chocolates on the dresser and steps out of the room.

"Good thing I get to surprise you with our date, then. I guess I should tell you our first stop, though."

"Since I'm driving, that might be best."

She closes the door behind her and takes my outstretched elbow, and we walk down the stairs.

"First stop is Well Read bookstore downtown. They're having a special blind date with a book sale." We stop at the front door and I help her slide her coat on before putting mine on as well, then I open the front door for her. "They wrap books from every genre in plain brown paper and put a few facts about each of them on the front. We like to read different things, but I thought it would be fun to pick out a book for each other based on what we know the other likes."

I pause at her car—we often drive that one on dates because it's easier to park her little sedan downtown than my Tahoe—and take her hand.

"That sounds perfect." Leaning down, I gently press my lips into hers, not allowing either of us enough time to deepen the kiss. Just a simple kiss to let her know how happy she makes me.

She smiles as I pull away and open her door.

"Good. Let's go, then."

The blind date with a book idea is brilliant, and I had fun going through the shelves of women's fiction, romance, and memoirs looking for the right thing for her.

I decided on a memoir about a woman in the public eye that was described as raw, honest, real, and relatable. I know how much Sarah loves reading things that connect with her and make her feel things. She's had a bunch of memoirs on her to read list, so maybe this will check one off.

Knowing I'm a history buff, she got me a nonfiction book about a soldier from World War II. I've been wanting to read more about World War II, so I'm excited to dig in, though we agreed we'd wait to unwrap them until this weekend, then we'd snuggle in bed with some hot cocoa and read.

"So, where to next?" I ask, as we exit the bookstore.

"We're headed to the art gallery a couple of blocks down." She wraps an arm around mine and we walk through the chilly February air, Sarah happily pointing out the white lights and red hearts along the street as we go.

The art gallery is hosting a flower and lights show with massive floral displays and coordinating colored lights featuring different shapes and patterns.

The floral arrangements are stunning and I can't imagine the work that goes into creating them, but paired with the lights, they create a romantic atmosphere. Perfect for Valentine's Day, especially since Sarah has had her hands on me the entire time.

At the end of the exhibit there is champagne, hors d'oeuvres, and chocolate-covered strawberries.

"Do you want anything?" I ask her.

She smirks. "Nope. We're on to our third part of the date now. Sizzling Dip."

My eyes widen. "Seriously? You got reservations there for Valentine's Day?"

A mischievous smile crosses her lips. "I called the first week they opened."

"That was in November," I say softly, realizing how long she's been thinking about this. That her promise of wanting more with me has never waned.

She shrugs. "I knew we'd want to do something special today. Just keeping with the tradition you started last year."

"You're incredible," I whisper, giving her a soft kiss.

"I do what I can," she says with a little shimmy of her shoulders. *Fuck, she's adorable.* She clasps my hand tightly in hers. "Let's go."

Sizzling Dip is a fondue restaurant. The first one of its kind anywhere within a three-hour radius. Which means it's been booked solid for months before they ever opened. That Sarah was planning ahead and got these reservations for us that long ago means everything to me.

The atmosphere is relaxed but still slightly upscale, with low lighting and small, cozy booths. I love it because it means I get to sit next to her. As I look around, I notice some signature phrases on the wall: *Dip It Low, Stick It In, Dip Baby Dip.*

"You know, this place is kinda naughty."

Sarah giggles, "I know. I love it."

I love you.

I don't say it. Again with those expectations. I let the words fall away, focusing on her gorgeous face, her pink cheeks highlighted by the low lights.

A waitress stops by and takes our drink orders, then confirms our choices. Apparently, it's a four-course meal, starting with salad, then moving on to cheese fondue—Sarah selected a garlic beer cheese for that. Next is a broth-based pot for cooking meat in. For that, Sarah selected a French-style featuring wine, scallions, and mushrooms as well. The final course is the chocolate. Sarah picked classic dark chocolate with cookies, marshmallows, and strawberries.

It all sounds delicious and the smell of the place is making my mouth water.

Once the waitress leaves, I decide it's time to give her the present I picked out. She's been planning this date since November, and I've had her present since the beginning of December. I thought about giving it to her for Christmas, but it seemed like a more appropriate Valentine's Day gift.

I take one of her hands in mine while pulling the velvet box from my interior coat pocket.

Her eyes flare when I set it in front of her. "Joel... we didn't talk about doing presents. I didn't get you anything."

I tuck a strand of hair behind her ear, wishing I could make her understand. Being here with her is all I need.

"Babe, you planned this whole night. That's more than enough of a present for me. Open it."

"Okay." Now I get her giddy smile.

She slowly flips the top open, and her mouth drops. "Oh. Oh my god. Joel... this is. Wow. It's beautiful. I can't believe—is that a real diamond?"

I chuckle at that and take the box, carefully lifting the heart-cut diamond pendant out and unclasping it.

"Yes."

I fasten it on her neck and she gently touches it before looking up at me with shimmering eyes.

"You're crazy. It must have cost a fortune."

"It wasn't that much," I insist.

"It's at least two carats!"

"A little over."

"How much did you spend?!"

"I'm not telling you." I kiss her nose and smile. She doesn't need to know I spent almost five thousand dollars on it. But what the hell is the point of being loaded if you can't spoil your girl with it occasionally? "All that matters is that you're worth it."

She continues staring at me in disbelief, then shakes her head. "Well, thank you. It's stunning. I love it."

I love you, I think again. But rather than say it, I softly kiss her lips, keeping mine pressed against hers until we're interrupted by the arrival of our salads.

I have no idea what the rest of the night will bring, but so far, everything has been perfect. As long as I'm with her, nothing else matters.

Sarah

I may have planned our date, but it was even better than I imagined it would be.

The necklace he bought me is stunning, and I was beyond shocked when I opened it. *A real diamond?* I hope what I'm about to give him is enough.

Joel opens the car door for me and offers his hand as I step out. My heart is beating obnoxiously as we approach the house.

It's almost time.

When we get inside, we take off our coats and shoes, then his eyes go to the stairs. I smile softly at him. I'm ready to be completely alone with him.

Surprisingly—or maybe not—the living area is empty. Everyone is probably busy with their own dates. Hand in hand, we walk up the stairs, taking the first left into the master bedroom.

As Joel swings the door open, excitement and anticipation overtake me. I'm ready. I'm so freaking ready for this.

I also wish I wasn't stress sweating. This is a good thing, but for some reason, my body is taking the tension surrounding me and responding with anxiety and fight or flight.

Joel takes my other hand, standing face to face with me, then slowly, he kisses me. The pressure is soft, his lips lightly brush mine as his fingers dig into my waist, pulling me closer. My body melts under his touch, and it takes everything inside me to stop myself from completely giving in, but I manage to retain some semblance of rationality.

"Joel," I say, lifting my lips off his.

"Hm?"

"I have something for you. A present."

His eyebrows lift and he takes a half a step back. "I thought you planning our date was my present."

"It was part of it. This is everything." I turn to my dresser, open the top drawer, and dig out a small white box with a red bow, then hand it to him.

He takes it from me and looks at it for a moment, then lifts the top off and looks down at the small, shiny, golden skeleton key.

"A key?" he asks.

My heart is slamming into my ribs so hard I'm positive it's going to bruise them, but I push past the feeling because I've been waiting for this moment and so has he. I'm ready now, and it's time to tell him exactly what he means to me and what I want more than anything.

Taking his free hand, I say, "I thought you needed the physical embodiment of something you already have." He tilts his head, looks down at the key, then back at me. "You've opened all of my locks, Joel. You have the key to every one, not to mention my heart and soul. You've been patient with me as I tried to figure out what I wanted and needed. Before Christmas, you told me I was what you wanted. Sorry, your present is a little late, but I'm ready to give it to you now. I'm ready for everything. I want to be the one who stands beside you in hard moments, the person whose hand you reach for, the one who takes care of you. I want your darkest thoughts and roughest moments. I want your sick days and early mornings, your middle of the nights and quiet moments. Most of all, I want you." I take the box from his hand and set it on the dresser, then wrap my hand around his. "I want us. If you're ready to be mine."

The moment his face goes from shock to pure happiness will be burned into my memory for the rest of my life. A smile blooms that could light the heavens. Then his eyes darken and that smile morphs into a devastatingly hot smolder. He steps in closer and slides a hand up the side of my neck, fingers twisting through my hair.

"Fuck yes," he mutters before slamming his lips into mine. "Fuck. Yes. I'm yours. You're mine. All fucking mine."

He grabs the back of my neck possessively, holding me in place as he claims my mouth again, pushing my lips apart with his tongue, letting it own me in every single way. I melt into him, my fingers winding through his hair as our tongues dance, letting out every ounce of pent-up tension and desire, begging for more with each stroke.

He pulls away suddenly and looks at me. "I love you, Sarah."

I smile as I finally get to say it. "I love you too, Joel."

His lips drop to my neck, his kisses now gentle. "I'm going to show you how loved, cherished, and adored you are. All night long." He traces the neckline of my dress. "Turn around," he breathes.

Trembling from the heat of his gaze, I slowly spin around.

His fingers dance over the zipper of the dress.

"Did you wear this for a reason?"

My breath hitches. He can see right through me.

"Maybe," I tease. "I recall you saying something about wanting to take it off me."

He undoes the zipper in one fluid motion. "That's exactly what I want."

Like he did on Christmas, he slides his hands over my shoulders, pushing the sleeves down, but this time his lips drop to the nape of my neck before kissing across my back, each kiss searing my skin and turning me on more than the moment before.

"Joel..." I moan.

"What babe? What do you need?"

I spin back to face him, letting the dress fall to the floor.

"You," I breathe. "Us."

I gasp as he swiftly lifts me up and lays me on the bed. He smiles hungrily, staring at my naked chest—I didn't wear a bra with the dress this time. Then he strips off his shirts and drops his pants to the ground before lying over the top of me in nothing but his boxer briefs.

His fingers twist through my hair as he looks deeply into my eyes. Though he doesn't say it again, I feel the words *I love you* radiating through my body, down to my toes, slamming into my heart, piercing my soul.

"You know this is it, right? Done deal. I'm never letting you go."

I bite my lip. He means it. I know he does. Still, I don't quite feel comfortable making the same sweeping and grandiose promise yet, so I simply say, "I know."

"Good."

He kisses down my chest, my navel, to my pelvis, then yanks my underwear off and dives between my legs.

Oh my god.

Shit.

Oh, it feels so good.

I whisper his name as his tongue owns me, showing me he meant every word he said tonight. I'm his. He's also showing *exactly* how well he knows me.

From the very first time I tried it, oral sex has been my favorite. Maybe it's because I need clitoral stimulation to fully enjoy myself. I don't know, but nothing fires me up as much as this.

He wraps his hands around my thighs as I roll my hips, matching the stroke of his tongue, feeling the intense pleasure more with each movement.

My fingertips dig into his scalp as he quickens his pace, focusing on the one spot—the one I *need* his tongue on.

"Yes," I breathe.

He tilts his head back, flicking me with the tip of his tongue, and it sends me flying over the edge. Every muscle tightens as I scream and moan before my body goes slack, blood pounding through me as I gasp for air. My hands slide off his head and onto the bed, but despite the incredible high he just gave me, he doesn't stop.

My legs are trembling as they clench around his head.

He still doesn't stop.

His tongue keeps swirling over me again, and again, and again. Until...

My stomach tightens and I fist the sheets, crying out his name.

He has his cockiest smile on as he slides up my body, effortlessly removing his boxer briefs and lining himself up between my legs.

"Still on birth control?" he asks.

"Yes," I manage to say.

The word has barely crossed my lips when he's deep inside me.

Round two of him knowing exactly what I like.

Slow, sensual sex can be nice, but I like going slow and sensual first—like he did—then going hard. Maybe even a little rough. Like pull my hair while you're—

"Fuck, Sarah," he groans, thrusting into me again.

He wraps one hand around the back of my neck, his fingers threading and tugging my hair as his thumb rests along my jawline.

I graze my fingers along his shoulders, then drag them down his back, digging my nails in as he moves faster, his sleek, muscular body rolling over mine.

His eyes glaze over as his breaths grow heavy.

Then he lets out a deep moan, turning me on more as I tighten around him.

Again, I drag my nails down his back, but only with one hand. With the other, I squeeze his ass. And his eyes slip closed. His movements grow choppy and then he shudders, moaning loudly through his release.

He drops on top of me, kissing my neck as he tries to catch his breath.

"That was incredible," he breathes.

"More than incredible." Our mouths meet in a sloppy kiss, but I quickly move to his cheek, then his neck. My kisses grow softer as I work my way over his body, kissing every inch, needing him to know how much I adore him. And that I'm not done with him yet.

I came twice. Now it's his turn.

By the time I've kissed him from head to toe, that muscle is hard and ready for me.

Do I have to cash in my feminism card if I admit I've dreamed of giving him another blow job? There's something ridiculously sexy about being in full control, making him moan, making him—

"Sarah," he groans, as I tease his tip. Then I take him deep and revel in the gasping noises I hear. With one hand, I gently caress his balls.

He lets me take the lead, enjoying every swirl of my tongue, until he sits up slightly, grabs my hips, and yanks them around toward him, guiding my thighs until I'm right where he wants me—in a sixty-nine position. His head dips between my legs again.

Holy shit.

I try to keep some control and focus on him again, but it's not easy. Right now, I don't think either of us is in control. We're just enjoying the moment, taking what the other gives until we're both spent.

After cleaning up, we end up naked in bed, bodies tangled together, hearts still pounding—not from the sex anymore, but the excitement of it all.

He gently grazes his fingers down my arm as I snuggle against his chest.

"Joel," I whisper.

"Hm?"

"I love you."

"I love you too, babe. Always."

And with those words, we both drift off to sleep, loved up and happier than we've been in a long time.

Joel

I peel my eyes open but snap them shut again as the bright sunlight hits.

Sarah's hand rolls over my stomach, and I no longer care about getting out of bed or moving or taking a piss or eating or anything else. She's here in my arms. *My girl.* Fucking finally.

Her lips brush my neck, and I open my eyes.

"Morning," I mumble, rolling over so I can see her beautiful face.

"Morning," she says with the most gorgeous smile I could possibly imagine.

Seeing her this happy is my favorite thing in the world.

She wriggles up my body and plants her lips on mine, giving me a deep kiss.

"I like waking up like this," she says.

"Naked?" I ask with a laugh.

"Naked in your arms. Because we're together. You're mine."

"Yes, I am." I rumble. "I didn't get to ask last night before we steamed things up." Her eyes dance as I say the words. "When did it change?"

She smiles softly, then kisses my chest. "It's been happening slowly, but the moment I knew was when Hyla was in the hospital. When I told you everything. That night... I just knew. I was ready for us. Didn't want to hold back anymore. Then I started planning. It had to be special."

"It was perfect," I whisper.

"Thank you for being so patient with me. It means everything to me. *You* mean everything to me."

She rolls on top of me, kissing me hungrily, like she'll never be able to get enough. I feel the same way. Our kisses are needy, frantic as our bodies connect.

When we had sex in October, it was amazing, but with nothing held back now, it's so much more.

After thoroughly enjoying each other's bodies, we took a shower. And maybe did some more enjoying. As we head downstairs for a late breakfast, we hear voices from the kitchen, talking and laughing.

When we get to the kitchen, hand in hand, everyone stops and stares at us. Rae gets a big smile and winks at Sarah, who winks back. Clearly, she knew what Sarah had planned last night.

Aaron smirks at me and does a slow clap. "It's about time."

"Coming from you," I say, wrapping my arms around Sarah and leaning back against the counter.

"Of course coming from me. After all the shit you gave us, I have to give some back."

"Does this mean it's official?" Amanda asks from the opposite side of the kitchen where she's leaning against Jamie.

"Mhm," Sarah says, smiling brightly. I love that our relationship is what's bringing that smile out.

"I'm happy for you two. And yes, it is about damn time," Miles says.

"No disagreements here," Sarah says, spinning around to face me and kissing me passionately. Actually, she's putting on a bit of a show, but I don't mind. Don't give a fuck about much of anything else when her tongue is in my mouth.

"Ew, get a room!" Rae says dramatically.

We pull apart and I throw my middle finger up at her.

She laughs as Aaron slings an arm over her shoulder. "After all the shit you've given us, payback's fair game."

"Well, I for one am just happy everyone's happy," Amanda says, raising her cup of coffee.

Aaron hands Sarah and I mugs and we all lift our cups and take a drink.

Here's to that.

Chapter Sixteen

My Future

Joel

"YOU WANT MORE?" MY voice comes out low and growly.

"Yes," Sarah gasps.

Wrapping my arms around her back, I flip her over, never letting our bodies disconnect. I know what she wants right now—what she always loves.

Thrusting my hips fast and hard, I wrap one hand around her neck, tangling my fingers in her hair as I reach between her legs with the other, adding the stimulation she needs.

"Joel," she whimpers.

"Yes, babe. God, you feel so good."

"Oh, oh..."

I rest my forehead against hers, looking deep into those endless blue eyes.

"I love you," I whisper.

And I get the biggest ego boost possible as she flies over the edge at those words.

"I love you too," she whispers as her high fades.

Fuck. It's those words that undo me, too.

I groan her name as my body tenses and shakes.

Gasping for air, I drop onto the bed next to her, pulling her close.

She kisses my neck while twirling a finger over my chest.

"Mm, I love waking up like that. Happy, in your arms, doing naughty things." She wiggles her eyebrows.

"Same. So far, we're nailing this relationship thing."

Her bubbly laugh makes my stomach clench. Thankfully, my dick is not ready for another round or we'd be in bed all day.

"You like *nailing* things? Or getting *nailed?*"

I roll on top of her again, dropping my lips to her jawline. "I believe *you* are the one who enjoyed getting *nailed.*"

I chuckle and hop out of bed. She swats my naked butt as I walk away from her.

The heat of her gaze is on me as I get dressed.

"Hey." She extends her hand out toward me.

I squat down and loosely intertwine our fingers. "Hm?"

"I'm really happy."

A smooth guy would hide his smile, but I can't. I'm beaming like a fucking moron at that, because it's all I wanted for so long.

"So am I, babe. This last month and a half has been incredible." I kiss up her arm, then press my lips against hers. "Mm, if I don't stop, we'll never leave this room."

Her eyes flare with excitement and she sits up. "And it's a big day." Jumping from the bed, she throws her arms around my neck. "I can't wait to watch you play tonight. You look so damn sexy in those baseball pants."

"Better than gray sweats?" I tease.

"Mhm. Gray baseball pants are *tighter.*" She brushes her hand over the crotch of my boxers, then scampers into the bathroom, pausing long enough to look over her shoulder at me as she bites her lip.

I'm going to get her back for that later.

As we walk down the stairs, Rae and Aaron's voices drift from the kitchen.

"That doesn't mean you need to get snippy with me," Rae says.

Sarah and I exchange a glance.

"I'm not being snippy. I just don't want to fucking talk about it anymore. There's enough pressure from everyone else. I don't need it from you, too. Leave it alone."

"Leave it alone or leave you alone?"

"Either is fine," Aaron says, slamming something onto the counter as Sarah and I tentatively approach the kitchen.

Rae sighs and gives us half a glance before folding her arms over her chest.

Given that today is the first game of the season—and Coach has made it clear Aaron will be playing—Aaron is more than a little stressed.

Sarah and I stand awkwardly at the edge of the kitchen as Rae stares at Aaron, who is leaning over the counter, ignoring her.

With a shake of her head, she walks over to him, then runs one hand up his back. He turns to look at her, but still doesn't look happy. Now facing each other, Rae wraps her arms around his neck. Though he still looks annoyed for a moment, as she looks into his eyes, his face softens and he wraps his arms around her back. She pushes onto her tiptoes and whispers something in his ear. As she does, his muscles relax and I can practically see the tension lifting off him.

"Okay?" Rae's voice lifts slightly.

"Okay." Aaron squeezes Rae tightly while saying, "I love you. I'm sorry."

"It's okay," she says, a little lilt in her voice, "I know you turn into a jackass when you're cranky."

He squeezes her tighter and kisses her neck. "Shut up."

"Mm, make me."

At this point, I clear my throat.

Aaron's grip on Rae loosens, but he doesn't let her go. She looks over her shoulder and sticks her tongue out at me.

I shake my head in response, but I'm proud of them. The little issues that used to become massive problems are now simply resolved with gentle words. It took a lot for them to get there, and they still fight. A happily ever after isn't always happy, but it's beautiful when two people believe in each other and their relationship and work hard to make it as strong as possible.

Wrapping my arms around Sarah, I feel that connection, the sweeping emotion telling me that'll be us too—in so many ways it already is. Not that I'm in any rush to propose, but from the moment she's been mine—hell even since before that—my commitment to her has been the same. I'm in this. I'll never give up on her or us, and I'll fight for us with everything inside me, whether she ever has a ring on that finger or not.

Sarah

"This is one of the few times I miss living on campus," Rae says as we huff it up the stairs to Chelsea's third-floor apartment. Since she only lives a few blocks from campus, it's where we're getting ready for the game today.

"At least Chelsea lives close, so we don't have to go all the way back to the lake house or get ready in one of the bathrooms on campus," I say.

"Yeah, that'd be a no from me. I'd rather get ready in my car," Mackie says as we get to the apartment.

Rae swings the door open without knocking—Chelsea's expecting us. Also, we've broken that barrier where unless we know Trevor is here, we just wander in. Thankfully, Chelsea is relaxed and fits in well with us. And especially Amanda—as evidenced by the laughter we hear as soon as we walk in.

We hang our coats on the rack in the hallway and slide off our shoes before rounding the corner into the living room, where we see Chelsea, Amanda... and Hyla.

"Oh my god!" Mackie shrieks, running over and hugging Hyla. "What are you doing here?"

Hyla smiles brightly—genuinely—and it warms my heart. I know she's still struggling in some ways, but she's been very dedicated to working on her mental health and her inner strength. Living with Trevor's mom has helped a lot, too, and as far as I know, she's had zero contact with her parents. Of course, she still has to deal with the drama of her father running for state senator, but she's handling it in stride, and I'm really proud of her.

"Like I was going to miss the first game. Especially since Trev is—"

Chelsea clears her throat and Hyla slaps a hand over her mouth.

"Right. Sorry. It's a surprise."

"Can't wait to finally find out what this surprise is," I say.

"Yeah, Trev's been teasing it for *months*."

"You're gonna love it," Hyla says. "Now, let's get ready." She claps her hands happily, and I can see the vibrant girl I grew up with returning.

Hyla and Chelsea are the masters of makeup. We all have the Sea Dogs mascot—a cute white dog with a black pirate hat—painted on our cheeks and on the opposite side, Mackie, Rae, and I have the numbers for our boys, like always. Rae and I are also decked out in the boys' Sea Dogs sweatshirts with lined leggings because it's freaking cold.

As we bundle up to head back to campus, I notice Rae has gotten quiet.

"You okay?" I ask.

She nods boisterously, letting us all know she's *not*.

"Rae baby."

"I'm fine."

"You sound like Ross Geller," Amanda says, wrapping a scarf around her neck. "You are not *fine.*"

"Can you blame me for being nervous?" she spits out. "I just want this game to be perfect for him. He deserves that much."

"He does," I say softly. "But you stressing will not make that happen."

"Yeah, well... have you met me?" She gives me a little smirk.

As we walk down the stairs to our cars, I ask, "Everything okay with you guys after this morning?"

"Oh yeah. That's all fine. Just my cranky husband needing a little soothing." Her eyes widen and a huge smile grows on her face. "My husband. I can't wait to cheer him on as his wife."

"You're adorable. You have the same look in your eyes as you did the night of the state championship game."

"Similar feeling. That was the first time I ever thought of him as my boy when I was watching him play. What about you? Are you excited to cheer Joel on as his girlfriend?"

My heart flutters at that word. After denying it for so long, it feels good to be living it now.

"I am," I admit as we climb into my car. Mackie is riding with Chelsea, Hyla, and Amanda. "It takes me back to senior night in high school."

"Do you ever wish you would've pursued something with him sooner?"

I glance at her as I pull out of the parking space and follow Chelsea's car up the hill toward campus.

"Sometimes. But I don't think I would've allowed myself to be as focused on nursing stuff if I had. I don't regret it. Sometimes, I do wonder what could've been. If we'd be married now too," I say with a laugh.

"Is that something you want?"

Chewing on my bottom lip, I nod. "I mean... not yet. Obviously. We just made things official. But at the same time... I don't know. There's not much point in waiting too long because we're already seriously committed to each other. Or maybe I'm living in the honeymoon period." I laugh nervously.

She shakes her head. "You know, it's okay to want that. You don't have to try to take it back in the same sentence you said it."

"I know," I say, turning onto campus. "But I don't want to rush. I know it's right, but I want to make sure we're settled into this too. I guess... I want it, but I want to work out any kinks first."

Rae laughs. "Maybe you should work *in* some kinks."

We're both laughing as I pull into a parking space. "You're naughty."

She shrugs. "What fun is it to be twenty and in love if you don't have some *fun* with it?"

We climb out and walk with the girls to the designated meeting spot outside the stadium where we see quite a crowd.

"There they are!" Mom calls, from where she and the entire group—including Dad, Grandma and Grandpa, Aaron's parents, Miles's parents, and Jesse—are waiting.

As soon as we finish exchanging hugs, Grandpa says, "If you're done with the greetings, let's take this inside. I want a damn hot dog and a beer."

We all chuckle and follow Gram and Grandpa as they lead the way into the stadium.

Joel

"Yo, AC, you ready for tonight?" Ricky, a junior who plays first base, asks Aaron.

Most of the upperclassmen on the team call him "Coach" or "AC" but the younger ones are a little scared of him and call him "Coach Cooper." Miles and I also call him that to annoy him. He doesn't need any extra stress today, though, and given his reaction to Rae this morning, I'm guessing he doesn't want any questions about playing today.

Of course, he's the picture of confidence in front of the team.

"I'll be fine. You worry about yourself. Make sure you're not tensing up at the plate."

"Sure thing, Coach," Ricky winks at him, then smacks his shoulder. "For the record, I think you're gonna kill it tonight and make sure we bring in the win." He holds out his fist and Aaron bumps it.

A sharp whistle pierces the room, and we all turn to look at Coach M.

"First game of the season, boys. Let's start out strong. Play hard, play smart, and don't let 'em in your heads. Get on out there."

Coach looks over at Miles, Aaron, and me. Aaron gives him a nod and Coach follows the rest of the team out.

Aaron looks between Miles and me. "No matter what else happens tonight, let's enjoy being on the field together again."

"Hell yes," Miles agrees. He bumps Aaron's fist, then mine. I bump Aaron's extended fist and the three of us walk to the dugout together.

The tension is high today. It's the first game, and the team we're playing, while not a rival, is as good as we are. It's always a toss-up on who will win when we play.

As the student who is going to sing the national anthem takes her place on the field, we make our way out of the dugout. Striding across the field with Miles and Aaron by my side feels fucking incredible. In many ways, it was a pipe dream I wasn't sure would ever happen. We all played together our senior year, but everything going on made it rough. The last time we played like champs together was almost four years ago. I'm ready for tonight. Ready to kick ass with my best friends and the rest of our team.

"Ladies and gentleman, welcome to the home opener of the Finger Lakes Sea Dogs!" the announcer calls through the loudspeaker. "Before we get to the anthem, I want to introduce my new co-announcer. He may be new to SUNY FL, but he's not new to baseball or to some of the players on this fine team."

Miles, Aaron, and I exchange a glance. *No way.*

"Ladies and gentleman, I have former Ida Warrior Trevor Matteny here with me."

Our section of the audience goes wild with whoops and cheers as Miles, Aaron, and I laugh.

"It's great to be here. I love the game and I have a few close friends down on the field tonight. I'm excited to be here and talk baseball for a few hours."

"Should've seen this one coming," Miles says.

"Probably," I say.

A moment later, the national anthem begins. We remove our hats and listen, and when it's over, we take our places—me at second, Miles catching, and Aaron in the dugout *for now.*

Sarah

"Girly, you have got to settle down. Having a heart attack is not the way to support your husband."

Rae stops wringing her hands and looks at Grandpa.

"He's right," Dad says. "You haven't even touched your nachos."

She looks down at her lap where her nachos are inevitably cold. Normally, she'd have pounded them within minutes of getting them.

"I know, okay? It's all anyone has told me all day. But this is my first time cheering him on since we've officially been a couple while he's been playing... like him again. I'm excited. And nervous. With each inning, I wonder if he's going to go in. They sent him back to warm up. I just—"

"Breathe, girly," Grandpa says, squeezing her arm.

Rae nods.

I take the nachos off her lap, dip a chip in the cheese, and hold it out to her.

She laughs, then takes a bite.

"Between innings, the Sea Dogs sent Aaron Cooper to warm up," the announcer says. "This is his first game pitching in years. Trevor, what can we expect?"

Trev laughs through the speaker. Announcing is truly the perfect gig for him.

"You can expect a lesson on the skill and finesse of a pitcher. Look, I've been playing with him since I was old enough to hold a bat, and I can tell you, he knows his stuff. There's a reason he became a pitching coach at nineteen. And it wasn't desperation. He knows this game. He knows the mechanics of pitching. Hand injury or not, he has tremendous skill. Now that he's back at the top of his game, any batter going up against him should be worried. He still holds the state title for most shutouts ever pitched."

"Here's hoping we get to see him play soon," the announcer says.

Rae rubs her hands together and takes the nachos back from me, eating slowly as she watches the team.

It's been a tight game. I have to admit, I'm a little nervous, too. Joel has been on fire, but the score is tied right now. And to Rae's nerves about Aaron going in, the pitcher is losing it. There's a man on first right now and one out from a pop fly. The batter up has not had a strike out all night, and it's the top of the seventh.

First pitch flies across the plate. Fastball, but not fast enough. The batter slugs it, but luckily, the outfielders handle it quickly and each player takes only one base.

Joel is on high alert as the next batter comes up. A line drive right now could make or break this game. Tied three-three with two men on base.

First pitch is fouled off. Second is a ball.

"They need to pull him," Rae says, voice tight. The nachos are gone and her nerves have faded. She's tense now, morphing back into the baseball girl who knows exactly when they need to make a change or get their shit together.

Third pitch. Fastball again.

It's a hit.

Line drive.

Joel's already in position. Lunges for it. Nabs the ball, spins around, tosses it to the shortstop at second. One out. We all stand as he sends it to first base. It'll be right at the wire. And... double play!

I'm screaming and cheering, my heart pounding at how sexy Joel looked plucking that ball out of the air like it was nothing. As they jog off the field, he glances at me and winks.

Damn him. He knows exactly how to turn me on. I'm gonna get him back for that later.

Gram squeezes my leg as the other team takes the field.

"You look very happy right now."

My cheeks flush, but I can't help smiling. "I am. I'm really happy."

"I'm proud of you," she whispers.

"For what?"

"For taking your time, trusting yourself, listening to your heart, and opening it."

I bump my arm against hers. "Well, I learned from the best. Thank you for always supporting me, being there for me." I rest my head on her shoulder. "I love you."

"I love you too, sweetheart."

We turn our attention as the Sea Dogs' first baseman, Ricky, steps into the batter's box. He's a little cocky, but in a funny way rather than an obnoxious one. Typically, he's a solid hitter.

Stepping up to the plate, he waits.

First pitch is low, and he doesn't swing. But the second, a curveball, lands right in his sweet spot, and he ends up with a double.

Joel's up next, and he's ready. The first pitch goes high and inside, but he nails the second. Line drive, close enough to first that it gets through. Ricky heads to third and Joel lands on first.

"He's gonna steal," Jesse says from behind me.

"Not yet," Rae says, intently focused on Joel's stance. "He'll wait a pitch and see what happens first. Joel's a sneaky stealer. He'll wait until the ball is in the right position."

Back when we all played together as kids, Rae and Joel were always the ones to steal a base.

The first pitch is fouled off. Joel cracks his neck, then turns his body slightly toward second base. He lets one foot drift off the bag, but shifts his weight back and forth several times. Joel's strong suit is his ability to steal a base without a big lead off.

"Now he's going to steal," Rae says quietly, as if a member of the opposing team might hear her.

Our eyes are locked on him as the pitcher assumes his stance. As his fingers tighten on the ball and he raises his arm, Joel shifts forward. Right before the release, Joel takes off. Too late for the pitcher to stop. The ball flies toward home, but Joel slides at the right time, and as the catcher throws—too late for an out—to second, Ricky takes off running for home. The batter jumps out of the box, allowing Ricky to slide headfirst into home and break the tied game.

We're all screaming and clapping as Joel brushes himself off and smirks at our section.

Miles is up next, and by the smile on his face, I can tell he's figured this pitcher out. He's itching for a big hit. Miles was the strongest hitter on the high school team. It may have been a while, but it's clearly been like riding a bike for him. Since the muscle memory kicked in, he's been on fire.

Miles has always been sure of himself in the batter's box and has a tendency to disarm pitchers.

And that seems to be the case this time when a slightly low fastball flies across the plate and Miles smashes it over the back wall. Home freaking run.

Joel crosses home base, then waits for Miles, sharing a bro-hug with him the second he runs across the plate.

The next batter up hits a pop fly, ending the inning, but our boys head into the top of the eighth up by three runs.

They *were* up by three runs.

Now they're up by one because of a homerun, a double, and a single—the guy on base managed to take two with that one. This pitcher has not thrown one strike this inning, as shown by the runs he's given up. Rae is about to have a coronary when the pitching coach steps in.

Finally, the call is made. Everyone in our area turns to look at Rae as the announcer speaks.

"After a couple of murky innings, the starting pitcher is headed out, which means... do you want to say it?"

I can imagine the massive smile Trevor has on right now.

"Ladies and gentleman, that means number three, Aaron freaking Cooper, is taking the mound!"

Cheers and whistles roll through the crowd as Aaron jogs across the field. He glances our way and winks as Rae blows him a kiss and whispers, "You've got this, Ace."

Aaron

If there's one thing in my life I know how to do perfectly, it's throw a pitch. I know the mechanics. I understand the finesse. I know how to read a batter, and Miles and I can practically communicate telepathically. There are a lot of things in my life I'm still figuring out, but closing out a game? This I can do.

I was nervous this morning, as evidenced by me snapping at Rae, then feeling ragey and antsy through most of my classes. But that was all pre-game nerves. Several years' worth. Once I was in the locker room, it all fell away, and now, standing here on the mound, everything else melts away. Except for her. I sneak one last glance at my girl. My *wife*.

I'm going to make sure we win this game. For Coach, for my teammates, for myself, but mostly for her. After everything, we both deserve this night.

After a couple of quick throws back and forth with Miles, the batter steps into the box, and I smile.

As Trevor rattles off my high school stats through the speaker, I throw my first pitch, a four-seam fastball.

"Strike."

The crowd cheers, and for the first time in way too long, I'm in my element. Coaching is amazing, and if I had to pick only one for the rest of my life, I'd choose that. But I'd pay someone to let me get on the mound once every month or two and feel this rush. There's nothing like it.

Two more strikes later, and we're one out in—one out closer to winning this game.

The next batter comes up. He gets a piece of the first pitch and fouls it off. Second pitch is a strike. As Miles throws the ball back to me, I hear the pad of footsteps behind me.

Oh fuck no.

The second the ball is in my glove, I pivot and send it straight to Joel. There's out number two by just a hair.

Joel winks at me and tosses the ball back.

Fuck, I've missed being out here with the guys.

Next pitch is another foul. He's determined to swing at anything, which means a curveball is a safe bet.

A moment later, the top of the eighth is over, and we're up to bat.

The opposing team has switched pitchers too, so we don't increase our lead at all, but we're still up by one.

"Easy peasy," Joel says, fist bumping me before we take the field again.

"Let's do this, A," Miles says, smacking my back.

We head onto the field and I throw a couple of pitches before the batter steps into the box.

I make quick work of the first two batters, but the third is one of the best hitters on the team—also a catcher. Catchers are notoriously the worst players to pitch against. They know how to read a pitcher. I've never met one better at it than Miles, but I chalk that up to the years of work he, Joel, and I spent learning the minutiae of the game. When we weren't playing, we were watching games on TV, going to the minor league team nearby, or studying more about the mechanics of the game.

He clips a piece of the first pitch, sending it foul. The second pitch I take a risk with, and it lands just shy of high and inside, leaving the ump to call it a strike. After that, he ends up with a streak of fouls, since you can't foul out. Five fouls later and tension fills my shoulders.

Nope. Gotta stay calm.

I roll my shoulders and take a few deep breaths, then look over at the stands.

My eyes connect with Rae's instantly. Even from a distance, it calms me.

For myself. For her. We're gonna win this game.

One more deep breath and direction from the pitching coach via Miles, and I'm ready for this.

In a split second, I remember everything I know about the mechanics of the game, how to strike out a batter, and then I forget it all again. Let it go. Focus on the ball in my hand, the feel of it, the positioning of my fingers, and throw.

The spin is perfect. It curves and drops so dramatically at the end that as he swings—and misses—he nearly falls over reaching for it.

"Strike."

The second the word is out of the umpire's mouth, cheers break out across the stadium. The team runs over and surrounds me, offering me congratulations and pats on the back, but Miles and Joel quickly push through everyone else.

"You fucking nailed it," Miles says, throwing an arm around my neck.

"Hell yes," Joel adds, squeezing my shoulder.

"We did it." I closed the game, but Miles and Joel and the rest of the team brought in the runs and got the outs.

Through the sea of purple and gray around me, I see her. A purple Sea Dogs hat on her head, wearing boots and leggings, my number and our mascot painted on her cheeks, and a sweatshirt with my last name on the back.

I push away from everyone else and open my arms as she runs to me, jumps, and throws her arms around my neck. Her legs wrap around my waist as she kisses me, then pulls away, smiling brightly.

"Nice pitching, Ace."

My heart thunders at those words.

"God, I've missed hearing you say that."

"Love you, Ace."

"Love you too, Beautiful. Let's go home."

Joel

After some praise from Coach and a quick shower, I make my way out of the field house, side by side with Aaron and Miles.

Outside, Trev, Hyla, Mackie, Rae, and Sarah are waiting for us.

Sarah looks so fucking adorable with her purple fleece headband and her hair thrown up in a purposely messy bun. And I love seeing her in my clothes. The possessive side of me fires up. Fuck yes, that's my girl. *Mine.* And even though I'm mature and cultured enough to know she doesn't belong to me, it's that she has my heart and I have hers.

She scampers over to me, wraps her arms around me, and kisses me deeply—in case the steamy kiss she gave me on the field wasn't enough. It's the first time I've ever had a moment like that. I've watched my friends have them over the years. I'll never forget how Rae ran to Aaron after we won state. This was my first time, though. The first time I ever felt claimed—and I love it. I love when she wants to show the world I'm hers. Sometimes, I low key want some girl to come hit on me in front of her so I can see her looking all sexy and possessive.

"You were incredible tonight," she says as we walk to her car. "That double play. Stealing that base." She's still gushing as we get to her car. I press her against the passenger door and lean into her.

"You liked that?" I ask, running my lips up the side of her neck.

"Mhm. And when you winked at me after... that was mm... panty melting. And I don't say that lightly."

Looking around and seeing no one, I slip one hand between her legs, feeling the heat. As I brush my finger over the crotch, I rumble, "I still feel some underwear here."

"Can you feel how wet it is?" God, she never misses a beat.

"Get in the car."

"Yes, sir."

Good God.

I open her door, swatting her ass as she gets in the car.

After tossing my stuff in the back, I climb into the driver's side. The second I put the key in the ignition, she climbs onto my lap and kisses me fervently, shoving her fingers through my hair.

"You looked so sexy tonight," she mutters against my lips.

Her tongue hungrily strokes mine. At the edge of control, I dig my fingers into her back, ready to throw her in the backseat and pray no one drives by and sees us.

"Mm," she mumbles, then slowly pulls her lips away, resting her forehead against mine. "I love you," she breathes. "Getting to watch you play tonight—not as your friend, or us messing around, or not knowing what we're doing, but as your girlfriend, the woman who loves you—it was so special to me. Seeing you do something you love, that you're so damn good at, it filled me with pride. You were incredible."

I brush my hand down her cheek. "That's how I feel watching you in your nursing program. Seeing you excel, completely in your element. You work hard, but I can see how much you love it. I'm proud of you every day, babe."

She loosely wraps her arms around my neck. "You amaze me every day. And the way you love me..." She pauses, emotion thickening her voice. "You were unbelievably patient with me. I know I've said it before, but it's hard for me to convey with words how much that meant to me. It made me fall harder for you, even faster than I thought I would. I promise I'm going to do everything I can to honor that and love you the same way."

"You already do," I mutter before crushing my lips against hers. "I love you so fucking much, babe."

After a thorough kissing, she hugs me tightly.

"Home?"

"Home."

She climbs off me and sits down in the passenger seat again.

As we drive home, her fingers twisting through the back of my hair, my mind flits back to our first home game last year. We were in limbo, no idea what the hell we were doing, but when she walked out of her bedroom with my number painted on her cheek, I saw my future. With each step we took toward a relationship, that future I saw with her changed and grew. Now, without a doubt, I see forever.

Chapter Seventeen

Twenty-one

Sarah

"IT'S READY!" I ANNOUNCE, walking into the kitchen.

"What is?" Miles asks.

"The Love Shack round two," I say with a smile. "Of course, unlike at my thirteenth birthday, most of us are in relationships, so it's basically a closet with a timer in it for making out—or more. Though there is a spinning board anyone who is single can put their name on and give it a spin."

"Should I take you in for a practice round?" Joel asks over his cup of coffee.

"Mm. I wouldn't argue with that," I say, striding over to him and rubbing my hands up his arms.

Miles gestures to himself. "I'm standing right here."

I stick my tongue out at him. "Obviously. Why do you think I said that?" I wink at Joel and take a step back. "I'm so excited for tonight. I can't believe we're celebrating our twenty-first birthdays."

For the first time in several years, we're having a combined party to celebrate all of our birthdays. Miles, Aaron, and Mackie have already hit the milestone, while Rae and Joel are up within the week, I still have another month. Sure as hell isn't stopping me from celebrating, though. I've always loved a good party. Surprisingly, this is the first big one we've thrown at the lake house. Some of our friends from college are coming, along with some friends from back home—Hyla, Nick, Leigh, Maia, Vince, and Braden. In case today isn't enough celebration, tomorrow the six of us, along with Amanda, Hyla, Trevor, and Chelsea, leave for five days in Charleston. It should be an amazing spring break. We're flying this time, courtesy of Amanda getting us a freaking steal on plane tickets. I'm not sure how she has connections everywhere, but it sure as hell has worked out in our favor.

"We come bearing food!" Rae calls as she and Mackie walk through the door followed by Aaron, whose arms are loaded with beer. Joel walks over and helps Aaron as I walk over to Rae and Mackie.

"I have this too," Rae says, holding out a manila envelope. "Mail from home."

Every couple of weeks, Mom sends an envelope with any mail Rae and I have gotten that we might need before we get home.

"Really? Love Shack round two?" Mackie asks. "Guess I shouldn't be surprised."

"Mm, maybe you can take Hyla in there," I say as we walk into the kitchen and put groceries away.

"Actually..." We all turn to look at Mackie as she hoists herself onto the counter. "Hyla and I had a long talk when I was home last weekend, and we decided to refocus on our friendship. She needs to heal, and I need to figure out what I want from my future. We both do. And we both need to take care of ourselves. The romantic stuff and staying in the between zone has been hurting us more than anything else. She doesn't need anything else harming her mental health. I don't either, for that matter. We agreed that we've loved each other and we care deeply for each other, but it's time to move on from our romantic relationship. It's going to be hard, but we both think it's the right decision. I don't know what the future might bring for us, but for now... it's time to move on."

"Wow," I breathe, squeezing her leg. "That's a lot. But very mature."

"Strong. Just like you," Miles says, kissing her head. "I'm proud of you."

"Thanks. Hopefully Charleston won't be too weird, but that's where the conversation came from. We didn't want to get sucked back into a toxic cycle. Anyway, figured you guys should know."

"We're all here if you need anything. A buffer. A reminder. A drink," Rae says with a laugh. "Whatever."

"I appreciate it. But, on to happier things. We need to get ready. Party time will be here before you know it." She hops off the counter and unpacks more groceries.

I grab the envelope from the counter. "I'm going to run this upstairs quick. I'll be back in a minute."

"Okay," Rae says as I walk out of the kitchen.

When I get up to the bedroom, I open the envelope, pulling out a few letters from the school that I already got emails about, a note that my dentist is retiring so I'll have to find a new one, and one more envelope with a large, lined Post-it wrapped around it. I unfold the bottom of the Post-it and read it.

Sarah,
This came in the mail for you the other day. I'll be honest, we considered not sending it, but we agreed you needed to be the one to decide what to do with it (even though your dad would've been happy to burn it). If you need to talk about this or need any help making a decision, call or text any time. Dad says he's always up for a three in the morning phone conversation. We love you so much, honey.

XO
Mom

With trembling hands, I pull the Post-it off and look at the envelope.

Then I see her name.

Vanessa.

I drop the letter onto the floor as nausea washes over me.

Why?

Why does she still elicit this reaction? I've been good. I've taken care of my mental health. Why does a letter from her make me feel this way?

I'm scared.

Scared it will trigger me. It'll make me slide down that slippery path. I want to follow Dad's suggestion and chuck it in the fire. Then I wonder if she could be sick. What if she's writing to tell me she's dying? How would that make me feel?

I pick the letter up again and stare at it.

What do I do?

My chest feels tight. Is this a panic attack? What's happening to me?

Tears fill my eyes as my body shakes, but I can't take my eyes off her name.

Vanessa Willis.

It's a different last name now, not that it's much of a surprise.

Bile rises into my throat, but I can't move. I'm stuck in place—how I always feel when she's involved.

"Hey, babe—Sarah?" Joel's in front of me in seconds. "What's wrong? What's going on?"

He scans my face, and I lift my eyes to look at him for half a second before my gaze drops to the envelope again. He follows my eyes, looking at the envelope as well.

"Vanessa Willis? Wait. Vanessa? As in—"

My nod gives the answer, but I can't say anything.

"Sarah? Shit," he mutters, pulling the letter from my hand and tossing it onto the dresser. "Come here."

He picks me up and sets me on the bed. The movement breaks me from my trance enough that I start crying. Hard.

Pulling the covers back, he climbs into bed with me and wraps his arms around me.

"Look at me, babe. Look at my eyes."

I turn slightly and our gazes connect. *His eyes.* They've always drawn me in.

"Breathe deep," he whispers, his arms tight around my body. In one of my classes, we learned about why babies like to be swaddled. They like firm touch and comforting pressure because it makes them feel cozy and protected, like they were in the womb. It's the same way Joel's holding me now. Making me feel safe.

I let out a long shuddery breath, then suck in another deep one.

After I've been breathing calmly for a few minutes, Joel asks, "Do you want to talk about it?"

"I don't know what I'm thinking," I say honestly.

"You don't have to. Let whatever you're feeling come out however you need it to. I'm here to listen and help you through it."

His words almost make me cry again. They prick my heart because I know their truth. My parents, grandparents, and Rae have always made me feel safe and beyond loved, but this is different. Even in the midst of their support and love, I sometimes felt alone, especially in moments like this. Right now, though, maybe for the first time ever, I don't feel like I'm facing it alone. I know he's in the depths of it with me, no matter what.

"I'm scared. And I'm angry. I'm really fucking angry."

"Tell me why," he breathes.

"I'm scared because of the feelings just holding the envelope brought up. I'm scared that whatever is inside it will make me spiral. I don't want to do that again. Then I'm angry. I'm angry she still holds this power over me. Angry she's contacting me at all. Angry she thinks she has any right to me or my life because she doesn't deserve it! She doesn't deserve me. She doesn't deserve to affect my life."

"No, she doesn't," Joel says softly, brushing his fingers up and down my arm. "But in all this anger and fear, you hold the power. You get to choose whether you open that envelope. You get to choose what to do with whatever is inside if you do. You get to choose what you allow into your life and how you handle it."

"The problem is, I don't know what choice to make."

He gives me a sloppy kiss on the cheek, his lips pressing firmly into my skin like he's trying to transfer an extra dose of love through them. "That's the best part, babe. You don't have to decide alone. You have me to walk through it with you, every step of the way. I love you."

I turn and throw myself against him, wrapping my arms around his neck and holding him close as some peace finally filters in. "I love you too. So much. Thank you for being the one by my side. There's no one else I'd want here but you."

"Babe, I'm always going to be here."

I give him a deep, emotional kiss. One I can feel flowing through my body, telling him over and over again how much I love him.

When our lips part, I feel a smile creeping onto my face. *I hold the power.*

"What do you want to do?" he asks.

"Right now, I want to let that letter collect dust. I can deal with it tomorrow—next week—there's no rush. I won't let her steal my joy today. I'm ready to go have some fun and celebrate."

He smiles brightly. "I love the sound of that. But if you need to talk at any point—"

I kiss him again. "Don't worry. I know where to find you. Preferably in my arms."

"Mm, that could be arranged."

"Thank you," I breathe against his lips.

"Nothing to thank me for." He nips at my lip and smiles. "Come on. Let's go downstairs. I'll make you a mocha with lots of whipped cream."

"You're the best."

He shrugs as he stands up, a dimple popping out as he gives me an adorable smile. "I do what I can."

He pulls me up and gives me one more kiss—one that says the last place he wants to take me is downstairs with other people—then we walk downstairs hand in hand.

Joel

"Hey! He's here!" Rae calls as Sarah and I walk down the stairs. "Oh, there you two are..." Her brow furrows as she looks at Sarah, whose eyes are still a little red and puffy from crying. "What's wrong?"

She gives me a look, and I take it as a cue to give them a minute. With a squeeze of her hand, I walk toward the front door.

From behind me, Sarah quietly says, "Cliff notes version because I refuse to let it ruin today... Vanessa sent me a letter—I assume. I don't know. I haven't opened it. Haven't decided if I will, but for today, I'm ignoring it and am going to have fun."

"I support this plan. Also, Vanessa can go fuck herself. I love you. Are you sure you're okay, though?"

The heat of her gaze lands on me as she continues talking to Rae. "It set me off, but I have a pretty amazing boyfriend who calmed me down."

"That makes me happy," Rae says, her voice getting squeaky.

The front door opens, and everyone turns toward it as Jesse and Dani walk in. I knew Jesse was planning on coming up early, but I'm a little surprised to see Dani with him.

"Hey big bro," I say as he pulls me into his arms.

"Little brother." He glances over my shoulder as he steps back. "Rae Rae. Sarah." He winks at them.

"What are you doing here?" Sarah asks, surprised.

"I told you I was coming," Dani says.

Rae and Sarah exchange a glance. "You didn't mention you were coming with Jesse," Rae says.

Dani glances over at him and shrugs. "We're friends."

Then she wanders toward the kitchen, but by the way my brother's eyes follow her ass as she goes, I'm not sure I believe her.

As everyone walks into the kitchen, Miles bumps my shoulder. "Think they're fucking?"

I stifle a laugh and shake my head. "Who knows?" I glance up at him. "Why? Are you jealous?"

"Nah," he says. He tries to hide it, but his face drops a little. "Hey, you okay?"

He gives a quick nod. "I'm fine."

That was convincing.

I grab his arm. "Since when do we lie to each other?"

He sighs and shoves a hand through his hair. "I *am* fine. I just wish I could be the guy I was a few years ago."

"What do you mean?"

His jaw ticks. "I wish a simple hookup sounded as fun as it used to. But living with all you happy assholes is a constant reminder of what I don't have. Most of the time it doesn't bother me, but sometimes it does. I'm thrilled for Rae and Aaron and you and Sarah. But I'm starting to think I'm going to be a thirty-year-old bachelor while all my friends are married with kids."

"Dude, you're twenty-one. And Mackie is single, too."

"Yes, but Mackenzie has had the big love already. I feel like I'm behind the curve."

"Because you haven't had your heart stomped on? Because you haven't had a relationship for the sake of having one? You did what felt right for you at the time. If that's not what you want anymore, then change it."

"Yeah, because finding love is so easy."

I tilt my head to the side. "I'm not saying it is. Even for Rae and Aaron, when it was right in front of them, it wasn't easy, but if you're ready for a relationship, you have to try for one."

"I don't want to waste my time on the wrong girl. Life's too short for that shit."

"So, what are you going to do? Keep hooking up and pray you meet a girl with a magical vagina who tames your dick?"

I raise my eyebrows and he laughs.

"That sounds like something Rae would say."

"Have you not met us? Practically twins." I grin at him.

"For the record," he says, smacking my shoulder as we walk toward the kitchen. "That's *exactly* the kind of shit that works in all those romcoms."

"Yes, because life is just like the movies."

He shrugs. "Eh, doesn't hurt to wait and see."

"And you're back."

"Yep. Thanks for pulling me out of that funk."

He walks past me into the kitchen as I shake my head. Someday, some girl is going to walk into his life and fuck him up. Can't wait to see that.

The party officially started about an hour ago, but people slowly trickled in all day. Now the alcohol is flowing, there's an insane amount of food, and everything has gotten loud.

There's an intense game of beer pong happening at the dining room table. Each time someone scores or misses, there's loud cheering or groaning.

Trevor appears to be winning, but who knows if it will last. Sarah, Chelsea, and Hyla are cheering him on as he plays against one of the guys on the baseball team.

Glancing around, I see Aaron and Miles laughing in the kitchen with Nick. Most of our other friends are in the living room area.

I tilt my head to look past the group of people blocking the full view of the living room and notice I don't see Rae. Spinning back around to make sure I didn't miss her at the beer pong match, I see her sitting alone on the back deck. It probably shouldn't worry me, but something about Rae sitting alone, especially during a party, always raises a red flag for me.

Grabbing my beer, I head out to the back deck, welcoming both the cool air and the instant quiet.

"Hey, everything okay?" I ask Rae, dropping into a chair beside her.

She stares at the darkening sky before turning to me. "I'm fine. I think I'm becoming more introverted. All the people and the craziness... I just needed a break."

"You've never been a party girl."

She laughs. "No. Definitely not."

"Well, good to know you're not upset about anything."

"It's a beautiful night with my best friends. What would I have to be upset about?"

I shoot her a knowing look.

"Yeah, okay. I've been through my fair share of shit at parties, but not typically *our* parties. At least not since the ill-fated eighteenth birthday party."

I groan at that. "Oh gosh. Don't remind me. Speaking of, is it weird that Jesse showed up with Dani? Do you think something is going on?"

"Oh. It occurred to me, but I really don't know. If they make each other happy, more power to them."

"It wouldn't be weird for you?"

"Since we have a... history?" Her voice cracks on that last word. "No. I mean, as long as Dani was fine with it, it wouldn't bother me."

"Even if it meant losing your backup husband?" I tease. "You never know how you and Aaron can fuck it up again."

She reaches over and smacks my stomach. "You asshole. You shouldn't even joke about that. We both know you don't ever want to see us be such dramatic messes again." She shakes her head. "Not that we ever would be. We're a lot stronger now."

"I know that. It's why I felt safe to joke about it."

"Wait. How did you know about the Jesse-being-my-backup joke? I don't think we ever said that in front of anyone else."

"He and I were joking around about it at one point. If you two were both single long-term, I could absolutely have seen you making that agreement, though."

She laughs lightly. "Yeah. It's funny... very different, but Jesse has always felt like my Trevor. You know, it didn't work out with him and Sarah, but in a different life, it could have. They still

299

care about each other deeply and respect what they had. Jesse and I never dated, but in a different life..."

"Yeah, I think he feels the same. That's why it was so hard for him when—" *Shit.* No. I've kept this secret for almost two years. Damn it.

"When what?"

Guess I might as well come clean.

"When you two slept together."

Her eyes bulge. "Wha—what? How do you—"

"He told me. The morning after it happened. He was pretty much crying in the living room over how fucked up his life felt. He was hurting over Carrie, then hurting because he was worried he'd lost your friendship."

"Oh..." Rae looks down, trying to hide her pain-filled eyes.

I reach over and squeeze her arm. "I'm sorry. I shouldn't have brought it up."

"It's okay," she whispers. "I can't believe you've known this whole time. Why didn't you tell me?"

"Jesse felt horrible telling me about it. He felt like it was betraying you. We were both trying to respect you."

"You Wilkinson boys. Troublemakers on the outside, sweethearts on the inside. Is that why you brought him over for that movie night? Jesse acted like he had no clue why."

"I didn't tell him why, but yes, that's why I brought him."

"Well, as much as I appreciate you two not wanting to embarrass me, you should've told me he was coming that night. I almost invited Aaron."

Can't help but laugh at that. "Might've made for an awkward evening."

"Little bit."

"Well, I'm sorry I foiled your plans."

"It's all good. We ended up right where we were supposed to. Aaron and I are married. You and Sarah are together."

"Hey. Why are we lumped in with your chaos?"

She smirks at me, lifting her beer bottle to her lips. "Because you slept in her bedroom that night."

She takes a drink as I stare at her. "You never forget anything, do you?"

"Nope. But in fairness, neither do you."

"Twins, like always."

"Yep." She holds her beer bottle out to me. "Happy birthday, Joelskies."

I clink mine against hers. "Happy birthday, Rae Rae."

Sarah

As parties go, this is one of our best. No fist fights. No relationship drama. It's a little weird, actually. Probably shouldn't jinx it. There's still plenty of time for that. Especially now that a game of truth or dare has formed in the living room. Since there are so many people, we had everyone write one truth and one dare on slips of paper. There's a truth hat and a dare hat to pick from when it's your turn.

Starting the game out strong, Rae volunteers to go first. Of course, she reaches for the dares.

"Okay," she says, closing her eyes and swirling her hand through the papers before pulling one out. She flashes her eyes open and unfolds the paper. She blinks a couple of times as her mouth drops. Then her gaze shifts around the room before landing on Trevor and Nick. "No," she whispers. "No way! This is rigged. It has to be."

She shoves the paper into my hand as she stares them down.

I glance down and read it.

I dare you to give an impression of an amazing orgasm you've had.

Oh my gosh.

The one dare she's never done. The one she got out of doing when Trev dared her years ago.

"Seriously! Is this rigged? Do all these papers say the same thing?"

I grab the hat from her and pull a couple of other ones out and quickly read them. "No. They're different."

"Unbelievable," Rae huffs as Aaron walks across the room to her.

"What does it say?" he asks, sitting down next to her.

She clears her throat, then locks eyes with Nick and Trevor and says, "I dare you to give an impression of an amazing orgasm you've had."

Nick and Trevor burst into a fit of laughter.

"Serendipity," Trevor says smoothly as Leigh smacks Nick.

"Ay! What kind of question is that? Do you want *me* to have to do something like that?"

"Easy babe. You were there. It's a little harmless inside joke. Right, Rae?"

"What's it gonna be? You going to go through with it this time?" Trevor asks. "I mean, say the word and we'll give you a pass."

"The word is this," Aaron says, standing up and taking the paper from Rae's hand. He crumples it up and shoves it in his pocket. "No."

Then he pulls Rae up and quietly says, "Certain things are reserved for only your husband to hear." He lowers his voice a little more, but unfortunately, I still have to hear, "Which is why I'm saving that paper for when we're alone later."

Gross.

Rae cocks an eyebrow, then jumps into Aaron's arms. "My knight in shining armor."

"Sorry, boys," he says, winking at Nick and Trev before carrying Rae out of the living room and over to the kitchen.

"Lame!" Trev calls after them. Then he looks at me. "You're up."

"Fine," I say. "Dare."

Grabbing the hat, I close my eyes and swish my hand through the papers before pulling one out. I open my eyes and unfold it, reading my own handwriting. I cheated a little because I used the same thing for both truth and dare. And it's coming back to bite me now.

I dare you to tell us a secret.

The only secret I have is one I have no desire to get into right now. The mere thought of it has made my stomach lurch. I fold it up and put it back in the hat.

"On second thought, I'm out."

Before anyone can respond, I get up and walk away. I don't realize where I'm headed until I'm standing in front of the drink cart.

Haven't had anything to drink yet tonight. *Maybe it's time to remedy that.*

As my hand hovers over the cotton candy vodka—my alcohol of choice, especially mixed with cream soda—something twists in my gut.

I don't want to be the girl grabbing alcohol to numb my pain or solve my problems.

I've done it so many times before. Given the choice between hurting or not feeling my pain, I usually take the latter, but it only works for so long before the pain hits even stronger than it would've been before.

This is the girl I never want to turn into again. The version of me I've been scared to turn into, knowing it's a version that would hurt people around me—especially Joel.

My eyes drift to the sliding door and floor to ceiling windows looking out onto the back deck. Joel is out there talking with Miles, Ricky, and a few other guys from the baseball team.

Rather than interrupt him, I turn and head down the hallway. A bathroom, Miles's room, and a small office are the only things down there. I slip into the office and close the pocket door behind me. It's more of a closet with a computer, printer, modem, and router, but it'll do.

Leaning against the wall, I slide to the floor and pull my phone from my pocket.

Me: I got a letter from Vanessa.

I send the text, then flick my screen off and rest my head against the wall, closing my eyes.

A moment later, my phone vibrates in my hand.

Flashing my eyes open, I look at it.

Gram: Oh my. This sounds more like a phone call to me than a text.

Me: Eventually. I'm not ready yet. I'm trying to ignore it tonight, but I'm struggling.

Gram: Why are you trying to ignore it?

Me: Because we're having the big birthday party celebration. I want to have fun. It's there in the back of my head, though. It won't leave me alone.

Gram: Not all that much of a surprise. It's normal that this would hit hard. What did it say?

Me: I don't know. Haven't read it. Haven't opened. Not sure I will.

Gram: Ah. Well, I trust you'll make the right decision.

Me: Can't you just tell me what to do?

Gram: Sorry, sweetheart. This is one you have to sort out for yourself. No matter what, you have everyone's support. Don't let this weigh you down. You have too much

brightness to let her dim it. Don't give her the power to do that.

Me: You always know the right thing to say.

Gram: Seventy-one years and I ought to know something. Go have fun with your friends. Love you, honey.

Me: Love you, Gram.

I turn my phone screen off again and sigh.

Gram's right. I think I give Vanessa too much power to hurt me. But why? Why the hell do I care what's in that envelope? Why does it matter? I've lived a happier, healthier life without her. What could she say that would change that?

Doesn't matter. Not tonight. My resolve strengthens again, and I stand up. Maybe truth or dare is not my game tonight, but I can think of some other things I'd like to do. As I reach for the pocket door, it slides open and Joel grins at me.

"There you are. Rae said she saw you walk down the hall here. The bathroom's empty, so I figured you must be in here."

"Not Miles's room?"

"Why would you be in there?"

I shrug. "Maybe I wanted a threesome."

He grimaces. "That's a hard pass, babe. Are you okay? Is there a reason you were hiding in the office?"

"I'm fine. I was reminded of what's sitting on the dresser upstairs. It caught me for a minute."

He sweeps some hair off my cheek, his gorgeous eyes peering deep into mine. "But you're okay?"

"Yeah. And I refuse to let her ruin tonight. Besides, I have more fun things I want to do."

"Fun things, huh?"

"Mhm." I run my hands down his arms, stopping to squeeze his biceps along the way. "Starting with taking you into the Love Shack."

"I won't disagree with that. Except..."

"What?"

He grins, then runs his tongue along his bottom lip. "There's a timer for the Love Shack." He steps into the room and slides the pocket door shut again, this time flipping the lock. Invading my space, he presses me against the wall and sinks his lips into mine.

Giving in to him, I wrap my legs around his waist and twist my tongue with his as I rake my fingers through his hair.

His kisses are long, powerful, and demanding. With every stroke of his tongue, he owns more of my body. More of my heart. More of my soul.

I give it all freely.

How did I ever hold back from him?

He rocks against me, groaning into my mouth.

I'm about to push him away, strip him down, get a little *dirty* when there's a knock at the door.

Joel groans—in frustration this time—and reluctantly lifts his lips off mine, gasping as he does.

"If you guys are... indisposed... feel free to not answer, but everyone is shouting that they want to cut the cake," Rae says.

"Jesse's waving a knife around, so we'd like to get this over with quickly," Aaron adds.

Joel scowls, but I kiss his nose.

"Give us a minute and we'll be out."

"Okay," Rae says.

Their footsteps fade, and I look at Joel. "We should probably..."

He sets me down, still breathing heavily. "Yeah."

I pop a kiss on his cheek. "Don't worry. There will be time for that later. Or maybe on the plane tomorrow. Might be fun to join the mile high club."

"You're killing me."

"You love it." A quick kiss to his neck, then I unlock the door and walk out. Teasing him is my favorite game.

The six of us are huddled around the cake, Miles wielding a giant chef's knife as we're blinded by camera flashes.

"Okay, I think that's enough pictures for a lifetime," Joel says, blinking as another flash hits right in our eyes.

"Fine, fine," Trevor says.

"Can we cut it now?" Miles asks.

"Not without a toast," Nick says. It's always Nick giving the toast. He raises his cup. "Here's to the six of you and your insane friendship that has lasted a lifetime and brought all of us together. Welcome to twenty-one, kids. Happy birthday."

Everyone cheers, and finally, we can cut the cake.

"Actually," Miles says, setting the knife down, "I've got a better idea." He pulls out some plastic forks and hands us each one. While everyone watches, the six of us plunge our forks in, destroying the cake as we all laugh and shove forkfuls in our mouths.

I hope someone got a picture because *that* is the one I want hanging on my wall for the rest of my life.

Chapter Eighteen

A Lifetime More

Sarah

"Being a flight attendant sounds fun," Hyla says, sitting down next to me and extending a coffee toward me as a group of flight attendants walk by as we wait to board our plane to South Carolina.

"Thank you," I say through an inhale of the heavenly scent of coffee.

"At least our little airport has a good coffee shop," Hyla says.

"Surprisingly." I take a sip and feel the hit of both energy and calm that only coffee can give. "So, a flight attendant, huh?"

She bobs her head up and down. "I've thought about becoming one. Meeting new people, seeing new places. Probably sounds crazy."

"I can actually see that being a great fit for you. You're bubbly, great at making friends, and people love to be around you."

She blushes slightly. "I'm not sure about that."

"Hey, it's true." I bump her arm with mine. "How have you been?"

She bites her lip before looking at me. "Pretty good. I feel stronger. Healthier. Not so... hopeless anymore. I still have my days where I struggle, but the reminder of what I don't want is right here." She flips one wrist over and traces the scar. "Whenever I have a moment where things feel dark, I try to remember my coping mechanisms, reach out to someone I love and trust—usually Trev or Liz—and I remember how I felt waking up in the hospital. How grateful I felt to be alive—the deep desire to live. Not survive, but thrive. I'm not quite to thriving yet, but I'm not just surviving anymore, either. That's progress."

I grab her hand and squeeze it tightly. "It definitely is. You should be proud of that. I know I am. You have so much strength inside you and so much brightness and beauty. I love seeing it all shine out of you again."

She leans against me. "For the record, so do you. If you ever need to talk about anything, you know I'm always, *always*, here for you, right?"

"I know. And it means a lot to me."

"You know, when Jenny and Greg got married, I didn't predict that my friendship with her would fade, but it's made me even more grateful for all of you. It's allowed our friendships to blossom and grow stronger, and I love that."

"Me too. And I'm glad you and Amanda get along so well now."

She laughs at that. "I can't believe how much I thought she hated me. We're kindred spirits." She smiles and shivers like she got a chill.

"What?"

"I just had one of those moments of complete and utter gratitude. I'm so glad I'm here."

"Me too. Life wouldn't be nearly as fun without you."

We share a laugh, then there's an announcement over the PA system that it's our turn to board.

Joel strides over from where he was chatting with the guys and grabs my carry-on and his in one hand before extending the other to me.

"Ready?"

His easy smile and mesmerizing eyes melt me and maybe put me in a little trance. It's not my fault he's so... dreamy.

Dreamy? What the hell is wrong with me?

"Babe."

"Sorry," I spit out as Hyla laughs. I elbow her in the side and stand up, taking Joel's hand. "Let's go."

I'm not sure how I feel about flying. I've only been on a plane a few times, and despite my adventurous nature, it's not my favorite thing. I feel a little claustrophobic knowing I'm in a flying metal box in the sky.

Nope. Don't go there.

I glance to my right at Joel, who is snoring softly.

Resting my head back against the headrest, I take a deep breath.

"You okay?" Rae asks from my other side. Aaron, Rae, Joel, and I are in a four-seat middle row on the plane.

I turn to look at my sister. "Okay enough."

She looks over at Aaron, who is also asleep, then at Joel, shaking her head. "How do they do that? Sleep anywhere?"

"I have no idea, but I wish I could, too."

"Are you thinking about the letter... or whatever it is?"

I nod slowly, glancing down at my carry-on that the letter might as well be burning a hole in.

"That. And I'm realizing I don't particularly like flying."

She laughs. "Yeah. I realized that about halfway to Spain. Luckily this flight is shorter. What are you thinking about Vanessa?"

"Can we start calling her *she-who-shall-not-be-named?* I hate even saying or hearing her name."

"Oof. I mean, I'm okay with that, but I hate seeing you like this. That she still has any power over you."

"Ugh, Gram said pretty much the same thing when I was texting her yesterday. I don't want to believe she still has any power over me at all, but clearly, she does, or I wouldn't feel like this."

Rae squeezes my hand. "She put you through a lot. It's been years since you've talked to her, and you've never had any closure on it. It's not that surprising it would still affect you like this. What did Grandpa say?"

I chuckle at that. "Honestly? Unless it's a phone call, I usually only talk to Gram. I group text them pictures sometimes, but Grandpa's snark—though lovingly intended—can sometimes be a little more than I need."

She chuckles at that. "Yeah. That sounds about right. See, I always text both of them because I usually need the kick in the pants. I can see where you need the calm, though. No one better at that than Gram."

I glance to my right again and look at Joel's sweet face.

"Maybe one person," I say softly.

Rae intertwines her fingers with mine and rests her head on my shoulder. "I'm happy you're happy. I've never seen you quite as vibrant as you are with him. He brings out the best in you."

"He does," I say softly, resting my head against hers.

I just hope it stays that way.

With this stupid contact from Vanessa, it has that feeling twisting in my gut again—eventually, I'm going to mess this all up.

Joel

"This place is fucking sweet. Why the hell don't you come here more often?" Trevor says as we make our way through the beach house and catch the view of the beach and ocean through the deck door.

"Seriously! I can't believe I missed out on all of this last time. I should've sunbathed while you guys did all the wedding stuff," Amanda says, eyes wide as she steps onto the back deck.

"This place is seriously gorgeous. Thank you for inviting me," Chelsea says.

"Of course. I'm excited to have everyone here with us this time," I say as we step onto the deck.

Hyla claps her hands. "This is going to be such a great vacation!"

"Hell yes, it is—" Amanda stops in her tracks as she stares off the back of the deck. "Oh my god!" She bolts down the stairs and across the large back terrace and into Jamie's waiting arms.

"What's he doing here?" Sarah asks in surprise.

"He managed to sneak away for a couple days. He has to leave on Tuesday morning," Aaron says.

"That's sweet, though," Rae says. Amanda and Jamie tip over, falling into the sand as they make out. "And maybe a little gross."

"Pot meet kettle." Sarah grins at her.

"I could say the same to you."

"Yes, you're all nauseating. Macks, shall we?" Miles says, grabbing Mackie's bag. One of the bedrooms has two twins and Miles claimed that one for him and Mackie so they could escape us being nauseating—his words, not mine. But probably fair. If I had to be here with Sarah and I not fully together still, I'd be a little bummed, too. For some reason, love is always in the air in

Charleston, and with four couples on this trip, that's sure to be the case.

"Let's all get settled. I had the cleaning staff put names on each door so everyone can find their room. There's an awesome fish taco place not too far from here where we can grab dinner, then have a bonfire on the beach. Let's all relax until then."

Everyone agrees and we head to our various rooms.

"This room is beautiful," Sarah says, looking around the master. "I've seen glimpses of it before, but I've never been in here."

The master is at the back of the house and has its own private balcony. I wrap my arms around Sarah from behind as she looks out the open door, taking in the sweeping views.

"I know we're not morning people, but we need to watch at least one sunrise on this balcony," she says softly.

"Mm. Agreed." Kissing her neck, I drag one hand up her body.

She spins around quickly, looping her arms around my neck. "We should probably christen this room, right?"

"Absolutely," I mumble against her lips, picking her up and carrying her to the bed to do just that.

"What do you think, Beautiful? Ready for a walk on the beach?"

Rae smiles brightly and hops out of her chair, grabbing Aaron's hand and pulling him up too. "Yes, please." She glances at us. "We'll be back!"

"Have fun," Sarah says.

They walk toward the water as Sarah twirls her fingers through my hair.

Everyone is meandering around the terrace. Trevor and Chelsea went to get ice cream. Hyla is sitting across the fire from us with Miles and Mackie. Mackie and Hyla seem comfortable with each other. Maybe slipping back into friendship won't be too bad for them. Amanda and Jamie are sitting on the beach, watching the stars and kissing.

"Everyone seems happy," Sarah says softly as I rub my hand up and down her back. I love the oversized Adirondack chairs around the firepit. Perfect for curling up with your girl on your lap.

"So... what do you want for your birthday?" Sarah grazes her lips over my cheek.

Palming her cheek, I look into her eyes which are almost as blue as the ocean in the distance.

"You."

"You already have me."

I shrug. "All I need." We share a soft kiss, then I ask, "What do you want for your birthday?"

"Happiness," she breathes, sadness creeping into her eyes.

Shifting so I can get a better look at her, I scan her face, seeing the pain behind her eyes.

"Babe. If this thing with Vanessa is going to affect your ability to enjoy yourself here, then we should talk about it now. Get it all out so you can have fun. You deserve that."

She nods. "Gram and Rae both said Vanessa still has power over me. If it's affecting me this much, they're right. But I don't understand why. Why can't I let this go?"

"Because she hurt you. Someone who never should've hurt you, broke you. And that comes with trauma and a lot of complicated feelings. You can't just turn those off."

"Cutting her off did that for me."

"But it didn't stop the feelings. It prevented the trigger for them. Maybe going forward, you need to start addressing those feelings and figuring out how best to deal with them."

"I wish I didn't have to deal with them at all. I don't want her in my life. I want to let her go."

"Then why are you worrying about what's in that envelope?" My voice is soft as I say the words. That's the question she has to answer before she can figure out what to do with it.

She opens and closes her mouth several times, then bites her cheek.

"I want her to feel bad. I want her to care. I want what's in that envelope to be her groveling, begging for forgiveness. She abandoned me, and I've had to deal with that every day of my life. Then I'm supposed to be the bigger person and let it all go? Forgive her? It's not fair. I want the closure, and I don't want to have to figure it out on my own."

I kiss the side of her head. "That makes sense. You deserve that."

"But?"

I chuckle. "She might never give you that. Even if she did, would it make you feel better? Make you want contact with her?"

"No. Not at all. I'm not sure there's anything she could say or do that would make me want to talk to her or see her again. I don't want her in my life."

The pain lifting off her is palpable. The energy around us shifts as her eyes widen, then fill with determination.

"I don't want to open that letter. Not even a little bit."

She jumps off my lap, and I quickly stand up as she tears off across the terrace toward the house.

"Where are you going?" I call, running after her.

"To get it!" she yells back.

I follow her into the house and upstairs to the master. She grabs her massive "purse" and digs through it, pulling out a folded envelope. She holds it up, smiling, then grabs my hand. "Come on. Let's go."

She leads me back downstairs and out to the terrace, stopping in front of the firepit.

Holding my hand tightly, she takes a deep breath, then tosses it into the fire, watching as the flames flare up around it, engulfing it, before turning it to ash.

Then she exhales forcefully and turns to me, smiling. It's brighter now, no ache in her eyes.

"Thank you." She loops her arms around my neck and looks into my eyes. "Thank you for knowing exactly what to say to help me process what was in my head. I think I knew all along what I wanted. I just needed to understand why. You helped me do that. You knew exactly what I needed."

Grazing my lips over hers, I mutter, "And you always know what I need. I love you, babe."

"Love you too." A quick kiss, then I see that joyful smile again. "Can we roast marshmallows? Then maybe go for a walk?"

"We can do anything that makes you smile like that."

I pull her into my arms, hugging her tightly. I love every version of her, but seeing her like this lights up my soul.

"Mm. Then definitely marshmallows. Ooh! S'mores. Rae got peanut butter cups to use instead of a chocolate bar."

"Sounds perfect, babe. Lead the way."

She takes my hand and starts off toward the house. I look over my shoulder, taking in the clear night sky over the beach mixed with the warmth of the bonfire and all of our friends surrounding it.

Charleston might not mean to me what it does to Rae and Aaron, but damn it, I love this place.

Sarah

My alarm beeps quietly, instantly rousing me from sleep. Somehow, I'm both a deep sleeper and a light sleeper—I can sleep incredibly deeply but still wake easily. I've never understood how, but it's always been the case. Unlike my sister or Joel, who both need to wake up gradually, I can go from asleep to awake in a second and be ready to go.

I turn off the alarm, then roll onto my side and poke Joel in the back.

He makes a groaning, grumbling noise, but rolls over.

"Are you awake?"

Again, I get a groan.

I slide down in bed and rest my head right next to his. "Happy birthday." I kiss his nose and finally, one eye opens.

"What time is it?"

"Midnight. Ish. I had to be the first one to wish you a happy birthday."

"You're crazy."

"Hey, you said you wanted me."

His other eye flashes open, and he smiles. Grabbing the back of my neck, he presses his lips against mine in a slow, controlled kiss before lifting his lips off mine, centimeter by centimeter.

"Fuck yes. Best birthday ever."

"Does that mean you're ready to open your present?"

"Mm. If I have to," he says, tugging at the hem of my shirt.

Wrapping my hand over his, I push back. "I meant your *actual* present."

"I thought that was you," he says, going for my weak spot—my jawline. He kisses it first, then licks across it.

I whimper as I try to keep my control and remember what I'm doing.

"I'm part of it," I get out, pushing him away so I can sit up.

My heart pounds as I climb out of bed, trying to ignore my body flushing and the heat coursing through my veins. I squat down next to my suitcase and open the hidden bottom compartment and pull out his gift.

What do you get the sweet, sentimental man in your life who already has everything?

Something that will make him cry, of course.

Inspired by the gift for Rae's bridal shower and the slideshow we made for the wedding, I've been slowly creating this gift for Joel over the last couple of months.

Sitting back down on the bed, I place it in his lap.

"You didn't have to get me anything."

"Shut up and open it."

He shakes his head. "So bossy."

"I thought you liked that."

He reaches over and squeezes my thigh firmly before unwrapping the present. Pulling the top off the box, he looks down at the faux leather scrapbook. A photo of us from prom is set into the front of it, and underneath it reads:

Patience (n): the capacity to accept or tolerate delay without getting angry or upset

He glances at me out of the corner of his eye, then flips it open to the first page. Two photos of us—one from childhood and a selfie we took a few weeks ago—sit on the page. Underneath is a note from me.

Joel,
The patience you've shown me has been the most heartfelt display of love I've ever received. Your steadfast love for me makes me feel safe, builds me up, and reminds me every day

what it is to care for and love someone.
Happy birthday. Here's to a lifetime more together.
Sarah

It wasn't easy writing those words—"a lifetime more"—but he's had so much faith in me, he deserves my faith in us in return.

He sniffs, then looks over at me. "I love you."

Wrapping one hand around his, I lean over and kiss his cheek. "I love you too. Keep going."

He flips through the pages, seeing photo after photo of us with little notes from me along the way.

"Sarah," he whispers as he closes the book, wiping his eyes. "That was... it's the best gift I've ever received. Thank you."

"Thank you. You never gave up on me. I know it wasn't easy for you, but it meant everything to me. It *means* everything to me."

"Damn, babe." He sets the present aside and wipes his eyes again. Reaching for me, he presses his lips against mine again. "Worth the wait. Worth every fucking second."

His kisses grow forceful, needy, and I melt under his touch.

He trails his fingers under my shirt and up my navel.

"Did you still want to open your *other* present?" I breathe.

"Mm. Do you want me to?"

Desperation fuels my response. "Yes."

He chuckles, pushing me backward onto the bed and lying over the top of me, pressing hot kisses into my neck. Then I feel how badly he wants this.

We go slow, taking our time, enjoying the feel of each other's bodies and the connection flowing between us. Joel is a master of the buildup. Of tantalizing me until I'm begging, then doing it over and over again. Bodies tangled, we revel in the heat between us. The lust. The love. The passion. We tease each other, driving each other to the edge before stopping and starting all over until finally we're flying over the edge together, eyes locked, hands intertwined, as we come apart at the seams.

He wraps me in his arms as he lies down next to me. "Definitely my best birthday ever." Then he laughs. "I've never had sex on my birthday before."

My eyes widen. "Seriously?"

He laughs. "Well, I didn't start seriously dating someone at fourteen like you did. And I'm not a random hookup guy like Miles. I think I did some other stuff with a girlfriend one year, but never sex."

"Glad I got to be the one who popped that cherry." I smile at him, unable to hide how happy I feel right now—not that I want to. I started this trip hurting and uncertain, but Joel's support helped me work through what I wanted and needed, and we've spent the last few days having a blast.

"Fuck, you're so cute." He kisses my cheek.

"Glad you weren't too mad at me for waking you up."

"You made it worth it."

"Good. Because I have more planned."

Yesterday, the girls and I went to a local bakery, and I got Joel's favorite cupcakes—spice with cream cheese frosting. I had to hide them in the back of the refrigerator under a giant bag of kale so I could surprise him with them.

"Oh really? Like what?"

"Get dressed and you'll find out."

"We're buying a dozen more of these before we go home," Joel says, moaning over the last bite of his *second* cupcake.

"Why don't you make those noises for me?" I playfully pout.

One eyebrow lifts, then he tackles me, pinning me down in the sand. "You must have a very short memory if you don't remember me moaning and groaning and saying your name. *Yes, Sarah. Fuck me.*" He drags his lips over my neck, then lets my arms go and sits back on his heels, grinning.

I prop up on my elbows and stare at him, tilting my head to the side. "You know, I kinda like some dirty talk."

"Oh, really?" He leans down again and whispers filthy things in my ear, things a lady should not repeat. Not sure how much of a lady I am, though, since I'm blushing at his words and wishing he'd take me back up to the bedroom and do the many naughty things he's suggested.

"You're pretty good at that. Maybe too good."

"Feeling a little hot?"

"Yep. Maybe we should cool off. In the ocean."

His eyebrows shoot up. "It's going to be freezing."

"That's the point." I shove him off and get to my feet. "What are you? Chicken?"

"Never." He stands up and takes my hand. "You want to do this? Let's do this. No backing out."

I twist my pinky around his. "Wouldn't dare."

"Three," he says.

"Two."

"One!" we yell together as we run toward the water.

A wave hits our legs as we run into the ocean.

"Oh my god! Oh! It's freezing!" I turn and jump into Joel's arms, wrapping around him like a koala on a tree.

"I told you," he grunts, bracing me with his arms as he runs out of the water and collapses on the sand.

"Cooled us off, though."

His eyes narrow as heat fills them. "Nope."

He pushes me backward, lying over the top of me again, hands in my hair as we make out in the sand.

It's crazy to think Charleston is where Joel and I had our first—unofficial—kiss. It wasn't some magical moment where everything changed, but it was still unforgettable. We've had a lot of amazing vacations here, but it's safe to say, this has been our best one yet.

Chapter Nineteen

Everywhere

Sarah

ONE MORE MONTH. I drag my finger over the calendar in our bedroom. Just under a month until graduation—the same day as my birthday. Three more weeks until my program is done, I take my boards, and hopefully become a registered nurse. First thing first, though. Tonight is a baseball game.

Stepping away from the calendar, I walk over to Joel's dresser and pull out one of his baseball tees. It's been a little warmer lately, so I think I can get away with one of his T-shirts over one of my long sleeve shirts.

On the bed, my phone rings. I spin around and grab it, smiling when I see Gram's name.

"Hey Gram. What's up?"

"Oh, not much, dear. You were on my mind is all. I don't mean to press a sore subject, but I was curious to know if you ever made a decision about that letter from Vanessa?"

Shoot. How did I forget to tell her?

I guess because I forgot about it in general. It's surprising, actually. I was sure I'd feel guilty about it, but I don't feel guilty at all. Like I did when I blocked her number years ago, I feel certain it was the right decision.

"Sorry, I forgot to tell you. I decided in Charleston not to open it. Joel helped me figure out how I felt about it all."

"Which is?"

"That nothing she could say or do would make me want contact. So, I tossed the letter in the fire."

Gram chuckles. "That's my girl. For whatever it's worth, this old lady thinks you made the right decision."

"You're not *that* old, Gram."

"Tell that to my seventy-one-year-old joints."

"Hey, baby, are you ready to—" Rae stops short in the doorway. "Oh, sorry."

"You're fine. I'm just talking to Gram. Come here."

Rae sits down on the bed and I plop down next to her, putting the phone on speaker as I do.

"Do I hear another grandbaby?" Gram asks.

"Hey, Gram! How are you?"

"I'm good, dear. How about you? What have you been up to?"

Rae shrugs. "Just school, work, cheering the boys on, and doing the wife thing."

Gram laughs. "Doing the wife thing. You girls make me laugh."

"Are those my girlies I hear?" Grandpa says.

There's some fuzziness, then the phone is on speaker.

"We're both here, Grandpa," I say.

"How are you two doing? Staying out of trouble, I hope."

"As much as we ever do," Rae says mischievously.

"Good. Just what I like to hear. Now, I'm afraid I need to steal your grandmother away. We're going to have dinner with your parents."

"Have fun," I say, wishing we could be there with them. Weekly dinner with my parents and grandparents was one of my favorite things growing up and something I miss having regularly now. All the more reason why I want to move back home when everyone is done with college.

"We will. Love you, girlies."

"Love you, Grandpa!" Rae and I call.

"I suppose I ought to go too," Gram says, her phone off speaker now.

"That's okay, we need to get ready for the game," I tell her.

"Wish the boys luck for me. Love you girls."

"Love you!" Rae says.

"Oh, Sarah."

Rae gives me a little nod and stands up as I take the phone off speaker and put it to my ear again. "Yeah?"

"I'm proud of you and the decisions you're making. You're growing into a strong, confident young woman. After all you've been through, it warms my heart to see you doing so well. I love you, honey."

And I'm crying.

"Thanks, Gram. That means a lot. I love you too."

"Have fun at the game, sweetheart. Talk soon."

"Bye."

I hang up and stare down at my phone.

"Everything okay?" Rae asks.

"Yeah. Just Gram telling me how proud she is of me."

Rae chuckles. "Oof, yeah. When she called on my birthday and said that, I started crying, too. The power of Gram."

I can't help but laugh at that. "She does have some pretty strong powers. Especially to keep Grandpa in line all these years."

Laughing at that, we get dressed and ready to go cheer on the boys.

I've been tossing and turning all night. For some reason, I can't get into a good sleep. Sighing, I open my eyes and glance at the time. Just after midnight. How is it only midnight? I feel like I've been in bed trying to sleep for hours.

Shutting my eyes hard, I try to relax against the bed and let the sound of Joel's breathing lull me to sleep.

Ugh. Now I have to pee.

After using the bathroom, I climb back into bed and try some deep breathing. Deanna Barnes, who runs an incredible yoga studio back home in conjunction with her husband's gym, often says, "breathe like you're filling your soul." She also pokes fun at how hippieish that sounds, but it weirdly makes sense. Or maybe that's my middle of the night tiredness talking.

Nestling in, I lie flat on my back, let my muscles relax, and breathe deep.

I'm almost asleep when the bedroom door swings open. "Sarah?"

I sit up straight in bed at Rae's panicky voice. Smacking my hand against the touch lamp on my bedside table, some light fills the room.

Rae sits down on the bed, phone in her hand.

"What's wrong?"

She shakes her head. "I don't know. Dad's on the phone. He wouldn't tell me anything until I got you."

I instantly wrap my hand around hers as Aaron sits down next to her. Joel rustles next to me, slowly pushing himself up to sitting.

Rae puts her phone on speaker and holds it out. "Okay, we're both here."

"Daddy, what's going on?"

Dad's shaky breath before he speaks makes my stomach twist.

"There's no good way to tell you girls this... We were having dinner with Gram and Grandpa tonight, and when they were getting ready to go home, Gram said she didn't feel well. She went to stand up, and she collapsed. We couldn't wake her. We called 911 right away and they got her to the hospital, but..." My breath hitches at his words. Dad takes a deep breath and continues. "She had a massive heart attack. There was nothing they could do. She passed away about an hour ago."

"No," Rae squeaks, tears spilling from her eyes.

"I just—I talked to her a few hours ago. I..." Joel wraps his arms around me, holding me tightly.

Rae's face is buried in Aaron's chest as she cries.

"I'm so sorry I had to tell you like this."

"How are Mom and Grandpa?" Rae asks suddenly, lifting her head off Aaron's chest. Then she looks at me, and I nod. "Actually, it doesn't matter. We're coming home."

"No. It's the middle of the night."

"We're not going to be able to sleep anyway," I say.

"I need you two to be safe," Dad says, voice breaking. Gram was a mother to him too. We *need* to be home.

"We'll make sure they are, Charlie," Aaron says, looking at Joel.

"Absolutely," Joel says, rising from the bed and grabbing bags from the closet.

"Okay. Text me when you leave. I love you both."

"Love you too," Rae says.

"Love you, Daddy." I sniff back tears as Rae hangs up.

We look at each other, both of us feeling the same thing—like the world is crashing around us.

"We need to get ready. Need to pack," I say, forcing myself off the bed.

"Yeah," Rae chokes out.

I turn back to her and lose all the control I was holding onto. Crawling across the bed, I pull her into my arms. She holds me tightly as we cry.

This can't be real. It's not fair. I just talked to her. She just told me how proud she was of me. It's not—I can't... what do we do without Gram?

Joel kisses the side of my head. "We're going to start packing."

"Okay," I say.

"Thank you," Rae whispers to no one in particular.

Aaron and Joel look at each other, then climb off the bed. As Aaron walks to the door, Miles sticks his head in. "Hey. I heard some noise up here—" He stops short, looking at us. "What happened?"

Aaron leans in and tells Miles what happened. At least, I assume he does. He says it quietly enough we don't have to hear it again. I don't want to hear it again. I don't want it to be true. She's only seventy-one. We were supposed to have more time. Grandpa was supposed to have more time with her.

Miles sits down on the bed with us and Amanda and Mackie walk in and Aaron fills them in as well.

"You guys are going home tonight?" Mackie asks.

"Yeah," I say.

"We'll come too," Mackie says.

"No. You guys have class tomorrow. You need to stay," I say. Miles and Mackie look at each other like they're going to disagree, so I continue. "Tomorrow is Friday. Come home after your classes."

"We'll all be there," Trevor says, appearing in the doorway.

Aaron looks at Joel. "We need to pack if we're going to leave tonight."

"We'll help," Amanda says.

"Yeah," Mackie agrees. "It's the least we can do."

Mackie helps Joel pack for me while Amanda follows Aaron back to his and Rae's room.

Trev sits down on the bed with us as well. "I'm so sorry."

Rae breathes out a shaky breath, then squeezes my hand tighter.

This wasn't supposed to happen yet. I'm not ready. I'm just... not ready.

Rae and I are tucked under a blanket in the back seat of her Corolla while Aaron drives us home, Joel sitting next to him, both quietly sipping energy drinks.

All I can think is that I don't want to. I don't want this to be real. I don't want Gram to be gone. I don't want to think about what comes next. I don't want to feel this pain.

"I hate this," Rae mumbles.

"Me too."

She wraps her hand over mine and rests her head against my shoulder.

"We should try to sleep."

"Yeah. Probably."

I rest my head against hers and close my eyes, but I can't sleep. All I can think is how unfair all this is.

Aaron parks the car out back and we all get out.

Dread fills my gut as we approach the back door. I'm not ready for this.

Joel wraps an arm around my waist. "I've got you."

Though the words don't stop the hurt, they make me believe I can face what's to come.

Rae goes first, Aaron's hand wrapped tightly around hers. She opens the back door and walks in. The first thing I notice when I step inside is silence. I *hate* when my house is quiet like this. It's unnatural. With Mom usually home and our friends in and out, this house was rarely ever quiet.

After shutting the door behind us, we slip off our shoes and make our way into the family room. Dad meets us at the doorway to the kitchen, hugging Rae and me tightly.

"They're in the front room. Come on."

He leads us through the house as if we've never been here before. A gnawing ache grows in the pit of my stomach. I want to scream and cry and run away.

Mom and Grandpa are sitting on one of the couches, talking softly, though Mom stops mid-sentence when we walk in.

Launching off the couch, she walks over to us and pulls both of us into her arms at once.

"You shouldn't have driven home in the middle of the night," she chastises, wiping her eyes. "But I'm glad you're here."

After she lets us go, we make our way over to Grandpa and attack him with a double hug.

"We love you," Rae whispers.

"I know, my girlies. I love you too."

The sadness in his voice breaks my heart. I can't imagine losing the person you love so suddenly—especially after fifty years together.

My eyes drift over to Joel. *I will not think about that right now. Or ever. I'm not sure how I'd survive pain like that.*

We sit down and quiet conversation resumes with Mom and Dad occasionally fielding phone calls from her siblings. Mostly, we sit together, drinking tea and eating sandwiches the boys made.

Around four in the morning, Dad announces it's time for everyone to get some sleep.

Rae looks at the front door and hesitates. "I know it's only a half block away, but I don't want to go."

"Sleep here," Mom says. "We put a new bed in your old room. Sleep up there. I'll feel better with both of my girls under one roof."

Rae nods and hugs Mom, then Grandpa, then Dad. I do the same, and the four of us make our way up the back stairs to our bedrooms. No matter where she's living, that'll always be her bedroom in my mind.

We exchange hugs, then go into our separate bedrooms.

I collapse onto the bed, tears streaming down my face. Joel lies down next to me and wraps his arms around me.

Rolling over, I bury my face in his chest.

"I hate this."

"I know, babe. I know."

He kisses my forehead and holds me tightly. That's the last thing I remember before drifting off.

Rae

Sniffling, I crawl into the bed in my old bedroom. It feels both comforting and strange to be in this room now. The walls are the same creamy tan they've always been, but now a plush-top queen mattress sits where my bed used to be. The bedding is new and cozy, yet also different from my patterned sheets and brightly colored comforters.

Aaron climbs into bed and immediately wraps me in his arms.

My safest place. Always.

What would I do without him?

Not a question I like to think, but it's on my mind. How could it not be in the midst of all this?

"I love you, Beautiful," he whispers as I sniffle.

"I love you too, Ace. I..."

"Don't. Babe. You're not going to lose me."

"You don't know that. I know you always say we die together like the old couple on the Titanic, but you don't know that's what will happen. My grandparents are the ultimate love story. They should've had longer. If they didn't, there are no guarantees for anyone else."

He kisses my forehead and squeezes me tighter. "They are soul mates. No doubt about that. But we're more than that. We always have been. I'm convinced we share a soul, and that's why we were always pulled to each other. And if we share a soul, then we die together."

I laugh through my tears. "You're ridiculous, but I love you."

"I love you too, Beautiful. So damn much. Let's get some sleep."

In the safety of his arms, for a little while, everything else washes away, and I manage to get some sleep.

Joel

"Go back to sleep," I whisper, kissing Sarah's head as I slide out of bed.

"Where are you going?"

"I know today is going to be busy. My mom texted me last night and said they came home from their trip early, so I wanted to go see them and let them know. I'll be back soon, okay?"

She nods, then pulls the covers up farther.

"Love you, babe."

"I love you too," she breathes, then nestles back into her pillow.

I head downstairs where I find Aaron in the kitchen with Charlie. Aaron hands me a mug of coffee.

"Thanks. I'm going to see my parents quick. I'll be back soon. Need anything?" I ask Charlie.

He shakes his head, looking exhausted. Aaron shoots me a look, then glances at my phone. He pulls his out and quickly types something. When mine vibrates in my hand, I look at it.

Aaron: Meet me at the bakery in fifteen minutes and we'll grab a bunch of food for everyone.

I look at him and nod, then walk through the family room toward the back door, sliding my shoes on before I walk out of the house.

Fog lifts into the air with each breath I take. It's cold and rainy today, matching the mood.

When I walk in my back door, I'm surprised to find not only my parents, but Jesse in the kitchen as well.

"Joel!" Mom says with a bright smile. "What are you doing here, honey?"

"Little bro? What's wrong?" Jesse asks, clocking the solemn look on my face immediately.

Everyone turns to look at me.

"Son, what is it?" Dad asks.

"Bea passed away last night."

"Oh no," my mom says softly.

"Shit," Jesse mutters, his face paling.

"What happened?" my mother asks as Dad whips out his phone and steps away.

"She had a heart attack."

"Poor Kara," she whispers, as my attention turns to my father.

I watch him out of the corner of my eye, listening as he talks.

"Charlie, I just heard. What do you need? How can we help?"

That's one thing my parents are good at—coming through in the clutch. They suck at the day-to-day stuff, but they're great in an emergency. And like always, they're more than willing to help how they can and are always generous with their money, using it to help those around them.

"What about the food?" he asks. "No, don't worry about that. We'll take care of the food. If there's extra, people will have leftovers to take. You don't need any extra stress. Of course. Give Kara our love."

"Hey," my brother says, looking sick to his stomach, "how are the girls?"

"Rough. They're rough."

He nods. "I've gotta go. But keep me updated? And let me know when the funeral is. I'll be there."

"Will do."

Jesse squeezes my shoulder and walks toward the front door as I turn to my mom.

"Glad you're home."

"I'm glad we cut our trip short. I was going to call you after breakfast to see if we could visit you at the lake house this weekend. Maybe next weekend instead."

"Yeah. You'll be there for Sarah's graduation next month, right?"

"Of course, honey. We wouldn't miss it."

Only because it's at the college and Dad's an alumnus.

I bite my cheek. Today is not the day for my complicated feelings about my parents.

I glance over at my dad, who is now on the phone with a caterer.

"I need to go meet Aaron at the bakery, but I'll talk to you all later, okay? Tell Dad thanks from me."

Mom gives me a hug and a kiss. "Love you."

"Love you too, Mom."

I leave through the front door, walking slowly around the block to the bakery and letting the crisp air cool me off.

When I get there, I find Aaron talking to Mackie.

"What the heck are you doing here?"

Mackie grins at me. "You didn't expect us to wait around when our friends needed us, did you?"

I chuckle at that. "Where's Miles?"

"On his way to see the girls. Figured I'd set you two up with all the good stuff before heading over. My mom started putting together trays of pastries, donuts, and bagels as soon as I texted her this morning. She also made some fresh English muffins and a quiche."

It's funny, our families didn't really know each other before we all met as kids. They may have known each other in passing, but our closeness brought them together, and though they may not all be best friends like we are, they support each other and show up for each other in the tough moments.

"Ready to head back, then? I don't want to leave them alone for long," I say.

"Me either," Aaron agrees. "Let's go."

Hauling all the trays of food, we make our way back to the girls.

Sarah

The bed feels cold without Joel. My heart feels heavier. I'm so thankful to have him by my side through this. I'm not sure I've ever felt an ache quite like this. Some people don't have close relationships with their grandparents, but they're everything to me. Gram and Grandpa were there through every hard moment in my life. And when Grandpa gave me tough love, Gram's hand was the one wrapped around mine, giving me calm, steady love.

I start sniffling again. The last time I remember feeling emotional pain so physically is when I broke up with Trevor, but even that doesn't come close to this.

My door creaks open, then closes again. A moment later, my covers flip back and Rae crawls into bed with me.

I roll over to face her and brush a tear off her nose.

"Been a while since we've done this," I whisper.

She nods and wraps her arms around me. We hold each other close as we cry, letting out all the horrible pain we're feeling—the heartache that feels like it might never stop.

After a little while, we decide to go check on Mom and head downstairs. When we get there, we see Mom on the couch in the front room with Miles' mom, Katie, snuggled next to her, arms wrapped around her. Dad is pacing back and forth across the room on his phone. He's been the MVP, fielding every phone call, figuring out what needs to be done, and contacting everyone who needs to be contacted.

"This is so hard," Mom sniffs. "And usually, when I feel like this, I call her. I always call her."

Mom breaks down crying, but Katie hugs her tighter. "I know, honey. I know."

We both smile wistfully at that. Over the years, Mom and Katie have become the kind of best friends that the six of us are.

"Sometimes you just need your friends," Rae says quietly.

"Agreed," comes a deep voice from behind us. We turn to see Miles smiling at us. "You didn't really think we'd stay away, did you?"

"Yeah, you should know by now we're shit listeners," Mackie says, walking down the hall from the kitchen. "Besides, what one of us goes through, we all go through." She smiles at us as Aaron and Joel follow her down the hallway.

"Thank God for that," I say softly.

The six of us stand together in a group hug.

"I'm glad you're all here," Rae says softly.

"Nowhere else we'd be," Miles says. "Sometimes what we really need is each other."

"Love you guys," I say quietly.

We stand, arms wrapped around each other, and for a moment, I feel like a kid again. The one surrounded by the love of her best friends—all these years later, it's still the same thing. The six of us, always in it together, no matter what. Moments like this, I couldn't be more grateful for that. As Joel's arm tightens around me, I'm also grateful that in that group of best friends, I found my love, my person, the one who makes going through this bearable.

After a day of visits from friends and much of my mom's family arriving in town, chaos has now taken hold. Rae, Aaron, Joel and I are sitting in the front room of my parents' house with Mom and Dad, Grandpa, all of my aunts and uncles—except Aunt Sylvia, who is on a video call with us—and several of my cousins as they intensely discuss funeral dates and plans.

The room quiets for a moment when the front door swings open, and Jesse steps inside. I'm confused until I realize his hand is intertwined with Dani's. She walks over and hugs Grandpa as Rae and I exchange a surprised look. Then we both look at Joel, who shrugs.

They sit down on the other side of Joel, and the intense conversation begins again.

Grandpa isn't actually discussing much. He keeps reiterating that we should stick to whatever Gram wanted, which is written in her will. My dad is the executor of the will, which means he's responsible for seeing her instructions carried out. The only problem is, she didn't specify every tiny detail, like the type of food, how many flowers to have, or how quickly the funeral should take place. Since Mom and Dad lived closest and spent the most time with them in adulthood, Mom has been the one trying to be the voice of reason and diffuse the arguments and think about what Gram would've wanted. Rae and I chime in to support her wherever we can.

Mom's family gets along pretty well, but someone is frustrated with something at every turn. Some people are grateful Joel's dad is taking care of the food, other people are pissed about it. Aunt Sylvia wants pink roses, but Uncle Chris thinks they're too fancy and Gram wouldn't have cared.

Mom presses the heels of her palms against her eyes, trying to take a steadying breath. Rae and I exchange a glance, and I'm about to say we should take a break when another fight breaks out over something innocuous.

Dad steps forward, opening his mouth to speak, when Mom stands up.

"Enough! Enough. We're supposed to be planning something that would honor Mom. Fighting like this would only disappoint her. The Wilkinsons are covering the food because they offered and they're good friends." She smiles softly at Joel. "The flowers will be white carnations and pink daffodils because those were Mom's favorites. Donations can go to Promise, where Rae works, or to The Trevor Project, because she was passionate about both causes. And the funeral will be on Tuesday with the reception at the farmhouse like she wanted. If you don't like it, don't come!"

Grandpa watches as Mom storms out of the room, but then nods.

"She's right. You'd all do well to think about what Mom would say right now."

He gets up and walks upstairs. He slept here last night, and may for the foreseeable future.

Dad looks down the hall as the back door slams. He turns to go after Mom, but Rae and I catch him first.

"Let us," I say softly.

He nods, pushing out a sigh. "I'll try to rein everyone in."

"Love you, Daddy," Rae says, then we walk down the hall to the back of the house.

Outside, we find Mom sitting on the steps up to the deck, crying.

"Hey, Momma," I say softly as Rae and I sit down on either side of her.

She sniffs, then looks between us.

"That wasn't my finest moment in there. Talk about not making Gram proud." She shakes her head at herself.

"Are you kidding? Gram could always dish it out when she needed to. How do you think she kept Grandpa in line?"

Mom chuckles.

Rae loops her arm through Mom's and rests her head on Mom's shoulder.

"You know, I always thought I got my ability to bottle things up until I explode from Dad. Maybe it was you all along."

Mom laughs again. "It's possible. I can't stand all the fighting. That's not how she raised us, especially over such petty things. I know everyone processes in their own way, but that was ridiculous. All she would care about is us being together as a family."

"And we will be," I say. "They'll settle down. Grandpa pretty much told them to shove it after you left. Everyone's hurting right now and it's showing off their worst sides."

"It wasn't supposed to happen so soon. I don't feel like I got enough time with her. I'm only forty-one. I'm still learning. There's so much more I wanted her to teach me," Mom whispers.

I wrap my arm around hers and take her hand. "Guess we'll have to muddle through it all together, then."

"I'm a great muddler," Rae says with a hint of a smile.

"I love you girls. I'm so grateful I have you both." Her eyes find mine as she says the words, and she gives my hand an extra squeeze.

"Love you too, Momma," we both say.

The back door opens and closes, and a moment later, Uncle Darren is standing in front of us.

"Hey, little sis. Everyone is calmer now if you're ready to come back inside." He extends his hand out to Mom.

Mom kisses each of our heads, then looks at Uncle Darren. "Yes. Okay." She lets him pull her up, then he quickly wraps his arms around her in a bear hug.

"I'm sorry. We're all hurting, but you've been through the worst of it. Love you."

"Love you too, you jerk."

Rae and I both laugh at that. It reminds me of how we talk to the boys.

As they walk back inside, Rae says, "Should we head back in too?"

I watch them go, then shake my head. "It's crazy enough in there. How about we get the boys, maybe Jesse and Dani too—I want to know what the hell is going on there—and text Miles and Mackie, and we can all go down to the coffee house for some coffee?"

A smile grows on her face and her shoulders soften. "Yeah. That sounds perfect. Let's go."

Joel

Something I've never done before: stood in a funeral receiving line. Well, we're in a sort of extended version of one in the front row of chairs. With so many people in the family, they opted to have all the cousins stand off to the side so people could visit with them if they wanted to. Most people have stopped to chat with at least a few of the cousins.

I was a little surprised when Kara and Charlie insisted I stand in the line with Sarah. It made sense for Aaron since he and Rae are married, but Charlie took me aside and said that I've always been like family and made it clear he knows that I eventually intend to marry Sarah. He's good at seeing through all the complexities to the clearest truth. Of course I want to marry her one day. I just don't want to push that. After everything, I think it's best to let Sarah set that pace.

Trevor and Chelsea walk in and wave in our direction. Trevor's grandparents have known Pete and Bea for years, so he makes his way through the entire receiving line before stopping in front of us. He gives Sarah a long hug and she starts crying.

I glance over at Aaron, who gives me a knowing smile. Rae and Jesse shared a similar moment when he first got here with Dani—still a little weird seeing them together. Maybe some guys wouldn't be so cool about it, but Aaron and I both respect the friendships the girls have with their—well, I guess exes isn't the right word for Rae and Jesse, but it's a similar sentiment. Despite what may have happened between Rae and Jesse or

Sarah and Trevor, we both understand the importance of the girls' friendships with them.

After two hours of standing and making small talk, the funeral ceremony begins. Taking our seats in the second row, we listen as various members of the family speak and tell stories, but Charlie gives the eulogy.

He gets up to the podium and puts his reading glasses on as he pulls out a piece of paper. "I'm going to do my best to get through this without crying like a baby." He exhales harshly. "Bea was a quiet force of nature. Calm but powerful, she could uplift you or put you in your place with one look. Her words were the most powerful, though. She always spoke with wisdom and an open heart, ready to offer words of encouragement or hard truths at any given moment. Like so many in this room, in losing her, I've wished for her words more than ever.

"To say she was a loving and devoted mother and grandmother sounds like a simple platitude. Don't people always say those things? But with her, it couldn't have been more true. Whether it was tea at the kitchen table or a middle of the night phone call, Bea was ready for it. She learned to text and video call to keep up with her grandchildren, who she always checked in with regularly. She was a true matriarch and the woman we were all proud to look up to.

"When I was eighteen, I left an abusive home and was welcomed by Bea into their family. She showed me love and compassion when I struggled and never judged me. This is the way she carried herself through life, and it shows in the legacy she left. A family full of loving, caring individuals who would do anything for each other or a stranger. I especially see her in the beautiful hearts of the women who learned from her. Her daughters and granddaughters share her kindness, love for others, and ability to give a withering stare."

Everyone laughs at that. And he's not wrong.

"I see her in my wife and daughters every single day. That is the ultimate legacy. Bea spent her life transferring tiny pieces of herself and her love into those around her, making the world a little brighter wherever they touch it. In mourning her loss, we should allow that to be our greatest comfort. We have not lost her spirit, her lessons, or her love. As we all move through life with her in our hearts, she's not gone. She's everywhere."

With a sniff, he steps down from the podium.

Sarah leans against me, tears streaming down her cheeks.

"He's right," I whisper. "She's a part of you."

Sarah nods, but whispers back, "I still miss her. I'd give back all the pieces of her inside me to have one more day—one more moment—with her."

I kiss her head as one of her cousins goes up to speak, but my mind is wandering to my own family. Bea left a beautiful legacy, and while seeing the girls mourn her is painful, it's equally painful to know I don't have that in my own life. Even with my parents. Of course, I'd be devastated to lose them, but I wouldn't be able to stand up there and talk about them the way Charlie talked about Bea. None of what he said was for show. She raised good kids and loved the hell out of them and her grandkids. It's what I hope to do someday, but there's a part of me that's sad I didn't get that.

＊＊＊

The reception at the farmhouse is as loud and full of love as one would expect from the Abbott family. More stories are told about the kind of mother and grandmother Bea was—even some fun stories from her siblings about what she was like when she was young.

I'm walking back to the living room from the bathroom when a firm hand clamps onto my shoulder.

I turn to see Pete, who smiles. "Come with me."

"Okay..."

I follow him upstairs and into his bedroom. He goes to a jewelry cabinet and pulls out a drawer, looking over it for a second before pulling something out. He closes the drawer and opens another, then pulls out a box. Turning to me, he places a ring in the ring box and holds it out to me.

"What's this?" I ask.

"Before everyone starts going through Bea's things, I wanted you to have this. I gave Aaron a ring for Rae. She wanted Sarah to have this one. I'm giving it to you for safekeeping."

My eyes widen. "Oh. Wow. It's beautiful." And it is. It's yellow gold with a large round emerald set into it. "It's meant to be an engagement ring?"

He smiles mischievously. "It is. Now this is where Bea would've said no rush. But in case today hasn't made it obvious, nothing is promised. Use it when the time is right. She knew, like I do, the right match for Sarah. I like Trevor, always have, but she never lit up around him the way she does with you. Take care of her."

"I will, sir. Thank you."

"Oh, don't start with the 'sir' crap, Wilkinson. Just do right by my girly. And don't wait around too long."

I chuckle at that. "I think that's more up to her than me, but thank you."

He nods toward the door. "Well, go on before she realizes you're missing."

I walk back downstairs, my heart beating faster than it should, but I can't help it.

I have her engagement ring in my pocket.

"Hey, where have you been?" Sarah asks when I get back to her.

"Ah, a couple of people stole me for more stories."

She wraps an arm around my waist. "I'm glad you're back."

A few minutes later, Charlie announces we're all going to walk down to Bea's favorite spot in the woods to spread her ashes.

As we walk, I hold Sarah close. Pain is welling up inside her again as we walk toward the final goodbye. It's an act meant to let Bea rest and bring the family closure, though I'm not sure you ever get closure from losing someone you love.

When we get to the spot—a small clearing nestled between the trees that overlooks the whole hillside—Sarah takes my hand and holds it tightly.

"I'm so thankful you're the one standing next to me for this." She leans up and kisses my cheek. "I couldn't do it without you."

"I'll always be here when you reach for my hand. Whatever you need. I love you, babe."

"I love you too."

Sarah

I'm not ready to do this. I made it through today somehow, but I am not ready for this. I don't want to say goodbye. I still don't want this to be real.

"This spot was Bea's favorite," Grandpa says, standing in front of everyone with Gram's ashes. "She'd come out to watch the snow fall, the stars grow in the sky, or the butterflies flit through the fields. It was where she always found peace." He looks down at the ashes. "This is where you get to rest, Ma. Your forever peace," he whispers through tears.

I'm doing my best not to sob, but I can't help it. Rae wraps a hand around mine as her body trembles, though Aaron does his best to steady her. How can you steady anyone through this?

Slowly, Grandpa turns and opens the small wooden box containing her ashes. In gentle movements, he spreads them as we all turn into puddles of tears.

When he's finished, he closes the box, but continues staring ahead, whispering a few words that the rest of us can't make out. As he turns back around, he wipes his eyes.

"Bea had one final request. She wanted this whole out of tune bunch to sing her favorite song—*All You Need Is Love*—my lord, she was obsessed with those damn Beatles. And I think she wants to hear us all sing it as one final laugh, but let's see if we can hold it together for her, huh?"

Grandpa starts, and everyone joins in, singing the song we all know because Gram sang it to us.

"Love's the most important thing," she'd always say. "Never forget that."

That would be impossible.

We're a mix of smiles and blubbering messes as we finish the song. After one last look at the clearing, Grandpa leads the way back to the house. A few people step up to the clearing and look out over the fields or say a few words before following him back through the trails to the house.

Rae looks between Joel and Aaron. "Give us a minute?"

They both nod and step back. Hand in hand, Rae and I walk over to the clearing, wrapping our arms around each other's backs as we take in the gorgeous view, tears streaming down both of our faces.

"Love you, Gram," I say quietly.

"Always," Rae breathes..

We take in the view for a moment longer, until a butterfly flits around in front of us, hovering in one spot before moving on.

Rae's eyes meet mine, and she whispers, "Now she's everywhere."

Cool water on my face feels refreshing, but there's no washing away today.

Looking in the mirror, I check to make sure I haven't missed any of my makeup.

I take in my reflection for a moment. My big deep blue eyes, light brown eyebrows, strays of blond hair stuck to my head, the soft curves of my plump lips, the mole just below my eye on my right cheek.

I wish I looked like her. I wish I could look in the mirror and see Gram.

"Hey, you coming to bed?"

I turn to Joel, who looks more exhausted than he'd ever admit he is. He's spent the last five days doing nothing but supporting not just me or Rae, but my entire family. He, Dad, and Aaron are the MVPs of this weekend. And at night, I know they were both keeping up on school work and figuring out what Rae and I needed to get done and how they could help us.

"Yeah."

I look down at the oversized tee that has swallowed me up. Joel's not a huge guy, but I'm small enough that his shirts are still big on me, and I love it. It makes me feel cozy and safe even when I'm not in his arms. Which I need to be right now.

I'm beyond tired, both emotionally and physically. I'm sad and angry. Angry that I have to go back to my life tomorrow like nothing has changed even though my world has shifted. Losing a grandparent might be nothing to some people, but it's everything to me. Gram loved me so deeply and profoundly before I was ever hers to love. I don't know what to do without that.

Crawling into bed, I sniff back tears.

"Come here," Joel whispers, wrapping his arms around me. I bury my face in his chest and cry.

"I'm not ready to move on."

"I know, babe. And you don't have to. But you have to keep living. Grieve, feel the pain as much as you need to, but don't stop living and loving—you know she'd never want you to."

"I love you," I sob. "How do you always know exactly what I need to hear?"

"I know you. Like you know me. We're not perfect, but together we are. And whatever you're feeling or struggling with, I'm here to hold your hand and love you through it all."

I wipe my teary, snotty face with my arm and look up at him.

He threads a hand through my messy hair and looks into my eyes. After a moment, he kisses my forehead and then my lips.

"Love you. Let's get some sleep."

I kiss him back, then nod.

With his arms wrapped around me, the heartache fades, the exhaustion takes over, and I quickly fall asleep.

Chapter Twenty

Ghost

Sarah

"I STILL CAN'T BELIEVE this..." I mutter, reading the short letter for the hundredth time.

Over on the bed, Joel laughs. "I don't know why. You've read it a thousand times, talked to your advisor about it, *and* accepted the placement."

Hands on my cheeks like the *Home Alone* kid, I turn to face him.

He laughs again as I climb onto the bed. "Maybe because the program is insanely difficult to get into? They only accept twelve students each year—from across the entire country! I wasn't even going to apply until my advisor suggested I should."

"I know, babe. You've told me many times. Just like I've told you, you were the most hardworking person in your program, not to mention you're insanely smart. In case I haven't mentioned it, that's very sexy."

He kisses my neck and I momentarily lose all thought process.

"Joel," I breathe as his mouth moves down to my chest. Then I smack his shoulder and jump off the bed. "I have too much to do! And you're trouble."

He half groans, half chuckles, falling against the pillows in my absence.

Grabbing my checklist off the dresser, I look over it.

Accept program placement. Done.

Make sure it's okay to switch locations and preceptors partway through the program. Done, noted in my file, and future preceptors for when we move back home have been chosen.

Graduate!

That's today.

I finished my program a couple of weeks ago. And yesterday I found out I passed my nursing boards. It's official. I'm a registered nurse with a Bachelor's of Science in Nursing. I worked damn hard for this. Now onto the graduate program. SUNY FL has an incredible combined Women's Health Nurse Practitioner and Certified Nurse Midwife program. They only take twelve people from across the country each year. I wasn't sure I'd have a chance, so I'd already applied and accepted placement elsewhere, when my advisor encouraged me to apply shortly before the deadline. Apparently, the teachers across the program were impressed with me. It's exciting, but nerve-racking. The other program I chose took place over two years with a few weeks off in the winter and summer. This program is extremely intensive, taking place over the course of twenty months with only a week off in the summer and two weeks in the winter. It makes me a little nervous since I already signed up to work at the hospital here on the OB floor a couple of nights a week. I made some great connections there when I was doing my clinicals, so I got a position easily. Hopefully, as long as I budget my time well, I'll still be able to handle it.

As I set the paper back on the dresser, I look at a framed picture of Gram and me that's sitting on top. *I miss you, Gram.*

Some days I still forget she's gone. I tried to call her when I got the acceptance letter. That led to a breakdown and Joel holding me in his arms for a good hour. Not sure what I'd do without him. Probably spiral and be absolutely miserable.

With a deep breath, I try to let go of some of the worry. Change isn't easy for me, and there's been a lot, but I can handle it. I'm strong enough.

I turn back to Joel.

He makes me stronger.

Crawling back onto the bed, I say, "Sorry. I'm a little... wired."

"It's only graduation day *and* your birthday."

I get a big smile when he says that. I *love* my birthday.

"Does that mean... you got me a present?"

He chuckles. "Yes. It's right here." He leans over to grab something from the bedside table, then sits up suddenly and whips his shirt off, making his pecs dance.

Laughing, I smack his chest. "Stop. You're goofy."

He cocks an eyebrow. "It's cute you think I'm joking. This is absolutely part of your present. But we'll save that for later. For now..." He pulls open his top bedside drawer—for real this time—and pulls something out, then tosses it to me.

I catch it and turn it over, seeing a brochure of Acadia National Park in Maine.

"A brochure?" I ask.

"Well, it was the only physical thing I could come up with to represent our trip there. In five days. I've heard it's crazy, but a lot less busy if you go before Memorial Day. I planned for four full days up there, hiking, whale watching, eating so much lobster, and all kinds of other fun stuff."

My eyes light up. I think it was last summer when I told him I'd love to explore Acadia, since it's the only National Park in the east. I shouldn't be surprised he remembered.

"You are amazing." I give him a soft kiss and look back at the brochure. "I'm so excited."

"Happy birthday, babe."

I wrap my arms around his neck and kiss him deeply until my brain decides to be rude and interject some reality.

"Oh, crap!" I leap away from him and off the bed, grabbing my checklist again.

"What now?" he asks, amused.

"Financial aid. This program is more expensive than the last one and I'd already filled out my application for the other one. I have to figure out how all of that works."

"Why?"

I spin to face him, brow furrowed. "What do you mean *why?* Uh, cause I need to pay for it or they won't let me go."

He climbs off the bed and walks over to me. "You don't need financial aid. I'll pay for it."

My eyes widen and I sputter. "What? No. Joel. That's crazy. You can't pay for it."

"Why not? We're in a relationship. There's absolutely no reason for you to take out a crazy amount of loans when I can afford it."

"Your parents can afford it."

"No," he says clearly. "My grandfather left each of us money. We didn't have access to it until we turned eighteen, but I have my own money. Plenty of it. My parents pay my tuition, but I'd be the one paying for yours. It won't even make a dent."

I push away from him. "No. It's too much."

"It's not," he says, grabbing my arm. "What's mine is yours. I mean that. We're not married yet, but we're going to be one day, right?"

"Yes," I say softly, the idea giving me butterflies and briefly making me forget our conversation.

"Then there's no point in you taking out a loan. Let me do this for you." He pulls on my arm, and I soften, letting him wrap his arms around me.

"What if I fail at it? Have to drop out? Mess up?"

"I don't care. I seriously doubt that's going to happen, but either way, this is important to you, and investing in your future and your happiness will never be a bad decision."

I look up at him, taking in the sincerity in his eyes.

Though it goes against my gut instinct that I need to work for the money, I slowly nod. He's right, there's no reason I shouldn't. He'd never hold it over my head or make me feel like I owed him. The only thing holding me back is my fear that I'll let him down. Like it's another way I could fall short—but that's my own discomfort, and I need to rise above it.

"Okay."

"Yeah?" he asks, a smile breaking out on his face.

That smile alone makes it worth it.

"Yes. Thank you."

"You don't have to thank me, babe." He runs his hand up the side of my neck and looks into my eyes. "Thank you for letting me."

He kisses me deeply. So deeply I feel a tingle roll through my body, landing in my heart.

"Joel," I groan, fisting the back of his shirt. "We have to leave in a half hour."

"We both already showered. Fifteen minutes for this. Fifteen minutes to get dressed. Simple."

I can't argue because his lips are on mine again and my body is melting into his.

Whatever. I can do my makeup in the car.

"There she is," Mom says, reaching for me as Joel and I walk over to where she's standing with Dad, Grandpa, Joel's parents, and

Aaron and Rae. She pulls me into her arms. "My birthday girl and my graduate. I'm so proud of you."

"That goes for all of us, girly," Grandpa says, hugging me next, and I do everything I can not to cry at the tightness of his hugs. I swear they've gotten stronger since Gram passed, like he's trying to hug us for both of them.

"Thank you. I'm glad you could all be here."

"Like we'd miss this," Miles says, ruffling my hair. I turn and thwack him in the stomach.

"No touching my hair. It took me forever to get it right."

Joel shoots me a look, calling me out on it. It took me five minutes of applying some anti-frizz serum to my mussed post-sex hair.

Mackie reads his expression and laughs, but takes my side. "Yeah, never mess with a girl's hair. You have younger sisters. You should know better."

Miles grins. "Why do you think I do it?"

Turning to Joel's parents, I say, "Thank you for getting tickets for everyone."

Joel's dad smiles. "Perks of being on the alumni committee. I'm glad I could get them for you. It's crazy how much people sell scalped ones for."

"Scalped graduation tickets? To SUNY FL? Seriously?" Rae asks. "When's Taylor Swift performing? I must've missed that on the ticket."

We both laugh at that.

"It happens all too often. We're working on a better way to do it. Hopefully, it'll be in place by the time the rest of you graduate next year," Joel's dad says.

It's a little sad graduating all by myself, but I'm proud of how hard I worked, and I'm thankful all my friends get to be here to see me walk across the stage.

There's an announcement telling us it's time for those watching to find their seats, and for the graduates to line up.

After a couple more hugs and a kiss from Joel, they head inside the building. Joel looks back and winks at me, and another flutter of excitement rolls through me.

I make my way around the front of the building to a different entrance and follow a group of graduates inside, looking around for the sign for nursing students.

When I finally spot it, there's a whole crowd in my way. Slowly, I make my way through, trying not to bump into people. As I wait for a line of graduates to go by, I notice a little girl laughing and spinning in place. She's maybe five or six. When she stops, her gaze lands on me. She smiles and waves as I stand there, gobsmacked. I glance around for a moment, wondering if I'm seeing things. She looks like a ghost from my past—like the ghost of childhood me. Big blue eyes, long blonde hair, and a cheeky smile. After a second, I realize she's still staring and waving, so I wave back. She giggles, then turns toward the crowd, running between the legs of a man and a woman.

As a path forward finally clears, I walk toward my group, seriously questioning my sanity.

Settle down. There are plenty of blonde-haired, blue-eyed little girls out there. You weren't seeing a ghost of yourself.

What would it mean if I was?

Nursing is my jam, not psychology.

One of my friends in the program greets me with a hug, and I return my focus to the ceremony that's about to start. Butterflies whirl again.

I'm about to be a college graduate. On my twenty-first birthday.

I don't know if anyone's ever mentioned it, but graduation ceremonies are *boring*. They're 50 percent people talking about the future in inspirational quotes from Facebook and saying, "carpe diem," and 45 percent is watching other people walk across the stage, then you get to have your 5 percent when you take your diploma, move your tassel, and everyone claps out of etiquette.

At least it's almost my turn. Although, with the last name McKinley, I'm right in the middle, so after the big moment, I have to sit back down and wait some more before I get to see the people I love and celebrate.

Slowly, the row in front of me empties, and with each name called, the anticipation in my stomach builds. Everyone in my row stands up and we walk down the side aisle, lining up by the stage.

Five more. Four more.

I wipe my hands against my robe to make sure they're not sweaty when I shake the hand of the assistant dean, who is leading the ceremony. Shake with the right, take the diploma with the left, right?

Stop, Sarah. Breathe.

"Rebecca James," they call.

I'm next, I'm next, I'm next!

"Sarah McKinley."

Standing tall, I make my way across the stage, smiling through the handshake, getting the diploma, and all the congratulations. As I get past everyone, the stage is mine for one small moment in time.

My moment.

The other cheers drown out, and all I hear are the ones from the people I love. My parents. Grandpa. My sister. Joel. His voice comes through the loudest, and I easily find him in the crowd.

He whistles as I stop and flip my tassel.

As I walk off the stage to the sound of their cheers and applause, my heart soars.

I fucking did it.

Joel

I'm not sure I've ever cheered louder than when Sarah walked across that stage. I'm so fucking proud of her. She has worked insanely hard to be here, *and* she was in the top three for her program. She fucking killed it, and I am bursting, ready to tell anyone who will listen that she's my girl. I can't wait to spend the rest of the day celebrating her in every way. She deserves to be showered with love and praise and all the good things.

As we finish our fourth round of pictures—first with her family, then mine, then with our friends, now a group photo—we make our way toward the door. It's hotter than hell in this gymnasium, especially in a long sleeve button down and a tie.

"Oh, Sarah," someone calls out to her.

We turn as one of her professors walks over to her.

"It's okay," Sarah says to us. "I'll meet you outside."

"Okay, honey," Kara says, and they all head out the double doors, but I stay.

Walking over to a nearby wall, I lean against it, watching as the professor speaking to Sarah calls several others over and they all fawn over and congratulate her.

I can't stop smiling, watching it all. I might as well have a name tag that reads, *Hello, my name is Proud Boyfriend*.

They talk for another ten minutes, and when Sarah turns to leave, she stops in surprise seeing me waiting for her.

"You didn't have to wait for me," she says softly, wrapping her arms around me.

"Of course, I did. I wasn't going to leave without you."

She laughs and shakes her head, stepping back and turning toward the door. As we walk, she says, "You're silly. It's just outside."

I take her hand and squeeze it tightly as we step into the bright sunlight. "Doesn't matter. I wanted to walk out of here with you." Leaning over, I kiss her head. "I'm insanely proud of you."

"Thank you. I can't wait to go celebrate."

"Me either. I intend to spoil you today."

"As opposed to all the other days?" she asks with a laugh. But before I can answer, she stops short. "Oh my god. It's her again."

"Who?"

She looks at me, eyes a little wild, then nods toward a little girl. "Can you see her?"

I cock one eyebrow. "Yes, I can see her, you weirdo. Why?"

She laughs. "Right. Sorry. I saw her earlier, and I thought I was hallucinating. She looks—"

"Just like you. Wow. She really does."

"Right?"

The little girl tugs on the pant leg of the man standing next to her.

Just then, we hear Charlie's voice and realize the man and woman standing in front of the little girl are arguing with Kara, Charlie, and Pete.

We exchange a glance right as the man turns around. He's carrying another little girl—this one with deep brown hair and brown eyes. But what catches me is his shaggy blond hair and his smile—one that matches Sarah's.

"What the hell?" Sarah mutters, squeezing my hand tighter.

Just then, all conversation stops as everyone notices us.

Slowly, the woman turns around and my mouth drops at the same time Sarah's breath hitches.

No. You've got to be fucking kidding me. It can't be. Not here. Not now. Not—

"Vanessa," Sarah seethes.

Holy shit.

To be continued in book six, Heartbreak Like This.

A Note from Bethany

Hello, my wonderful readers! Sarah and Joel are officially here! I hope you loved the beginning of their story. Has Joel won your heart? When I started writing their story, I had no idea Joel would become one of the swooniest boys I'd ever written, but now he might just top the list.

If you're mad at me about the cliffhanger... sorry? (Don't hurt me). I promise there is still so much more to come for Sarah and Joel's story in book six, Heartbreak Like This. Don't let the title fool you, there will still be plenty of sweet, swoony, and fun moments in there too (amidst some hard times). I can't wait to continue their story and maybe introduce the next friend's as well. ;) if you can't wait, you can pre-order Heartbreak Like This on Amazon right now!

Until then, and as always, you can find some bonus chapters on my website. These flashbacks tell the story of Sarah and Joel's pivotal moments in high school and how they affected them.

Also, if you want more details about what happened at Rae and Aaron's wedding, you can find their bonus novella, Married Like This, on Amazon & Kindle Unlimited

P.S. If you need more from Ida, check out the Freaking Love and Ida Romance series for more!

P.P.S. If you enjoyed this book, please consider leaving a review. Reviews, especially on Amazon, help indie authors like me get more readers!

As always, thank you SO MUCH for reading. All the love!

XO

Bethany

Bethany's Books

Friends Like This series

Friends Like This

Falling Like This

Broken Like This

Love Like This

Married Like This
(a Friends Like This bonus novella)

Together Like This

Heartbreak Like This

Freaking Love series

Part One: First Love

Part Two: Real Love

Part Three: Forever Love

Ida Romance series

Reckless for You

Faking It for the Holidays

Everything for You

Running Back to You

Lacy Creek series

Finally Yours

Always Mine

Only Ours

Complete Novella Trilogy

The Music of Together Like This

You can find the Together Like This playlist on Spotify
- Every Side Of You- Vance Joy

- Take It From Me- Jordan Davis

- The Only Exception- Paramore

- Sunrise, Sunburn, Sunset- Luke Bryan

- Wanted- Hunter Hayes

- Chance- The National Parks

- Why Don't You Love Me- Hot Chelle Rae, Demi Lovato

- Give You Love- Forest Blakk

- God Gave Me You- Blake Shelton

- Anti-Hero- Taylor Swift

- Let Me Love You (Until You Learn to Love Yourself)- Glee Cast

- I'd Be Lying- Greg Laswell

- Take My Breath Away- EZI
- Baby, It's Cold Outside- Vanessa Williams, Bobby Caldwell
- Hard To Love- Lee Brice
- Family- Track45
- Mirrors (Acoustic)- Beth
- Closer to Love- Mat Kearney
- Forever- The National Parks
- Just A Kiss- Lady A
- Dress- Taylor Swift
- Can't Take My Eyes off You- Frankie Valli
- New Year's Day- Taylor Swift
- To a T-Stripped- Ryan Hurd
- Thank God- Kane Brown, Katelyn Brown
- Brendan's Death Song- Red Hot Chili Peppers
- Say Goodnight- Beth Nielsen Chapman
- All You Need Is Love- The Beatles
- Part Of It- Jordan Davis
- Pointless- Lewis Capaldi
- Lover of Mine- Louyah

- ...Ready For It?- Taylor Swift

About the Author

Bethany Monaco Smith is a writer-mom. When she's not busy hanging with her boys, she's writing cozy small town romances with lots of heart, a bit of steam, and all the feels.

She loves happily-ever-afters and cries at every emotional moment, whether reading, writing, or watching. When she's not mom-ing or writing, you can find her binge-reading on Kindle Unlimited, supporting fellow indie authors, and having sushi dates with her SIL. Bethany survives on coffee, rewatching the same TV shows over and over, and her KU subscription. She lives in the Southern Tier of NY with her husband and two sons.

For more about Bethany and what she's working on, follow along on Instagram (@bethanymonacosmith) or on her website, www.bethanymonacosmith.com. Stay in touch by joining Bethany's exclusive Facebook group, Bethany's Book Nook & signing up for her newsletter.

Acknowledgments

First and foremost, Cassie, thank you for being an incredible friend and PA, my sounding board, and a constant support. Thank you for listening to every rant and meltdown and for reminding me to stop overworking myself. You are amazing!

Lacey, as always, thank you so much for being my kick-ass editor and helping to make these stories shine. You are the best ever, and I can't thank you enough!!

Amber, thank you for continuing to be my hype woman, and telling me I don't suck at this, even when I think I do. ;) XO

Shani, for loving these characters as much as I do, letting me hype you up with all my crazy ideas, and for making all the mockups (an occasional dream catchers) that make me smile & keep me going!

Special shout out to the BOD Squad. You guys are the greatest cheerleaders and supporters ever & I'm so thankful to have you!

Jenni, thank you for loving Aaron freaking Cooper and letting me steal a few of your characters to hang out with some of mine.

To my supremely awesome ARC/Street team, THANK YOU. You ladies are the absolute best and I could not do all this without you!

To all my amazing betas for helping me work out the hard stuff, for loving these characters, and helping to make this story shine!

To the incredible author/bookish community I'm lucky to be a part of, thank you. You have been a source of camaraderie, support, and hilarious memes that keep me going on the rough days and celebrate with me on the awesome ones. Y'all are the best!

Finally, to all of you for reading and loving these characters! I'm so grateful for your support and how you've embraced these characters and this world. Can't wait for you to read what's (and who is) next.

Made in the USA
Las Vegas, NV
05 February 2025